In Times Like These

Gail Kittleson

ISBN-13: 978-1532968853

ISBN-10: 153296885X

Cover by Castle Creations, www.jackiecastle.com

Chapter One

*S*omeone wearing Burma Shave hoisted Addie from a rickety oak piano stool into a polka's wild pulse. One minute, she did her best to keep up with George Miller's accordion tempo. The next, she flew around the crowded town hall's wooden dance floor.

His strong arms pulled her out of a twirl, and laughing brown eyes sparkled at her between deep-set matching wrinkles.

"Your feet are almost as talented as your fingers on those old ivories, Mrs. Bledsoe."

She gathered her wits. "George?"

The rural mailman's laughter melded with aromas from the food table, where aproned women plied homemade chocolate cake, lemon pie and other delicacies. Nearby, the steady *glub glub* of every percolator in Halverson, Iowa kept time with the music.

Over on the makeshift stage, somebody else belted notes from George's bright red accordion, but before Addie could figure out who it was, he lunged her through the Wooden Heart Polka.

An old fellow on the tuba and his wife on the concertina zipped into foot-tapping melody. More onlookers took to the dance floor and a whirr of excitement buzzed the high-ceilinged room.

Above it all, a wide paper banner announced the reason for the festivities. *Red Cross Annual Roll Call—Halberton County Goal for 1941—$10,000.* Below, someone penciled in earmarks: $500, $1,000, $1,250, and on to the final amount.

George pulled Addie to the side of the dance floor and grinned down at her. "If you weren't married, I'd take you up to New Ulm, Minnesota to hear The Six Fat Dutchmen. Been in the business since '32. They spruce up the beat so, I can hardly make it through the moves."

"I can't imagine that."

Furrows crinkled his brow. "How's your mother-in-law these days? Has Orville improved any?"

"If anything, he's gotten worse. Berthea has to feed him now."

"Umm . . . she's got a mighty heavy load."

The piano started in again and perky crescendos added an upswing. The pianist's flaming hair fit right into the gala atmosphere. Leave it to Fern to blend an oompah beat with runs she normally played on the church organ.

Then Kate grabbed Addie's hand, her eyes flashing as blue as an Iowa summer sky. George threw up his palms in mock dismay and waved Addie off with her best friend.

Kate grabbed a chair and pulled Addie down beside her "Hey—you haven't forgotten how to dance."

"The last time I attempted a polka was at . . ."

"Our senior formal. Harold wouldn't lower himself to polka, so Joe took you out."

"While Alexandre swooshed you around Canadian style. And a few months later, he *took* you to Canada."

Back on the stage, George strapped on his accordion. "George cleaned out our driveway every winter morning before his mail route. It's sad his wife died so young, but we never know . . . "

Kate's grimace sent a pang through Addie. "If only I'd been here when Aunt Alvina passed, but after Alexandre got called up . . ."

"Your mother-in-law needed you. Remember what you said yesterday? What's past is past. Regrets are a waste of . . ."

Kate's grin returned. "Time." She sashayed Addie through a line of Schottische dancers three abreast, until someone caught Kate's arm and whizzed them both into a line.

"So many folks I haven't seen for so long are here tonight."

Ponytails flipped from side to side on the hop steps. "Yeah. One of the girls said her brother left today—still in high school—he and three others from the senior class joined up."

A snippet of conversation caught Addie's ear. "Our boys'll tear those Germans and Japs limb from limb. It'll all be over soon."

4

"I sure hope that's true, but it's hard to think of so many off to war. Come on, we hafta dance even faster, for them. My brother said to keep on living, because that's what he plans to do."

They joined the dancing crowd, and ten minutes later, Addie panted. "Kate, my collar's as wet as if it just came from the clothes wringer.

"How about an apple cider?" Kate led the way to a gleaming silver punch bowl.

"You leave tomorrow—are you all packed?"

Minus a hairpin in her wispy blond hair, Kate filled two cups with cinnamon-laced cider. Addie grabbed some cookies and plopped on the stage steps beside her.

"Can't believe how fast the time has gone. December fourteenth already—one last fling before I board the train. I'm so glad you're here, kiddo. This way, I won't upset Harold by coming out to the farm. Heaven knows he won't show his face here with all these Germans."

"He only let me come because my playing would raise money for the troops, and it's hard to say no to your banker. But Harold certainly expressed his doubts, especially after Germany declared war on us yesterday."

"Oh, I can imagine. 'You're playing German music? Don't you know the Krauts are the enemy?'" Kate lowered her voice to a mocking tone.

"That's pretty close. When I reminded him polka music is as Polish as it is German, he hit the roof."

"He said, 'German, Polish, what's the difference? They're all mad, but Hitler keeps stirring the pot.'"

"Harold's opinion, exactly."

"Still, he chose you—never mind that your mother said 'Yah vol' with the best of them."

Addie chuckled. "Maybe he accepted me because our name was Shields. Still, Daddy wasn't much of an English gentleman."

At that ludicrous idea, Kate choked on her cider, so Addie smacked her on the back. "No more joking for you tonight. Here, eat one of Berthea's famous sugar cookies. You need energy for your trip."

"She's the best baker around." Kate replied through an enormous, unladylike bite. "How could her son have turned out so sour, growing up with cookies like this?"

Her comment increased the lump in Addie's throat. The evening was almost over, and they'd spent so little time together. "How long will it take to get to Canada?"

"Probably two times forever, with the bulging troop trains. Chances of finding a ship are better there than in New York, though, but when I do land in England, I still have to find Alexandre."

"They didn't give you any clue where he is?"

"A makeshift hospital somewhere in London. Guess I'll get to know the city, eh?"

The heavy iron clock keeping watch over the banner announced only an hour left. "I'm so glad we caught up with each other yesterday at the cemetery."

"Great minds—and hearts—run together. I couldn't believe it when I saw you standing beside your mother's grave, with time to talk without Harold hovering. I believe the afternoon warmed up just for us."

The music stopped and the bank manager balanced midway up a wooden stepladder. He scrawled $1,575 on the bottom of the banner and someone handed him the megaphone.

"Thanks for coming out tonight. When we reach two thousand, the bank's going to kick in an extra hundred dollars to give us a head start on next year's goal." A cheer broke, and the trumpeter plunged into the Wooden Heart again.

"Oh, remember this song from German class? Come on, let's dance again." Kate crooned in Addie's ear, "*Sei mir gut, sei mir gut, sei mir wie du wirklich sollst . . .* Be good to me, be to me how you really should . . ."

"How can you breathe that evil tongue?" Addie arched in fake protest and stifled a giggle as they wove through the dancers.

"You sound just like Harold. Don't let him influence you too much."

"How will I even know that's happening?" Addie shivered in spite of the room's warmth. "Oh Kate, I'm going to miss you so much."

"I'll write, I promise. But how will you keep Harold from finding my letters?"

"I usually go after the mail, since his mother's afraid to leave Orville."

"Berthea, afraid?"

"Being stuck in the house has changed her. I'll just have to find a spectacular hiding place, that's all."

After another song, Addie took Fern's place until Fern, drenched in freshly applied Emeraude, switched with her again. Then Kate and Addie danced 'til they collapsed in oak chairs set up around the room.

"I sure hope you find Alexandre soon."

"German ships still sail the Channel, and Wailing Winnies keep buzzing over London, and oil bombs . . . sure hope one doesn't hit wherever he's staying." Kate's sigh tore at Addie's heart. "The next time we see each other, Addie, you'll have little ones running around."

"Not according to Harold—he doubts I'll ever fulfill his desire for children."

"Hey, you've only been married three years." Kate gave her a hug. "He's coming for you at ten?"

A mash of emotions swarmed Addie—so many things she should say, but words forsook her. At nine fifty-five, the banker scrawled another five hundred dollars on the banner.

"With the bank's donation, we've got a solid foundation. Bravo to you generous people. Dig deep for the cause."

Like clockwork, Harold entered the hall, but before he spotted Addie, the banker grabbed his elbow—a reprieve.

"There's your prince, as cheerful as ever."

Addie clung to Kate's hand. "I'll watch every day for your letters and write as soon as you send an address."

"You don't know what that means to me, Ad." The glint in Kate's eyes belied her determined expression.

Now, words inundated Addie. "I hope you have a safe trip and find a ship with no trouble, that no Nazi subs spot you, you don't get seasick, and you find Alexandre right away."

From the corner of her eye, she saw Harold fidget as several other folks approached him. "If anyone can manage this, you can, Kate."

"You think I'm the strong one, but you're my anchor. Since Aunt Alvina died, I've felt so . . . lost. And now, with Alexandre's crash . . ." Kate's voice cracked, but she forced a smile.

"Now, go join the gathering crowd around your football hero, debate champion, ultimate farmer husband, Addie Bledsoe. I'll slip out, so he'll never notice me."

She let her fingers trail the air, then hurried back and whispered, "Watch out for him, you hear? I don't trust Harold for one minute."

Addie brushed her eyes with the back of her hand. All the things she should have said swirled in her head. Suddenly, her feet felt heavy, but she slipped next to Harold.

"What do you think about Germany declaring war on us, Harold? That devil Hitler has to be destroyed, that's for sure. And those Japs—can't believe one of our hometown boys might've perished last week in that harbor. We'll show 'em, won't we?"

Even from a distance, Addie noticed the little muscle in Harold's cheek go wild. It could be a long night.

"Your little wife has added so much to our evening. Thanks for sharing her with us." The banker's compliment alerted Harold to Addie's arrival, and Harold gestured her closer.

"You're welcome. My Addie's quite the gal, isn't she?"

One of the women in the circle turned to another. "Oh, wouldn't it be nice to be young and in love again?"

Over by the exit, Kate scanned the crowd for Addie and gave her a secretive wave. When she left, a draft of bitter cold swept the room. Addie unconsciously rubbed her thumbnail—winter stretched ahead like an eternity.

Chapter Two

*H*arold burst into the big farm kitchen with a practiced scowl and accepted a steaming cup of coffee. He took a miniature spiral notepad from his overall pocket and scribbled, speaking as he wrote.

"January 13. Temperature -22. If it gets any colder, we'll lose some stock."

"Did you get all the sheep out of the drifts?" He flung back the shock of sandy hair brushing his steel-gray eyes and disregarded Addie's question. Maybe this pie would ease his mood, but today's crust turned as cantankerous as the weather.

Berthea's warning . . . *more than two tries toughens the pastry* tensed Addie's shoulders.

Aware of snow clumps from Harold's blue and white striped overalls forming pools on the faded gray linoleum, she muttered, "Come on, you stubborn crust—cooperate."

Fern, the Esther Circle leader, said cleanliness and good food made for a happy husband, but those muddy splotches on the floor would have to wait. Harold moved closer, jutted out his chin, and spread his feet wide apart.

"Last night I read about the unjust judge finally giving in to the persistent widow. Maybe today, the draft board'll take me, although if Pearl Harbor didn't change anything, I don't know what would."

His volume increased as cinnamon wafted like incense. Addie stirred an ample spoonful into the apple filling. She folded the crust in half, lifted it into a glass pie plate and patted the soft, curved edges.

The Golden West Coffee tin holding her egg money caught her eye. Its beaming cowgirl belied the tight knot cinching her stomach, and the irony struck—like this gaping pie shell, she waited to be filled.

Trembling, she poured in the apple mixture, dotted butter across the surface, and positioned the delicate top crust. Berthea fluted her crusts, but under Harold's piercing stare, pressing a dinner fork around the edge took less time. Then Addie slit the center with a paring knife and dabbed on fresh milk with a clean rag.

The oven's hot gust circled over her knees as she slid the pie onto the middle rack. Harold's inadvertent touch quickened her heartbeat.

"Let's sit down for a minute." She fumbled for a chair near the glittering windowsill. Behind her, ice slashed the glass, but he kept pacing. Addie flattened her hands on the table. Hopefully, he wouldn't take his anger out on the plates again. Sharp ceramic shards still surfaced between the floorboards from his outburst a week ago.

If only she could think of something to quiet him, but reminding him the county enlistment board harbored no personal contempt had produced the broken plates. And now, every point she considered second-guessed his scriptural interpretation.

Harold hadn't won the county debate tournament for nothing, and he made Halberton history at the state contest. Even after three years, Addie could never anticipate his barbed switchbacks.

Her forefinger traced her thumbnail, back and forth, and she picked at a food speck on the yellow tablecloth while Harold's size fourteen boots forged a rhythmic route across the kitchen. A stanza from last Sunday's final hymn came to mind, so she broke into muffled humming. At a pause in the melody, she anticipated Harold's pivot, creating an extra floorboard squawk.

For all the saints, who from their labors rest . . . The song eased her racing thoughts and made her think of Mama, enjoying peace at last.

"Aren't you going to clean the counter?"

She jumped up and scraped flour and lard leavings into the slop bowl for the always-ravenous hogs. *Oh blest communion, fellowship divine; we feebly struggle, they in glory shine.*

Harold's crossings accelerated. "Will you stop your infernal humming? A man can't even think."

Addie swallowed the music. "Sorry." An undeniable urge to leave thwarted her determination to remain calm. But then her mop pail called from the corner. That's what she could do—clean the stair landing.

Half filling the pail from the hot water reservoir, Addie added a pinch of Borax, Berthea's answer to every challenge. She added cold water from the black iron pump set into the countertop, grabbed her scrub rag, and tied her brown wool scarf over her hair.

When she crossed under the dining room archway, Mama's words came strong and sure. "Find something good in everything." Harold's agitation motivated her to clean a neglected space. That was a good thing, wasn't it? The water-stained dining room ceiling reminded her that maybe Mama watched right now from glory.

Circling the table to the stairway door, Addie sent a smile heavenward, just in case. On the last cold step of the first flight, she pulled her wool socks over her knees before kneeling to poke her rag into the railing's nooks and crannies. Her rag made a soothing swish over the inlaid oak pattern.

With the scrub water dingy brown, she sat back to enjoy the carpenter's artistry in this six-by-eight foot space. A master craftsman invested painstaking work in this landing, used only to pause before continuing up or down.

Even here, loud squeaks from Harold's pacing echoed like squealing piglets, so she carried her pail up the second flight. She ought to have cleaned out the storage room months ago. Why not today?

As she and Kate once did on the frozen river, she slid down the long hall—a person could make work fun in an old rambling house. The transoms above five tall oak bedroom doors cast dancing shadows the entire length of the hall.

Just before she set down her pail at the final bedroom, the toe of her shoe caught an uneven place, lurched her into the door and onto her backside. Water splashed everywhere, but surrounded by dripping walls and baseboards, Addie broke into a giggle.

"Kate would appreciate this." A banging door downstairs sobered her. If Harold came up and saw this mess, he'd throw a royal fit. She scurried to the linen closet for cloths, wiped the floor, and stuffed the evidence down the clothes chute.

A shiver took her head to toe, and her freckles greeted her in an old broken mirror Berthea abandoned when she and Orville moved to their new house across the driveway. A fine mist covered the speckled surface, but Addie still glimpsed straggling dark curls that framed her near-black eyes. Even the wide space between her eyebrows and hairline reflected the deep rose of her cotton dress, the hue of her dad's nose on his worst days.

"Please keep Kate safe and help her find Alexandre. They love each other so." She touched her chin to the frosty mirror. "Addie Bledsoe, you'll catch a cold right here in your upstairs. Get down and check on that pie."

But she detoured into her room, slid open the top bureau drawer, and fished for an old photograph that Kate's Aunt Alvina took eight years ago. She captured Kate dressed up as Barbara Stanwyck and herself as Myrna Loy. *Snap.* The happy memory fortified Addie to face Harold again.

A newsman's voice trickled up the stairway. Oh, no—Harold already tuned in the radio, though the evening war report wouldn't air for hours.

"Once we asked if Wilsonian idealism or Jacksonite common sense would prevail. Pearl Harbor, my friends, is now a moot question."

Down the stairs, wet boot prints embellished the dining room floor, so Addie swiped them with her rag and left it in the soaking bucket. Harold's eyes caught hers like a German bomber circling a hapless Allied aircraft. At least from newspaper accounts, she imagined that's how it would feel.

He shadowed her to the back porch steps, where she flung the remaining scrub water on a snowdrift. Falling ice rat-a-tatted against the pail, and Harold's ragged breath hit her neck en route to the kitchen.

"The Japs are taking Singapore. They've called on Percival to surrender."

"Oh, my." She refilled his coffee cup and pulled out a chair. "Sit down, won't you?"

He swung his head around. "How many times have I told you . . . ?" Scraping the floor with her chair bothered him. She forgot again.

He tore at his hair, standing Wildroot-plastered sections on end. "Impregnable Fortress, my foot—so much for Britain's Far Eastern imperial power. The Brits blew up bridges while the Japs used bicycles to maneuver!"

Addie's throat burned with desire to wash the wildness from his eyes.

"I don't care what they think. I'm going down there again." He raked his chair over the floor with a glare. "I am!"

"Maybe they'll take you for the February quota."

"You know it's hopeless."

"I'm sorry. I wish . . ."

"You always wish, but you don't know what it's like to be branded a cripple."

True, she didn't know, but no cripple could pace like Harold, or do his heavy farm work. If only he'd been called up before Orville's stroke, he wouldn't be fighting this 4-F status. Why did he have to be the only one able to work the family farm?

His chin poked over the white long-john triangle showing at his flannel shirt opening. "They take riff-raff like Alexandre." He punched the wainscoting with his fist.

Addie hovered near the kitchen doorway. She could point out Kate's husband's Canadian citizenship, but Harold already knew. A sick sensation swept her.

"You stand up for him for her sake, but where's her big strong pilot now?"

A cloudy streak monopolized Harold's eyes. "The RAF let the Japs take Malaya and now they're letting Singapore go. This war needs Americans who can fight, yet they refuse me."

His head grazed the doorway as he ran out, and a rowdy wind banged the storm door against the frame three times before it latched. Addie secured the heavy inside door and smoothed the rough wool of Harold's coat left on its hook.

A flash of the blue bubbletop pick-up sailed between barren lilac bushes and the corncrib, his torso thrust forward in the cab, broad shoulders swaying in the crackled leather seat. He careened down the lane and made a run up a slight incline onto the road without checking for traffic. Of course, in this storm, few would risk driving to Halberton.

An accident might take his life. The thought sidled in like a snake. No—she refused to entertain the idea. She counted to ten and drove her fist into her palm. "I will find a way to make him happy. I will."

The mailbox at the end of the driveway beckoned, and she reached for her gray and brown plaid wool coat. Maybe George brought her a letter to read before Harold returned. By then, she would have time to hide it, and he might come home in a better frame of mind.

Navigating the slick driveway, she retrieved a few letters and a package of mail tied with string. A glossy ice patch dared her to try it out, but she skirted it to deliver Berthea's mail as fast as possible. Berthea's slick front railing stuck to Addie's mittens, but the door opened before she knocked, exuding warm, yeasty air.

"Miserable cold, isn't it? This mail'll be our excitement for the day." Addie handed Berthea the packet and stood in the three-foot entryway to let her skin thaw while Berthea broke the taut string with her teeth.

"Not much here but bills. Guess you know that already."

"No, George keeps our mail separate. I never look at yours."

For a moment, the corners of Berthea's mouth reflected Harold's glower, but she shook her head like a wet dog and motioned Addie in.

"Being cooped up like this makes me downright irritable."

Her admission came the closest to an apology Berthea had ever offered.

"Well, I'd better get back home and start . . ."

"Supper? What're you having?" Berthea veered close enough to waft the aroma of coffee and beef gravy on her breath. "I'm so sick of cooking. Orville won't eat anyhow, so what's the use?"

The beginnings of a smile played on her lips as she fumbled with an envelope. "What a considerate sort that George Miller is to tie our mail like this." She glanced back at Addie. "Did you say what you're cooking?"

"Something with chicken . . ."

At Orville's high-pitched call, Berthea jerked away. Her fleshy neck propelled her head forward, aligning her chin with the top of a full-length flour sack apron that covered her ample bosom and gave off a rendered lard odor. Not exactly heavy, she rounded out more than adequately.

Always find a kind word, Mama used to say.

"Where'd Harold go?" Stray dark hairs on Berthea's chin wiggled with her conspiratorial question.

"He's upset about the battle of Singapore."

"He's applying again?"

"Yes."

Berthea's shoulders drooped. "How many times will they let him?" Her dark hair streaked white during the past year, and a green cotton housedress aged her stocky form.

"When that boy gets something in his head . . . " Another urgent call sounded. She opened her mouth, shut it again and turned away.

Addie let herself out. Halfway across the yard she pulled out the letters, and her heart skipped a beat at Kate's unmistakable handwriting on a pale blue envelope. An unexpected array of fuzzy snowflakes replaced the icy onslaught, and an enormous flake perched on the tip of her nose.

"Montreal, Canada, January 4, 1942. Three weeks ago."

Two at a time, she galloped the porch steps. In the kitchen, she edged a paring knife blade under the envelope's seal and breathed deeper.

Chapter Three

"*G*oing out to the barn to check on that ewe." Harold shoved back his chair and squinted in Addie's direction.

"All right." Would he accept her offer to help or get upset? Anything she suggested these days received a tart look at best. Better to wait. Later, he might welcome some coffee.

After she cleaned up the kitchen and knitted a while, she tucked a thermos under her arm and stole into the barn. In faint lantern light, Harold sat cradling a newborn lamb. His head rested at an odd angle against a couple of hay bales, and an old Coke bottle topped with a foamy black rubber nipple leaned against his knee.

The lamb, pink-nosed and healthy looking, snuggled into the crook of his arm. Not far away lay a motionless wooly gray mound—the mother. Addie bit her top lip. This loss would trouble him, but at least he saved the orphan.

Sleep mellowed the harsh lines of his face. In this quiet moment, Harold seemed like a little boy, and Addie imagined away the years.

"Oh, Harold . . . this is who you really are." On a crossbeam, a barn swallow's forked tail flicked in its cup-shaped mud nest.

"You're as headstrong as Orville and as tight-lipped as Berthea, but I know you're hurting for Joe, somewhere out there in the Pacific."

A bitter draught razed the dusky alleyway, stirring the tight scent of oats in feeding troughs, a tinge of blood and water from the birthing, and the warm, acrid aroma of fresh manure. So far, the cold restrained the dead ewe's rancid smell, but by morning, the stench would permeate the building. Harold shifted against the bale and snored, so Addie set the thermos near him and backed away.

"He might not hold me like he does that lamb, but he's consumed by the war. He can't think of anything else but Joe going down on the Arizona." Her bulky chore coat caught on a splinter, so she wrestled it loose. "In time, he's bound to change. Doesn't love believe the best and never give up?"

Her whisper bounced back at her. She wanted to help him to bed, but knew better. No, until the old Harold returned, she'd bide her time and practice her own kind of loyalty.

* * *

"German U-boats sank an Atlantic Coast liner last night." Astride the straight-backed wooden chair, Harold's eyebrows flurried up and down like snow sailing over the yard in a strong wind. A few minutes later, he almost knocked himself and the chair into the radio.

"No! This cannot be!"

Addie grasped her mending needle tighter. If the wind hadn't drifted the driveway shut, he would be driving the hog he butchered early this morning to the locker. Why did the weather refuse to oblige?

"They mock us. Our citizens watch our own ships burn and sink." Harold flailed his arms in the air.

"Oh, Harold. That's the worst news yet." She rose and touched his shoulder, but he yanked away just as a dark streak hurtled along the floor.

In his stocking feet, Harold leaped and stomped, shaking the thick curved glass frames of his grandparents' portraits near the front door. Then he twisted toward Addie in victory.

"Got him."

Bile rose in her throat at his sudden glee. He poised his thumb and forefinger over the small, furry gray lump, and swung the creature by the tail like a pendulum. His eyes locked on hers.

"You're not glad to be rid of this little pest?"

She pushed on her chest to catch her breath. "Yes, I . . . I am. You move so fast—I've never heard of anyone catching a mouse that way."

"You grew up in the filthiest house this side of the Rockies, and your dad didn't do anything fast, much less chase mice." A strange fire burnished Harold's pupils. He glanced from the mouse to her. "I bet you caught more vermin than he did."

She nodded without thinking.

"Then why do I handle them around here? You should take over the job, with all your experience." He edged near, suspending the limp animal like a shoestring.

"Harold, I don't . . ."

"Don't think you could measure up to my remarkable feats? The fellow who's not good enough to fight for Uncle Sam, but can still be trusted to kill mice?"

Something about his look sent an odd quiver through Addie. She backed against the crushed velvet davenport.

"Harold, please . . ."

But he swung the mouse so close that tiny teeth set against pink gums oozed a mineral scent. Addie's heart pulsed in her ears.

"Maybe Harold Bledsoe ought to join the circus or a traveling show so everyone can see him and laugh. Maybe Jack Benny could use such an accomplished guy."

Her teeth chattered under his smirk. He wouldn't toss a dead mouse at her . . .

But he did. She shrieked and spun away. Her neck burned as the mouse tumbled to the floor, and Harold's rowdy hoot resounded.

"Oh, Harold, how could . . .?"

"Easy. I'm tired of throwing out mice. I'll make you a new deal, just like that blistering Democrat in the White House. You set the traps and cart off the prey from now on. Harold the Great has better things to do."

His legs bent like saplings in heavy snowfall as he slumped into his chair. The broadcaster droned on, as unremitting as winter. "We have Kaiser Wilhelm, Queen Victoria's grandson, to thank for creating the German Navy—Kaiser means Caesar, after all. Perhaps his Netherlands asylum will end in just deserts for his crimes."

Addie stumbled to the back porch for the dustpan and her old broom. But when she returned, the tiny body had vanished. Her skin turned to gooseflesh as she made a slow circle.

"Figure it out." Harold leaned toward the burgundy fabric of the speaker, his tone dull. "I only stunned him—the remarkable Bledsoe fails again."

In the corner, Addie tipped the magazine rack to check a trap they kept set year-round, but the wooden contraption sat empty. Aware of Harold's eyes on her, she wavered.

"It's only a mouse. There's a war going on, woman."

The curl of his lips propelled her toward the davenport, but her skin still crawled. The wounded mouse might have sought refuge in the springs below her. Fifteen minutes crawled by before a sharp click came from the corner.

Immersed in radio chatter, Harold gave no sign he heard, so Addie crept to peer into the shadows. No second wind for the little fellow this time.

Harold usually emptied the trap for the barn cats, but the floorboards announced him leaving. Addie couldn't bring herself to remove the critter from the metal clamp. The porch door slammed, and though Harold wouldn't approve the waste, she whisked the trap into the dustpan. The cats would have to go without.

Metal scraped against gravel out in the yard. Finally, the wind died down so Harold could start shoveling. Satisfied the floor was clean, Addie checked her apron pocket and ran upstairs to the small bedroom at the end of the hall. Its blackened brass knob quarreled, but she rammed her shoulder against the hardwood until it gave way.

Dust floated up when she shoved aside some boxes and pulled open the heavy closet door. The frosty room echoed her sneeze, and with her thumb, she edged a bit of colored paper from the baseboard. *We Fight Together* splashed the bottom of a Great War victory garden postcard. A faded ink scrawl showed on the back.

October 1917

Dear Bertie,
    Thank you for writing. I'll never forget our good time in your garden.
                    Friends always, G_____

Berthea had a good time with a friend? The concept seemed foreign, like Hitler's radio speech cuts. Through the half-iced window, Addie glimpsed Harold's parents' house. Maybe back then, Berthea knew a soldier who called her Bertie.

Even on this frigid February day, natural light warmed the space. How could sunlight, through miles of sub-zero atmosphere, still produce heat? That was a *Kate* kind of question.

Hell-bent on getting to town, Harold demolished three-foot drifts piled across the driveway. At the same time, her dearest friend crossed an ocean peppered with Nazi submarines. The idea stiffened Addie's nerves like the iced electrical wires strung from posts along the roadside.

"No use thinking about it. All I can do is pray." She pulled Kate's first letter from her deep apron pocket, thankful she'd discovered the perfect hiding place—this little room at the top of the stairs. The day of their wedding, Harold declared the space too small for anything but storage.

True, there wasn't even an iron grate in this room to let in a little heat from downstairs, but warmth flooded Addie as she bent over the letter. Just like Kate to begin with a puzzle, as she did in their junior-high note passing.

December 28, 1941

Dear Addie,

Hope this finds you well. Will embark from __ in a few hours (think Q as in question). Earning my way with a capital T, and glad I came here, since this wouldn't have been possible from the U.S. after what happened in December.

Did you hear that Winston Churchill addressed both houses of Congress two days ago? Clearly, he spoke for the Brits, Canadians, and Australians, who unanimously welcome us with great relief. "Hope has returned to the hearts of scores of millions of men and women, and with that hope there burns the flame of anger against the brutal, corrupt invader. And still more fiercely burn the fires of hatred and contempt for the filthy Quislings whom he has suborned."

There's a new word for us—I think it's taken from a Norwegian collaborator. Even Norway, with a history of shunning war, can't help but get involved. Knowing you're not alone in an uphill struggle means everything. I remember feeling that way the day we met—my first day of school in Halberton. When you came to sit by me in the cafeteria and turned those friendly brown eyes on me, I knew things would be all right.

Have you heard any more about Joe Lundene? Who else has been called up? Any change with Harold's status? I pray for him to be accepted daily, and hope for an early spring there.

That will mean less brooding time for him and more for you to cheer on those recalcitrant hollyhocks. I think this summer is your time, Addie. Surely they'll cooperate with you this year.

Love always,

Kate

The day this letter came, Addie dusted off her interpretative skills—Kate sailed from Quebec. By now, her ship might near British shores. *Busy aboard* could mean anything, but her capital T must refer to typing. The star pupil in their tenth-grade business class, Kate could type with her eyes shut.

That new skill provided release for her incessant ideas and today, facilitated her search for Alexandre. The world beyond Halberton now reckoned with Kathryn Isaacs.

Addie stared out over the frozen yard from the west window, and her breath cleared the pane enough to reveal her teetering wooden garden fence, where her down-the-road neighbor Jane Pike's hollyhock starts resisted growing. Though Harold refused to let her order any seeds from Berthea's seed catalog, Addie could at least dream. Come spring, she'd renew her efforts to camouflage that unsightly fence.

Kate's letter crinkled as Addie pushed a heavy box into the closet and raised the edge enough to slip it underneath. Just in time, since Harold emerged from the barn and threw two massive pork quarters into the bubbletop. In two weeks, shiny white meat packages would line Berthea's new International Harvester deep freezer.

An uneasy place below her collarbone released as the engine turned over and Harold left the yard. She shut the door and shoved several more boxes in front of the closet, then scooted down the stairs and through the back porch to the basement.

In the fruit cellar, jars full of vegetables reminded Addie that by summer Kate might be back. She chose a few ingredients for supper, all the while listening for the mail truck. Surely George would stop by before Harold returned.

And he did, leaving another letter from Kate in the cold metal rectangle. Addie raced home and dropped into a kitchen chair without even removing her boots and coat.

Chapter Four

January 21, 1942

The Chancellor Hotel, Room 27
126 Bristol Street
London, England

Dear Addie,

Hope this finds you in a blessed thaw. First, details from the train. A friendly passenger offered me cinnamon rolls she warmed on the wheel housing. I can still taste them.

Fresh-faced GIs filled Illinois Central Station and a sign proclaimed "First Chicago USO Station Opening in April." On board again, a stitch in the engine's rhythm gave me pause.

What if the train crashed? I expected to see farms, but gray buildings lined dismal streets. "Passengers transferring at Union Station, disembark for Indianapolis, Cleveland, Detroit, Mont . . ."

I thought I'd already boarded the fast train, but the conductor waved me on. "Up ahead, Miss. Leaves in ten."

An arm steadied me when I bumped into an elderly man. A tall young fellow eyed me. "May we help you?"

"I need the train through Detroit to Montreal."

"Wait right here, Pa." His father mumbled in Italian while my rescuer peered at my ticket.

"Straight ahead." He grabbed my case, so I carried only my travel bag from our clandestine Cedar Rapids trip—remember?

"Take good care of this young lady." He handed over my case and disappeared. A Chicagoan? I'll never know.

The conductor announced a fifteen-minute delay. Near the restrooms, a sign declared the SECOND USO station, to open in May. From then on, it was sleep, eat, read, sleep . . .

I was sad to hear of Carol Lombard's death. Did you hear she was on her way to raise war bond money? Poor Clark Gable.

I must stop for now. Evelyn, whom I met yesterday, is showing me around London.

This letter will find you via a charming red sidewalk postbox. By now, you've figured out my first letter's clues, so please write soon.

My very best,

Kate

Tires screeched. Addie buried Kate's letter in her apron pocket and waited until Harold clambered to the basement to stoke the furnace. When he went back out for chores, she tiptoed upstairs to conceal her second treasure.

* * *

Clenching a small paper, Harold paused beside the kitchen door with his birth certificate in hand. Not again.

"The death count hit two thousand. A Japanese bomber dropped one right down the Arizona's smokestack, blew it like a volcano. The board just *has* to take me now." His cheekbones became blades in the ceiling bulb's glare.

"Have Joe's parents heard for sure?"

"No, but he's gone." The diagonal vein crossing Harold's forehead pulsed blue against his year-round tan.

Addie poured hot water into a cup. What if Joe escaped somehow? Why not hope for the best and save room for surprise, like Kate?

"Still don't believe me, do you?" Harold shook a ragged fingernail in her face. "You're making tea? This war calls for sacrifice, and you'd better get used to it."

He marched out, and she stole up to the landing to observe his gait past lilac bushes protruding like toothpicks from massive snowdrifts. Transplanted from Mama's soon after their marriage, the rows formed a demarcation line between the two houses and added balance to the farmyard. Deep red dogwood branches complemented the lilacs' brown and beautified the long driveway toward Berthea and Orville's new house.

Harold's broad stride showed no hitch. "I swear, fury improves his bad leg. If this would convince the draft board, I'd find a way to tell them." The hallway clock showed just enough time to write Kate before George delivered the mail.

February 6, 1942

Dear Kate,

SO glad you're safe, and thank you for the report. You brought those kind strangers to life for me. Yesterday, I slid down the driveway expecting only bills, but your letter awaited me. I hope you soon find Alexandre—can you imagine his surprise when he sees you?

Mrs. Morfordson asked about you at the Mercantile the other day. I still miss her English literature class. How did you know where to go in Montreal? The encyclopedia says it's actually Mont Royale. Did you see a castle? Tell me about your ship—any submarine sightings?

Cold and more cold here, and Harold haunts the draft board. I'll turn to happy thoughts—one day long after this war, we'll pore over these yellowed letters in my backyard.

Sisters at heart,

Addie

The letter occupied her apron pocket while she deboned a chicken, keeping an ear out for George's truck. But a sudden knock distracted her.

Maynard Lundene hunched on the top step, cavernous hollows lining his cheekbones. He shoved his knitted hat over his blue-tinged hairline, and seeing his pale, watering eyes, Addie's voice forsook her.

"Is Harold home?"

"He should be soon. Would you like to come in?"

Maynard's mouth worked as if he chewed tobacco. "Well then . . ." His rough knuckles scratched under his cap.

"Have you had any word . . .?"

"Today." His voice thinned to half a whisper. "Our Joe went down with the ship."

Addie touched his wool coat sleeve. "Oh, I'm so sorry."

Maynard held his cap over his heart.

"You're sure you won't come in? I have coffee on."

"Might wait in the barn a while." He reached for the door handle with a shy half-turn, revealing feathery late-afternoon whiskers. "War's an awful thing."

"Yes."

He let himself out and tackled the ice covering the yard. Addie gripped the doorframe—she'd better alert Berthea, who surely suspected the truth when she saw Maynard's truck.

Might as well check on the hens, too. She stuck her arms into her stiff chore coat and coerced her cold metal overshoe buckles. *Our Joe went down . . .*

Joe Lundene's face, so lively and full of good humor, swam before Addie as she broke ice in the hens' water pans, refilled the grain tins, and shared awkward tears with Berthea. Orville's snores from the couch punctuated her mother-in-law's voice.

"Send Harold over right away, will you?"

He screeched the bubbletop to a haphazard stop and entered the barn as Addie hurried home to make dumplings, Harold's favorite. A little later, the clash of buttons told her he dropped his overalls beside the washtub, so she piled them into rinse water saved from the last washing and rubbed Fels Naptha soap into the stains.

He lingered on the porch, so she reached for him. "I feel so bad, Harold."

"I told you he was dead. I'm going over to tell the folks."

"Your mother already knows."

He glared at her.

"I knew she would wonder, with Maynard's truck here."

"You told her?"

"I thought it would be hard enough, without . . . "

"You knew I'd want to break the news."

Surely, he heard her heart thump, just like he read her mind. "I was trying to . . ."

He stomped his foot, growled and ran out.

Addie caught the flailing door and sputtered. "Why do I always make him so angry?"

George's truck wavered to a stop beside the mailbox, so she dug out some egg money and raced along the tall pines' shadow to make the clandestine exchange. Amazing how a few coins could pay for postage to carry her letter all the way to London.

Minutes later, she ran upstairs and pulled the familiar photograph from her drawer. The image stilled her trembling and took her back to October,1934. Aunt Alvina's faint lavender still drifted to her, or did she imagine it?

That day after school, Kate had faked a dramatic swoon. "We have the house to ourselves." She spun around, chandelier sparkles in her eyes.

"Let's bring Myrna Loy to life. Come upstairs and hang your coat on my bedpost."

Kate sped upstairs, Addie followed, and soon faced a pink wonderland—white wrought iron headboard with a lacy bedspread, matching nightstands with identical lamps, a tall highboy and a shiny dressing table complete with a gold mirror and brush.

A faint, sweet scent enveloped the room. Addie stared in wonder—the new girl in school had chosen her for a friend.

Kate bounced in and bowed with a flourish. "Sit here, Miss Loy. I've wanted to meet you ever since your fans voted you Queen of the Movies. I feel privileged to work on your hair and lovely face."

Addie hung back, but Kate continued. "I'll just tweak your eyebrows and apply a few powder sprinkles on your nose."

Unable to resist, Addie sank on the bench.

"Relax, now. A bit more color here, and . . ." Kate pulled a pair of tweezers from a sack. "A few less hairs in the arch."

"Oh, my—Dad wouldn't . . ."

"Miss Loy, in that latest Thin Man episode, you were wonderful."

Fifteen minutes later, she stepped back. "There. With that cute nose tip and your hair drawn up, you could pass for Miss Loy's twin."

The mirror intensified the chicken pox scar on Addie's nose, her hesitant eyes and abundant freckles. But she mustn't disappoint Kate.

"Why, you made my eyebrows arch like Miss Loy's."

"Admit it, you're a raving beauty. Now, here's a challenge for you." Kate pointed to her own reflection. "See what you can do with a straight nose and stringy hair."

Addie fingered the gold hairbrush.

"Go ahead, it's not made of glass."

"How about Barbara Stanwyck? I think she's as pretty as Myrna, don't you? I could bobby pin some waves . . ."

By the time Aunt Alvina stood in the doorway, they'd ransacked the attic for satin dresses, hats, shoes and fur stoles. Kate pretended to smoke the eyebrow pencil and made eyes at Clark Gable under heavy lacquer.

"Girls! What have you . . .?"

An alarm buzzed low in Addie's eardrums. She winced when Aunt Alvina raised her hand, but a peal of laughter broke and Kate's aunt gasped for air.

"Let me get my camera." She bustled off, Kate giggled, and the tightness in Addie's shoulders gave way.

Snap. The girls rolled off the bed and laughed until tears smudged their thick powder.

Forever after, they referred to it as Myrna Loy Day.

* * *

Berthea waved Addie into a chair at the kitchen table, where a letter spread out, with photographs of Harold's brother Bill's children.

"Bill and Sue wrote that Collins Radio has expanded their radio production down in Cedar Rapids, so Bill's company is hiring more workers."

"What wonderful pictures of the children, Berthea."

Berthea's short-lived smile faded to a frown. "Bill thinks if Harold could work there, he'd feel better."

"Humm . . . but doesn't he have to keep the farm going?"

Berthea pinched her forehead and pushed a cup of coffee toward Addie, who held up her hand. "I've had enough for one day, thanks."

"How about tea?"

"You have some? Oh yes, I'd love a cup."

"Was your mother a tea drinker?"

Mama's sparsely supplied, lopsided cupboard flashed before Addie—the tea jar stayed empty most of the time. But Berthea had something else on her mind.

"Sue wrote about her cousin in California, maybe near your sister. They've had some bad wildfires out there, and with the CCC firefighters gone to war, the danger's worse."

"Rose lives close to San Diego."

"Did you know Japanese submarines fired on an oil field out there, and even tried to start forest fires up in Oregon? Don't mention this to Harold, though."

"You don't need to worry about that."

"Sue's father knows a forest ranger there whose co-workers spotted the Japanese off shore. Aren't you glad we live here?"

Taken by a sudden longing to be with Ruthie out in sunny California or Kate in London, Addie drowned her reply in pungent green tea.

"We Iowans are definitely doing our part. Did you notice Maudie Reicherts drove out to see me this morning? Says they miss me at the Ladies' Circle. Now wasn't that nice? Says the Maytag Company is making military equipment, and even children save stamps for war bonds."

"Rghsh . . ." Berthea started up at Orville's emission from the back of the house. "Go right ahead and enjoy your tea. I'd better check on him."

Addie poured a second cup. Not one to run out of anything, Berthea's pantry door hung open, with laden shelves promising a continuous supply of pies, cakes, and cookies.

The table held stacked letters, newspapers and bills, as well as the Sears Wishbook catalog, opened to a child's wooden dollhouse in Modern Colonial Style. Seven rooms only $1.99.

Maudie's visit made such a difference—Berthea hadn't shown this much life in months.

Chapter Five

*H*arold liked fresh starch in his Sunday shirt, so Addie left the ironing until Saturday night. When his collar stood alone, she hung the shirt near his creased suit pants.

Her buttercup linen dress needed no ironing. Her brown cardigan ought to be warm enough in the drafty sanctuary, even though Harold thought sweaters tacky. Last winter, she shivered through services, but when Berthea started wearing her sweater, he relented.

A shaving brush smoothed the lapels and she checked for wrinkles marring the pleat. Small price to pay for Sunday's hymns sweeping her away.

The next morning, First Methodist's gold organ pipe scrollwork and flourishes on the wooden pulpit satisfied some nameless longing in Addie. Fern's organ trills distanced Harold's misery and lightened her heart.

"For now we see through a glass, darkly; but then face to face: now I know in part, but then shall I know fully, even as also I am known." Pastor Taylor scanned the crowd. "No one can predict what lies ahead, but war rouses us."

Harold jitterbugged his foot on the varnished floor, but Addie resisted the urge to clamp down on his knee. He stared straight ahead, eyes gray as stone.

"During these perilous times, evil ravages the earth and conscience calls us to stand and fight. We see the conflict darkly, but our duty is clear."

Throughout the sanctuary, women's brown, tan, gray and dark red hats dipped like hay in an August wind. Men gawked at the elaborate heathery-green organ pipes as if seeking heavenly signs.

"Turn to page 327, *A Mighty Fortress is Our God*. In uncertain times, we can count on this truth."

Harold hissed, "That's a German hymn." His conversation with the pastor later might leave Addie time to play a hymn or two on the piano.

Were they to take our house, goods, honor, child or spouse, though life be wrenched away, they cannot win the day . . . A shiver coursed Addie's spine.

Fern outdid herself with extra chords. . . . *a bulwark ne-ver fa-ay-ay-ling. Our hel-per He a-mid the flood of mor-tal ills pre-vai-ay-ay-ling.*

Chaos might trouble this old world, but by the final refrain, Addie turned toward Harold, hoping the music raised his spirits. But she faced only polished wood and Berthea's scrunched forehead.

After the service, Berthea chatted with a friend, so Addie played four verses of *Trust and Obey*. Harold still shook his finger at the pastor in the frigid entryway. When Berthea tugged his sleeve, Addie joined them.

"Harold, I can't leave your dad alone any longer."

Harold huffed, but tore himself away. Berthea gasped when he skidded the Chevy full circle on the ice at Second and Main.

She invited them over for dinner, and afterwards, Harold fell asleep with Orville in front of the radio. With the last clean dinner plate in the cupboard, Berthea covered an enormous yawn.

"You need a nap, too. Thanks so much for dinner." Addie went for her coat, but Berthea snapped.

"I need some fresh air, but I'm so afraid of the ice."

"How about teaching me to make those soldier cookies you mentioned the other day?"

Berthea brightened. "Why, I could . . . "

"I'll get your coat."

"Must've made fifty batches during the Great War." Berthea rummaged through her pantry. "Condensed milk and coconut, some nuts—I'll be right out."

Snores issued from the two matching profiles, and Addie's heart went out to Harold. He worked so hard.

Two hours later, six dozen chocolate mounds cooled on Addie's kitchen table. "I'll go get some packing boxes. Harold should be in soon to listen to Jack Benny."

"Does he still tune in to *Charlie McCarthy and Co* after Jack? My, how he and Orville argued about that." Berthea hunched her shoulders like Orville. "'We already listened to Roosevelt, why waste time on that Edgar Bergen dummy?'"

She mimicked Harold. "'Dad, anybody making a go as a radio ventriloquist must be smart.' Oh, the disagreements they had."

From the back bedroom, Addie brought an armload of boxes, and Berthea continued. "When they switched from the Chase and Sanborn Coffee Hour, Harold became furious.

"'How can they take off W.C. Fields, Don Ameche, and Dorothy Lamour? It's not fair—now, it's just Charlie and Mortimer Snerd.'"

"What did you say?"

Berthea shrugged. "I don't remember who won most of the time. Did you have arguments over radio programs at your house?"

"We . . . ah . . .we didn't listen." No use saying they had no electricity.

"Harold took to the radio as a boy, tromping around like a soldier repeating everything he heard. His memory always amazed me." Berthea clucked her tongue. "The Great War, without all these battle reports, was far easier. The details can be hard on a person, don't you think?"

"I wish Jack Benny aired every night instead of the war news."

While Berthea taped boxes, Addie printed soldiers' addresses. At five fifty-five, she turned the dial to WHO, Des Moines, and rattled the box for a better signal.

>   The Jell-O Program, starring Jack Benny, Mary Livingston,
>   and Phil Harris. Jell-O, the most colorful dessert in the world. Each
>   beautiful, delicious color has its own genuine fruit flavor: strawberry,

raspberry, cherry, orange, lemon, and lime. There's
only one genuine
Jell-O. Look for the big red letters . . . and now, join
me in welcoming Jack What's His Name..."

Berthea opened the door when they heard Harold outside. "Is your
dad all right?"

"Still sleeping when I left to do chores."

"If you walk me home, Addie, I'll get some money for George. He
won't mind mailing these for us tomorrow."

"I don't know if I ever mentioned that he asked about you and
Orville at the fundraiser in December."

Berthea's eyes crinkled. "Really?"

An early moon prevailed over a glistening landscape, and Old
Brown nosed Addie's leg as she steadied Berthea and spoke to the
dog. "Hey, fella. You're cold too, aren't you?"

"Orville says that's crazy talk. Dogs were born to endure the
elements, just like cows or foxes. But I feel better if Old Brown stays
in the barn on these bitter nights."

"How long have you had him?"

"Years and years. He straggled into the yard one day and stayed."
They slowed to navigate an ice patch a few feet from Berthea's front
steps.

"I ought to let him in tonight, but you know how Orville can be. I
try hard not to set him off these days. Come inside a minute."

Orville yelled as she opened the door, and her voice constricted.
"Oh, no—I'm always here when he wakes up." In the living room,
Orville sprawled over the edge of his chair, in an unmistakable urine
smell.

"Buddy Weham, Beedma and Taye Roseva. Tucka nose in evwons
bizna."

"Yes, that Bloody Kaiser Wilhelm and Bismarck. Teddy Roosevelt
stuck his nose in everyone's business."

"Fankin's gonna kiw aw sons."

"Franklin's not going to kill our sons, Orville. You've been
listening to the news again. But Bill's vital to his company—

remember, they're making some tank part now, and Harold's classified 2-C now. The war board knows how much we need him here."

But she couldn't budge Orville, so Addie hooked his belt loop with her finger and pulled. Inches at a time, they righted him. "Smoka matches aida axis." Spit flew on Addie's arm.

"He must've heard that on the radio again while we were gone."

"What was it?"

"*Smoking matches aid the axis.* They've mentioned a danger out west lately—the Japanese might set forests on fire in Washington and Oregon."

Berthea whispered into Orville's ear. "That's a long, long way from here—nothing to worry about." Orville touched Addie's elbow. "You remember Addie, don't you?"

Berthea tucked his hand down. "I'll be right back."

She went into the kitchen and returned with ten dollars. "Give this to George for postage. He'll know the exact amount, and I want you to keep the change."

"Oh, that's not ..."

"No, I mean it."

"Why, thank you."

"Thank *you.* I had a lovely time."

"Do you need help getting Orville into bed?"

"We'll manage."

Addie gulped at Berthea's unexpected hug and crossed the yard in wonder. Hearing laughter from the living room added to her relief.

Jack Benny put Harold in a good mood that lasted until Monday, when he drove to town for some chicken mash. Addie decided to do the chicken chores while she waited for George to bring the mail. Sure enough, he knew the exact amount, and she carried almost five dollars home.

Better yet, George handed her a letter from Kate. As she checked on the chickens, a strong March wind whipped around an ice-coated Studebaker and Jane Pike stuck her arm out. Addie latched the coop door and hurried toward the green car.

"George plowed us out—been shut in for days." Jane's verdant eyes, a deeper shade than her vehicle, bore spring's sure promise.

"I know that closed-in feeling. Can you come in?"

"No, thanks. Nothing left to scrub at home, and I've baked enough to last a month. Going over to clean at the church. Here's some stepe pierogi for you." She hoisted a brown cardboard grocery box through the window.

"Oh, thank you, Jane. Umm, still warm on the bottom. I can't imagine how much this will cheer Berthea. She's got cabin fever too."

"Don't worry about the bowl until spring comes. I miss your visits."

"I miss you, too." Jane rolled up her window, let out the clutch, and waved good-bye. Berthea must have been watching, and opened the door before Addie hit the top step.

"Jane brought something for us?"

"She couldn't stay inside any longer, she said."

"Here, let me get a pan." Addie ladled a healthy portion of the savory sauerkraut, dumpling and onion blend.

"That was real thoughtful, especially when her Simon's so cantankerous. Compared to him, Orville's a Teddy bear."

"We won't have to cook supper—that's a treat, isn't it?"

Berthea jerked away when Orville called her, so Addie left.

In the back porch, she kicked off her boots. Only four-fifteen, and no supper to cook. She took the stairs like a hungry cougar and skidded to a stop at the end of the hall, where a needlepoint plaque proclaimed, "The Lord is good, and his loving kindness endures forever."

Mama quoted that verse even when her final sickness reduced her to a skeleton. Her tongue thickened, yet she seemed stronger-spirited than before. "No matter what happens, Addie, remember that God never leaves us." She repeated the verse, emphasizing different words each time.

"*The* Lord is good . . ."The *Lord* is good . . . The Lord *is* good."

Today, Addie echoed her. Seeing Jane, even for a few minutes, gave her hope. Having her for a friend meant so much. The winter would pass, and then she'd ride her bicycle down the road to Jane's often. They'd exchange plant slips, and then Kate would come home.

Leaving the door open so she could hear the motor sputter when Harold parked the bubbletop, she wrapped in a blanket and sat on a box. Then she feasted her eyes on Kate's precise handwriting.

February 26

Dear Addie,

I'm washing dishes in the hotel restaurant for my board, but will lose my sanity if a hospital doesn't ring me up soon. The cook weeps over losing Singapore, the last Nazi bombs ruined a local cinema, and a madman murders single women here.

But even worse, two weeks ago, Germany humiliated the Brits in the Channel Dash. Three big Nazi battleships surprised our Navy and passed through the Dover Straits.

The RAF was slow to react. This will mortify Alexandre. The grim atmosphere shows on the streets, here in the hotel, everywhere. The manager says we've suffered the worst disgrace since the American Revolution—worse than Dunkirk.

I zip my lips, if you can imagine, and seek something positive to say. Guess I hadn't realized this nation's pride—after all, the Channel between France and England has been called ENGLISH for centuries. Now, with stories of Russian bravery circulating, and relying on the U.S. to bail them out, Londoners look awfully grim.

Hitler's audacity in the Channel feels like the last straw.

But France has suffered this way for two years—they caved to the Huns so easily. On to more cheery news. Yesterday Evelyn found an ad for a typing position, so I applied, to keep me out of trouble. And now for your questions—your letter encouraged me beyond words!

Our ship was lend-lease, transporting necessities, from food and munitions to paper products and medical supplies. (Now I see how much they need food here—

when I move into a flat, I'll beg you for supplies. How can one live without cheese?)

Between icebergs and U-boats, we zigzagged across the Atlantic. I typed reports, yet never saw the ship's name or code number, and only glimpsed Mount Royal (less than a thousand feet). Sorry, no castles this trip.

Landed at night and lugged my suitcases to the train in heavy fog. The inspector eyed me with suspicion after I dropped a case on his toes, and spat a perfunctory, "Do get on, Miss."

I miss our literature class, too, and wonder if Mrs. Morfordson has forgiven me for skipping graduation.

Take heart in spite of your worrisome husband.

Love,

Kate

When the barn door slammed after Harold drove in, Addie sat for a few more minutes, digesting all the news. There must be something she could do to lift Kate's load. Cheese would mold on the way over there, and so would apple pie, Kate's favorite.

But maybe she could send some fudge, or . . . cookies, that was it. She'd make Berthea's recipe, the peanut butter recipe Kate raved over the night of the fundraiser. She had the peanut butter, and if Harold took her into town on Saturday night, she'd buy some chocolate chips with her surprise gift from Berthea.

He'd never find out, because she'd do the baking on Monday, when he promised to help Mr. Lundene sort his cattle.

Chapter Six

"*S*orry, no letter from Kate today. Such a perky, chin-up gal." George's infectious grin heartened Addie from his pick-up's friendly warmth. "Want me to keep her letters back 'til I can put them right into your hand?"

Blood pulsed in Addie's ears. She focused on his mustache, but jumped when the barn door slammed. She met George's eyes, and his brows formed an upside-down V.

"Don't worry. Maybe you'll be able to do me a favor some day." A reassuring grin showed his dimples. "I remember the day Kate came to live with Alvina. Can't believe how fast that little orphan grew up, and always with such fire in her eyes.

"Now she's in London. Spent some time there myself, during the last war. Has she heard anything about her husband?"

I'll never forget the good time we had in your garden . . . Did George write that note to Berthea?

"She's still searching for him."

"I'll watch for her letters—and I won't say a word to anyone." George shifted and steered down the gravel road.

Realizing he knew her secret made Addie's spine tingle. Her breath issued in white mist as she calmed herself. "But Kate and Berthea always speak well of him, so there's no reason to be anxious."

Late that afternoon, freezing rain coated the farmyard again. Addie skated to the barn to fill water pails and see how else she could help Harold. They simply had to get to town for church tomorrow.

The Lord is good, Mama's version throbbed through her mind. "Please let the ice subside during the night."

A smooth, shiny glaze stuck the chicken house door together, so she pried it open with a crowbar and filled the shallow cement trough. Only a few hens fluffed their wings, and the day's droppings filled only half a pail.

The hens stirred, and Addie rested the shovel tip on her boots. "I startle easily, like you girls, but can you imagine being fearless enough to tackle London like Kate? From what Berthea says, Jane puts up with a lot, too, yet she's always so cheerful. Oh, to be as strong as them."

She lifted the latch. "See you bright and early in the morning."

After supper, she ironed their church clothes and barely stayed awake through *Truth or Consequences* at 7:30. Before daylight, while Harold snored, she sanded the paths for him and whizzed through chicken chores.

En route to the barn, she heard a "Whoohoo!" and glanced up. Berthea hailed her from her front step. "Orville's got the sniffles. I'm afraid I'll have to stay home."

When Addie was halfway through distributing the grain, Harold took over, so she returned to the house. While she dressed for church, a bat or mouse skittered through the crawl space where the back bedroom had been added on—did those creatures feel trapped, too?

When Harold came in and cleaned up, she stopped holding her breath. They would really be going to church. With persistent rays breaking through low eastern clouds, the bubbletop slid into town toward arched leaded glass windows that blinked from the red brick building. The stained glass half-circle above the altar illuminated the sanctuary, and Addie sank into their pew.

Maybe today, the sanctuary's serenity would seep into Harold. He needed it so desperately. He refused to talk about Joe, but had thrashed half the night.

Sitting here brought to mind the joy Addie felt when Mama said yes to one of Aunt Alvina's requests. Yes, Addie could ride with them to her country church. Addie's *unanswered* file contained so many "whys" about Mama, but that day, her love shone through.

As Fern plunged into her prelude, other memories drifted in. Addie's question file bulged with Mama's death, but only a week after the funeral, Harold invited Addie to Methodist Youth Fellowship. The group met on Thursday nights, he said, and they could bring guests.

She couldn't believe a senior, a football player, even noticed her, and Harold was less than pleased when she brought Kate along. Earlier that day, Addie begged her to say yes.

"You have to come, Kate. Harold Bledsoe invited me, and I've never been on a date. He said, 'You have nice pins.' What does that mean?"

"He said that to you? It means legs—I didn't think he would ever go gaw-gaw over any girl. Didn't I tell you you're the spitting image of Myrna Loy?"

The youth group discussion on "Peace and the League of Nations" interested Kate, who participated right away. After listening for a few weeks, Addie spoke up one night.

"Wasn't it President Wilson's refusal to negotiate that caused all the trouble?"

The adult leader shrank back when Harold raised his voice. "If you look into it deeper, you'll see he suffered a stroke."

Kate saw Addie flush and whispered, "I think he's wrong—it was Wilson's stubbornness."

The next week, Harold's roving hand under the table broke Addie's concentration. Still, she liked having a destination one night each week, with only Dad's snore and her "slow" brother Herman for company after Mama died. Ruthie, the oldest, took their youngest sister Bonnie with her when she married Reginald and moved to Minnesota.

To the opening chords of "Are Ye Able," sunshine created a glorious effect on Fern McCluskey's fiery hair. Her playing was just as attention-catching, and her black velvet hat perched over her widow's peak in military style, highlighting the upswing of her victory roll hair-do.

Beautiful Carole Landis may have pulled off that look in Hollywood, but only Fern would attempt it here in Halberton. Now that Addie thought about it, hadn't she seen Carole's latest photograph feature Fern's exact bejeweled earrings? If only Kate were here to confirm her hunch.

Next to her, Harold straightened and looked askance at her. She folded her hands like his and set her mind on churchly things, but for some reason, Orville's words on her first Sunday here came blasting in.

"You're Presbyterian?"

"Mama's parents were, but Dad grew up Lutheran . . ."

"Watch out for them Lutherans. Bad as Catholics—worship a statue."

Later, Orville revealed other biases. "Watch out for them Baptists, they're out to getcha. Watch out for them Holy Rollers . . ."

Addie relaxed and gave thanks for Fern's fervent playing and this chance to leave the farm. The beauty of flickering candles on oak grain generated warmth in her chest as a graying man strode down the center aisle.

"This is the day that the Lord hath made. Let us rejoice and be glad in it." The guest speaker prayed for the troops before facing the congregation. "I commend you all for braving this weather. I received very short notice, so we'll sing a couple extra hymns. First, 'Trust and Obey.'"

Voices reedy with the cold produced feeble results, so he took the pulpit after the first song. His smile wavered like the singing.

"On second thought, we will sing only one hymn." He fluttered his notes and Harold stretched his long legs under the pew.

"Today's text, 'Love endures all things,' includes war. Love endures even that great evil." The speaker sneezed into his handkerchief.

"Here, love functions as a noun, but in 'Love one another,' we discover it shows action, and bids us question ourselves. Do we show love to the elderly, the infirm, and the backslider? Do we love youth and children? But most of all, do we love the stranger?"

A woman two rows down clasped her brown gloves. The net trailing her gold velvet hat brushed her nose. Next to her, Mr. Olson, the café owner, fumbled with his hymnal.

"Would you love a black-skinned stranger?"

Harold lunged his elbow into Addie's ribs. Her cheeks scalded as his whisper carried. "In Halberton?"

The speaker paid no attention. "If I entered your church smelly and hungry, would you keep your love in your pockets? If my ancestors hailed from a country you detest, how would you treat me? To be disciples, we must care for the outcast."

Harold struck again. "Oh, this is deep . . . nouns, verbs and adjectives, even."

The guest pastor took his lonely seat near the organ pipes. Walt McCluskey stood, gathered his pinstriped lapels, and cleared his throat.

"In lieu of our final hymn, I have an announcement. Pastor Taylor has now joined our troops, like all true patriots of a rightful age."

Harold stiffened. Addie held her breath as a stir traversed the congregation.

Diffused window light revealed a perfect part on the left side of Walt's scalp. "Besought with requests, the national church office has no shepherd to send us. But among us sits a young man with a scholarly bent and the desire to serve."

Harold's knee began a riotous bounce. Addie followed Walt's scan of the scattered members as the guest speaker slunk down the side aisle. Then her focus returned to Harold. So he knew Walt was up to something, but hadn't said a word to her.

"Infirmity deters Harold Bledsoe from fighting, a bitter blow to one so zealous." Harold's history with the draft board shuttled through Addie's mind. Last May, he went with Joe to sign up for the first time, and she'd lost count since then.

Walt's dramatic upsurge drew Addie back to the sanctuary. "The solution seems as clear as the ice on our sidewalks. Harold, would you consider First Methodist your battlefield?"

Harold's foot halted in midair. Everyone knew Orville's stroke forced Harold home from college during his freshman year, and many may have viewed his return as comeuppance. But today, his aspirations acquired transcendence in the light from a purple and gold leaded window.

As Mrs. Morfordson often said, "In literature as in life, perspective makes all the difference."

This congregational son could lead them through war's tumult and cost far less than a full-time pastor. Fern, the Sunday school superintendent, surveyed today's sparse flock. She'd instructed most of them at one time or another. Finally, she fixed her eyes on Harold.

"We all are well aware that you can think holes through anything, Harold, like you did on the debate team."

The little muscle in Harold's cheek beat a fixed rhythm. He might be pleased, or he might storm out of the building—Addie had no idea which.

Fern forged ahead. "We attest to your football leadership, too." She swooped her bosom upward, causing her silver sweater pin to sparkle. "We beseech you to use your God-given gifts on behalf of First Methodist."

Applause exploded, and Fern beamed at Walt, who ushered a speechless Harold to the basement. As everyone dispersed, Fern paused near Addie.

"My, my dear. Such a big day for you. I'm so thrilled my dear husband had such a wonderful idea." She stepped closer. "Aren't you excited?"

A puzzle of emotions prevented an honest answer. Fern cocked her head and waited, but Addie still couldn't think what to say.

"Well!" Fern shrugged and bustled off.

Foyer chatter swelled, but Addie veered to the piano. After playing every verse of "A Mighty Fortress" and "The Old Rugged Cross", she thumbed through the hymnal for another favorite.

But Harold approached her, hands folded. "I agreed to preach and visit the sick." His bland expression revealed nothing.

Worms navigated Addie's stomach. She hadn't expected to have any say in the matter, like that farmer by Benson stuck in a stall with his prime bull. After his goring, local farmers took more caution with confined animals.

But an hour ago, Harold walked through these doors a parishioner like everyone else. Now he'd become the leader. He hummed an old tune driving home, but the back of Addie's neck tightened. Brown fence posts etched endless white fields all the way as she plotted when she could write Kate for her opinion.

* * *

Berthea traced her fingers over the kitchen table after supper. "It's March eleventh already. We're almost through the longest month of winter."

"Easy for you to say. Every month's the same for me, Ma. Did you hear they extended the draft age to forty-two a month ago? Bill's company makes munitions now, so he won't go, and I can't, either."

Berthea rose for the peach pie she asked Addie to bring, based on her belief that pie cured most ills, and cinnamon improved almost anything. But just then, the newscaster jerked Harold like a puppeteer.

"Congress entertains welcoming females to the army—the Women's Army

Auxiliary Corps already trains at Fort Des Moines."

Harold's wail roused even Orville. "Right here in Iowa, yet they refuse me."

Berthea tried in vain to soothe him. "They're nurses, dear, and Congress won't pass it. Besides, you've got your sermons to write now."

She shrank from Harold's glare, and Addie startled when he jumped up. His coffee cup overturned, drenching his pie.

Sermon writing might help, but might just as easily upset him.

* * *

The last week of March, Berthea knocked one morning with a Burpee's seed catalog tucked under her arm. Her boots formed perfect mud tracks to the table as Addie eyed the catalog she'd coveted all winter. The company designed the pages for midwinter dreaming, but she still wanted to see it.

"Is Harold around?"

"I'll get him." She called him through the archway, and he twisted from his books. "What do you want?"

"It's your mother."

Berthea eyed her muddy tracks. "I thought I cleaned my boots off well enough . . ."

"I needed to scrub anyway." Addie plied her rag as Harold sat down. From her perspective on the floor, Berthea's right shoulder sloped more than normal today.

"Your father wants to sow oats where we border Alfred's land."
Harold's eyes glazed over.

"The Farm Bureau paper says we ought to conserve soil." Berthea pulled out a dollar-sized yellow paper. "Here's last year's tax stamp for growing marijuana. It costs a dollar—shall we renew it?"

Addie stilled her urge to respond for Harold. With Berthea representing Orville, he would only resent her butting into "men's business."

"Harold?"

He fiddled with the paper. "Number 6451, fifteen acres. The Navy needs hemp for ropes. Go ahead."

Addie threw her rag in the pile near the metal washtub and turned into the dining room. But Berthea hailed her and held out the catalog.

"Thought you might like to take a look at this, Addie. They've outdone themselves this year, what with all the emphasis on victory gardens."

"Thank you. I've been wanting to see the new flower bulbs."

With a full-fledged scowl, Harold suddenly came to life. "Don't dream us into poverty, now."

"Harold, there's nothing wrong with dreaming, you know." Berthea raised her eyebrows in Addie's direction.

"Don't worry." Addie sailed from the kitchen with the precious catalog in her clutches.

Chapter Seven

March 30, 1942 RED LETTER DAY!

A Salvation Army warehouse produced Alexandre. Only scars evidence his downing. Besides that, our navy convoys avoided the German Tirpitz, said to be heavier than even the Bismarck.

On to Harold. His anger scares me. Men full of mortification and introspection sometimes take out their inward strife on their wives. As I've said before, WATCH HIM.

I can well imagine his reaction to the war reports. Even after the Blitzkrieg, calamities scale new heights. Surrender seventy thousand Commonwealth troops to the Japs? Enemy slaughters over three hundred patients in Alexandra Hospital? Unthinkable. Unimaginable. Stunned faces fill the streets here.

Alex rejoins the fight in a few days, and I choose to believe the European front less dangerous than the Pacific. (But what do I know?)

You never flit far from my mind, friend. Thanks for your prayers. You have mine, as well, and I can't thank you enough for the PACKAGE—yummy! Took exactly three weeks. I'll hoard those cookies for weeks.

Love,

Kate

*A*ddie devoured the news and slid the envelope under the box in the upstairs closet, with a last glance at the postmark—eighteen days in transit. She hurried downstairs to fry some beef and chop vegetables for stew.

While the meat browned, she turned to Burpee's red, white and blue middle section, where Berthea introduced her to victory gardens the first winter of their marriage. Mama loved flowers, but lacked the energy to create a garden, so Addie learned what she knew from Aunt Alvina.

"War gardens, Mr. Burpee called them. My mother had one, and my aunt, too. The way things look, we might need to resurrect them."

The catalog's array energized Addie, and in preparation for warm spring days, she hung the washing on her clothesline in spite of the muddy yard. Then she leveled her ironing pile, stacked sheets and pillowcases on the shelf and underwear like hay bales in Harold's drawer.

Following Berthea's lead, he bought her an electric iron last year. Using a flatiron took much longer, so she couldn't complain about this job.

Before long, George's truck idled at the driveway. Addie closed the last drawer and threw on her sweater. He waved as she slogged to retrieve the mail, and then toward Berthea's house. Mud sucked at her boots, but letters could make such a big difference in her attitude.

Two knocks brought no response, so Addie inched the inner door open. Eerie quiet enveloped the house.

"Berthea?"

The kitchen clock's steady tick-tock offered no clues, nor did the family pictures. Bill's carefree dark hair fell onto his forehead in his wedding photo, but Harold brooded in his graduation picture. Down to his full lips, so like Orville's, worry stalked his countenance. No one mentioned pictures on their wedding day, so there weren't any.

A noise from the hallway summoned Addie, and she peeked around the corner to see Orville's bony feet splayed on the floor, stockings drawn up under his robe. Berthea cradled his head, but her eyes told the tale.

"Shall I send Harold for the doctor?"

"He's gone."

"I'll . . ." Addie half-turned toward the front door.

"Be careful." Berthea's stern look flashed a warning—even she couldn't tell what might set Harold off.

Something pricked under Addie's ribs as she swallowed down her trepidation and gathered her courage. Who knew how Harold might lash out at her when she told him the news? But Berthea seemed so calm. Mama's passing came to mind. Now, she hurried through the mud toward the barn, and found Harold. The day Mama died, Dad was nowhere to be found, though Addie searched high and low.

Harold leaned over the soupy swill, stirring with a long stick. When he spied her, his lower lip curled. "What're you doing out here?"

"Your mother needs you right away." Addie took the stick. "Hurry. Let me finish this."

She'd never done such a thing. Never given him an order like this. Harold drew a long breath, eyed Berthea's house, and then let go.

* * *

April 16, 1942

Dear Kate,

    I don't envy you saying good-bye to Alexandre again. By now, I hope you've found work.

    On Tuesday afternoon, Orville died. The Norwegian Lutheran pastor held the funeral today. Orville would protest the choice, but the Presbyterian minister developed pneumonia.

    At least it wasn't your German Lutheran pastor, since people suspect his Germanness. Pastor Langly said life is our chance to do something beautiful, and also to become beautiful inside.

    We paused at the back of the church, and I heard Harold catch his breath. Then, Fern's hymnal crashed on the organ keys. I was glad Bill kept a hand on

Harold's shoulder. He seems calm, and content with his lot in life. If only Harold could borrow his outlook.

More on the funeral later. The weather's warming. Daffodils and crocuses poke hesitant heads in our yard, bringing hope, and so will your next letter. Tell me about the flowers over there, please, if the Luftwaffe left any.

Expectantly,

Addie

A week after the funeral, Addie rolled up Harold's overall legs and let the sun drench her as she impaled the first weed crop. After a while, the crunch of two sets of shoes lifted her head as Berthea and her three-year-old charge approached.

"Willie, meet Miss Addie, working in her lovely garden."

"Wuvwee darden." Chubby arms spread wide, Willie glowed.

"Miss Addie loves her flowers."

"Fwowers."

On her knees with her head slung to the side like a cow seeking grass, Addie worked back on her knees.

"Willie's tired of Grandpa George's mail truck, so he's staying with me for a while today."

The little boy's chocolate-toothed grin captivated Addie.

"Nice to meet you, Willie. Auntie B gave you some chocolate, I see."

"Bee. Shokate."

Berthea put her finger to her lips. "Don't tell Harold."

"How old is Willie today?"

He held up three fingers.

"Three. Oh my, so big!"

Berthea flashed her best smile since the funeral. "Don't you love his chubby cheeks?"

Addie poked one, and Willie gave her a grin. "Willie, shall we pick a flower for Auntie B?"

"Fwower. Bee."

She pulled some violets and Shasta daisies. "For Auntie B."

Tears sprang in Berthea's eyes. "Thank you very much, sweetie."

Willie reached on tiptoe to kiss her, and she touched the slobbery spot. "Oh, my—would you like to give Miss Addie one?"

But his mood took a turn. He shook his head and stamped his feet in the grass.

Addie chuckled. "It's okay. Today's your day for kisses."

"Willie, let's go play with the toys. Tell Miss Addie good-bye."

"Toys, toys!" He pressed against Berthea's skirt.

"Bye-bye, Willie. Come over and see me later, all right?" Addie caught Berthea's eye. "I'd be happy to watch him for a while."

She shook her head. "Thanks, but I need time with this bit of heaven."

Addie returned to her weeding, certain that down the road a quarter-mile, their neighbor did the same. Three years had passed since they met, on the day Addie married Harold. Afterward, Harold carried her belongings into the farmhouse his parents vacated for their new Sears and Roebuck number 115.

A week earlier, Berthea had invited Addie to view the groundbreaking before they dug the basement and set the limestone foundation. Thanks to Sears and Roebuck's ingenuity, by Monday morning, Orville and Berthea took up residence in their newly painted home, and turned the old farmhouse over to Harold and Addie.

The workers connected the old basement cistern to the windmill, and Harold transformed a walk-in closet into a bathroom. No more toting water pails or using makeshift potties on frigid winter nights, no morning dumping or stench.

On their wedding afternoon, Addie and Harold moved some of the furniture Berthea left, and Addie stared out an upstairs window at Berthea and Orville's bright white coat of paint. Maybe someday she would paint this old house yellow to complement the flower garden she planned out back.

Some of his parents' clothes still hung in the largest closet, so Harold carried them to the new house while Addie cleaned. After supper, he dropped into a bedraggled armchair with a book.

Addie peeked into the living room after washing the dishes. "Want to take a walk?"

He frowned over his reading glasses, and she got his message. He wanted to be alone this evening, and his stare dismissed her from the room. Her eyes burned as she backed away. Not what she'd foreseen on their wedding night, but the beautiful evening beckoned her outside to an old bike sitting in the shed.

She pedaled south down the gravel road as a fine mist rolled over rustling corn. Mama and Ruthie used to say you could hear corn grow. With every turn of the wheels, Addie practiced her new name—*Mrs. Harold Bledsoe.*

Now, three years later, she pulled out some quack grass, thankful that Jane taught her to space flowers and vegetables for optimum sunshine. When they met, Addie never would have guessed how much the outspoken older woman would show her.

On Addie's wedding night, a tangle of half-grown hollyhocks straggled up Jane's ditch, forming perfect camouflage, so Addie didn't see anyone outside at first. But the flowers drew her, so she parked the bicycle, entered a vast, abundant garden and exclaimed, "Oh, these will be gorgeous in July."

Farther in, an older woman straightened. Knee-deep in a yellow, red, and purple tulip bed, her one hand grasped a cane, but she offered Addie the other one.

"You must be the new bride. I'm Jane Pike. Glad to know you." Her warm, substantial fingers enveloped Addie's, wafting the pleasant scent of new earth.

"Your garden—how wonderful!"

Mrs. Pike tottered to a wooden bench, well concealed by flaming tulips. "Have time to sit a spell?" She descended with a thud amidst violent knee pops.

"Thank you, ma'am."

Mrs. Pike covered half the bench, a slatted affair held together with iron supports. "Been moving in today?"

"Yes, it didn't take long, but I needed to get some fresh air tonight. I found an old bike out in the shed and pumped up the tires."

"Now that's something I would enjoy. But with my bad knee, I might break my neck learning to pedal the thing." Mrs. Pike rubbed the joint and grimaced.

"Yet you maintain this lovely garden. I simply had to stop."

"I'm glad you did, Mis . . ."

"Call me Addie. We lived south of town, on the old Reser place. My parents were Avery and Betty Ann Shields."

"Don't believe I've heard of them." The bench creaked as Jane shifted her weight, with a ramshackle shed forming a backdrop for her square jaw and short-cropped salt and pepper hair.

"Mind you, I don't know many folks." All the while, she worked at a mix of green and black lining her fingernails.

Now, Addie glanced down at her own nails, sporting the same stain. That first afternoon, Jane earned her immediate trust, so words came flooding out of her mouth.

"Mama died, but Dad still lives on the home place with my younger brother Herman. My oldest brother Reuben left years ago, and my little sister lives with my older one in Minnesota."

"And now you've come to our side of the world." The lines around Jane's eyes crinkled like a daylily's innermost folds.

"We only lived a few miles away, but I don't know anybody up here. I'm happy we have such a close neighbor."

"So you're all settled, then?"

"Harold's mother left plenty of furniture. I cleaned out the closets, and the dust . . . "

"Old houses collect it like old women my age collect wrinkles." Mrs. Pike put her hand to a roll that blanketed her middle. "And fat."

Her deep chuckle enveloped them and Addie relaxed. Before she knew it, she'd spilled out the day's details to this new neighbor, and the sun hung golden orange over the horizon.

"I've never cleaned with Harold underfoot. He said Berthea kept the drapes closed, but I whacked them with a broom over the clothesline, and they're a shade brighter already. I like a lot of light, don't you?"

"Drapes, in my opinion, serve to keep the cold out in winter and let sunshine in the rest of the time."

"I probably shouldn't have said all of that." Addie's cheeks burned for telling family tales. "My chief fault is impatience, and I talk too much. I know it'll take time to get used to . . ."

"There's plenty to adapt to in any family. And rest assured, what you say is safe with me. I hardly ever see Harold, and since Orville's stroke, Berthea, either."

Mrs. Pike rubbed her crusty palms together. At the same time, fiery speckles appeared in the cornfield. "Dusk is such a pleasant time of day, isn't it?"

"Oh look—lightning bugs—the first I've seen this year."

"They bode well. My grandmother used to say fireflies signal a bountiful harvest. I have no idea if that's true or not. Anyway, I've always felt there's something magical about them."

Something magical. Addie stretched out the small of her back and tackled some creeping Charlie intent on overtaking her daylilies. *Maybe those lightning bugs when I met Jane were a sign—she's brought me good luck with my garden.*

Her eternal war with the weeds showed progress, but pails clinking in the barn told her she ought to start supper. She hated to stop reminiscing, since Jane had become such a bright spot in her life.

"My Mama called fireflies starlight come down to earth."

"That's lovely."

"Your garden inspires me, Mrs. Pike. I'm going to plant one."

"I'm Jane, just plain old Jane." The heavy flesh under Mrs. Pike's arm swung as she waved over the garden. "You're welcome to starts of anything here. What kinds of flowers would you like?"

Earlier in the day, Addie might have said, "It doesn't matter, just flowers." But surveying Jane's array, a clearer answer formed.

"Ones that let the light in to others, some of every height. And lots of yellow."

Jane beamed, and a reverent pause cloaked them as the sun dipped lower. Then an engine sputtered from the direction of the farm, and Addie's heart flip-flopped. That might be Harold.

Leaning on her cane, Jane came to a stand. Like emeralds, her green eyes reflected waning sunlight ...and warmth.

"I'd better get going. It's almost dark." Addie ran a few steps and turned. "But I'll come back."

"See that you do, Addie Bledsoe. Glad to have you for a neighbor."

Addie finished weeding and scanned in vain for the hollyhock starts Jane gave her for the second time last spring. To her words of thanks, Jane remonstrated.

"Never say thanks for plants, or they won't flourish."

Smiling at the old wives' tale, Addie set her trowel on the shelf in the shed. Maybe it was time to pay her neighbor this season's first visit.

Chapter Eight

April 12, 1942

Dear Addie,

When Harold's so unsettled and irritable, remember Mrs. M's advice—some things are better left unsaid. There's no need to tell him everything that comes into your mind.

You've heard we bombed Lubeck, Germany because of its timbered medieval buildings, to decrease morale? But the RAF responded in kind to Luftwaffe strategy. Now London's fire wardens expect raids in retaliation. Sounds like children, doesn't it?

The March 28 bombing, a 5.5% loss, included Alexandre's Spitfire, so I await word again. Thousands of orphans need homes, and fearing Nazi incendiaries, many older folks sleep in the tunnels. They stand in line in late afternoon, holding their spots.

Have you heard about the Easter Sunday Ceylon Raid? With anxieties so high after Singapore, an Australian unit reported a large sea turtle as a Japanese amphibious vehicle—now Harold can taunt them, too.

Though we lost the Dorsetshire, the Cornwall, and nearly five hundred men, the fleet survived, thanks to Admiral Somerville and a new hero, Leonard Birchall, who radioed the Japanese position and strength before being shot down.

But the U.S. has bad news, too, with the fall of
Bataan. Maybe our generals aren't perfect, either.

Halberton seems a peaceful oasis, though I know
you fight your own battles. Your letters cheer me, and
remember, spring is on its way.

I promise a brighter outlook next time.

Kate

*A*long the fence, short sticks marked where the renegade
hollyhocks should appear, but they seemed to come up wherever they
pleased. Berthea called them biennials, but you never knew what to
expect—would they disappear for one year, two, or more? Arms
akimbo, Addie sighed.

"Where are you? I know I should be patient, and Jane would say
it's only May."

Forget-me-nots' miniature periwinkle blossoms splashed around
the big front porch like paint dabs. Bleeding Hearts spread magenta
and white under the eave spouts, and daylily clumps promised a
golden June spectacle. Even Johnny Jump-ups already showed, though
they often sprouted later.

Harold called from the shed, so Addie hurried over. "Hold this
hitch while I find a bolt." He handed her the heavy iron bar. "It's all
lined up, and I don't want to do it all over again."

She concentrated on keeping the small holes in line, but five
minutes later, her back complained.

"Harold?" No answer, and her discomfort became pain. She yelled
again and looked around for Berthea, but the old Chevy was gone.
Easing the hitch to the ground. Addie checked the shed, barn, and milk
house, but found Harold leaning over a book in his new study.

"Harold?"

His head pitched like a pump handle. "Didn't I tell you to hold that
hitch?"

"I couldn't any longer. My back . . ."

He slammed the book down. "I give you one simple duty and you
suddenly develop back problems. I was just checking something."

"Are you ready now? We can try again."

He rushed past her. "I'll do it myself, like everything else around here. You're so set on your garden, you're worthless."

His pronouncement settled over her as she drank a glass of water and studied him through the porch window. His sermonizing hadn't lessened his irritation, that was for sure.

"Worthless like those hollyhocks." She rubbed her lower back and went back outside, where she examined the trumpet vine. Last week she asked Jane if she should prune it.

"No, wait. Those dried-up twigs will turn into green leaves any day."

The vines now crawled the fence top like invading snakes. Several pithy branches still protruded, but the whole plant would soon leaf out.

Yet not one hollyhock broke through the black soil. Each spring the garden sprites forced her to beg Jane for more seedlings. Could it be that the fence's rotting wood resisted hollyhocks?

April 21, 1942

Dear Addie,

I may have found work to keep me from the Dover cliffs.

Tomorrow's interview with a Mr. Tenney will give me some idea—had to reassure you all is not gloom and doom, as per my last letter. Maybe the sun will set on the British Empire, but England will survive.

Dig For Victory flyer enclosed. Even the lawns around the Tower of London have been transformed into vegetable gardens, creating a green oasis in the dismal grayness. And we have sparrows, pigeons, and robins. They tell me another paler robin comes in winter from Scandinavia, too.

Keep up your good work and as they say here, Cheerio, dear friend.

> Love,
> Kate

After Harold left to sow oats, Addie studied Kate's flyer showing a hearty British woman wielding a spade in the midst of towering buildings. Imagining gardens throughout the great city of London led her outdoors.

Maybe today her hollyhocks would appear. Their blossoms laced her childhood memories, floating in the wind like bright-skirted ballerinas. Her sister Ruthie taught her how to drill buds into broken-off blossoms to create women bedecked in red, pink, rose, yellow and white flower skirts.

The delicate ladies kept them company all day long. What other flower could star in a stage play or inspire an impromptu tea party?

But Mama called them weeds, scrunching her sunburned nose.

"Blamed things will overrun my green beans."

As much as her mother detested hollyhocks, Addie wanted them to grow. She squatted, looking for babies, but as Mama would say, it was either feast or famine.

"You silly plants. Don't you know Jane says this is your year?"

She squished through the low area between the house and garden. One last bitter March snowstorm had preceded rains that seemed endless, but finally, heat pressed on purple lilac buds, releasing their heady scent.

The big yellow daisy bush she strategically planted doubled its girth every year, hiding an ugly, rusting pipe near the back porch. Dogwoods ranged beside the driveway, and even when blizzards bore down, their red bark splashed against the snow like cardinals' feathers. Now, summer brought blossoms.

"Harold calls my work a waste, but how else could I create something beautiful, like Pastor Langly preached? Anticipation is half the fun, except with those hollyhocks."

"In due time," Mama often had announced, or "We'll see."

She often uttered one of her fixed responses while studying Dad draped across his stuffed armchair, his incoherent stare fixed on the broken radio. In due time, perhaps, he would come to life. *We'll see.*

The red Farm-All sputtered into the driveway, and Addie leaned over to pull a thistle. Three summers ago, Harold might have caught her eye from the bouncy seat. Once, he leaped down, threw her over his shoulder and made for the corncrib during the middle of the day.

Remembering how he carried her up the homemade wooden ladder, Addie's face heated. The solid oak floor creaked under them and she felt the effects in her back for days.

Back then, the star of Halberton's 1938 class, his educational hopes curtailed by Orville's stroke, still entertained a passion that matched his anger at life, and his intense declaration satisfied her. "You belong to me, Addie."

His blue eyes changed to clouded gray, relaying another message she could never decipher. Back then, feeling needed satisfied her. But now, did desire for her even enter Harold's mind?

He hooked up the plow, and she turned her attention back to the garden. Jane seemed not to mind being bothered. Maybe she would ride over after dinner.

A run-down truck turned in, and a man chatted with Harold. When he left, Harold waved her over.

"A man in Halberton is dying, and someone needs to make sure he takes his morning pills. He's not elderly, just looks that way after his Great War experience. Ride in and check on him, all right?" He focused just above Addie's head. "His name's Mr. Allen. He lives on Third, two houses down from Mrs. Raney."

His eyes shone steel gray. "And while you're in town, pick up a can of oil at Carson's station."

Addie rubbed a jagged place on her cuticle and went for the bicycle. Morning sun eased her jitters over meeting Mr. Allen, and since she passed the station on the way to his house, she stopped for the oil. No one manned the office, so she went into the shop, where a voice came from under a dark green farm truck.

"Can I help you?"

"I need whatever kind of oil Harold Bledsoe usually buys."

The grease monkey rolled his dolly out, got to his feet, and gestured to lines of cans on the far wall. "For his tractor?"

"I think so."

The tall, slender worker led her to the counter and turned to face Addie.

"Why, Glenora—is that you under all that grime?"

60

The young woman's good-natured chuckle made Addie smile. "Yep, it's me, doing my part, since my brother went to off to the West Coast last week."

"No—Pinky, too?"

"Yep, and just about everybody else too, hon. Ira Yates got rejected, so he moved to Waterloo to work at the John Deere plant—making tank parts."

"Good for him."

"Harold's got a file here, I think." Glenora thumbed through a grimy recipe box. "Yep. I'll just write this down."

"What's this?" Addie studied a handwritten note taped to the counter.

Here are three high purposes for every American:

    1. We shall not stop work for a single day. If any dispute arises we shall keep on working while the dispute is solved by mediation, conciliation, or arbitration - until the war is won.

    2. We shall not demand special gains or special privileges or special advantages for any one group or occupation.

    3. We shall give up conveniences and modify the routine of our lives if our country asks us to do so. We will do it cheerfully, remembering that the common enemy seeks to destroy every home and every freedom in every part of our land.

    This generation of Americans has come to realize, with a present and personal realization, that there is something larger and more important than the life of any individual or of any individual group - something for which a man will sacrifice, and gladly sacrifice, not only his pleasures, not only his goods, not only his associations with those he loves, but his life itself. In time of crisis when the future is in the balance, we come to understand, with full recognition and devotion, what this Nation is, and what we owe to it. Franklin Delano Roosevelt, February, 1942

"Dad's enamored with the fireside chats—cut that out himself. With Pinky gone, he can't stand anyone griping about the war. Figures this might shut somebody up before they start."

"Not a bad idea." Addie picked up the can of oil. "I thought . . . didn't you win a scholarship to some college in Nebraska?"

Glenora wiped a soiled handkerchief over her forehead. "Iowa State. Guess I wasn't destined to go after all."

"Maybe when this is all over . . ."

"Everybody makes sacrifices, that's for sure. Harold's been in here going on about the board. Any change yet?"

Gnats flew in Addie's stomach. "No, but I keep thinking maybe he'll resign himself someday."

Glenora grinned. "Eternal optimism, huh? I went through twelve years of school with him, and I'd say Harold doesn't know the meaning of resign."

* * *

May 7, 1942

Dear Kate,

Through ups and downs, you hold on, as always—I hope Mr. Tenney finds your typing scores irresistible. Corregidor has fallen now—Harold makes sure I never miss a report. But that's enough about the war.

I'm still catching my breath from an adventure. Harold sent me to check on a sick man in Halberton, Norman Allen. His sister is visiting her daughter in Florida, so I only have to go for a couple of weeks.

Norman scratched a peculiar reddish-blue design on his scalp the whole time I was there this morning. I wanted to tie his hand down. The county nurse left instructions for six different pills, one with water, one with food, two before breakfast, two after.

I asked Norman if he liked eggs, so he opened his right eye and part of his left. I don't know if he can see with that one, but it certainly has a life of its own.

"Over easy, two or three."

The toaster tch-tched, so I turned the bread. Then his breath grazed my neck, and I jumped two feet. "Scaredja, didn't I?"

A big black ant ran from a greasy crack in the pale green linoleum, so I smashed it with my shoe, and the second tch-tch-tch stopped.

Norman's bent frame hit just above my shoulder, and his wheeze made me pull out a chair for him. When I set his coffee cup down, he latched onto my arm and said he learned to sneak up on people in the Meuse-Argonne.

Our world history lessons flooded in—Mr. Blaine called the Meuse-Argonne Hell on earth, remember?

My patient started to eat, but I recalled my mission and reminded him to take his pill first. Brown spittle spewed on his whiskers, and I thought of Berthea nursing Orville for three long years. Since you love suspense, I'll save the ending for my next letter.

Stay far away from the Dover Cliffs.

Love,

Addie

Chapter Nine

"*T*urn the crank while I clean out the sieve. The sows wreaked havoc with this water tank mechanism." After half an hour, Harold lowered himself to cussing and Addie tried in vain to ignore him.

Finally, he looked at his watch. "Aren't you supposed to be in town?"

Grateful for deliverance, she pedaled straight to Third Street, cooked breakfast, and called Mr. Allen to the table.

"Good morning, sir. Here's your breakfast." She pointed at the line of white dots beside his plate. He eyed her askance, but popped one behind a chipped brown tooth and gulped some coffee.

"Set yerself down."

She avoided looking at his left eye. "You fought in the Great War?"

He coughed as if to bring up a pyramid. The tremble in his shoulders hurt to watch. Should she pound on his back? No, a fragile bone might break.

Harold said Mrs. Allen died years ago, but a hook still held her apron, stained with what looked like splattered angel food cake batter. Creamy tan wallpaper featured brown teapots and cups faded almost to white. Near the stove, the small Frigidaire listed south.

Finally, Mr. Allen stopped hacking and wiped his sleeve across his mouth. He ate three bites of egg, some toast, and took the next two pills. Addie's hopes rose, but then he turned inquisitive.

"Who sentcha here?"

"My husband, Harold Bledsoe."

"Oh, yeah. Likes to talk about religion and the war." He balanced his elbows on the table, his shoulder blades like wing joints.

"Did I tell ya how good it was t' see Fernella when I come back from the troop ship?"

"Fernella?"

Another cough let loose and he lost what he'd eaten, maybe a pill, too. The nurse said if he missed one, not to give him another, so Addie put the lost pill out of her mind and cleaned the table.

"Fernella McCluskey."

Addie felt her eyes open wide. "Fern's real name is Fernella?"

He put a quivering finger to cracked lips. "She'd kill me if she knew I told. Don't know if I'd-a made it without Fernella."

"You mean Mrs. McCluskey at First Methodist?"

"Who else?" His expression registered impatience. "I'd camped out in the woods through the Battle of Saint-Mihiel . . . rained five days straight . . . had to leave our food behind in the mud. My buddy got trench foot even 'fore we dug the trenches . . . "

His head drooped, but then he jerked awake. "Met Fernella at the church, helpin' returnin' soldiers. Only place her folks'd let her go. Worst thing she coulda done, 'cause she met me."

The clock made Addie edgy. She had to clean the chicken house and bake pies for the church council meeting tonight, but wanted to hear the rest of the story.

"Wasn't good 'nuff for her daddy, but she thought she wasn't good 'nuff for anyone a'tall. Sometimes, we slipped away b'fore her daddy picked her up. She didn't mind my eye, neither." His wounded eye watered over a grin that meandered his face.

"She showed me I could still do somethin' 'sides kill. Never forget how good she made me feel—like I was alive again."

Addie's imagination went wild. She leaped up and sent Norman's cup flying. A tepid coffee smell and his startled look washed regret over her as she mopped up the mess.

"I'm so sorry. You need to take three more pills, right away. I— it's so late. I have to get back home."

She stood over him until he swallowed the pills. His Adam's apple bulged and she poured him more coffee, threw the smelly goop on his plate into the wastebasket, and backed toward the door.

"Comin' agin tomorra?"

Something came over her, like when she and Kate watched the boys turn over their cranky Latin teacher's outhouse on Hallowe'en one year. Even though she didn't do a thing but watch, a thrill went through her when the stinky contraption smashed to the earth.

"Maybe." She opened the door like Jean Harlow. "If you behave."

Her heart practically beat out of her chest. She could never, never talk like that to Harold. She pedaled home and parked her bicycle in the shed, where he greased the plow.

"Did Mr. Allen take his pills?"

"Yes."

"You would make a fine nurse, hon." He squinted at her like he was planning something, but it had been so long since he'd called her honey, she took heart.

While her pies baked, Addie shoveled chicken manure on her raspberry patch and her mind wandered to an advertisement in Berthea's newspaper.

> Install Cel-o-glass. Attracts ultra-violet rays, and gives you the most eggs at the lowest cost.

A sketch showed a chicken coop with big new windows and happy hens laying piles of eggs. Could sunshine make that much difference in egg production? A few years back, Harold brought home ideas like this from Iowa State, only to be rejected by Orville. But he wouldn't even give the Cel-o-glass ad a second thought.

His only comment was, "Now there's a money-making deal, eh? But will it make *us* money?"

She took a bath, ironed his shirt, and wrapped her pies and a platter of ham in newspapers. Headed toward the pick-up, Harold gave her a pinch, an improvement over last month's council meeting when he demanded she re-iron his shirt at the last minute.

That night, she feared he might burst a blood vessel and gave silent thanks that she lacked her older brother Reuben's illogical laughing urge when Dad lost his temper. She wanted to clamp her hand over Reuben's mouth so Dad wouldn't strip off his belt and go after him.

But Reuben seemed destined to laugh at such inopportune times. No wonder he lit out at the first opportunity. Harold might get furious, but surely he'd never hit her.

The potluck went fine except for Marge Calease's pineapple and shredded carrot gelatin salad. Wilbur thought she made a hot dish and put the bowl in a direct line with the car motor, melting her creation into a strange brownish liquid. Marge wrung her hands as all the women offered their contributions.

But Fern rushed to her rescue. "Let's not waste it, Marge. Someone will drink it." She poured the slime into several cups and her prophecy proved true.

Hello again, Kate.

I'm still tending my patient. You'll say I should've put my foot down with Harold, but hear me out.

Tonight, the women stormed the church kitchen when their husbands went to the council meeting. A little later, Walt tapped Fern's shoulder and said he needed me for a minute. Oh-oh.

Harold wouldn't like this at all. He's a one-man show, though one sweet older lady insists, "Harold's sermons inspire me so, Addie. You make such a wonderful team."

She raised her eyebrows at me as if to say, "I told you so."

I joined Harold under the picture of a missionary who sank with her ship after donating her lifeboat seat to another passenger. Strangely, Harold beamed and pulled me so close the metal folding chair cut into my leg.

"You do so well as Mr. Allen's nurse, dear, that I suggested you continue until Mr. Allen's sister returns."

My heart plopped into my shoes. Go back to that hot, stinky place? I spared you the odors, but you can imagine, with no indoor plumbing.

The voice in my head knew what to say: "You've gone too far this time, Harold. Get Fern—I'm sure she'll manage just fine."

But I wilted like my clematis leaves when I trimmed their ground cover too much the other day. Harold twisted his fingers in my side, so I mumbled okay, if they couldn't find anyone else. Mama always said that suffering reaps rewards, remember?

I have to fix supper, but will write again soon.

Take care,

Addie

* * *

Mr. Allen scratched his scalp. "Doubted I'd ever see ya agin."

"Why? I'm honored to help out a Great War veteran."

He blinked hard and took four pills without complaint. "Told ya 'bout Fernella yesterday, didn't I?"

"Yes, but if you eat two bites right now and take another pill, you'll only have one to go."

"Ahhhhh, that gal was somethin'. Looks a little stern now, but in those days, she smiled like a princess."

"Sir, your eggs?"

"'Magine what she meant to a flea-bitten soldier." He looked Addie squarely in the eye. "If you're thinkin' I didn't love my wife, you're dead wrong. I woulda married Fernella in a second 'cept for her daddy, but I waited three full years t' marry Millie."

"I wasn't thinking that." Actually, she'd been wondering how Fern could ever have seemed so beautiful.

Mr. Allen's bad eye roved the ceiling. "Can't tell by lookin' what somebody's been through."

The county health nurse bustled in. "Now, we're going to have our bath, Mr. A."

An insistent question troubled Addie. What had Fern been through? She tried to recall when she'd seen Fern smile. What took her beautiful smile away?

For dinner she roasted pork, mashed potatoes and made gravy, cooked corn, and took out an orange gelatin salad. As the hired men passed the bowls around, Harold frowned, but couldn't accuse her of frivolity, since Berthea brought over two boxes of Jell-O yesterday.

One of the hired men paused before leaving. Busy clearing dishes, Addie didn't notice him until he cleared his throat.

"That was real good, ma'am."

His smile seemed genuine, and she managed to say thank you. When the dishes were finished, she bagged cookies for the three o'clock lunch, fixed chicken salad sandwiches, and squeezed lemons for lemonade. Harold told her he'd like a fresh cherry pie, but she hadn't found time to pick, much less pit the cherries—maybe later, after she took lunch to the field.

Feeding Old Brown some scraps, Addie heard a low bawl from the wrong direction. Down the driveway, six milk cows strung along to the road. Her stomach tightened—Harold would be so upset. He hired the men today because both fields came ready at the same time and the forecast included rain. He wouldn't want to waste a minute.

Thankful to see the Chevy, she raced back to Berthea's. "The cows are out, but I'm not sure . . ."

"It's not the first time. Ride your bike for Harold, and I'll shoo them toward the pasture." Berthea launched down the driveway hollering, "Come bisey, Come bisey!"

Down the old lane behind the barn, sun glinted off the baler. Addie bicycled as far as she could and then loped through the jagged stalks toward thehay rack. Harold scowled.

She bent to catch her breath. "The cows are out. Your mother . . ."

"How did that happen?"

"I don't know. I noticed them a little while ago and your mother is . . ."

"You left her alone?"

Addie strummed her thumbnail as her chest tightened. Harold spoke to the driver and propelled toward the farmyard faster than she could ride. By the time she reached home, he and Berthea had corralled three cows.

Harold barked instructions. "Hold your arms out wide and act big."

Hoping the sturdy animals wouldn't charge, Addie flapped her arms and yelled. Twenty minutes later, the last one entered the pasture and Harold wired the fence. Without a look her way, he loaded the lunch into the bubbletop and took off for the field.

Flushed and panting, Berthea caught up. "We did it—good work, Addie! I need to get out like this every day." She started home, but turned. "Do you think it's too late to plant dahlia bulbs? I found some I'd forgotten."

"I'll ask Jane—she'll probably say it can't hurt to try." Berthea's praise rang in Addie's head for the next half hour.

Chapter Ten

*A*fter a humid haying day, Addie weeded until sunset, when Harold and the hired men drove into the yard. She washed up at the outside pump and made supper. Harold went straight to the living room and flipped on the news, so she took his plate in and picked up her knitting. A few minutes later, the broadcaster struck an alarm.

> Finally, the woman's Army Auxiliary Corps bill has passed.
>
> Introduced by Edith Nourse Rogers a year ago, the law fell into gerrymandering, even with Mrs. Roosevelt's support and the nurses' brilliant work at Schofield Hospital. Not even the events at Hickam Field could sway our legislators.
>
> The Chief Nurse earned the Bronze Star and Purple Heart for meritorious service. The Navy, Marines, and Coast Guard now authorize women's training, so chins up, boys, our women will soon join you. Authorizing Negro women to join up will be considered next.

Harold ran his fingers through his hair. "Your Kathryn will love that."

Addie focused on her stitch.

"Aren't you going to answer me?"

"I wasn't really listening."

"Ach . . . you don't care about the war at all. I said Kate would support a women's corps, probably even the Negro women."

71

"Our men need help, don't you think?"

"What do you mean?"

"What would have happened in the Battle of the Coral Sea without a hospital ship?"

Harold kicked his chair into the corner. Addie cringed, but Kate's advice sustained her. *You don't have to say everything you think.*

"Kate's addled your brain—you don't know right from wrong anymore. The Bible reveals women's rightful place, and it's not in the Army."

Though her needles quivered, Addie spoke up. "Pick up that chair, Harold. If you want to discuss the war, go talk with your mother."

His fingers undulated along his thigh, and her heartbeat staggered against her breastbone. The click of boots on waxed linoleum echoed, though the cloud of Harold's rage lingered.

Weariness descended like a driving rain, and Addie switched off the radio. Then she shared her thoughts with the room. "No wonder he dislikes Kate—he puts all women in one sub-male category. But what was I thinking to sass back like that?"

She wracked her brain trying to think what she could do to make amends and pull Harold from his brooding rage. Why did he assume he was the only one suffering?

Donuts? They made a mess, but he loved them. She could try Bertha's recipe again tomorrow. She leaned her forehead on the icy windowpane. "*Donuts won't fix what ails him.*"

A quick shiver went through her as Joe's voice spoke unbidden truth in her head, and a memory snapped into view. Joe had come to help sort the pigs on a wet spring day with biting wind that sliced between the buildings. Addie bundled up and trudged down to the barn with a basket of warm cinnamon rolls and a thermos of coffee.

Sweet Joe moaned with delight at the treat and said he didn't know how Harold had gotten so lucky to end up with someone as thoughtful as Addie.

She could still remember Harold's eyes narrowing as he glared at Joe. After that look that always froze her on the spot, he stuffed a roll in his mouth and grunted. "Goin' over to check on Dad. He'll want to know how it went." He stomped off.

Another slap in the face that didn't leave a mark.

Joe looked away for a moment, and then murmured, "Addie, I'm sorry."

He spoke so quietly she nearly missed the words.

She brushed away escaping tears and faced him. "No, it's ok. It's been a long morning, and he's tired. I understand."

Joe gave her a steady look and blew out his cheeks for a moment before he replied. "No, you don't . . . *understand*."

It took him a long moment to continue. "You know Harold and I played football together in high school."

She nodded.

"And you know he went with Clara Schmidt for a long time."

She nodded.

"You know why he broke it off with her?"

Addie could feel color rising in her cheeks. She opened her mouth, desperate to change the subject. This was private, Harold's business. What if Joe told her . . .

He interrupted her flashing thoughts. "She missed a big game. He scored the winning field goal in the last 5 seconds."

"I can understand him being upset, Joe. Football meant a lot . . . "

"Carla missed that game because she'd gone to help her sister who'd just had a baby. She hemorrhaged and nearly died."

Addie remembered studying the toes of her galoshes to avoid eye contact.

Joe's voice came to her again today, gentle but firm. "It's all about him, Addie, *always.* Wouldn't even say it was his fault . . . his folks had him late and Orville spoiled him rotten. Oh, he'd get after him at times, but let anyone else say a word and he'd rip them apart. That included Harold's mom."

April 30, London

Dear Addie,

Alexandre returned whole and has flown off again. For the moment, gratitude outweighs my anxiety.

Mr. Allen intrigues me. I never pictured you as a nurse, but you can do whatever needs doing. Next report, please.

Drumroll . . . I got the job! Evelyn and I celebrated with dinner and stopped by a park that escaped the bombs. I wonder how things looked here before, as you must wonder how dapper Norman once appeared in his Great War uniform.

Evelyn finally divulged her history. Her mother's health failed the past few years. After the first bombing, Evelyn rushed home to nothing but rubble. She says the bombs detonated her emotions, too, but she's adopted her mother's habit of hope.

I can't feel sorry for myself, and can't help but think destiny had you meet Mr. Allen, even with the horrid smells. As Evelyn would say, "Da—a—astardly, dear, yet onward we go."

However, Harold standing you before the council goes beyond fair or right. Remember Mrs. Morfordson's challenge to our class: "Consider the question each moment poses?"

Evelyn would say "Blaahst the council." She wears a bright red scarf, the only thing left of her mother's, and often exclaims, "BLAAHST those Nazis!"

Practice it. "Blaahst them!"

Harold's getting worse. Here's a question for you: why do you let him treat you disrespectfully?

Awaiting your response,

The Typist

Harold refrained from shoving his chair back when the minute hand hit seven a.m. Addie reached to clear his plate, but he held her wrist. "We need to pray."

She sat down so fast that the plate spun like a top. When he said they needed to pray, she'd always done something to disturb him. How many times had she asked, "What is it we need to pray about?"

Suddenly, she knew the answer to Kate's question—fear made her accept Harold's behavior. Her statements often antagonized him, but this time she didn't know what she'd said wrong, and she determined to keep quiet.

Harold ran his tongue along his teeth. "Harrumph!"

She jumped, but steeled her resolve. A stubborn itch began between her shoulders—something to focus on besides Harold's drawn expression.

His tongue finally settled down and the uneven edge of a mismatched tooth extended over his lower lip. "We must beseech God for children. 'For where two or three are gathered . . .'"

"...together, there am I in the midst of them." The rest of the verse flitted from Addie's mouth before she could stop it. Harold stuck out his chin.

"Yes, smartie."

She stared at the bright tablecloth, the one thing in this room she picked out herself.

"Addie!" Harold let go of her wrist, sending tingles all the way to her shoulder.

The lines in his neck protruded. Tendons, their high school biology teacher called them when Kate sat next to her and gashed the leg off a chloroformed frog. Mr. Mertz wasn't exactly pleased with Kate that day.

Harold thrummed the tabletop, creating a muffled beat not unlike the Halberton band at the last parade. At the same time, the clock's tick grew far too loud.

"Harold . . . Harold?" The screen door squeaked open. "Is anybody home?"

Usually quick to do Berthea's bidding, Harold glared at Addie as though she arranged for his mother to come.

Yes, I told her we'd be asking a blessing on our efforts to conceive, and she agreed to interrupt us.

"Oh good, you're still here. The engine's making such a racket, I thought you'd better check it."

Harold sucked in his cheeks. If he took Berthea's statement the wrong way, Addie would hear about it later.

"I'll be back." He focused over Addie's head to the yellow checked curtains floating in a brisk spring breeze.

"Did I come at a bad time?"

Harold grabbed his hat, leaving Addie to respond.

"Oh, Harold likes to start work early."

"Just like his father."

"Would you drink a cup of coffee?"

"No, thank you. I hope he can find the problem soon and . . . I did interrupt something didn't I?"

"We were just . . . ah . . . praying for a child." Addie clapped her hand over her mouth—Harold would be furious. She changed the subject. "I'm going to visit Norman Allen soon. Can I pick up anything for you if he can't fix your car?"

"No, thanks. I have a meeting to attend, that's all." Color rose in Berthea's cheeks.

A meeting so early? The churchwomen always waited until midmorning so they could serve food.

Berthea pulled at her collar and Addie noticed her jacket complimented her figure, or she had lost weight. "Did you get a new jacket?"

"Goodness, no. It's something I found going through our old things." Berthea fidgeted with her skirt and Addie searched for something to say.

"That shade of blue matches your eyes."

Perspiration ranged Berthea's forehead, although the morning temperature stayed cool. It wasn't like her to be at a loss for words. Addie filled in the silence.

"I think I'll plant some more beans this afternoon, and the lettuce is almost ready. How are your radishes doing?"

Berthea jerked her head toward clatter from the yard and dabbed her forehead with her hankie. "Fine." She turned back, and it seemed less flesh moved than normal. "I'd better see how Harold is doing."

The seams of her hosiery divided the backs of her calves perfectly as she navigated the porch steps and walked toward Harold. She hadn't been over much this week, but at the mailbox two days ago, Addie noticed how her elbow rested on George's open truck window. Berthea had startled when Addie neared.

"I must be going, George. And here's Addie to fetch their mail."

The flush on Berthea's cheeks might have been due to the day's heat . . . or was it? But the egg truck turned down the driveway just then, so Addie put it out of her mind. In retrospect, the scene piqued her curiosity.

The kitchen's walnut-stained oak wainscoting met a waist-high lip, and brittle varnish peeled off when Addie traced it with her finger. She fingered a transparent, golden-brown piece the size of her thumbnail.

Her coffee didn't sit well, increasing her hankering for some tea. Her sister Ruthie used to brew a pot for Mama when things troubled her. She could point out to Harold that coffee was rationed too, but might as well control her tongue, as Kate mentioned. What good would it do to say anything?

To rid herself of the vile taste, she leaned over the slop pail. Harold would frown on this, too. Women shouldn't spit, sit with their legs uncrossed, or . . . She shook out her yellow tablecloth, the same brash shade as her late daffodils.

Kate would say where there's a will, there's a way. But would it be right to pray for tea in wartime?

Chapter Eleven

*B*erthea roared off in a terrible hurry, and Harold took his place at the table again. He cleared his throat, and as if someone jogged his memory, reached for Addie's hand and closed his eyes.

"Dear heavenly Father. We thy humble servants desire a child to brighten our home, as Thou hast promised those who serve Thee."

Heaven knew this place needed brightening. Before they married, Harold told her his vision of a table full of sons and daughters, as the Psalms pictured.

"We long to bear fruit for Thy kingdom, and faithfully carry out our duty. Now we beg Thy beneficence, if it be Thy will." Harold squeezed her hand, but before she could gather the right words, he uttered "Amen."

Eyeing the clock, Addie waited. Harold's terse jaw announced her failure—three years and no child. And now, the clock proclaimed a late start on a prime workday.

Harold's prayer replayed as she pedaled down the road against a sharp wind, and questions surfaced like the pebbles flying up on her legs. Did he mean since they did their part, God must do his? The Psalmist gave a snapshot of a believer surrounded by children, but could everyone expect bountiful offspring? That principle didn't seem to play out in real life.

Take Mama, who got plenty of exercise, yet every year, her midriff grew and she walked a little slower. By the summer between Addie's seventh and eighth grade year, huge sores broke out on her legs.

When Aunt Henrietta drove her to visit Ruth and Reginald in Minnesota, Ruthie took her to a doctor. Addie, left to care for Herman and Bonnie, learned about this when she received her very first letter.

After the opening paragraph, she sat down on the log where they watched for the school bus. Her breath stopped in her throat.

"Tumor in the womanly parts . . . nothing they can do. Don't mention anything to Herman or Bonnie." Addie could barely whisper the news to Kate at lunchtime.

Mama's face told the story when she came home. She never walked outside again. Two months later, she died, though the Presbyterian women prayed for a miracle.

The night before, Mama smiled. "God is with me. Do you sense Him here?"

Lying sent you to the lake of fire—how could Addie say yes? If only they'd had some tea, she'd have brewed Mama a cup.

There she went again, thinking of her own wants. Maybe Harold was right about her being selfish. The wind blew her chastisement back into her face.

As June sunshine welcomed her to Mr. Allen's, she set aside her thoughts of tea. Maybe her patient would answer her question about Fernella today.

June 3, 1942

Dear Kate,

Your recent exploration of that wonderful bookstore made me hungry to see London. Speaking of food, the McCluskeys invited us for dinner the other night. Fern said I shouldn't bring a thing.

The day of the dinner, Harold came in early and shaved for the second time. I wore my yellow Sunday dress, his favorite, though the shade fades my skin.

Fern served an apéritif right away. We were sitting ducks on the davenport as Walt described a new seminary program that certifies laymen to preach.

He said it was to meet the strain, with so many becoming chaplains. Harold asked him how the program works. Fern asked me check on the casserole with her.

Harold shoved to help me rise, and his eyes glinted. My heart sank at the word casserole. Fern pronounced it *casserolay*. I'd hoped for something lavish, like salmon loaf. The first time I tasted that, I wished we were Catholic, so Harold would demand fish on Fridays.

Fern handed me her cookbook and my outlook changed. She asked me to check the time for the steak en fromage on page 62.

The ingredients enticed me— olives, mushrooms, dry mustard, Worcestershire sauce, ketchup, and Tabasco—all expensive. The meal might prove a treat, after all.

By the way, Olson's café boasts a new sign, Stop in and 'ketchup' with the best, with a wife toting ketchup to her husband. Harold would strangle me if I wasted money on such a luxury.

But back to Fern and the casserolay. She told me she wearies of potatoes and waltzed across her waxed tiles to the biggest Frigidaire I've ever seen. Before she opened the door, she rolled her little finger in a curlicue, accentuating her sharp brassiere points.

Then she flung open the door and offered me a taste of chiffon salad. Wow—Jell-O and whipped cream.

I practiced my dignified pose (I can see you laughing) and said I wouldn't want to ruin my appetite.

When she pulled a scalloped dish from the oven, the crust shone tawny brown, and Fern sprinkled cheese like molten gold. The crust's perfect flutes reminded me of Berthea's pies.

Mrs. M would be proud of my metaphors and similes, don't you think?

My mouth dropped at that casserolay set on a folded towel beside the stove. Fern peered right into my eyes and asked what I thought.

I said Harold would love it, since we're used to plain old farmer food at home. But why should Fern be nervous about our opinions?

Norman's words resounded in my head: "I made Fernella feel like she was somebody, but when Walt came back from the war, her daddy latched onto him like scales on a fish. Wish she hadn't let him make her choices for her."

I couldn't help myself. I asked if he'd proposed to Fern.

He said privates don't enter the officers' mess and that no one could've stood up to Fern's father for her.

His story replayed as Fern's casserolay satisfied my taste buds. Fern seemed satisfied, too. She leaned on Walt's shoulder when they watched us leave.

Courage, and all my best,

Addie

* * *

Early Tuesday morning, Harold took Berthea to pick up Decoration Day flowers, but forgot to sharpen the lawn mower blades before he left. Addie put her muscles to the ancient tool, and when she finished mowing, she attacked the weeds, though her mending pile called her.

Last night when she drooped on the davenport, Harold eyed the corner sewing machine. He stuck his elbow up, showing bare skin through his shirtsleeve. Once again, she was remiss in her responsibilities.

"I know I'm behind, but could you look at the treadle? It keeps sticking."

Harold went to work under the machine with a groan, so she must get started today. But now, she needed to check on Norman. Finding him snoring, she cooked breakfast and counted his pills.

What difference could they make with him so close to death? When she took his tray in, his wicked blues swept her.

"Good morning, Mr. Allen."

"Call me Norman. Glad to see ya." He hacked for a few minutes.

On impulse, Addie patted his hand, the shade of sweet Williams, Grandma Shields' favorite flower. Hundreds of black and brown marks ranged his forearm. White, gray, and a few black hairs put Addie in mind of an oak forest in March, his skin as fragile as melting snow crust.

Norman slept while she did dishes, but later she found him awake.

"Millie used to smile like you. I'd hate for her to see me so useless. That's what she said when she got so sick. Wish't I coulda done better by her." His eyes stopped at the bedroom door.

"We lived here for . . . almost twen . . . " A coughing spell claimed him. Addie wiped his chin. ". . . almost twenty years—she made my life heaven, always smilin'. Made up fer . . ."

Coughing wracked him again, so Addie ran for fresh water.

"Now Fernella . . ." He turned toward the front window. "That girl didn't smile, not without good reason." He pressed his palms down to push his head higher, and Addie added an extra pillow.

He drifted off, so she cracked a window and studied the room's three wall hangings—the Allen's wedding portrait, Millie's parents, and Norman's army discharge. The sun hid under a cloud, which was just as well in such high humidity.

All of a sudden, he sputtered, "Wish't Millie could've borne children." A few minutes later, he opened his eyes wide and sipped some water. "But Fernella didn't neither. I made her smile, 'til . . ." He dropped his hand on his chest.

"Until what?"

He snored. Mystery roamed the room like a trapped ghost, and a glow enveloped Norman's countenance. Addie lingered at the transformation, like late-blooming bittersweet over the back gate.

Chapter Twelve

Several mornings later, Addie kept hoping Norman would waken. Then Harold stopped in and walked her to the kitchen door, employing his preaching voice.

"Uncertainty about Mr. Allen's eternal destination troubles me." His cheeks hollowed. "Nothing is so important."

Yesterday, Norman bemoaned hurting Fernella, but whispered "yes" when Addie asked him if he believed in forgiveness. Wasn't that a good sign, and shouldn't they be glad his suffering would soon end? Hadn't Harold heard their missionary speaker last Sunday?

On her confirmation day, the pastor said the same thing. "Each of us is human, and we all make mistakes. But faith overcomes our worst errors."

But she held her tongue with Harold, and pedaled home when the nurse came. In the fresh summer breeze, the world seemed alive, and Jane waved her into the yard.

"We have a new project for the troops." She handed over a cellophane packet complete with instructions.

1. Obtain hanks of yarn from your local Red Cross chapter.
2. Follow instructions according to color (olive drab for army, navy blue for navy)
3. Once sweater is finished, wrap in brown paper and send to address below:

"Have you made one yet, Jane?"
"Four, two for each branch. Did your Mama teach you to knit?"

"No, but Aunt Alvina's friend did. Her name started with an L."

"Letha Cady? Then you'll have no trouble." Jane's overall buckles gleamed in the sun. "All this time, I thought you looked familiar. You visited our church years ago, didn't you?"

"Emmanuel Lutheran out in the country?"

Jane chuckled. "I learned more from the questions you asked Alvina than from the sermon."

"You heard me?"

Jane grinned. "Did you know Alvina called you her second blessing? Having Kate come when she'd lived alone for so long sent her into a spin. But she cherished Kathryn's new little friend Addie—said you had more curiosity than anybody she'd ever met."

Jane's question brought Addie back. "So, how is your garden?"

"Last week's heat scared me, but I watered every night and covered some of the plants in the hottest hours."

Tuesday's wind did even more harm." Jane leaned on a fence post. "You're still going to Norman's?"

"Yes. Everyone says he'll die soon, but he's hanging on."

Jane's laughter created a pleasant stream.

Addie recalled how Berthea once said Jane's husband, Simon, used to growl. In her opinion, he was the meanest man in this county. She even suggested that Jane might have shot him and buried him in the grove behind their house.

Addie wondered why she'd never glimpsed Simon, but stifled her questions. Today she reflected on Jane's ready sense of humor. Somehow, she rose above her circumstances.

"Well, Addie, I wouldn't be surprised if it takes more to kill Norman than an ordinary man, after all he's suffered."

"Did you know him before he left for Europe?"

"Sure did. His father died, so he left school to work full time and provided for his younger sisters. But the army still called him."

Harshness entered Jane's tone. Did she refer to Harold's draft status? No, if she had something to say, she'd say it, like Kate.

"Where did he work?"

"Drove the early morning creamery truck, then loaded coal for the railroad. After he came back we didn't see him for a while." She rubbed her bum leg. "Would you like some tea?"

"I'd better get back. I have a beef roast in the oven, and Harold will be home soon." Addie glanced down at the knitting packet. "What time does the Red Cross office open?"

"You thinking to ride in for yarn?"

"Maybe in the morning, after I go to Norman's."

"How about I pick some up for you?" Sunlight sent a glitter through Jane's eyes. For a second, a younger woman shone through, a red-haired spitfire.

Kate's suggestion in her latest letter popped into Addie's mind, that every once in a while, we should do something new, maybe even a little risky.

"Okay, thanks. And I've changed my mind. I'd like that cup of tea."

Later, she pedaled home to the aroma of cooked beef. After she added some potatoes and carrots, went back outside, and slipped her spade into the loose soil around a scraggly pine planted in an inhospitable spot.

The stem moved, so the taproot hadn't developed. That would make the transfer easy, but it was a bit late for a good start. Still, the weatherman forecast steady temperatures until July.

Three years ago when she'd transplanted this tree from the ditch, Harold spouted, "What're you doing, fortifying the lilac barricade?"

"But I thought your dad would enjoy the scent."

His eyebrows shot up. "You think you know what's best without asking anyone else?"

That night she made the mistake of trying to answer him, but they'd been married only a few months. She hadn't wised up yet.

"Don't you suppose my father would rather see what's going on here?"

"But he can see the barn and hear the motor turn over when you start the tractor. Even Jane can hear that clear down the road, and I thought . . ."

"What does Jane have to do with it?"

Addie retired in defeat. Now, she situated the pathetic pine in its new hole and thoroughly doused the roots, exactly as Jane would. Her philosophy was straightforward. "I've lost a few prize plants, but that's how you learn."

Addie spaded extra soil around the stem. Jane said it helped to talk to plants, so she bent close.

"This location gives you more light, so this is your time. Grow!"

The bubbletop entered the yard and she prepared for battle with that dratted sewing machine.

June 18

To my friend afar,

I've begun to look forward to seeing Norman.

According to Doc, he should be buried by now. His sister broke her leg, so I'll be with him for some time.

He talked nonstop today—the Midway victory renewed his will to live. The news lifted our spirits after the Decoration Day Pearl Harbor speeches.

Harold turned the volume up double at the report and raised his fist in a victory salute. "Got the Japs' flagship and two aircraft carriers. That's one for you, Joe."

He raised his fist in a victory salute and seized me, which led to more efforts to conceive. But Kate, I really think it's hopeless.

Otherwise, there's not much news. Berthea keeps so busy, some days I don't even see her. And every day, I wonder if you've heard anything from Alexandre, and what else is going on there. So glad you've found a new friend, Kate.

Until next time,

Addie

* * *

Norman plunged into another story. "You know Mrs. Engelbrit, lives down by the railroad tracks?"

Addie shook her head.

"She come by yesterday. Said her Amos always held me in high regard—died a few years after the war, from the trench gas. Never made thirty."

"Would you like a glass of milk?"

"Don't pay that nurse no mind." He stared toward the window. "Amos never come back to hisself after his tank hit them new-fangled mines."

"What happened?"

"Head wound, worse'n mine. His brother went out East and talked him out of his hospital bed. Married a nurse and moved back here. Mrs. Engelbrit's one fine lady. Her citified speech riled folks, but she was good to Amos."

Norman's bad eye lurched as if it longed to relocate.

"Tell me more about him."

"Hit a twelve-pound German mine, just a wooden box fourteen by sixteen with twenty two-gram 'plosives, could destroy a tank. Germans buried 'em ten inches deep, and wham. Bang!"

Addie rescued his coffee cup from his flailing arms.

"Wish I'd'a gone to see Amos, but I could only think about Fernella." A tear rolled from Norman's good eye. "You wouldn't believe how beautiful she was."

Right. Hard lines run from below Fern's eyes clear down to her jaw, and her forehead wrinkles like a newborn puppy.

When Norman snoozed, Addie made some coffee, and spied Millie's tea can on the shelf. One whiff doubled her desire.

Norman stirred, so she peeked in. "Would you mind if I made tea? I saw some out here, and . . . "

"Help yourself. Millie liked tea."

If only Harold could see me now. She'd only taken a few sips before Norman woke again.

"That tea's pretty old."

"Oh, it's fine."

"Was talkin' 'bout Fernella. Beautiful, that she was." He studied the ebb and flow of the lace curtains. "Wish she'da kept the baby."

Addie sat bolt upright. Her cup clattered against its saucer. *Baby* swirled between them, an April twister, and Norman's eyebrow dipped like cobwebs along the wall.

"If I could do it over, I'd charge up her front steps, make her pack a bag and drive her outta this place."

"Don't know how her daddy found out, but by the time I went for her, they'd already left. Her mother had no time for me, and the station men said her daddy took an early run down to St. Louis."

Norman's chest fell something fearful. I ran for a cool cloth and prayed he wouldn't fall asleep. A shiver took him, but he opened his eyes.

"I stared down the tracks with my worst feeling since the war. Even if I borrowed the creamery truck, I'd never find Fernella in that city."

He drifted off into a snore, leaving Addie with those empty tracks—true love found, but lost. She wanted to surprise him, to change the end of the story, but could only watch his nose hairs quiver.

In a few minutes he roused and fixed his good eye on her. "Don't have t' know everything 'bout the future to do somethin' today. When ya feel somethin' strong, it's time to act. Wish I'd known that back then."

Norman dozed off again and Addie sat there wondering if she'd understood the stories Mama tried to tell her near the end of her life.

The nurse came and cast a wary eye on her. "Did Mr. Allen take his pills?"

"Yes, ma'am, without a struggle."

Her cool stare dismissed Addie, who hid the tea behind a bag of musty horehound drops. Those empty tracks Norman faced haunted her all the way home, along with a question.

Why did Fernella's father take her to St. Louis?

Chapter Thirteen

"*W*hat time shall we leave for the Farm Bureau barbeque?"

Harold kicked at stones in the driveway, while Addie attacked some stubborn weeds by the windmill.

"I can't afford to leave. The mare could foal any minute."

Berthea's face fell. "But the speaker's from Iowa State, an expert on hybrid seed corn. I know your father hated hybrids, but now . . ."

Addie walked over. "I can watch Daisy, Harold."

"Oh, yeah—right." His tone matched his eye roll, but Berthea jumped to Addie's defense.

"She can ride to get you if anything happens, or run over to Alfred's. He won't go to the meeting—far too set in his ways."

"Well, all right, if you insist, Ma."

"Good—let's go at five-thirty."

Harold went about his business, but Berthea paused. "You're so good at weeding, Addie. You never give up. Beside my back door, there's a jar with a Borax solution that'll kill these—makes them a whole lot easier to pull a couple of days later."

"Thanks—I need all the help I can get."

Addie went for the bottle and was spraying the unruly growth beside the corncrib when Harold came out of the barn and yelled, "Be sure you don't forget. Can't watch mares too closely at times like this."

Berthea got in the car and Harold joined her. Addie waved them off. Though he checked Daisy five minutes earlier, she went out again, just to be sure.

Then she raced to the house for some paper and leaned against the barn wall to write Kate about today's time with Norman. She barely looked up, and four pages later, an uneasy feeling plagued her.

Better not keep this in her apron pocket overnight—Norman said to listen to one's intuition. Harold had no inkling about her correspondence with Kate, and she had to keep it that way. With the thick enveloped addressed and some egg money in her pocket, she pedaled to Jane's, who worked outside, as usual.

"Hello, did you come to help me weed?"

"I would, but Daisy's about to foal, and Harold left me in charge."

Jane found her bench and sat down. "Nothing like a baby foal—I'd like to take a peek when it's born."

"I'll let you know, and would you please mail this for me tomorrow?" Addie handed over the letter and a quarter.

"It won't be that much unless you're sending it four times."

"I want to be sure you have enough—it would never do for George to bring this back."

Jane flicked away a black picnic bug. "Pesky things showed up early this year. How's Kate getting along?"

"Alexandre's flying again, and Kate's friend is helping her find a job."

"That girl needs to keep busy. Never saw such a wiggly little thing. Turned out pretty well, though, don't you think?"

"Oh, yes. She can manage whatever comes her way."

"Um. How about some tea?"

"I'd love to, but I'd better watch Daisy. Next time?"

"I'll hold you to it. Say, I'm out of yarn again."

"Me, too—it went so fast."

"Want to drive into town for more tomorrow? One o'clock?"

"Okay. Harold should be out in the field by then."

* * *

"Mornin', Glory!" Berthea's smile lighted her face as she exited the Chevy.

"You look chipper today."

"Going into town for coffee energizes me. Today, your old teacher, Mrs. Morfordson, told a tale on Harold."

She sat down on a stump near the garden, so Addie rested her trowel and waited.

"That woman can hold an audience better than anyone I know. This one would embarrass Harold, she said, but she had to tell it with me there. Brought back a good time, Bill just out of high school and Harold in the sixth grade."

Addie planted her hands in the grass—she needed to hear about good times. Berthea folded her hands over her knee and grinned.

"Mrs. Morfordson assigned a poem to Harold's class and gave them three days to compare two objects, use rhyme and rhythm, and focus on a down-to-earth topic. They had to read the poem and write a paragraph describing the connection between the two objects."

Sun warmed the backs of Addie's arms and Berthea chuckled, such a lively difference from last spring.

"Reading his paragraph, Harold was dead serious.
Roses are red.
Grass is green.
My teacher's built
Like a B-17."

Berthea cackled, "Can you imagine how that poor teacher controlled herself?"

"Mrs. Morfordson always maintained her dignity, and knew how to handle boys. But she's tall and thin. How did Harold justify his comparison?"

"She said she's thought about his logic for years. He described the plane as purposeful, useful, and necessary for the USAAC's defense. He even held up a sketch.

"He never referred to size. When she asked him to tell the class more about the Air Corps, he said the world's best military aviation organization held the keys to the future, just like their teacher. Without her grammar instruction, how would they fare in their high school classes?"

Berthea hee-hawed and slapped her knee. "We laughed 'til we cried. Fern even came over from another table when she saw how much fun we were having."

"You tell a pretty good story yourself."

"I don't hold a candle to Myrtle Morfordson. One of the women asked what grade she gave Harold. She said with his accelerated vocabulary and adult descriptions, how could she give him less than an A?"

"Will you tell Harold about this?"

Berthea eyed the wooden silo where Harold wet down alfalfa and leavings from the oat field.

"I don't know. The time would have to be just right."

* * *

Harold's hair, normally parted and slicked down with Wildroot crème, showed bits of bedding straw as Addie placed three perfect over-easy eggs on his chipped white china plate. Four sausage patties sided a stack of toast, sliced down the middle and arranged so the halves formed M's.

She touched his shoulder. "How did it go with Daisy last night?"

"This birthing will be a tough one."

How do you know? She swallowed her question, knowing he would think she doubted his wisdom. Just yesterday, she read, "Set a watch before my mouth" in Psalms.

He balanced a piece of toast and scanned the table before resting his eyes on her. What had she forgotten?

Then she noticed—the jam jar. She reached for the cupboard, but the jar sat a little too high, so she slid her chair back. When she set it down near Harold's plate, the jar slipped and plunked down. His fingers tightened around his knife.

"Sorry. I didn't mean to set it down so hard."

There, she'd said *sorry* again. One of Kate's recent stories catapulted through her head. Kate's new boss, Mr. Tenney, started her working the very day of the interview. In the afternoon, he sent her on an errand to a bookshop:

The other day, I visited Mr. Firth, the bookseller.
He fought in the Great War with Mr. Tenney's father.

The recent defeats have disheartened him, but he focused on past victories. He recalled the anniversary of the Blitzkrieg's worst and final bombing. Bombs fell in batches, hitting Westminster Hall, the Abbey, and the Houses of Parliament.

Fires raged out of control and the whole city spent all night in terror. But the British survived, and Mr. Firth said W.C. taught them to refrain from apologizing and celebrate their tenacity. Otherwise, they would look down on themselves forever.

Refrain from apologizing . . . Addie quieted her nerves and spooned a little scrambled egg onto her toast. The other day, Berthea mentioned how often she apologized. "Addie, you're a good worker. Do you realize how often you say you're sorry?"

She had no answer, and now she'd said it again.

Weariness showed in the puffy shadows beneath Harold's eyes. But with him getting up three times to check on the mare, she lost sleep last night, too. Still, while he slept a little longer, she'd finished the chicken chores, checked on Norman, and cooked this late breakfast.

Why did forgetting one inconsequential jar of jam count more than all the things she did *right* this morning? She'd even carried extra water for the pigs and checked on Daisy.

With this world's life-and-death struggles, why concentrate on such trivial things? Time lapsed as Harold finished his breakfast, but she could tell he waited for something. Normally, she repeated her *sorry* if he was still irritated. But she made her decision—she'd apologized enough.

He looked away before she did, and silence dogged them until he left with a terse order. "Keep watch on that mare."

The chair ridge hit Addie's back in exactly the right place as she leaned back. The play of eastern light in this room would be beautiful if that old wainscoting were brighter.

Mr. Firth's quote about all the British military failures went through her mind as she pictured Kate sipping that precious rationed cup of tea. Through her letter, strength flowed into this kitchen, even across the Atlantic Ocean.

Chapter Fourteen

*B*etween picking string beans, baking a pie, and preparing dinner, Addie checked on Daisy. After eating, Harold dashed to the barn. She wiped her hands on her apron when he peered through the screen before heading back to the field.

"You won't forget the mare, will you?"

"I watched her all morning, Harold." She wished he'd call Daisy by name. She stacked the plates and pans to dry, though he wouldn't approve. A few minutes later, the door screeched and he stuck his head in again.

"She left a couple of manure piles in her stall. You could clean them up too."

Addie simply stared at him. When had she failed to notice extra jobs around here? The other day, he left the tank water running, and if she hadn't happened into the barn for a shovel, the pump would have worked five extra hours.

Something swirled inside her, dark and burgeoning, and words fumed like strong horseradish roots boiling for relish. What would Harold do if she let those words go?

He tapped his fingers on the screen, but finally swiveled and left the porch. Addie checked the strawberries, since they ripened fast in this heat. Before she reached the high-arched barn, perspiration pooled in the small of her back.

The familiar odor of animal waste spread from Daisy's back stall, along with an odd grating sound. Well-organized tack, feeding troughs and milking stools lined either side of the wide, dim alleyway.

No wonder Harold attracted her—he kept the barn as clean as some women kept their houses. But that same careful nature chafed on her nerves. Did other married people realize too late that they differed so greatly? Did other women discover that such weak stitching held things together?

But her most haunting question had to do with Mama. What motivated her to marry Avery Shields, about as responsible and organized as an infant? Had he seemed strong and protective to her back then, like Harold, only to change over the decades, until Mama became the strong one?

She would give every flower in her yard for one afternoon to chat with her. Maybe in her heavenly form, she would voice what she couldn't back then. *No one but Avery ever paid me any attention. My father died when I was young, so I was hungry for someone—anyone.*

A steady scrape joined Daisy's urgent rubbing, so Addie quickened her pace. Daisy rubbed her hindquarters across the far wall, back and forth, back and forth.

With all her inner stretching, itching made sense. Pungent fresh manure singed Addie's nostrils, but she saw no piles.

On closer look, small flakes peppered the whole area—Daisy's agitated crossings must have dispersed the warm, wet droppings. Her nose felt hot, so Addie hurried for some water. When she poured it into the trough, though, Daisy shook her head and kept scratching.

For a moment Addie wished Harold were here. Mama's sparse wisdom on birthing came waylaid, like a message advanced through several people. Once, she commented to Ruth.

"Don't worry, Ruthie, you'll be fine. My babies all came easy."

In home economics class, Mrs. Belwith added little to the tight textbook paragraph. "Modern science works to sanitize delivery, resulting in better health and a lower mortality rate for both mothers and newborns."

Addie waved her arm to shoo flies from the mare's caked eyes. Maybe she should crack open the back door for some fresh air.

Humidity flooded in, so she barred the door again, and smoothed Daisy's velvety muzzle. Then she checked outside for Jane, shading her eyes from a blaze of light. Early this morning, the sun, hidden in mist, resembled the moon— a sure predictor of a scorcher.

Lazy black and white sows lounged in their shady pen. The spring litter grew so fast that Harold moved them to the pasture in little wooden tents he nailed together to keep off the worst of the heat.

The hollyhocks she'd planted by the windmill grew almost waist-high by mid-June. Now they flowered, yellow and white, deep rose and pink. But the garden fence stood barren except for the trumpet vine. Maybe Jane would have a suggestion when she stopped to pick her up for their yarn run.

When Addie opened the barn door again, the creaking had stopped. Seeing Daisy reach for her backside with her muzzle sent panic through Addie, but the Studebaker horn blasted from the yard, so she ran to Jane's open window.

"She's about to give birth, and . . ."

Jane turned the motor off and bailed out when Addie opened her door. About halfway down the alley, an unearthly cry stopped Addie in her tracks.

"Keep moving." They rounded the stall divider and Jane inspected. "The head and two hooves. Perfect."

Near enough to touch Daisy, Jane found a spot on the floor and in a flurry of flying straw, lowered herself against the wooden divider. Addie dropped beside her.

"Will everything be all right?"

"No need to worry, child. Let nature take its course."

"But Harold said this would be a hard birth."

"What does he know?" Jane rolled her eyes.

Did she ever have children? She'd never mentioned any. Addie shadowed Jane as a tiny hoof became a leg, then two, and finally the front quarters protruded. For a while, Daisy licked her foal's face, and then the hooves struggled with the white sac. Stroke by stroke, the foal finally gained full freedom, alerting the world with a high-pitched squeal.

"Good, girl, Daisy. You have yourself a filly."

After a while, the baby struggled to rise to its feet. Jane squeezed Addie's hand, her eyes like sparkling green lanterns.

"The yarn can wait—wonder doesn't come along that often."

* * *

97

Halberton's emergency siren went off as Addie dumped the supper scraps in Old Brown's dish. She ran inside and motioned to Harold, but he ignored her. Finally, she turned the radio down long enough for him to listen. Eeriness descended as they pulled drapes and shut off lights. Normally, the Saturday night party line ring reminded them of the black-out, but this must be something new.

He hunkered on one end of the davenport, so Addie picked up her knitting. But her mind traveled to London, where Mr. Tenney instructed Kate on air raid precautions. Injured early in the war, he now headed an important government office.

Harold would be quick to point out that at least Mr. Tenney's country *allowed* him to serve. He'd also say that lately, a few other men who might have been classified sole providers shipped out, too.

During the latest war report, she slid a little closer to Harold, hoping he would put his arm around her. But he moved away and cupped his chin in his hand.

A little later, she jumped when he slammed his fist on the cushion, puffing dust all over.

"D*** Japs! I hope they burn in h***."

She slipped through the dining room and kitchen for a twilight stroll around the yard. Evening light sometimes revealed vestiges of the skulking weed crop. Even if she'd gone over the same area that morning, she might notice a weed she missed. If she failed now, the next generation would overrun her flowers and vegetables.

Last night, she hovered near the fence, where a yellow trumpet vine testified to its will to live. Not much more than a spike of brown last spring, now green tendrils spiraled halfway up the wire she strung over the fence.

When Jane gave her this plant, she added, "You don't often see a yellow one, Addie—this is for your birthday. Mind you, plant it away from the house, or it'll eat at your foundation."

Last year, the vine sent all its energy toward its roots, this year to its leaves, and next season, yellow trumpets would cheer the raspberry patch. Thanks to Jane, so many plants flourished here, and yesterday, they shared the wonder of Daisy's foaling. Yet Jane's secret about her husband still seemed as deep as the Atlantic.

The joy of the foal's birth lingered, like Norman clinging to life as his sister Lucille took over his care. But when Addie pedaled to town on an errand, she still stopped to see him. One morning last week, Lucille asked if she could stay for an hour while she grocery shopped. Addie prayed Norman would divulge more about Fernella, but he flitted in and out of sleep.

At least Kate bore the suspense with her. A whippoorwill cast its song from one of the tallest pines and a squirrel darted along a fallen log. She weeded until darkness encroached, then went inside to bed.

The next morning, she would have forgotten it was July fourth, but Harold shooed her to Berthea's after chores to listen to the radio. For once, he sat through a broadcast without fidgeting.

"Friends, we bring you our President. Following his example, government workers take no vacation today, to propel the war effort. And now, we move straight to Washington, D.C."

Papers rustled into the microphone as Berthea brought in some coffee and cookies. President Roosevelt's voice sounded more nasal today.

> For 166 years this Fourth Day of July has been a symbol to the people of our country of the democratic freedom which our citizens claim as their precious birthright. On this grim anniversary its meaning has spread over the entire globe—focusing the attention of the world upon the modern freedoms for which all the United Nations are now engaged in deadly war.
>
> On the desert sands of Africa, along the thousands of miles of battle lines in Russia, in New Zealand and Australia, and the islands of the Pacific, in war-torn China and all over the seven seas, free men are fighting desperately—and dying—to preserve the liberties and the decencies of modern civilization. And in the overrun and occupied nations of the world, this day is filled with added significance, coming at a time when freedom and religion have been attacked and trampled upon by tyrannies unequaled in human history.
>
> Never since it first was created in Philadelphia has

this anniversary come in times so dangerous to everything for which it stands. We celebrate it this year, not in the fireworks of make-believe but in the death-dealing reality of tanks and planes and guns and ships. We celebrate it also by running without interruption the assembly lines which turn out these weapons to be shipped to all the embattled points of the globe. Not to waste one hour, not to stop one shot, not to hold back one blow—that is the way to mark our great national holiday in this year of 1942.

To the weary, hungry, unequipped Army of the American Revolution, the Fourth of July was a tonic of hope and inspiration. So is it now. The tough, grim men who fight for freedom in this dark hour take heart in its message—the assurance of the right to liberty under God—for all peoples and races and groups and nations, everywhere in the world.

Berthea turned down the volume. "I guess that explains why we have no parade or fireworks this year."

"Makes me at least want to work in a munitions plant somewhere." Harold paced to the window and stared out. "Didn't hear Roosevelt mention farmers contributing anything."

"But where would the troops be without food?"

"Where they are right now. It sickens me not to be there with them."

"Think about it, Harold, those hogs you sold last week went up to Austin, Minnesota to make Spam for the troops." His groan did nothing to deter Berthea.

"Look at this newspaper article about Joe Dimaggio's parents. Remember when they were declared enemy aliens? Sounds like they're going to be pardoned now, since the President says the Italians have passed the patriotism test."

"So some Italians lost their house and their boat—what do I care? They deserve whatever they get. You don't see Joe Dimaggio enlisting, do you?"

Berthea shrank back when Harold threw the newspaper on a pile of magazines and left the house in a huff. Berthea raised her palms and sighed.

"I thought maybe it would make a difference—Harold has always thought so much of Dimaggio."

"That's for sure. Last summer he listened to Joe's winning streak as much as he does the war news now. I thought he'd never stop describing his statistically impossible record."

Addie reached for the top magazine. "Gary Cooper playing Lou Gehrig—Kate would sure want to see this movie. Would you mind if I borrowed this issue?"

"Any time, Addie, and LIFE is there, too—there's a convoy on the cover. Orville thought magazines were a waste, but I saved my egg money for them all those years. There's nothing I like more than reading in the evening."

"I'd say you earned that right." Addie patted Berthea's hand and looked up to see tears in her eyes.

July 18, 1942

Dear, dear Addie,

Your letters remind me of my old home, but Halberton holds little for me now, except you. *Mrs. Minniver* released here on the tenth—boy, would I love to see it with you.

When Alexandre kissed me good-bye this time, my heart nose-dived. Hush-hush plans, he said. "Military schemes prosper in secret, my love. But with your conniving, you'll figure it out."

Conniving . . . me? It's ingenuity, don't you think?

Another nasty defeat in North Africa last month, when everyone thought the Canadians would hold the city. Now Rommel's headed for the Suez Canal. Mr. Churchill spoke about the situation, but did little to hearten his listeners. That day, I moved into Mr.

Tenney's mother's house in Westbourne Grove, and she had her ear to the speaker.

Evelyn stopped by the office a few days earlier and mentioned me working evenings in the hotel kitchen. Mr. T overheard and blustered, "I am well aware of the shortage in flats, but you're in a hotel? You'll do no such thing under my employ—I shall ring Mum up this instant."

I now enjoy a room on the second floor, down the hall from his mother. Mrs. Tenney's quite proper, so I watch my P's and Q's. Her circle of friends, fundraisers, and bandage-rolling keep her busy.

It's wonderful to be back in a house, where I make my own tea (if there is any), and have some toast at will. Sweet rationing has begun. It may never reach the States, but enjoy your cookies and pie while you can.

Our office "integrates imperial and foreign forces on our soil." In other words, we provide necessities for Polish, American, Canadian, and Norwegian uniformed personnel.

I type and post messages at the nearest Royal Mail pillar-box, a shade of pure red reserved for the Post. The closest box bears the initials V.R. for Victoria Regina, the reigning monarch at its installation.

If weather permits, I pack lunch to eat outside. In the afternoon I type replies, receive deliveries, open mail and scoot it to Mr. T through a hazy-glassed door.

He often emerges with more dictations, errands or filing. Mrs. Culver, the chief secretary, distributes the jobs.

At five, one of the other girls walks me home, fourteen refreshing blocks. (Except for the bombing sites still hanging open like a tornado just struck.) With everyone seeking escape, reopened theatres have extended their hours. Window displays flourish for quadrupled pedestrian traffic. Have you located a London map yet?

Fire scares everyone, decreasing motor traffic. Before the war, the London county council managed sixty fire stations and 3,000 officers. Now there are 25,000, not including volunteer compulsory fire watchers (I've always liked a contradiction in terms). Mr. Tenney oversees ancillary ambulances, evacuation and rescue, rest centers, debris disposal, billeting, fire reports, meals, decontamination, first-aid posts, stretcher parties, shelters, and air raid wardens for civilian defense. No wonder he never stops working.

The debris service employs nearly 24,000 to demolish unsafe structures. First, the rescue service extricates victims (500 parties equipped at 100 spots).

Mr. Tenney says London's bombing exceeds all of England's, with more than 40,000 houses destroyed and half a million needing repair, extensive damage to sewers, gas and water pipes. From tenements to estates, everyone fears fire.

No doubt, "class" will resume with peace, and "better people" will once again look down their noses at the masses. One day, I may become the first woman Lutheran pastor, to proclaim lessons from this horrid war.

Did I mention we had an alert recently? An ear-splitting wail sounds, everyone takes shelter, and wardens begin their patrols until the all clear. Great damage this time, but not near here. This gives you a snapshot of my life in London.

Don't worry about the bombs, please. Mrs. T and her warden friends have everything in hand, and actually, it's not so different from your situation, where at any second, Harold might blow up.

There's a metaphor for you, and I think Mrs. M would give you an A for yours.

Craving your next letter,
Kate

Chapter Fifteen

*T*his morning Harold sowed a second oat crop on the creek bottomland, and after picking the strawberry bed clean, Addie hurried to town. A little before eight, she wheeled around Main and Third and followed Mrs. Heber into the library.

The dignified librarian untied her black and white checkered scarf. "This dratted late July humidity flattens my thin hair." She folded the silky fabric into a square and slid it into her pocketbook. "Don't know what I'd do without my scarf."

"Yes, ma'am." Addie leaned against the chest-high counter.

"What might I do for you?"

"I need a map of London, please. Kathryn Isaacs wrote me, and I'd like . . ."

Mrs. Heber's eyebrows danced.

"Hummm . . . surely we have one somewhere. Thumb through the reference section under L, or E for England, or G for Great while I try a few other places . . ."

Addie entered the reference section where Harold once researched his debate topics. She seldom found anything she could use, but this morning, she eyed the leather volumes with resolve.

Reproducing a detailed copy by hand would take some time, so she should have specified that she needed to check out a map. She'd have to add the book to her letter stash, for times when she could draw with Harold gone.

The unmistakable tenor of Fern McCluskey's voice gave way to Mrs. Heber's monotone. Addie paid no attention until a phrase caught her ear.

" . . . wild little alley cat, ran after that Canadian boy when he visited her aunt, and now she's in London. Couldn't wait, like Liz Sweeter, whose Anthony fights over there, too. But would Liz up and head to London? Mercy me, no!"

The insults made Addie's head spin. What did Fern know about Kate or Alexandre? And compared to Fernella's younger days, Alexandre and Kate's *wild* would seem mild.

"Well, I never! Do you suppose they keep in regular contact? I'd think Addie would keep busy enough on the farm, now that Orville has passed. Harold bears all the farm work besides his new ministry.

"With his upcoming seminary interview, I wonder if he realizes his wife's connection with that Kathryn Isaacs. I doubt he would approve—can't be too careful about appearances, don't you know? These orphan types—one never knows what sort of stock they hail from."

"Keep in mind that Addie is still a *Shields* at heart, Fern."

The emphasis on her maiden name swelled Addie's throat. She rubbed her thumbnail to calm her reckless pulse. What would Kate do at such a time? She wouldn't panic, for one thing, and would come up with a plan without divulging unnecessary information.

Would she slink to the other side of the clerk's desk and wiggle toward the door at the level of Daisy's new foal? Addie tried to think through the results. Mrs. Heber would wonder where she went, and perhaps realize that she'd heard. But then, that precious London map would never materialize.

"No use throwing the baby out with the bath water," Mama used to say.

Or should she confront the obnoxious women head-on with an innocent question. What could she ask? "Have you found any maps of London yet?"

Then she could continue, "Oh, Fern, I didn't recognize you with that new hair color. What do they call it, *Brazen*, like the stuff you put on your eyelids?"

That was Kate's style, and these old gossips deserved exposure, but Addie knew she could never pull it off. She hunched in the reference section, fuming at her ineptitude. Maybe she ought to write scripts for other people, since she took so little action in her own daily life.

In the end, she decided to sit still until further notice. That is, until the clock showed eight twenty-two. She'd promised to take Lucille's place for a while this morning, and it wouldn't do to turn up late.

Mrs. Heber's heavy footfall vibrated the floorboards. "I've found just what you need, dear." She held a book in front of Addie's nose, upside down.

"What good work, ma'am. I appreciate your kindness."

Addie turned the book and memorized the page, 264, and followed Mrs. Heber to her desk. As if by magic, Fern appeared not six inches away.

"Why, hello, Addie. How do you do on this fine day?"

"Good, thank you. And you?"

Fern swung her lashes low to reveal an outrageous amount of black coating. "I am well. Do you still visit Mr. Allen in the mornings, dear?"

Like the imperceptible rise in barometric pressure before a storm, something happened inside Addie. Mrs. Heber set her purple stamp on the take-out card and readied her fist to trounce the silver handle to produce an inked *date due*. As she made her move, Addie took a deep breath and hardly recognized her own voice.

"I do visit Norman, no longer for First Methodist, but as a friend. His war stories, especially from *after* the war, intrigue me. My, how that poor man suffered, and he has such a remarkable memory for details."

Mrs. Heber handed the book over, but Addie stayed a moment longer to savor the drop of Fern's lower lip and her stunned silence. She wrung her perennial white gloves in her hands as Addie continued.

"Thank you so much. I'm certain Kate will appreciate any information I can send her. By the way, have you heard the enemy shot down her husband's plane twice?"

"Indeed?" Mrs. Heber's fingers flexed. Fern clung to the wooden counter.

"Ah, yes . . . Who knows what injuries Alexandre sustained, or if he's even alive—so sad. Harold knows him well from his visits here. They share a liking for Tom Mix movies and World War I airplanes. Can you imagine his courage, piloting a Spitfire?"

She turned on her heel, and near the door, glanced back. Fern's attempts to arrange a normal expression on her face weren't working.

"Thank you again, Mrs. Heber, and so nice to see you, Fern. Perhaps our paths will cross sometime over at Norman's house."

* * *

A friendly breeze scuttled the library steps. Addie straddled her bike and sped east on Second Street. Her heart still pounded as she made a right turn and pedaled another block. All the way, she chattered to herself out loud.

"Well, old girl, now you've done it. If Fern goes to see Norman and he thinks you gave anything away . . ."

But an unfamiliar calmness quieted her fears. On her left, in the shade of a weeping willow, little Billy Hayes played with his cherub twin sister in their yard, and the innocence of their hand waving touched Addie. She waved back and rounded the turn toward Norman's place.

"But you didn't give anything away. No—you kept your dignity. You only hinted enough to unsettle Fern. Nothing wrong in that."

No nurse's car at Norman's. Addie breathed a relieved sigh, parked her bike and stuck a bobby pin in her windblown curls. "So, no more thinking about that—what's done is done. Kate would be cheering for your performance. After all, you stood up for her and Alexandre."

A deep breath later, she tapped on the back door and faced Lucille, whose uncombed hair resembled a hay field after a bad storm. Thick bags drooped below her watery eyes.

"Sorry if I'm a little late, ma'am. Are you all right?"

"We've had a bad night, but Norman finally dozed off a few minutes ago. Never thought I'd say it, but I do wish he could pass. He suffers so, and there's so little a body can do for him."

"Would you like to go over to your house for a while?"

"You're an angel, Addie. Norman always speaks well of you. I admit, I haven't a clean dress in the house."

"I don't need to head back home until eleven. Will that give you enough time?"

"Oh, a bath would feel so good right now . . ." Lucille grabbed her sweater and Addie tiptoed into the kitchen. From the living room, a mixture of honk and snore issued from Norman's slack mouth.

Still dazed by the powerful instinct that overcame her in the library, she poured the kettle half full and set it on a burner. For once, she said what she meant without raining fire down on her own head. A peculiar satisfaction swept her.

Even Mrs. Allen's wilted wallpaper sent her a quiet message: *we only have today, better make the most of it.* Like those faded pink teapots on the wallpaper, Norman couldn't last forever. This might be the last time she saw him.

A tender awareness overcame her, something akin to what she experienced when she entered the First Methodist sanctuary. *Her final time with Norman.* Though she wished the foreboding away, something inside her insisted.

With the teapot beginning to burble, she pressed her forehead against the cool cupboard door. The leaden scent of outdated baking ingredients inundated her.

"Oh God, please allow Norman to wake up, and if it be Thy will, direct his mind to where he left off in the story. It sounds selfish, but I really want to know what happened, and so does Kate."

The clock measured human undertakings and desires in seconds. The bottom of the kettle clicked faster as the water heated, like Norman's old toaster. Addie sat at the table and folded her hands, as a Sunday school teacher once instructed. "When we fold our hands and pray out loud, children, our Father in heaven sees our earnestness."

It couldn't hurt to repeat her request. Afterward, she opened her eyes to the faded teapots. "I wish we had met, Millie. I think we'd have been fast friends since you loved Norman and you loved tea, too."

The kettle whistled. Breathless, Addie ground a fistful of crumbly black tea leaves into a cup, covered them with boiling water, and carried her steaming concoction and a cup of coffee to the living room.

"Yer back. What took ya so long?" Clarity stoked Norman's eyes as if he'd treated himself to a shave and haircut down at Libersky's barbershop.

"I've been working—Harold's been baling hay, and I tend a large garden."

"Um—good coffee, just like Millie's. She planted a victory garden with her mother, ya know?" He gestured toward an end table. "Look in that newspaper. My niece won the 4-H Sears Roebuck garden contest over in Cerro Gordo County."

Addie fetched the paper, replete with a large photograph of a girl with a flagrant ponytail. Rows of enormous cabbage plants and string beans flanked her.

"Mind readin' it for me?"

> Joanie sold over two-hundred pounds of cabbage
> for almost ten dollars. She's fifteen and a half, she says,
> not fifteen or sixteen, and that precise, exacting nature
> led to her victory. She sold forty-six pounds of green
> beans, too.

"Wow, that's a lot of produce."

"Yeah. Some rich lady in Mason City bought most of it, with house help for all that canning. Joanie's my brother Hank's girl, and she's entering the northeast Iowa contest now. Might end up in the national one, too." Addie set the paper down and sipped her tea.

"Yup. Right proud of her. Hank come to see me a couple days ago." Norman smacked his lips. A bird brushed the front window just below the glass diamond.

"Do you have other brothers and sisters?"

"A few, scattered around the state like chicken feed." Norman lapsed into a fog, and Addie imagined his siblings passing before his mind's eye.

"Been waitin' for ya, Stopped the story standin' there watchin' fer the train, didn't I? Been stuck there ever since, 'cause nobody else listens like you."

His left eye popped in its socket, seeking an eternal home. He struggled to maneuver his arm, so Addie pulled up his pillow. A bit of caramel-colored earwax decorated his striped pajama collar and hair oil stained the pillowslip.

The open window let in air still cool from the dew, but Addie's knees went weak. A sick wave took her and she gripped her teacup. She would miss Norman. He reached for his cup, took another sip, and something about the quiet in the room soothed her.

He sniffed. "That Millie's tea you got?"

"Yes."

"Take the rest home, ya hear?"

"Oh, no. I couldn't, why it was . . ."

"Millie's. She could care less in Paradise, where tea ain't scarce." He chuckled. "'Sides, I'll be with her real soon. I can tell."

"You can?"

"Yeah." He chewed the insides of his mouth with his three good teeth. Some squirrels fought in the side yard's maple, and Norman's sucking noises fit right in.

The sensation that she landed in the right place at the right time washed over Addie. . . . *Where two or three are gathered . . .*

A profound soundlessness held her when the ancient phrase tumbled through her mind, as though heaven broke through. Maybe this was what Mama meant about feeling God with her before she died. *If only I'd been older, or wise enough to understand.*

Did Norman sense this divine presence too? Addie patted his pale fingers and his voice blossomed like her daylily bursting with flowers at the end of August last year, when she thought for sure the plant had already given its all.

"Fernella come back. Not that night, but a few days later. Three times I called at the house, but her Mama said she was real sick. Then Fernella found me at the church one night, her cheeks white as maggots.

"'The baby's gone,' she said."

"Gone?"

"'Daddy paid a man to take care of it.' She run out the back door, but wouldn't let me come near."

His trembling sigh quaked forth. "My heart busted in two. But I had to know more." His wild eye traveled the room and he brushed it shut with the side of his hand.

"A strong gust blew up right then. Maybe the Almighty felt sad, too. Fernella's voice wavered like a haunt's when she whispered she was sorry. Then she bent double and held her insides like she was dyin'."

Norman chewed on his bottom lip with a single tooth. "Even after the Argonne, I couldn't take it in. Fernella commenced to sobbing so hard, it like to have killed me."

Salt niggled Addie's throat, in tandem with the knot in her stomach. Norman stretched his neck from side to side, revealing the success of Lucille's ministrations on his scalp.

"When she finally let me, I rocked her and talked to her real soft, but she shook so hard I feared she might stop breathin'."

He stared at the diamond in the window, a lighter pink in this light. "Did the same thing once with a buddy in France. Don't hafta say much at times like that, ya know."

The tea's steam cleared Addie's eyes. Norman sank back against his pillow. Some small animal scrounged in the honeysuckle bush south of the house.

"When Walt come on the scene, I give up hopin' Fernella would talk to her daddy and he'd change his heart. When I went into the railroad office for my pay, I always felt somethin' between us, like those wooden trench walls in France.

"It was all on my part, though—a person can 'magine somethin' into bein' real. Just before her wedding, Fernella said her daddy still didn't know who I was, and she'd found her peace. But that feelin' never quite come to me, though meeting Millie helped me put it all behind me." His moan fractured the morning quiet.

"Fern never had children, and I always wondered if . . ." Norman's breathing thinned and Addie thought he slept.

She refreshed her tea and remembered her prayer, right here at this table. Dim teapot outlines uttered *amen* to Norman's story, and hope entered her gradually, like dawn's light overtaking the horizon during her early chicken chores.

If God answered such a selfish request, maybe He'd answer her prayers for Harold. Those pleas seemed selfish too, but what if the Almighty noted a person's honest desires?

When she rejoined Norman, a verse flashed through her mind. "For he knoweth our frame; he remembereth that we are but dust . . ."

Norman's eyelids shuttered open. "Yer husband asked me if I wanted to be forgiven." He said it so matter-of-factly, as though mentioning something new about his niece.

"Said I already was, but he didn't like it one bit. He wants to say he done it, so's he can tell the story after I'm gone, so's people will know he done good." A cardinal chirruped outside the window.

"Well, he won't git the chance, I seen to that. But you know how to keep a story, I can tell. Know anything 'bout forgiveness?"

At the very top of the far wall, a small black spider hung in limbo between floor and ceiling. How could she answer? A full minute passed before the pink diamond caught Addie's eye, and finally words came.

"Maybe forgiveness is more about knowing than feeling. You said the feeling never quite came to you that it was all right about Fernella and the . . . the baby? Yet you told Harold you've been forgiven, and the other day, you said you believed, remember?"

Norman's hair scratched the yellowed pillowcase, and for the first time that morning, his left eye tracked in sync with his right.

"Forgiveness goes deeper than feelings, I think. We can be awful hard on ourselves—harder than on anyone else. I'm like that, Kate says, so that makes it tough to believe God would forgive me.

"What if God fulfills our desire here on earth, but the feeling finally comes to us on the other side? Maybe that's what it means for all our troubles and doubts to vanish when we finally see things clearly."

Norman pressed her hand in his. The fragile blue lines traversing his temple made her crazy heartbeat knock against her eardrums. He spoke once more as the screen door squeaked and Lucille burst into the kitchen.

"Take that tea 'long now, Addie girl. Doncha forget."

She leaned close, stroked his cavernous cheekbone, and planted a kiss on his forehead. "Thank you, Norman. You're such a good friend to me. Good-bye."

Chapter Sixteen

July 26, 1942

Dear Kate,

I'm out on the back step in a strong east wind, wondering about Harold traveling to St. Louis. Will the wind slow his train's speed?

Probably a question our math teacher would relish, but even Mrs. M would entertain that idea. Old Brown wriggles my way, and the sun seems to be shining just for me.

How lovely to write wherever I want, with Harold off to St. Louis for his interview. I'm thinking of the months ahead in a positive light.

Our old pooch misses Berthea, who goes to town often. After Orville's funeral, she volunteered for church committees, joined the garden club, and the library board. The county fair committee needed new judges for the 4-H projects, so now she's all excited about that. The old Chevy doesn't get much rest.

Berthea asked George to help with chores this week. She's a smart cookie, Kate, had it all set up before Harold could say no.

I hope his interview goes well—if the seminary likes him, he'll spend most of the winter there. Can you believe it? You prayed for something to happen, but I never dreamed of such a long vacation.

The other night, Harold said he thinks a person's death corresponds with finishing our earthly work. I'm inclined to agree, since Norman lingered another day after our final talk, the day Fern finally visited him.

She told me about it right after the burial. I started walking home as soon as Harold pronounced his part. "Ashes to ashes, dust to dust."

Norman's nephew gave a short sermon, and Lucille read the scripture. Limited to the graveside service, Harold pouted all day when he found out and ridiculed the nephew the night of the funeral.

"He has no training whatsoever. Did you notice he used the lilies of the field passage out of context?"

The nephew said Norman knew war first-hand, but still gave him a model for a worry-free life. Never one to complain, Norman enjoyed peace and contentment in spite of hard times. Wouldn't you say that sounds like the lilies of the field theme?

I kept my opinion to myself instead of pointing out Harold's own lack of training. You know where that would have led. But my silence pleased him as much as my opinion, and he read the protest in my eyes.

"It's impossible to discuss anything meaningful with you. You're hopeless. I'm going out to chop wood."

He left and I gave thanks to his back. Come winter, the pump house burner will eat all the logs we can feed it. Anyway, after the service, I longed for a walk, and cut through the cemetery. I didn't even notice Fern until she hailed me from the bench near Aunt Alvina's grave.

The black she puts on her eyelashes colored her tear lines. She looked so sad patting the seat beside her, I sat with her a while. She mentioned Harold seemed nervous and I replied that it didn't help when he realized his tie matched Norman's.

Then she asked if I thought Norman died at peace, and I said I hoped so. But that didn't satisfy her, so she pried some more.

I knew we were getting into risky territory, and said I was pretty sure Norman found relief from things that bothered him for a long time.

Fern withered against the bench and demanded I speak more clearly. So I asked if she was related to him.

She said she wasn't, but that she'd known him for a long, long time and was concerned about him. What could I say? I mumbled something about him feeling he'd hurt people, though he only meant to love them.

Her forehead became a geographic map full of wrinkles, and my heart sank. When she asked what I meant, I would've given anything for you to take my place. You always come up with something.

I launched into my best explanation—the time I planted lilac starts between our house and Berthea's, thinking Orville would enjoy the blossoms the next spring. But Harold was furious and said his dad would rather see everything going on here.

Fern stared at her lap. A cardinal and his mate perched on the gravestone to our right—that's rare in the open, but they both landed like two pretty geraniums, one brighter than the other.

A cardinal came to the window the other day when I said good-bye to Norman, too. Maybe it was the same one—do you think it was a sign?

I felt sorry Fern didn't even notice them. When you're tormented inside, you miss so much right in front of your nose. (I'm not saying she's tormented— she might have buried things so deep that . . . well, I'll leave the analyzing to you.)

My story prompted Fern to ask how Harold was doing with all his new responsibility, which led to me asking if she and her father were close.

She said yes, since her mother was 'quite flighty', but he always maintained control. Just what he did in a seedy St. Louis doctor's office.

In the end, we agreed that at least Norman can rest. Resting brought to mind Harold's sleepless night before his "Dust to dust" in front of half of Halberton. He showed more nerves than when his debate team advanced to state—paced half the night and spent the other half in the bathroom.

If this is a prelude to the rest of his career, I don't know that it's such a big chance, Kate. What if his nerves worsen?

Right up to the service, the toilet called him. I know because I went around back to wish him well. From the smells sailing through the moon cutout, he hadn't moved closer to heaven. I delivered my best wishes, ill received, and hurried away.

He must have practiced his words over thirty times, which brings me to a scurrilous reality. Maybe scurrilous isn't the right adjective, but this does involve danger and foreboding.

Harold guards his church work with furtive secrecy. He didn't even tell me when Norman died. Jane did, hours later, when Harold holed up in the living room writing his sermon, before he learned he didn't need one.

You're my favorite sleuth, so tell me what you think about this behavior, please.

Here's another question—what is it about me that bothers him so much?

Cheers to you,

Addie

As Addie crossed the yard the next day, Harold drove the Chevy down the driveway. He gathered his suitcase with new light in his eyes, but Berthea made the announcement.

"The interview went well. I just knew it would."

Harold swung by toward the house. "Aren't you going to tell Addie, Harold?" He kept walking, so Berthea shook her head. "Tomorrow the fair starts. I'd better get busy."

Addie picked green beans and scrubbed potatoes for supper. Harold dived into his food as if he hadn't been gone, and went outside. Later he waved a sweet corn stalk at her.

"The leaves have rolled, and this ear looks almost full." He tore off the stiff green husks, and pale yellow kernels felt full to her touch.

"If we leave this in the field any longer, the raccoons'll get it."

Canning corn took a day and an evening, repeated at least twice more until the basement shelves held enough jars for winter. Harold planted several pickings, so when they depleted this first one, plenty more waited.

"Let's pick all we can." Addie ran to the house for his old cotton shirt, though afternoon heat still hung in the air. She left the supper dishes on the counter and grabbed Harold's second set of overalls, too, though he would disapprove. Too many times, sharp leaves had slashed at her legs like forest-green swords.

Harold took the "dead road" that bisected Bledsoe land north to south, with a view of the Pike farm. Deep ruts created by decades of cows, wagons, and tractors made for a bumpy ride, so Addie gripped her door handle. She held back her questions about his trip, but maybe now he would tell her about the interview.

The distance passed through a hole in the floor. "Run a truck into the ground," was Orville's philosophy, so Harold plastered the rotting vehicle together with wire. "Milton," as Addie called the bubbletop, would probably serve them for years to come.

"Why Milton?" Harold asked when she first christened it.

"After a neighbor of ours who gave Ruthie and me odd jobs when times got rough."

Harold whistled Hoagy Carmichael's *Stardust,* and the melody made Addie want to touch his fingers. In spite of everything, riding beside him gave her satisfaction. But he gave no sign of considering the melody's romantic lyrics.

At the edge of Jane's grove perched a small cabin, like those on the old Mill road southeast of Halberton. People still used them for camping along the river, but Berthea said Depression families lived in them full time.

At the corn patch, Harold headed in the opposite direction. Scratching filled the evening air—rough leaves clawing at trespassers. Hungry mosquitoes buzzed Addie's ears as she and Harold dumped load after load of corn into the truck and headed home.

The short trip took Addie back ten or twelve years to when Milton offered Mama whatever remained of their sweet corn before the coons took over. She helped Ruthie and Reuben pick and husk until fireflies lighted the yard and skunks lent the night their odor.

Afterward, if times were good, they split a sarsaparilla and sometimes took her along to wash off the sticky corn silk in the creek. She hadn't heard from Ruthie for weeks now—better write to her.

The pick-up bounced down the driveway and Harold parked near the tank, where she could husk and wash the ears in the morning. Before he walked toward the barn to get a head start on tomorrow's work, he turned. Maybe now he would share something about his trip.

"Pack me a double lunch for tomorrow. I won't come in at noon."

Not ready to go in yet, Addie eyed Jane's place. Harold pulled the barn door shut with a finality that made her cringe, so she shed his overalls and ran to the shed for the bike—still an hour of light left.

In a few minutes, a churned-up breeze cooled her arms and legs. The sight of Jane in her flowers, backside in the air, brought a grin. Some things she could count on.

August 10, 1942

Dear Addie,

Your long letter came so fast this time. I'm celebrating your little break from Harold.

You and Norman became so close. That doesn't surprise me one bit—Mrs. M always said you have a winning way with folks.

And Fern . . . I have to feel sorry for her, guarding her secret all these years. But Norman's passing brought up the whole thing again.

News here—the Huns are using a new phosphorous bomb. That's all I'll say about it, but now, people fear enemy pilots will drop fighters right into London. Mrs. T's circle discussed what they'd do in the event.

To see that proper lady assault the air with her fist made me consider her capabilities. I can't imagine what I'd do if a bomb landed nearby on my way to work, but can easily see Mrs. T and her circle pummeling a lone Nazi to death.

Right now, we're enjoying an abundance of fruit to satisfy our longing for sweets. Mulberry boughs hang heavy, and Mrs. T seems to have connections to the owners.

Too bad you're not here. You could give her a taste of the best pie possible. We've had ever so many cherries, but never too many. I fixed up a screen in the courtyard to dry thousands for next winter.

The Japs have taken India--such dismal news. What will happen next? No word from Alexandre for weeks. Waiting for his letters drives me to distraction.

I'd hoped to stay away from war news, but it always wedges its way in. Enough until next time, and cheerio, my friend.

Kate

Chapter Seventeen

*P*iles of husked corn covered every inch of Addie's kitchen table. Last night when she mentioned her plans for the day, Jane offered to help. With Harold gone all day and Berthea busy judging fair projects, they plunged into pan after pan.

Pop, pop, pop . . . slap. Holding her knife parallel to the top ear, Jane slid the sharp edge through the kernels like a professional. When the knife contacted the pan in her lap, it made a slapping sound, and she threw the cob into a metal pail on the floor. *Bang.*

In real time, the *pop, slap, bang* came from one deft movement. Jane did the same thing when she knitted, instead of throwing the yarn over the needle like most women. She called it the pick method.

"Modern knitters frown on it, but Mama knitted this way and it works for me."

Toward midday, they'd worked themselves into a rhythmic fever and the muggy air made it hard to breathe. Jane paused to wipe her forehead with a rag.

"Wish I could do more for our boys, like work for John Deere or make Spam? Better yet, I'd like to work for an airplane factory. My cousin's boss said she does better inspections than the man she replaced."

"My sister Ruthie works with munitions in California. Her last letter said they even found jobs my brother Herman can do."

"Is that the Herman who worked out at the gravel pit?"

"Yes, in their busy season. Dad worked there, too, on and off."

Jane's left eyebrow asked her next question.

"Dad worked from May through October, except when they fired him. But Mr. Andrews always relented, and stopped by for Dad's promise to show up every day.

"Dad would glance toward Mama, with Ruthie's arm around her, and then at the rest of us, on our best behavior. He would work steady for a while, but then one day after school, Ruthie would cradle Mama in the kitchen corner again.

"She'd gesture toward the living room, or outdoors. That meant Dad had gone off again and I needed to watch the little ones. Mr. Andrews would stop again and shake his head. 'Don't know what more I can do, Betty Ann.'"

Addie replaced the full cob bucket with an empty one and headed to add the cobs to the swill. Her thoughts raced. "Dad could've fed pigs and milked a cow."

For a while, they did have a cow that Reuben taught her to milk. She even named her Harriet, but one night after school, the barn sat empty.

"I lost her." Dad turned tightlipped.

"How did he lose Harriet?" Addie waited to ask Mama until he sprawled in his chair, oblivious to his three older children scrambling to organize socks, shoes and books for school in the morning. Mama burst into tears and Ruthie chided Addie.

"Your questions only make things worse."

The pigs squealed in delight at their newfound treasure, but back in the kitchen, Jane's forehead puckered. "Your dad sounds a lot like mine, Addie. Did you know a Chicago bookie followed a regular route here? Drove a little carriage with a white horse."

"A bookie?"

"A gaming man—sold tickets on races in Chicago . . . horses and dogs. The local men knew his schedule." She shaved another ear— s*lap . . . bang.*

"That's how we lost everything." Jane's lips formed a ruler and she stared out the east window as if checking to see that her house still sat down the road.

"House, land, and my brother to a badger attack when he hunted for meat one cold night. Dad was off with the bookie, and my brother had no experience night hunting. Mama and I got him to Doc Wilson's, but he'd already lost too much blood."

She sawed through two more ears. "That night, Doc cried, too. Said what an awful waste of human life."

Norman talked about times like this, when comforting words meant little. Jane strummed an empty corncob with her knife, wasting valuable seconds, and the clock ticked too loud. Addie kept cutting as if her life depended on it. Then Jane's voice came, soft and warm, like butter on an ear of hot sweet corn.

"Mama never forgave dad, though he sobered up and earned our place back. About killed himself doing it, but he knew he'd already killed her."

"It was just your brother and you?"

Jane nodded.

"Did you live in the same place back then?"

"Yes." Jane emptied her pan into the big cooker. Her movement cleared the air, and her verdant eyes flashed.

"I'll never let a man lose it again. Sometimes a woman has to take charge of her own life with the brain God gave her."

Questions teased Addie, but she clamped her mouth shut. If Jane wanted to tell her more, she would.

Jane wet her dishcloth, wiped the table, and scanned the clock. "I do love corn in winter, but on sultry days like this, it's even stickier to work with than jam or pickles."

"Please, will you take some jars home with you?"

Jane dried her hands. "Maybe some day when they're sealed for sure. Remember, I have my own patch to put up."

"Let me know, so I can help."

"You're a trooper. I'll see myself out."

She gave the kitchen a last look. "This room could sure use some paint. I've got two-thirds of a gallon left from doing mine. If you want it, let me know."

After Jane left, Addie realized how her feet ached. Jane must be sore, too, after such long hours, but rows of jars lining the table and cupboard testified to a day well spent.

Yellow kernels against green glass made a pleasant sight. Now, the timer clicked away a twenty-minute hot water bath as Addie considered supper. Maybe bacon and eggs, though Harold would lift his petulant chin. Against that familiar image, Jane's words rang.

A woman has to take charge of her own life . . . Until today, Addie had no idea Dad gambled, but Jane's conjecture made sense. How else could anyone lose Harriet? A ring of truth traced her spine—her dad gambled away their best food source.

Ruthie revealed his drinking after he and Herman moved to California, when she wrote that she forbade alcohol in her home. "I don't want my children living with a drunk like we did." When Addie expressed surprise, Ruthie's crisp reply shocked her.

"Why do you think he disappeared every few weeks with his paycheck? Didn't you smell the whiskey in his coffee cup? Why, instead of fixing holes in the ceiling, did he throw a box of crackers into the attic for the rats every once in a while? Did you walk through life asleep, Addie?"

Clear, yellowish liquid filled the cup her dad kept close at all times, but Addie didn't recollect the smell. If she missed something so obvious, she could easily have missed a gambling habit.

She dropped her head on her arms. Harold didn't like Herman or her dad, so she avoided the old place after they married, but last spring, Dad stopped by with train tickets from Ruthie. When he and Herman left, she knew she'd never see them again.

Herman's excitement showed in his eyes. He sleepwalked through life, too, although not by choice. The more Addie thought about it, maybe Ruthie's assessment was right. She'd sleepwalked through her youth.

Ruthie planned to stay in California only until Reginald returned from the war, but her last letters highlighted opportunities she hated to leave.

"Maybe I'll never see her again, either."

The timer announced the end of the long day's work, but Addie still sat. *Maybe you're still sleepwalking.* She could almost hear Ruthie's voice.

"Maybe I am." She studied the kitchen walls. "Jane's right about this dark wainscoting. I might just take her up on her offer."

* * *

Humidity laced the hot August afternoon, so Addie carried the mail to the wide front porch. In May, she'd set some wintered-over geraniums beside the steps and dragged a rocking chair from the living room. In the evenings while Harold leaned toward the radio, she sat out here.

The first time she did, he quizzed her. "You don't care about the war?"

"It's such a beautiful evening, and I can hear fine from out here."

She waited, thinking he might join her. After the first night, she took a book along to read, or rocked to the mourning doves' evening song.

This afternoon, yellow-green leaves swayed above, melded by sunshine. Behind them, pine tops tickled the sky. A lazy ladybug traversed the floor, and the dry scent of ripening crops drifted through the porch. Addie leaned her head back against the rocker.

The memory of Jane's steady cutting rhythm and their conversation brought a smile. Maybe later she'd bike over with a quart of fresh raspberries.

An envelope's local return address enticed her, but weariness sat at her collarbone. Rustling leaves and the rocker's gentle beat against the slanted wooden floor lulled her into a nap.

The crunch of rubber on gravel woke her. She started up. Harold was home for supper already? She peeked around the corner. Yes, he headed the Farm-All for the barn—still plenty of time to peel potatoes and reheat the meatloaf.

A letter hit the floor when she straightened the cushions, so she tore open the envelope to a single, hand-typed sheet.

Masterson and Masterson
Attorneys at Law
614 Second Street
Halberton, Iowa

Mrs. Adelaide Bledsoe
Rt # 2
Halberton, Iowa

Dear Mrs. Bledsoe,

We request your presence for the reading of Mr. Norman Allen's last will and testament at eleven o'clock a.m. on August 15, 1942. Please observe utmost confidentiality. Mr. Allen has requested that not even family members, including spouses, be notified.

If for some reason you cannot attend, please contact us. Otherwise, we look forward to your attendance.

Yours truly,

Mortimer F. Masterson
Attorney at Law

Concealing the letter in her apron pocket, Addie sped to the kitchen and lit the fire under the skillet, poured water into a pot and held a match to the second burner. Not a second too soon, she opened the potato bin. The porch door squeaked and Harold's head appeared.

"How long 'til we eat?"

"About twenty minutes."

"I'll grease the baler before I come in."

With each knife stroke, curiosity assailed her, and with it the weight of wrongdoing . . . *utmost confidentiality* . . . It was one thing to conceal Kate's letters, but this had to do with official business. The idea set Addie's heart racing.

Besides, she'd snoozed away the day's last working hour. That would upset him, too. *You don't have to tell Harold everything ...*

Steam drifted from sizzling potatoes and onions, meatloaf bubbled in cornstarch gravy, and a hopeful thought surfaced. Since Jane wasn't related, she might clarify the lawyer's instructions.

After supper, Harold cranked up the radio and plunged into the world of war and theology, so Addie cleaned the kitchen and headed to Jane's. Corn leaves on both sides of the road accompanied her like an applauding audience, and she thanked God for giving her a trustworthy friend.

As she rode into the yard, something—or someone—flitted through the grove, toward that old cabin she saw when they picked corn. She looked again, but maybe her eyes played tricks on her—no need upsetting Jane, who waved her into the kitchen. She set her dishtowel aside and motioned to a chair.

"Is something wrong?"

"I need your help, Jane. Would you please read this?"

Jane centered her magnifying glass and after a few moments, a grin lighted her face. "Why, child, Norman left you something."

"Left me something?"

"He included you in his will. Best make sure you remember this meeting." She peered through the glass again, an excited tremor in her voice. "The fifteenth. I'll drive you in."

"But I ought to tell Har . . ."

"No!" Jane shook her head with a vengeance. "This letter's addressed to you. They could have written Mrs. Harold Bledsoe, but did they?"

Her green eyes glittered with intensity. Usually she avoided giving her opinion, except where it concerned flowers.

"But this kind of business . . . What if I need to ...?"

"Norman had good reason for his instructions. Maybe he knew more about Harold than you think." Jane made a fist on the table. "Did your mother have one single thing she could call her own?"

Addie shook her head twice, once for Mama's two dresses, every day and church.

"Mine didn't either, a crying shame, after all their hard work. Maybe Norman willed you his kitchen table, or maybe a whole lot more. You mustn't go against his wishes. A person's will is a solemn trust."

She stared into Addie's eyes. "Obey his instructions and remember, a woman has a right to something of her own."

Cheerful white wainscoting backed her declaration. Those final words reverberated between them like a sinful pleasure.

"But Harold can read my mind. How will I hide this for so long?"

Another thought interjected Jane's harrumph. That wainscoting—she really ought to paint it. Next week, Harold would drive Mr.

Lundene's grain to Cedar Rapids. Maybe then she could borrow Jane's leftover paint.

"The same way you took care of Norman. At first you thought you couldn't manage, right? And the same goes for Daisy's birthing." Jane crossed her arms over her apron.

"I wager Norman learned as much about you this summer as you learned about him. Death sometimes brings clearer sight, more than meets the eye." Jane's agitated toe tapped the thin crackly linoleum.

"I may be old and ugly and half-crippled, but I've learned a thing or two in this life. I've known Harold Bledsoe since before he could walk, and he's always been willful, Addie. Sometimes men grow up thinking they always have a right to their own way."

She leaned closer, revealing gravy splatters across her apron yoke. "But no one gets to win all the time. You don't know what lies ahead, but the Almighty does, and maybe He whispered it to Norman Allen. Right now, you need to practice a little faith, and that may mean letting go of what you think you know."

The queasiness in Addie's stomach gave way at the image of the Almighty sharing secrets with Norman. She could almost see Him bending down to whisper in Norman's hairy ear. But could she go two weeks without looking Harold in the eye?

"Would you mind keeping this letter for me?"

"Gladly. You can do this, Addie. I know you can." Jane waved the envelope over the table like a banner.

Chapter Eighteen

*D*ark clouds rumbled in the northwest. Addie parked her bicycle in the shed and checked on the chickens on their roosts, cocking their heads and fluffing their feathers.

"You girls know a storm's coming, don't you?" A communal cackle swept the coop like the women at a Ladies Aid meeting. Out in the back yard, her garden, at its lush peak, encroached its boundaries. Melon vines intertwined with mature potato plants and flowers trespassed snaggly bean rows.

Satisfaction swept Addie at the sight of fledgling string beans hanging low on the bushes. She smoothed a tomato leaf between her fingers, simply to enjoy the clean scent, like geranium leaves.

The living room window revealed Harold frozen in place over his books, and the radio blaring. With every porch step, her head throbbed. Deceiving him couldn't be right, yet Jane's injunction swirled up the stairs with her. If only she could talk this through with Kate, she'd feel better.

But Kate's instant response still ran through Addie's mind. "Jane's right, and you wouldn't disobey a lawyer's injunction, would you? Even I wouldn't do that."

Jitters in her stomach, Addie went to bed, but at midnight, a cannon blast split the sky. Addie lowered the south window against a driving wet wind that sent notice: summer's oppressive heat couldn't last forever. In each shadowy room, she shut south windows as wildness whipped the grove.

Another boom intermingled with similar distant warnings until they blended in one long explosion. *Pow!* An even louder growl ripped the heavens. Ever since Ruthie stood with her in the doorway whispering, "Thunder and lightning are God's power on display," Addie had loved storms.

Lightning lit the farmyard and something smashed. Through the big bay window facing the yard, a brilliant flash radiated, and a giant hard maple branch cascaded to the earth.

"What're you doing?" Addie jumped at Harold's voice.

"Just listening and watching."

"I'm going out to check the stock." He rummaged on the porch for his boots and coat, and she watched him run. He might have been a child, at the mercy of forces far beyond his reckoning. Another crash jolted the house, and something scratched the back bedroom window. The next flare revealed another enormous branch torn from its moorings.

From the kitchen window, Addie saw a forty-foot walnut tree—not just a branch—covering her garden. Ungainly saw-toothed branches held the trunk up from the ground like so many enormous caterpillar legs. Her breath caught in her throat.

"Oh, my tomatoes, and . . . " Another bright stroke showed the trunk settled over her melon and squash patch.

The fruit and vegetables, fresh, beautiful, and well formed, needed only a few more weeks to ripen. She nurtured each plant until golden blossoms transformed into tiny gourds, folded in on themselves and thickened by the day.

So many velvety orangey-gold blossoms. Just yesterday, she shook out the bees and flattened the flowers to soak in egg and milk. Dipped in cracker crumbs and fried them for supper, what a treat they made.

"Just like a tenderloin," Mama used to say.

Maybe in the morning things wouldn't look as bad as she thought. She didn't even hear Harold come in, so he startled her from her reverie. "That big walnut tree almost hit the house. But we're lucky. Other than that, there's not much damage."

"Yes, we were lucky." Her words drowned in another thunder roll and Harold reached for the light switch.

"Power's out. I'm going to try for another few hours of sleep. You coming?"

"In a little while." She turned back toward the window.

"Worried about your garden?" He answered for her. "You are, aren't you?" He flopped his arms at his sides. "Don't you realize that tree could have walloped the house? And for all we know, the corn crop's ruined, or the soybeans flattened."

He filled his lungs. "But you only think of your garden—you're sick, you know."

Something tugged at Addie's insides. He knew what her garden meant to her. *I've known Harold Bledsoe since before he could walk, and he's always been willful ...* Even if he thought of all her gardening as a waste, didn't he still relish eating its produce?

He snarled. "No faith, that's your problem. That's why we don't have children yet."

My problem . . . no faith. She swallowed down his meaning and blinked back tears.

In fifteen minutes, the storm subsided, so Addie reopened the windows and stood a bit longer, massaging her thumbnail, before she crept to the davenport. Ragged branches waved across a slim moon, so gentle no one would ever know a storm had swept through.

At the grain elevator tomorrow, farmers would discuss the results. "This late rain made the corn crop," or "A man can't win—lost my lower forty acres of corn last night."

A nameless sensation, cold and insistent squeezed Addie's chest, banning sleep. She'd felt alone before, yet this was different. Her mind rebelled, a useless ball of gray yarn in her head.

Think about something happy. Myrna Loy Day came to mind, and all her giggling with Aunt Alvina and Kate. But her heart still ached.

Then Jane's advice flowed through the living room on the breeze. *Practice a little faith.* If only practicing faith were more like practicing the piano, with clear results.

* * *

August heat blistered the daylilies with brown scabs, rendering Old Brown even more lethargic. He languished under the porch this morning.

At midmorning, heavy haze still hid the sun. Cobwebs laced the window screens and created little dewdrop tents in the grass. The humidity sucked every drop of moisture and gouged deep cracks in the earth. Leaves curled in on themselves in survival mode.

Bushy growth now hid the damage to the melon patch. After Harold, Mr. Lundene, and another farmer pulled away the walnut tree the morning after the storm, the garden looked better than Addie imagined, with some crushed melons and tomato vines, but more that survived.

Yesterday, she stumbled through a patch of thigh-high weeds west of the grove. If she whacked them off now, snow might not linger so long there next spring. Even a week made a big difference in Harold's attitude, so why not do what she could?

Over the scythe's hiss, Addie heard her name. Past the garden, she rounded the house corner as Berthea joined Harold behind the tractor. She rarely donned Orville's trousers, but today, thick denim touched her boots.

Harold pointed to the power take off attached to the tractor. "Look here, Ma, you just push this lever down when I wave. I've covered the connection with this casing, see?" He pointed to a contrived metal cover. "The shaft can't come loose. Nothing to fear."

Berthea chewed her lower lip. "This makes me nervous. I've heard too many stories of men's pant legs caught up in there and . . . "

"The power take off makes a lot of noise, but it won't fall apart." Harold squinched his eyes. "Would you rather we spend twenty dollars hiring a man?"

Berthea's sigh melded with the roar.

"All right, then." Harold turned to Addie. "I need you up in the haymow."

Glad she put on overalls to ward off mosquitoes in the grove, Addie trekked the alleyway. Her overalls snagged on barbed wire coils strung beside the barn ladder.

Already in the mow, Harold motioned her near the open door. "The elevator drops the bales right here." He toed the spot with his boot.

"When a bale peaks over the elevator, shift it aside. I'll unload twenty, shut the machine off and come up to stack them. Get each bale out of the way before the next one comes." He studied Berthea. "If Ma can hold her own, we'll finish in a couple of hours."

Each bale weighed about forty pounds, so Addie used her legs to steady herself. The heavy mist finally lifted into perfect blue sky, and she tossed up a prayer.

A few yards away from the elevator, Harold tossed a bale from thehay rack onto the conveyor belt and waved to Berthea. Addie's thirty foot vantage point reduced Berthea to a gnome, and she was sure Jane could hear the ear-shattering racket.

Harold said Orville, slow to accept timesaving innovations, had conditioned Berthea's leeriness toward new machines. But she could see the elevator's value, so she rode along to Benson to order it last month. Yesterday the implement company delivered the long, slanted metal monster resembling a giraffe's neck and head.

Harold's arm strength made up for any lack of agility and transferred the second bale with ease. Addie planted her feet, slipped her fingers under the twine, hefted the weight over the haymow lip, and pushed the bale as far across the wooden floor as she could.

Thirteen bales crossed the lip before one entered the conveyer crooked. Harold failed to notice, but Addie automatically threw out her hand. Visualizing the domino effect ignited fear, and she shrieked, though she knew Harold couldn't hear.

"Harold, that bale's cattywampus!"

He'd already bent to retrieve the next one, but she couldn't just stand there and watch. She made a megaphone of her hands and screamed again.

"Berthea!" Somehow, Harold heard and turned in time to see the misaligned forty pounds gain altitude and nosedive off the elevator toward the back of Berthea's head.

The next moments, like a scene from a silent movie, cast him in the star role. Seconds before the bale plunged into Berthea, Harold intervened.

His knees dipped as his shoulders bore the weight. The bale glanced off his left side and he regained his footing as the would-be killer bounced on the ground. The twine split, cascading hay in a fireworks display.

Aware of something amiss, Berthea flipped the lever. The urge to shuttle down the ladder and smother Harold with hugs overwhelmed Addie. This was the strong man she married, the guy who taught himself to kick a football after his coach counseled him against signing up for the team his freshman year.

Instead, he gave himself to kicking and not only made the team, but kicked the winning point in three close games. And won the heart of every young Halberton girl.

"What I wouldn't give to feel those biceps around me," one of Addie and Kate's classmates swooned when Harold passed them in the hallway. Muscles did little to attract Addie, but after Harold introduced her to his parents, Berthea pulled Addie aside one day.

"Come over here by the corncrib." Knobby indentations marred the paint, like deer markings left from rubbing their itchy nubs on the uneven boards in springtime.

"Harold flung himself at the corncrib every night after supper to toughen himself for football practice. See where his shoulder protectors hit the boards? He threw himself at the crib all summer long for four years." Addie's admiration grew.

Now, below her, Berthea wiped her forehead and yelled up to the mow. "We need a break—I've got roast beef for sandwiches."

Harold gathered the wayward straw, retied the twine and threw the bale on the hay rack. Addie maneuvered the ladder and caught up with him at Berthea's steps.

"Harold, that was amazing."

His eyebrows met in a frown. "Stupid, you mean? I ought to have been more careful."

He opened Berthea's door, his profile lost in shadow.

"Your quick reaction saved your mother's life. I saw the whole thing, and it seems impossible that you got there in time."

"Oh sure, a real modern-day miracle." His sarcasm pierced her. "You coming in or not?"

Something still urged Addie to hug him, but since the night of the storm, he pushed her away.

"I need to check my apple butter. I'll eat some leftovers at home."

He shrugged and slammed the screen door. Addie trudged across the yard, her boots heavy as lead weights.

The apple butter she'd simmered since dawn drew her inside. The recipe required a full day, so she picked yesterday and soaked two pails of quartered apples in salt water overnight.

Early this morning, she drained the salty water and set them to simmer in her deepest pot. Gradually, they turned into rose-colored mush, lending the kitchen a heady, mellow scent. Every time she stirred the mixture, she added cinnamon.

With her overalls stripped off like fetters in the noonday heat, Addie breathed in the pungent aroma. The texture of applesauce by now, the butter only needed to cook another few hours. On this stirring, she added a teaspoon of cloves and tapped at the translucent skins with her paring knife, their original color now given over to the whole.

Mama pressed the sauce through a sieve to remove the peelings, but leaving them in added consistency, and if they cooked long enough, they disappeared into the butter. With rationing, Addie left out the sugar, which made little difference in taste.

Harold disliked apple butter, but she'd already made him two apple cobblers and frozen three pies for a rainy day. She pictured him at Berthea's table, wolfing down roast beef sandwiches, and batted back tears. Why wouldn't he accept anything she offered, even praise?

Her stomach growled, so she sliced a piece of whole wheat bread and set it in the toaster. *Tsk, tsk, tsk.* The sound brought Norman to mind, and while she waited, Addie imagined this wainscoting painted white.

Slathered with butter and the hot apple mixture, her toast became a feast. Harold would never taste sweet cream butter and homemade apple butter like this, never appreciate this slow simmering treat.

"But I do, and surely that counts for something. I might take some to Jane after supper. I just might."

Chapter Nineteen

July 25, 1942

Dear Addie,

Reading your letter proved an ambivalent experience.

The massive dictionary in our office defines ambivalence as a simultaneous contradictory attitude or feeling toward an object, person, or action—my reaction to Harold's recent behavior.

What bothers him about you? I don't know how to convince you that it's nothing you've done. You've worked so hard to please him, Addie. In your heart, you surely know that's true.

What irritates Harold is who you are. You're honest, sincere, and you have opinions of your own. Granted, you've stifled them to keep the peace, but he knows you don't agree with him on everything. That's such an unrealistic expectation, don't you see? Who could ever agree with anyone on every single question?

But consider this: why would someone who loves you refuse to embrace your exuberance for life? You're witty—your tongue only ties when you're intimidated, so why intimidate you?

Insecurity leads some folks to bully. Harold's done great things in spite of his accident, so I doubt his

behavior arises from that. Here's my take on this—
what if he can't abide your strengths?

Why do I trust this instinct? Because our intuition
exists for a reason. Didn't you trust Norman's
perception that God forgave him long ago?

What if Harold fears he can't hold his own with
you? You're too quick-witted, and a thinker. Have you
two ever argued? If not, his intimidation has worked.
And he knows it.

He only has to huff, puff and withdraw to crush
you. In spite of your intelligence, you came from the
south side of Halberton and your dad rented instead of
owning land.

Did you know that no one from south of town ever
received the Valedictorian award? The spring of our
graduation, I researched old Press issues under the
guise of writing a history report.

Though I was orphaned into Halberton's system,
my grandfather distinguished himself as a judge. The
British openly claim their pecking order. If you're titled
and own land, you count more than ordinary people.
Well, small towns have their own "landed gentry."

Our grade points tied, and the Valedictorian
committee's finagling infuriated me. Their decision to
choose me motivated me to run off, and Alexandre
proposed we elope at just the right time.

By missing graduation, I also missed the looks on
their faces, and the pleasure of graduating with you. In
my befuddled-by-romance state, standing before a
magistrate across the state line looked far more
exciting.

When I heard that Mrs. M filled in for me at the last
minute, I felt terrible. Then someone told me your dad
didn't even come. That made me furious—at him and at
myself.

Back to Harold. The picture of a perfect woman in
his brain, a mix of his doting mother and some dishy

brunette from the magazines in the school furnace room, is real only to him.

You fit the pretty part, and so does your sweet "it doesn't matter" attitude. But Harold's inner picture never challenges him, so if you do, he intimidates you and conjures ways to blame you.

If he ever saw this letter, the truth would send him over the edge and halt our correspondence. Heaven forbid—please burn it right away.

Every show of strength in you unsettles him. If you look him in the eye and state your case, he must reconnoiter, since bullies back down when confronted. The sooner you stand up to him, the better.

My fingers have quite worn out, as Londoners say. Please don't let my analysis send you into a dither. This is how I see it, limited by prejudice. I'm cheering for you.

Kate—'the analyst.'

"Do you have time to run into town this morning? I need some more yarn." Addie waited outside Jane's screen door.

"Not today." Jane's glance shifted at a faint sound from the living room. Her watering can lay beside a rose bush, dribbling from the spout.

"I don't mind riding." Addie backed down the steps toward her bicycle, but Jane lingered. "Could I pick up anything for you?"

Jane strummed the screen. "Could you . . . would you mind taking a note to Dr. Townsend? I can write one quick."

"Take your time. I'll look at your hollyhocks. Heaven knows I can't enjoy them at home."

But Jane didn't smile at Addie's little joke, and a few minutes later, she stepped out with a sealed envelope. "Would you mind dropping this off right away?"

"All right. See you soon." Addie pedaled faster than normal. Doc answered her knock and opened the envelope, his kind dark eyes shifting from the note to her.

"Take some time to catch your breath, Addie. Let me get you a drink of water."

She accepted, and he smoothed his white mustache. "I'll take care of this right away, don't you worry."

On a whim, Addie leaned her bicycle on the fence circling the high school and wandered to a row of wooden swings beyond the football field. She sat down and pushed the next swing back and forth with her toe. Along with Jane's uncharacteristic agitation, Harold's sour reaction yesterday when she tried to build him up nagged at her.

How could she fathom Jane when she couldn't even understand her own husband? Kate's letter showed that she comprehended so much about Harold. That perfect woman in his head made sense, but what to do about her?

Brooding only wasted time, so she gulped down her heaviness and continued on her way. Under the striped awning of Olson's Café a new corkboard replaced one that had fallen apart last winter. The announcements tacked here hadn't changed much.

"Home grown pecans from my Georgia cousin, ten cents a pound. Elmer Sweeney"

"Passel of six-week old pups. If someone don't take them, they ain't long for this world. Got kittens to send along, too. Theo Thorson"

Ride the bus to Cedar Rapids on Friday nights at five p.m. to help out at the USO Hall. Free ride leaves from Town Hall.

Another, scrawled in childlike letters, magnetized Addie.

LOST: new mattress on Benson curve August 3. Reward. Contact Denny Hayes

How could anyone lose a mattress? Wouldn't a driver notice such a cumbersome object flying from a truck or the top of his automobile?

"Truth can sometimes be stranger than fiction." A man's voice startled her, and she turned to see Walt McCluskey. "Hello, Addie. In town to shop today?"

"No, I'm picking up some extra Red Cross yarn for sweaters."

"For the troops? How good of you. My Fern's too fidgety to settle down long enough to knit. How's Harold these days?"

"He's busy haying."

"We're mighty pleased with that young man. Yes, indeed." Walt rocked back on his heels. "You must be awfully proud to be his wife."

Proud to be Harold's wife. A simple *Yes* refused to come forth, and in Walt's puzzled gaze, Addie felt the back of her neck heat.

Finally, he looked away and cleared his throat. "Nice hot weather we're having, isn't it? Well, then, we'll see you in church on Sunday." He gave her a nod and sauntered off, the successful banker in his pinstriped suit.

But his words stayed with Addie. He expected her to be proud of Harold. Did other people find their inner truth so at odds with what other folks thought?

Outside the Red Cross station, signs advertised far-flung volunteer positions. The long list intrigued Addie, as if assigned by Mrs. Morfordson and penned by a classic author. So many possibilities—farm laborers, replacements for Civilian Conservation Corps firefighters drafted into the military, factory workers in corporations modified into war plants.

Just reading the needs energized her—all across the nation, people of all ages joined together to support the war effort. With all these opportunities, why was it so hard for Harold find his niche?

A few minutes later, yarn in hand, she braked in front of the hardware display—a shiny paint can pyramid. Something clicked inside her, a puzzle piece slipping into place. She'd put off painting the kitchen wainscoting all summer, but tomorrow Harold would be gone with Maynard Lundene the entire day.

August 10, 1942

From my bright white kitchen, the plot thickens.
Oh, Kate, Harold will be furious when he comes
home from Cedar Rapids. But Jane stands ready, should
I throw myself on her mercy.
　　She offered free leftover paint. I prayed for a sign
and Berthea liked the idea of whitening the kitchen, so I

plunged ahead. The room sparkles, and Berthea loves the change. But I'm biking this letter to Jane, so she can mail it in case my treachery drives Harold too far.

I do hope I live to obey my summons to the lawyer's office concerning Norman's will—I'll tell you about that later, but back to the paint.

Why did I risk Harold's fury? Covering those dark boards brought a sense of . . . what? Adventure? Victory?

You'll remember who wrote, "Unless we act on our dreams, life becomes puppet play."

Well, I acted on my dreams, and for better or worse, white walls surround me.

Always . . . or at least a few more hours,

Addie

After eating a sugar cookie she baked for Harold that afternoon, Addie did the chores and rode to Jane's.

"Harold won't even turn on the light tonight. In the morning, you'll be able to handle his reaction better." She offered some fresh tea, and Addie stayed until sunset. At home, she left a glass of buttermilk and a plate of cookies for Harold on the table.

Moonlight streamed over the landing, followed her up the stairs, and decorated her thin rose chenille bedspread. But when she closed her eyes, her thoughts erupted. What had gotten into her? Why had she let her desire to paint the kitchen overwhelm her?

Kate would say God ordains our desires and feelings, so she could trust her instinct to lighten the room. Then why did she shiver on this hot August night?

Harold would counter Kate, "By your logic, anyone could validate their actions, any old murderer—even Hitler."

"You're taking the parallel too far."

"Hogwash!" And to that, Kate would say . . .

The next thing Addie knew, sunrise streaked the horizon and Harold snored beside her. She skulked downstairs. Jane was right. He must not have noticed the paint. His trail left boots, cookie crumbs, and the sour odor of spilled milk.

While she made coffee and sniffed the dawn, the last star faded. She smoothed the white wainscoting and willed away the tension that rose in her chest.

Outdoors, Old Brown rubbed against her leg. "No matter what happens, boy, it's good to be alive on this fresh new day."

Before Harold found her, she fed the chickens and cleaned their water pans. When he entered the chicken house, she froze. He must be furious—he never came in here, since chickens pecked his legs when he was young.

But now he faced her, with the rising sun at his back. Goosebumps traced Addie's arms.

"You painted the kitchen." Harold took two steps, letting in more light.

An odd calmness descended over her. Harold's muscular torso pushed his arms out from his sides. In the yellow rays, his legs took on a stick-like appearance, and though one measured an inch shorter, they looked the same from where she stood.

He hadn't put on his overalls yet, which said a lot. Nothing kept Harold Bledsoe from donning his overalls first thing in the morning. With his thumbs hooked in his pockets, he looked like the little boy Addie visualized when he held the orphan lamb.

In the aura, his features went hazy. So this was why the hens' eyes dazed every time she entered. From their perspective, any random intruder might be entering.

Her voice chirped from some deep well, like the one where Joseph's brothers threw him when their jealousy turned into revenge. She tried again.

"Do you like it?"

Harold stamped his foot. He ought to have known better—the sudden movement startled the hens and one of them grazed his face. He startled back as another crisscrossed his chest, and the birds set up a cackling chorus. Their comradeship widened the opening in Addie's throat.

"Your mother liked the idea. She said the varnish was as old as Methuselah, and white would make everything look clean."

Harold tilted his head like a carnival bobble doll. She wished he would lift his hat and scratch his head, make a sound—something. An image of her dad surfaced, whipping off his belt and ordering her closer. She had to obey, even when he bent her over his knee. She held her breath as he pulled up her dress, whisked off her panties and stung her bare buttocks.

Once, Ruthie's tears shocked Addie when she checked her backside and legs. "He bruised you with his buckle. I've gotta get you out of here." But several years passed, and Ruthie fell in love. Before she married Reginald, she held Addie's hand in the Presbyterian church narthex.

"You're in high school now. It won't be that long before . . ." Addie finally escaped when she married Harold, but today, she almost choked on the same suffocating sensation Dad's whippings produced.

"Don't look at me with those innocent eyes. There's nothing innocent about you."

"What do you mean?"

"You always go your own fool way, changing things that have served us well for a long time. Worse yet, you've stooped to using my mother to shield yourself."

"But it's true, Harold—she said the whole house needs painting. She said rancid coal smoke caught in the old hopper assembly your dad replaced when they built their new house, and everything's dingy."

Harold's forehead vein bulged even more. "Now you're using my father, too! I'm fed up. You spend money we don't have. This has to stop."

With each accusation, his voice rose. He jabbed his finger at her. "You don't know how hard my parents worked to pay for this farm. Dad almost lost it during the Depression. You think we have money to waste on paint? I'm fed up, do you hear me?"

Addie's throat clogged. Where was the courage she felt yesterday when Jane's pig bristle brush transformed the kitchen's darkness? After she put away the can, she fetched Berthea, whose mouth fell open when she stepped in.

"Why, it's beautiful. I can't imagine Harold not liking it."

"You really think so?"

"Once he gets used to the shock. But he never would have agreed to this. That's how Orville acted about moving, yet once we did, he liked the new place."

By the moment, the sun beamed brighter. Addie pictured Berthea still enjoyed her morning sleep in her back bedroom, insulated from outside noises. The coop's walls loomed in and she wanted to crumble into the dirt floor. The hens hunkered down in their roosts as morning mist reached the far wall, and Harold moved three steps closer.

Chapter Twenty

Harold could see into her soul. He read her deepest motives like his sermon notes—she was selfish and egotistical and immature. Addie felt ten years old and braced herself for a blow.

But like an echo from a deep cavern, Kate's voice rose in her. "When you stand up to a bully, he always backs down." The hens' tittering calmed her, and her voice flitted high and soft, but at least she found it.

"The paint didn't cost anything."

"Bah!" Harold tensed his biceps.

"Someone gave it to us."

"Who?"

Mentioning Jane would only make him angrier, so she kept quiet.

His spittle landed at her feet. "You hide things from your own husband." Her cheeks burned, for if he discovered she'd been included in Norman's will . . . Shame bore down, no matter how positive she felt yesterday, or how the paint improved the kitchen. If she stood in a police line-up right now, any random observer would declare her guilty.

"You're an unfit wife. You vowed before God to honor and obey, but you've made our marriage an offense in His sight." Harold's voice soared as it did one Sunday in June when he preached about the end of the world.

Unfit wife, an offense in God's sight . . . how did the topic alter so fast, from paint to their marriage? But she had no time to consider. On his next indictment, Harold's eyes turned metallic.

"Bill and Sue are expecting another baby and you haven't even had *one* yet." He flipped his hair back. "You're under God's curse. You can't bear children because of your disobedience."

Cold fingers squeezed Addie's chest. Harold raised his hand. His chin jutted inches away and a rush of air made her blink.

Then he stepped back. "No. I will not let you cause me to sin. You ought to be my help-meet, as God ordained, but you've become my test, my Jezebel." He turned on his heel and slammed the door, sending the hens into another frenzy.

An odd serenity enveloped Addie, though her hands shook and her eyes smarted. She leaned on the doorframe as Harold advanced toward the barn. Her theory proved true again—in his fury, his limp disappeared.

Behind her, hens fluttered their wings. Such flighty creatures, just like her. But Harold did back down, as Kate foretold.

Addie fought for breath. "At least I didn't cry."

Light manure swished under her chore shoes, and Harold's charges pulsed in her ears. *Under God's curse* ... He spouted the very fear that kept her awake in adolescence, pleading for God's forgiveness and protection.

If I should die before I wake, I pray thee Lord, my soul to take. What fate could be worse? When sleep evaded her back then, she finally visited the Presbyterian pastor.

"You believe Jesus died for you, don't you, Addie?"

"Yes, but I have doubts and terrible thoughts."

He patted her shoulder. "Nothing changes God's love. He sent His only Son to die for us. Don't you think he can handle a little doubt?"

The fear that haunted Addie for weeks diminished a little. The pastor scanned his bookshelf and handed her a slim volume, *Grace Abounding to the Chief of Sinners.* "You've read *Pilgrim's Progress.* John Bunyan wrote this too. He wrestled with fierce doubts and thought he was destined for Hell.

"Our sin reminds us we're human. By comparison, shame says there's no hope. But with God, there's always hope. Read the book of First John. God's love is greater than our hearts when they accuse us."

She and Kate read both of the books, and gradually the condemning voices died down. But Harold's fresh accusations revived them. Outside the chicken coop, sunlight loosened Addie's shoulders. So did the sight of her garden, with bounty weighting every branch and vine.

Her daylilies, ragged from battles with the weather, hunched over, their stalks crisp and brown. With a good rain, though, they would bloom again. You couldn't judge the future by the present. Sometimes flowers withdrew to regroup, not to die.

A speck of blue hidden under a hydrangea bush caught her attention, so she leaned down for a closer look. Periwinkle blossoms. Somehow a seed landed here, and though all the other plants blossomed in June, this one, spritely and vigorous, sent out its color weeks later.

Forget-me-nots spoke of friendship. An ache wrenched Addie as she touched the five-petaled flowers. A talk with Kate would take the sting from Harold's biting words.

"Think of the positive. He didn't hit you," Kate would say. "You stood your ground, and he backed down. Good for you, Ad!"

The eggs still waited, so Addie returned to the chicken house. Harold leaped onto the Farm-all and when the engine fired, he spun from the yard, towing a spreader full of manure.

Berthea's door opened and shut, but Addie looked away. Her shaky fingers still rattled the eggs—this was no time to talk. But when Berthea crossed the driveway, she had no choice.

"Didn't Harold just take off without milking the cows?"

"He . . ." Addie's voice broke.

"Addie, what is it?" Berthea grasped her hand. "Why, your fingers are freezing. Look at me, honey. What's wrong?"

Her brow knit, and Addie bowed her head.

"Did you and Harold fight about the paint?"

Addie's breath came in spasms. "I can take care of the cows. Don't worry, everything will be all right . . . "

Berthea gathered her in. "Now, now. He'd better get back here and do his work. Did he . . . did he hurt you?"

Addie buried her face in Berthea's soft shoulder. She wanted to say, "He said terrible things and threatened to hit me," but stifled the torrent.

The tractor motor hummed beyond the grove, and Berthea pursed her lips. "Let me handle him. I know he can be difficult."

"Please don't say anything."

"I won't, but I will tell him the paint is a big improvement, and he'd better start appreciating all your work around here." Berthea's eyes widened. "He's just like his father. I put up with his attitude far too long, and you shouldn't have to do that for the rest of your life."

She set her jaw as Harold drove back in. "I'll invite him for breakfast. Let me know if he troubles you any more, all right? We women have to stand together."

She swung across the yard, her bathrobe brushing the gravel. A robin warbled from a branch, his sturdy legs supporting his own melody. Addie's next breath came a bit less haggard.

Sunlight glinted on something shiny down the road, and Berthea was making Harold breakfast. Why not ride over and let Jane know she survived?

* * *

For a week, Addie left Harold's breakfast in the skillet while she went out to do chicken chores, but today he waited at the table, his expression sour. She broke the silence.

"In a little while, Jane's picking me up to get yarn, just so you know."

The admission made her feel better, though he gave no indication he heard. She would also visit the lawyer's office, but at least she told him part of the truth. Did lies come in large and small sizes? A question for her next letter to Kate.

Jane beeped the Studebaker's horn as Addie dried the last plate, and she hurried out into the front seat.

"Feel all right about this meeting?"

"I've never seen the inside of a lawyer's office."

"You're not on trial—just listen and nod." Jane dropped her off and headed to the Red Cross office.

"I'll sit here and knit when I get back, so don't worry about me."

Addie shut the door, but turned back.

"You'll be fine. Masterson will do the talking. You can ask questions later, if need be."

"Harold drove to Benson this morning. What if he drives by?"

"Fiddlesticks. Why would he pay any attention to me? Worry about something worth your energy, Addie."

Seeing Fern sitting in the waiting room surprised her, but Fern's jaw dropped and a red-hot flush surfaced under her make-up. "I didn't expect to meet you here."

Mr. Masterson opened his door and tipped his fingers. Fern rose, but Addie waited.

"Come in, both of you." He led the way into a spacious room with light cascading from two directions onto a walnut desk seven feet wide. He gestured to a wooden chair on his right. "Sit here, Mrs. Bledsoe."

The plush paisley rug tripped Addie, so she stumbled in while Fern took the other chair. Fern's pale blue suit complemented her hair's red highlights. Her fine-grained leather purse sat primly in her lap, but her white gloves couldn't hide the way she kneaded its handles.

Suddenly aware of her plain calico shirtwaist dress, Addie worked at her thumbnail. The lawyer's salt-and-pepper hair and his casual tone testified to many such meetings.

"Mrs. Bledsoe, may I call you Adelaide?"

"No, sir. I mean, please call me Addie."

Once he explained what would occur, her pulse stopped rattling in her ears. She still wished Jane or Kate sat beside her, but so far, Jane was right—Mr. Masterson seemed friendly and kind. He opened a file on his desk and leafed through some papers.

"Are you ready, ladies?"

Fern looked anything but ready. She crossed her legs, but the toe of her white pump wiggled back and forth, a little like Norman's left eye.

"Norman Allen, being of sound mind, made out his will with clear purpose. I propose to read you his wishes for his holdings here in Halberton." Mr. Masterson smoothed his mustache. "Is that agreeable?"

Addie's tongue twisted, but the lawyer accepted her nod.

"To Addie Bledsoe, I leave my 1937 four-door red Ford coupe, in the back shed. Before she decides whether to keep or sell it, I want her to learn to drive and try it out a few times.

I also bequeath the contents of my house to Addie Bledsoe, to be removed before auction and dispersed as she wills. If she decides to sell the household goods at the auction, any and all material profits go directly to her."

A '37 Ford coupe—she didn't even know Norman owned a vehicle. *Household goods.* The term floated through her mind like goose down. That must mean the furniture and a few pictures on the living room wall. Then she remembered. Norman had already given her a treasure, Millie's tea canister.

Fern re-crossed her legs and chewed on her upper lip through dazzling red lipstick.

"Now, to you, Mrs. McCluskey." He shuffled the papers. "Let me repeat, these gifts must remain absolutely confidential. Do you both agree?"

Stinging started behind Addie's eyes. Norman must have a reason for his wishes, but how could she possibly keep a car secret? She'd hoped things could return to normal, but now, she would have to hide even more.

Then she recalled something Jane said when she first read the letter. "Down the road, you will have a need for whatever Norman gives you."

Mr. Masterson awaited her reply. "That means no slips, even to your husbands. Is that perfectly clear?"

"Yes, sir."

He slid his glasses up his nose. "Mrs. McCluskey?"

"I know how to keep a secret, Mort."

"Then, in Norman's own words:

Sell my house at auction and donate all proceeds to an orphanage, to provide for newborn babies until they find a home. I charge Fernella McCluskey to manage these funds, trusting any concerns to her judgment."

Mr. Masterson raised his eyebrow in Fern's direction, and she shrank back. "He adds an endnote.

'My sister, Mrs. Theodore Schultz and her children have been amply provided for in other disbursements. Thus, I require that even she have no knowledge of these proceedings.'"

Fern's facial muscles fluctuated. She froze when Mr. Masterson said *Fernella*, but then her lips puckered as if she fought tears. Addie turned her attention to the rich Oriental rug beneath their feet, an intriguing mélange of dark reds, purples, blues and gold.

"Lawyer Masterson," as Addie's dad called him, angled back so sunlight struck his bald spot. "Any questions?" Several cars passed by as a large circular clock maintained its steady rhythm.

"In here, you'll find the keys to Mr. Allen's auto." He handed Addie a bumpy gold envelope.

"And Fern, if you desire help with the auction, we have workers available. Best to hold it before winter sets in." He turned back to Addie.

"I suggest you look things over and make your decision about the auction soon, say . . . by September first? Let me know, and I will inform Mrs. McCluskey."

"Is . . . is his house locked?"

"Yes. Come by for the key any time."

"If you have no further questions . . ." He slid his chair back and walked around the desk. Fern's expression became a caricature of Harold when he heard news of a fresh Allied loss—distress and something else. Was it anger?

A pang skittered Addie's abdomen. She felt as though she ought to offer Fern some sort of assistance, but not here and now. Fern marched out, and the outer door banged.

The lawyer angled his head. "Good day, Addie."

Thank you, sir." Taking extra care on the thick rug, Addie made her exit.

Chapter Twenty-one

Jane handed Addie a small brown paper sack when she got in.

"Brought you a treat."

"A Snickers bar—I haven't tasted one since . . . way before Kate left for London. Aunt Alvina didn't seem to mind us raiding the candy shelf when I stayed overnight. But you shouldn't have, Jane."

"It's a big day, so why not celebrate a little? How did it go in there?"

"Fine. You'll never believe what Norman left me." Addie shut her door and Jane revved the engine.

"Well?"

"A coupe."

"You mean an automobile?"

"Yes, a '37 coupe."

"Well, I'll be hornswoggled. Who would have thought he owned such a thing? Is it here in town?"

The reality of the past hour started to sink in, and Addie nodded as she sank back against the seat.

"Let's go have a look." Jane headed the Studebaker toward Norman's corner.

"I don't know . . ." Addie's voice faltered, as it had with Harold in the chicken house.

"If you'd rather wait, fine. But a quick peek wouldn't hurt."

The bag rustled in Addie's hands. Jane bought her a candy bar— she couldn't believe that, much less that a red coupe awaited her. Jane slowed the Studebaker.

"What'll I do with a car, Jane?"

"What do you think Norman had in mind?"

"The will says I have to learn to drive before I decide whether to keep it."

"Then you don't need to decide right away."

"I guess you're right. It's just that I . . . Where would I hide a car?"

"How about finding out what you have to hide?"

Jane turned into Norman's alley and bustled out to tackle the heavy wooden sliding doors. "Lift on your end, now. These rusty runners haven't moved in a long time."

They lifted and tugged, heaved and shook. After a mighty lurch, Jane's half finally gave way amidst complaints from the worn boards.

"Will you look at that? Makes my old green bird look like a relic."

In spite of a dusty film, the coupe's polish shone like Fern's waxed floor. Jane made her way around the treasure with Addie in her wake. Nothing here except mice had stirred for a long while. Traces of the pesky creatures peppered a pile of boards.

Cobwebs slung from rafter to corner, posts to ceiling. How long had it been since Norman came out here? And did he smooth his fingers over the coupe's smooth finish like Jane?

"What do you think?"

The coupe matched Berthea's unfolding blood-red dahlias—that was all Addie could think of.

"Hum?"

Addie shook herself back to the coupe . . . her coupe.

"Think you might want to learn to drive it?" Jane's grin started slow and spread.

"Maybe I can come over and sit in it a few times first."

"No time like the present." Jane opened the driver's side and bowed low. "Have a seat in your new car." Addie bit her lip and slipped against the cool, soft leather. Jane went around the other side and sat down, too.

"Oh, my goodness, Norman knew what he was doing. Look at these pieces of shed snakeskin scattered on the floor to keep mice out."

Addie sank into luxury—an interior even cleaner than Aunt Alvina's car. "I wonder if Norman ever drove this. It smells brand new."

"If he did, he certainly didn't leave a speck of dust."

When they got out, Jane winked. "Pretty nice, eh?"

The cranky shed door challenged them again. Rust flaked in Addie's palm when she turned the latch.

Back in the Studebaker, Jane headed toward home.

"It's not just the coupe, Jane. Norman left me his household goods too."

"He really took a liking to you."

What could she say? The whole scenario seemed impossible.

In Addie's yard, Jane shifted into neutral. "Give yourself some time to get used to this, Addie. Sometimes, even good news takes digesting."

She handed Addie the Snickers bar before she shut her door. "Enjoy your Snickers, and don't you dare share it with Harold." Her grin flashed again. "Say, have you heard that the Mars family named Snickers after their horse?"

Addie stared at the brown paper wrapping.

"Go ahead, eat it right now. Then I can have the pleasure of watching."

Addie took a bite. "Um . . . scrumptious. You're too good to me, Jane."

"Pfft. No one could ever be too good to you. Now enjoy that candy, and come on over if you need to talk."

* * *

Late August colored the red sumac along the fencerows. The corn's rustling turned into an insistent scratch. Silence stalked Addie up the steps past Jane's rosebush, still brimming with fragile, pale pink petals. She pressed her nose against the screen.

Jane sat at the table, her head folded into one arm. Her fingers poised near her radio dial. Addie's heart skipped into her throat—maybe she suffered a stroke like Orville. The scent of roast beef wafted out. *No, please.*

But Jane stirred, so Addie knocked again.

"Oh, Addie. Come on in." Her voice lacked its normal lilt, so Addie sat down without a sound.

"Is something wrong?"

Jane's long sigh sent a quiver down her spine. "Have you heard? A few days ago, our forces launched a horrible battle in a town along the French coast. More than thirty-five hundred, mostly Canadian and British boys, died." She rubbed her jaw line. "Kate's husband is Canadian, isn't he?"

"Yes. You mean the attack on Dieppe." Harold repeated the details ever since the first bulletin crackled across the airwaves. He slugged the living room wall with his fist and shrieked.

"Don't the commanders care about wasting human life?" Last night, he ranted for over an hour before Addie went upstairs.

This latest debacle rolled around inside her like a giant, fire-breathing dragon. So many soldiers dead, so many planes shot down, and such a mighty victory for the enemy.

"Almost a hundred planes lost—how can our forces bear this?" Harold yelled the statistics into the porch as she swayed in her rocker last night. A thousand crickets chirped around the porch and fireflies lighted the grove and cornfield.

If only she could talk with him about what was happening. But she might slip and mention Alexandre—she'd never hear the end of that.

Harold poked his head out again and again to spew each dire report. Why insist on repeating everything when she could hear it well enough herself? And why start talking to her now, when he'd barely spoken to her since she painted the kitchen?

She almost said, "The Brits are our *allies*—they're doing the best they can." But his eyes clouded from blue to gray, so she held her tongue.

The whole time, another unsettling truth nagged at Addie. Chances were, Alexandre flew in the Dieppe raids, and Kate most likely awaited word.

"Sometimes it seems like the whole world will dissolve in flames." Jane's wide cheeks fell in downward wrinkles. "We went through this in the Great War, with such high hopes it would never happen again. Today, things seem even more impossible. For every victory in the Pacific, an hour's worth of agony happens in Europe."

A shadow flitted outside the window—maybe a raccoon, although they didn't often appear in daylight. Jane didn't seem to notice.

"My uncle was never the same after the Great War. Most of those men, like Norman, picked up where they left off, but some of them couldn't shake the memories."

Her sigh filled the morning stillness, backed by the fixed ticking of her clock. After a while, Addie brought up another topic.

"Your rose bush still has blooms—even through this awful heat."

Jane brightened, and glanced out the screen door. "That tea rose has been there as long as I remember." She gave her first smile. "How about a cup of tea? I have a little left. Why hoard it when we can drink some together?"

"I'd love that."

"You're out early this morning." The gas burner flamed under the kettle and Jane scooped fine black tea into her strainer.

"Harold had to leave at six to help the Perrys bale hay. You heard Earl broke his leg falling off a hay wagon the other day? Berthea went along too, to help with dinner. I did the chores, but got to thinking about the lawyer's meeting. I wanted to talk something over with you."

"All right."

"Sunday after church, Fern pulled me out behind the building and made sure we were all alone. She asked if I'd gone through the household items yet, and was upset that it's been a full week since the meeting. She said I should quit putting it off.

"Something told me not to tell her we already looked at the coupe. I guess Kate would call it my intuition. But I think Fern might complain to Mr. Masterson if I don't hurry up."

Jane filled the teacups and brought them to the table. "Wonder why this matters so much to her."

"She pushed me for a specific time, but then Harold announced something from the front steps, and I reminded her I couldn't tell him, and it might take time for me to get to town."

Jane shifted her weight in her chair. "She pressed you?"

"Yes. She set the auction for September, and said I need to decide about the household goods right away. She even offered to help slip things by Harold—putting me on some church committee so I'd have a reason to go to town."

Jane rubbed her chin. "How did Fern know you hadn't already gone over there? Has she posted a guard at Norman's back door to keep watch?" She gave a cynical grin.

"Maybe the lawyer mentioned I haven't asked for the key. She said surely Norman has some treasures in his house, and aren't I even curious? She even offered to help me organize things."

"Did she now?" Jane refilled their cups.

"I said no, but she grabbed my arm and said to let her know when I go. But I . . ."

Jane's eyes shone emerald gold. "Sounds like she wants to snoop around. She's married to the richest man in town, so what would she be interested in? Maybe something she'd rather the rest of the world not see?"

Addie's collarbone itched. Jane's intuition was right on the money. The only thing Fern might seek would be a photograph. Yet with all the secrecy surrounding their relationship, the young Fernella surely would never have allowed a photograph of them.

"I don't have a thing planned today and could sure use an outing. Harold's gone until tonight, right?"

"Yes. He and Berthea won't be back until after dark, so I need to start his chores. The churchwomen serve the evening meal too, so the balers can get as much done as possible before nightfall. And that means Fern will be busy supervising."

"Did you have any big jobs planned?"

"I thought I'd can some tomatoes, but they can wait."

Jane downed the rest of her tea. "Enjoy another quick cup and hurry home. I'll take care of something and pick you up in half an hour."

She disappeared into the next room. Fresh steaming tea calmed Addie, and she feasted her eyes on the flowers outside the window.

Beyond the lovely bed of orange and yellow zinnias east of the house, a shadow fell over a beaten-down path. When it took the shape of a man, Addie's heart flip-flopped. Could Harold have . . .? She leaned back from the window.

Under a black beret, a short, weathered man approached the house. Patched overalls hung from his thin shoulders, and his rounded boot toes turned up at the ends. Shoulders rounded, he waited like a timid child outside a side door. That door opened, and a thick arm extended—Jane's.

Addie squeezed nearer the window. The man's wrinkled face and downcast eyes carried a vacant look, like the upstairs windows of abandoned Depression farmhouses marking the route between here and Benson.

Jane handed him a plate covered with a dishtowel. They chatted, and he slipped a basket over his hand before shuffling toward the grove.

Addie extricated herself. Was he Jane's husband? If so, why lurk out there like a stranger? He might be a vagrant following the rail lines—Aunt Alvina used to feed a couple of those men regularly. But the railroad passed south of town—why would a hobo walk all this way?

Long ago, Addie set to rest her questions about Simon Pike, but they all flooded back. The day she took the note to Doc Townsend, she determined once again to leave the mystery to Jane. Now, she renewed her resolve, hurried outside and pedaled home as fast as she could.

Chapter Twenty-two

*A*ll the way home, Addie wrestled with the stranger's presence. But she had something else to consider—going inside Norman's house for the first time since he passed. In one way, Fern had spoken the truth. She'd put off facing those empty rooms far too long.

At least Jane, as unshakable as anyone Addie knew, would go with her. Addie ate an apple and gave the chickens a little more grain. With no meals to cook, the day seemed peculiar.

Down by the rocky incline to the dry creek, two dark horse tails swished together, one much lower than the other. The foal was growing by the day. Addie toyed with names, but nothing seemed quite right.

Old Brown lingered by the back porch steps, so she took him some water and a chunk of leftover beef and petted him for a while.

"Good dog. Enjoy the peace and quiet while you can." The dog's yellowed eyes communicated understanding. "Watch out for things while I'm gone, all right?" Old Brown stretched out and settled his nose on his paws.

Not long afterward, Jane chugged into the yard. At the law office, Mr. Masterson came into the waiting area as Addie entered, and reached to some hooks on the wall.

"Here you go, Addie. Hopefully, we'll get this taken care of soon."

During the short ride to the house, Addie's throat constricted. If only she could trade this task with someone else. Lately Mama's favorite tune, "*This is My Task*," kept coming to mind.

"To do my best from dawn of day 'til night . . . and smile when evening falls. . . this is my task."

But this task, going through someone's things—especially Norman's—bothered her. When Mama died, there'd been little to go through, and she and Ruth worked together. But those things belonged to her mother. This was different.

On Addie's third try to unlock the cantankerous back door, Jane took over. "Probably hasn't ever been locked before. I imagine after his time in France, Halberton seemed like safety itself to Norman."

The air was stuffy, so they opened as many windows as they could and set to work. Three hours later, Addie sank on the floor near a dented army trunk. Jane occupied the armchair in the corner where Norman's hospital bed once sat.

"Well, what do you think of all this?" She glanced at a wad of dollar bills in a wooden cheese box on her lap.

"I don't know what to say. Stranger things have happened, I keep telling myself."

"I imagine they have."

"But not to me. I never pictured this much money. Do you think I ought to tell Mr. Masterson?"

Jane pushed deep into her chair. "No. Everything in the house belongs to you, and Norman was no fool—he knew how much money he had."

She ruffled the bills. "It's time for you to do some thinking. What do you need? Or what might you like to do some day?"

The living room seemed larger without Norman's bed. But his scent lingered, like the pink diamonds fluttering on the far wall. And his words still lived in Addie.

"No one could've stood up to him for her."

Kate's philosophizing matched Norman's. In her own way, Jane expressed the same concept when she read the lawyer's letter. *A woman must take charge of her own life with the brain God gave her.*

But the huge cash pile and the Ford coupe and the furniture in this house overwhelmed Addie. Before this came about, she had nothing to call her own except Mama's sunshine and shadows quilt, her photograph, and her clothing.

Now she possessed more than she imagined owning in her entire life. Why would God allow this if Harold's accusations were true— that she was unworthy, disgusting, disobedient? And yet, those condemnations burrowed like wasps in a fencepost, eating away at her a little more each day. How could she move ahead when her foundation teetered like rotting wood?

Jane slid forward, expectant. Finally, Addie blurted, "How can I want something when I don't deserve anything?"

"Where did you get that idea?"

"Harold said God is cursing me—that's why we don't have children yet." A tremor took her, but the truth was out in the open.

"Why, that . . ." Jane's face reddened.

"He called me his test and said I'm not a fit wife. He said I'm a Jezebel, a temptress."

Jane gritted her teeth. "You have about as much in common with Jezebel as Eleanor Roosevelt has with Betty Grable."

"Our adult Sunday school class is studying evil women, like Potiphar's lustful wife and Delilah, who ruined Samson."

"Who teaches that, Walt? I wouldn't wonder. Potiphar's wife, phooey! Delilah? Yes, she connived, but Samson allowed her to shatter his defenses little by little."

Jane sputtered on, but Addie remembered her comment the morning after the painting incident. "If he ever hits you, tell me. I'll make him real sorry."

The sun shifted, sending rose diamonds further up the wall. Stillness descended on the room. The glass over Norman's discharge papers sent out reflections, doubling the diamonds' effect. If only Kate were here to watch them dance.

She would decry Harold's accusations in a minute. But Kate couldn't fight this battle, and for some reason, Addie still hadn't written her about the chicken house confrontation. The thought of penning Harold's harsh pronouncements made her squirm, and she felt like a traitor for letting them slip to Jane.

They replayed most often at night, an ever-ready snake's hiss. Insistent questions stalked her. What if God had cursed her? What if her disobedient attitude did keep her from bearing a child?

When weariness should have guided her into sleep, these taunts stole her peace. The onslaught struck in the daytime sometimes, too, but she dealt with it by throwing herself into her work.

Jane's eyes flamed with fresh passion. "You not deserving anything—that's an outright lie. Who does Harold think he is to talk to you like that?"

She squashed the chair's nubby grain with her thumb. "If you could, what would you do right now, Addie?"

For the moment, new questions nudged out the old. Who *did* Harold think he was, her father, or her lord and master? And what would she do if she could? Finally, one forbidden answer bubbled up.

"I'd go far away."

The invitation in Jane's eyes led her to let everything out.

"I'd find a way to get to London to see Kate. I've tried so hard to make Harold happy, but nothing works. He accused me of wasting money when I painted the kitchen, even though I told him the paint was free.

"He said I don't honor him as the Bible says women should treat their husbands, but I've tried to. Really, I have. I just can't seem to get it right."

Jane leaned forward and flexed her fingers. A sob started low in Addie's chest, and the next thing she knew, Jane's arms surrounded her. When her tears subsided, the diamonds danced even brighter against the wall.

In the same tone she used to quiet Daisy that day in the barn, Jane shushed away her fear. "There, now. Nothing like a good cry to cleanse the soul." Addie's first deep breath confirmed Jane's pronouncement.

"Seems to me your logic's askew, child. Was Harold right about Daisy's foaling?" She answered for herself. "No, we both witnessed that he wasn't. So why should these things he says about you be right?"

For a moment, Norman lay there in his hospital bed. Hadn't he questioned Harold's assumptions, too? Why should he know her motivations better than she did herself?

"I believe you met Norman for a reason far beyond these household goods, Addie. What if he came into your life to show you an honorable man's opinion? Obviously he thought you worthy of an inheritance."

... you know how to keep a story, I can tell. The curtains blew in a sudden breeze, wafting another recollection. *Take that tea 'long now, Addie girl. Doncha forget.*

"He called me Addie girl . . . "

"Norman proved to be a good friend, didn't he? Maybe today, here in his house, you're getting another chance to say good-bye to him."

"I wouldn't trade the hours I spent here for anything. What Norman gave me—this money is nothing in comparison."

"And who knows what else waits around the corner? You're being watched over, child, I swanny. I'm no prophet, but I'm certain things will turn out all right."

Jane pulled at her overall buckle. "And for the record, if a woman's cursed for not having children, then I'm cursed right along with you. In fact, if everything Harold says is true, I'd say all of us are doomed."

So she didn't have children. The curtain rolled in on itself as the wind shifted, and Jane smoothed Addie's tousled curls. "Be that as it may, Addie Bledsoe, something's being born here, and you're the mama."

August 27, 1942

Dear Addie,

Hopefully you still count me your friend after my melancholy letter. Still no news of Alexandre, but I hold out hope.

This disastrous battle produced intelligence—now we know the enemy can intercept communications, that they watch for an increase in vessels on our side of the channel, and that we need more naval fire and armored vehicles. Dieppe was a test, finding a way to enter the continent.

Canadian forces were more than eager to prove themselves, after two years of waiting here in England. Alexandre's friend Arnold was one of them—he told

Alexandre he envied his crashes. At least he was in on the action. But very few in Arnold's unit survived.

Two days before the raid, the Telegraph's crossword puzzle contained the target city's name—can you believe that? Gives me shivers. Do spies communicate through the Daily Telegraph? Mrs. T says it'll be cold in August before she buys another copy.

The command knows they need new codes. Perhaps they should hire us, with our note-passing experience. There. My sense of humor has returned—it always does when I write out my feelings.

Still, couldn't they have learned this at far less cost? Perhaps waging war is like living, fraught with uncertainty and inevitable error. Do you feel that way? Probably your next letter will tell me—you often answer my questions before I ask them.

Mrs. T says I carry myself well, but the turmoil I share with you. Thanks for bearing it. Speaking of that, did you hear Clark Gable enlisted? It's quite the story— a private at age 41, earning $66 a month.

And speaking of famous people, London grieves the Duke of Kent's death two days ago. He was in the Navy I think, on the water in Scotland, and ran into a cliff or hill. Remember what I wrote about landed gentry?

Mrs. T and her friends know this Duke only from the newspapers, but the whole nation mourns a royal family member.

I'm assuming the furor over your kitchen paint has passed? And how did the lawyer's meeting go?

I'm dashing this off at lunch, since they keep us late. Evenings find me too nervous and exhausted to wield a pen.

> Still in hope,
> Kate

All day long, tension hung in the air and sultriness invaded every space. The ants in the old sidewalk crevices had a heyday, so when Berthea drove in, Addie ran over.

"Do you know any remedies for ants?"

"Outside or inside?"

"Out."

Berthea wriggled from under the wheel. "Sprinkle two tablespoons of sugar with two tablespoons of Borax down their hills. The sweet smell and taste deceive them."

"Sounds easy enough, although I hate to waste sugar."

Berthea's chuckle heartened Addie. "Two tablespoons won't make or break this war, and with all the misery over in France, won't it feel good to carry out a successful offensive? I did that with the mold around my bathtub the other day, and still go in there to stare at my success."

"Do you think it'll storm?"

"Sure feels like it. Maybe you should wait with the Borax 'til afterward. If you don't have anything for supper, come in for some sausage rings I'll never use."

"All right, thanks. One less meal to plan."

Just after chicken chores, a late August rain swept the yard, relieving the humidity that made breathing difficult. Harold raced from his tractor to the barn, which meant an early start on his chores, so Addie peeled potatoes, onions and turnips to fry with the sausage. The downpour slowed to a steady drizzle, and a strong breeze tossed the curtains against the gay white wainscoting.

Something about yellow checked curtains on white beaded board satisfied, like a perfect pie or Fern's casserolay. Remembering that dinner with its chiffon dessert gave Addie the urge to make something sweet. She found a bag of raisins in the pantry yesterday, and since Berthea brought over extra sugar and flour last week, she didn't feel so guilty about baking.

Harold loved raisin cookies. If he balked, she'd remind him she left out the sugar in her apple butter. Stirring up a double batch took no time, and when he entered the back porch, drenched, one pan already cooled. He grabbed three on his way to the living room.

She ought to have known. He never protested something he liked, but if he caught her drinking tea, the sin of waste had occurred. The Golden West coffee girl, always optimistic and sassy with her pert orange scarf, lifted her coffee cup and winked at Addie from the egg money can.

On a whim, Addie addressed the chipper cowgirl. "Wouldn't it be nice if he would say thank you, just once?" She turned the can in her fingers and read, "If you are not completely satisfied with our product, ask your grocer for a refund."

She imagined Minor Randolph's reaction if she tried to make good on the offer. His pinched face and the shock in his eyes contrasted with the mercantile's full shelves.

A chuckle burst out. "Refund my money—Minor Randolph? Like my hens will grow beards."

She flipped the sausage and checked to see if the potatoes had browned enough. From the living room, the radio roared the nightly newscast.

"If only I could write Kate tonight."

Grease splattered, so she leaped back. "Don't be foolish. It wouldn't do for Harold to uncover your secret now."

Her thoughts went back to the other day when she met Berthea at the mailbox, and George handed her a letter from Kate. A look passed between George and Berthea, and later, Berthea stopped by.

"Peeling potatoes for supper? Wonder how many we've peeled in our lives? Let's see, forty odd years and ten potatoes a day . . ." She took a chair at the table. "By the way, I think it's wonderful you correspond with Kate. It must be so hard for her now."

"Yes. But . . ." How should she begin? As if she understood, Berthea winked.

"Don't you worry, I'll never mention this to Harold. The way he talks about Kate's husband bothers me, and she really needs you now. I've learned the hard way that sometimes, friends can be our real family."

Berthea stared out at the chicken house. "Orville never liked me to have women friends either. I was so focused on being a good wife I didn't argue, but now I wish I'd ignored him. How was I to know most of his anger was just bluster?"

"You gave up a friendship?"

"For all practical purposes, yes. What I wouldn't give to relive that part of my life."

"That reminds me of something. One day I was cleaning the spare room closet and I found an old postcard. Let me run and get it."

Berthea's forehead folded as Addie handed her the card, and she took a few moments to read the message. Then she turned the card over and over in her hands.

"I can't believe you found this. It's from Geraldine Thomason, an old friend from school days. We always had such fun together. Thank you so much, Addie." She stared at the address again.

"I remember when this came, back when the first war still had a dreamlike quality. But Geri was one of those brave nurses who followed the troops to France, and soon enough, she made the war plenty real." She wiped her eyes with her sweater sleeve.

"The influenza took her. I learned later that disease killed more people than battle. This card was the last I heard from her, and it touched me that she remembered the fun we had together. I figured this had vanished forever."

Sometimes, friends can be our real family. The broadcast grated on Addie's ears as she filled a bowl with fried potatoes. She dreaded supper with Harold's sober countenance across from her, and Berthea's wish that she'd ignored Orville's wishes produced a sour taste.

This was no way to live, but how could she break through his anger and make a new start? No time like right now to try.

"Come on, Harold, supper's ready."

He ladled his food in sulky silence. She passed him the gravy bowl, the breadbasket, salt and pepper, and the butter dish. Intent on eating, he managed not even a word, and the fulfillment of her longing seemed as likely as the Allies winning the war before Christmas.

Yesterday they listened to the President's Labor Day address with Berthea. Afterward, Berthea turned down the volume and leaned toward Harold.

"He mentioned the farmers this time, dear."

"So what? He's bringing in foreigners to work in the factories and fields. Why doesn't he send some here, so I can fight? Americans would have changed the outcome of that Dieppe raid, I tell you. That General Montgomery has about as much sense as . . ."

"But some Americans did fight, Harold, for the first time in Europe."

"Aw, what do you know about it, Ma? They only used fifty of our men, with a British lord in command."

Berthea took a breath and squared her shoulders. "Harold, I listen to the same news you do. Those Churchill tanks were supposed to make the difference at Dieppe, but less than half of them made it through the German resistance.

"Half of the forces were captured or killed, even though the Canadian commanders believed they could achieve success. Their names are McHaughton, General Crerar and Major-General Roberts. Is that enough information for me to form an opinion?"

"Hogwash. You're as impossible to reason with as Addie."

Berthea shrugged as the door slammed. "Well, at least you and I are in good company, Addie."

But right now, Addie's usual evening company—a glum Harold and the war report—seemed unbearable. She fiddled with her food while her mind traveled to London. Writing Kate would have to wait until tomorrow, when Harold attended an elevator meeting in Benson.

Chapter Twenty-three

September 10

Dear Kate,

The waiting must be abominable. I wish I could help you pass the time.

Harold obsesses over Dieppe, but acts now as if the paint incident never happened. Since last night's council meeting, I've become the Thin Man's perfect wife.

The seminary agreed for him to come home to plant crops, so from December to April, he'll attend classes in St. Louis, and George will help with chores. I didn't ask how Berthea got Harold to agree to that.

He actually grabbed my hand when he told me the news. But acting too happy upsets him, so I tempered my emotions, as Mrs. M would say.

Your letter enlightened me—Harold chose me, knowing I'd never fight back. Your analysis made me think, and brought Shakespeare and Mrs. M to mind: "Go to your bosom: Knock there, and ask your Heart what it doth know."

Harold goes there less and less to remind me of my responsibility to produce heirs, but what more can I do? If it didn't cost, I'd visit Benson's new doctor.

Rest easy, your letter perished in our burn barrel and didn't send me into despair, but the Allied defeat put me in a black mood. Do you walk in the evenings? I think I'd have to.

Please send a description of Mr. T—nose, coloring, earlobes, etc. I picture him blue eyed and unmarried?

I'm so thankful for your job, and can't get discouraged when I think of you waiting, Arguments battle in my head, but you're one to take action. I merely think about it.

The Enquirer posted an ad for a reporter. A chance to write, but Harold says he needs me, especially with Berthea "gadding about." Yet when I manage things, like Daisy's birthing, he's furious.

That day, I feared for the prominent vein crossing his forehead when he groused, "You allowed a stranger in the barn?" I reminded him that Jane has lived down the road forever.

He glared at me as if I'd exited a Messerschmidt that just strafed our cornfield. His reaction baffles me—this calls for another analysis, oh, wise one.

His seminary news rendered him friendly again, but that may change tomorrow. I never know. At least he's leaving in December. (Never say this out loud, lest we jinx the possibility.)

Have I taken your mind off your fingernails and the Cliffs of Dover for a few minutes? I'll be praying.

Addie

"Find out if the Benson elevator has storage space—Halberton's full." Harold gave no more details before swinging onto the tractor and chugging down the driveway. Berthea drove away in the Chevy earlier, so Addie secured a quart jar of water in her bike basket with some twine and took off on her bike.

Seven miles of dusty gravel later, knowing her white blouse and everyday work skirt stood out like a red Farm-all in a dry hay field. Stained denim farmer caps topped farmers' heads in a row to the counter. Peeling lime green paint near a grain scale absorbed local gossip. Men-talk, Jane would call it, but gossip nonetheless.

Kate would dub these fellows dirt philosophers, definitely not landed gentry. Some of them lined First Methodist's pews yesterday to acknowledge the Almighty as ruler over all, but now demanded fairer prices. Their conversations followed two eternal topics—the weather and money.

"Rain's comin' Thursday. Gotta get the crops out by then, but where kin a man put 'em? Runnin' outta room, don't wanna drive t' the Mizippi, neither. Prices run a nickel higher there, but gasoline's up three cents a gallon, so I figger. . ."

"Cedar Rapids pays a pretty penny. Think it might be worth renting a truck? If it rains in the next six days, we could lose th' crop. Blamed if these elevators don't own our hides, Mervin."

At noon, Addie delivered Harold's answer—no room in the inn. He scowled, so she gave herself to weed chopping and jam making. After washing supper dishes, the evening seemed perfect for a neighborly visit, so she popped her knitting needles and yarn in a paper sack.

Luscious late Queen Anne's lace and sunny ditch sumac danced in an early evening breeze that hinted of fall, her favorite season. Spring was glorious and summer prolific, but September golden and mellow. From an electric wire, a cardinal sent three strong low notes: "Agree, agree, agree."

"I could transplant some sumac near that old fence, but it grows so tall, the roots might suck up all the water from my garden."

This afternoon gave her breathing space—no hired men to feed, no lambs to tend, just soft, plump ewes eyeing her from the field beside the grove as she cut weeds growing into the raspberry patch. Then she picked berries and spread old newspapers on the front porch floor.

Pouring them out on the papers coaxed black hard-shelled picnic bugs, masters of deception, from the succulent berries. Light and fresh air always won, since the insects couldn't handle their dark, cramped quarters any longer. They crawled forth only to be crushed under Addie's thumb.

Jane kept a little wooden mallet on the outdoor table where she dumped her berries, but enjoyed smashing them, just the same.

"Makes me feel good every time I squash one, exactly how I felt when the Justice Department executed those German spies."

Addie could have recited every detail of Operation Pastorius, since Harold repeated the spies' names over and over. He still exulted in their demise.

Today, Addie carried four jars of fresh preserves to the basement. Counting them warmed her heart—thirty-three altogether, and the patch showed no sign of letting up. Above them sat forty-two quarts of green beans, sixty-seven of corn, thirty of carrots, and fifty-one of dill pickles.

Her blue and white enamelware canner still overflowed with jars of tomatoes every other day. So far, she stored enough tomato soup for a jar every week this winter, plus more juice than she could possibly drink.

With only beef and a few chickens left to can, depending on when Harold butchered, a weight tumbled from her shoulders. She could manage the chickens, thanks to his ingenious system of lining up four nails about the width of a chicken's neck, on the tree stump chopping block. With a fowl's pulsing neck between them, the nails steadied the bird, simplified her axe stroke and saved valuable time.

The rest of the way to Jane's, she let her mind wander to her childhood. Twice a year, Mama arranged knives, pans, and vats of cold water out beside the barn in the evening. Mama's sister Iva came to help, with her brood of five. The cousins flapped their arms, mimicking the headless chickens circling the yard, sometimes colliding with each other.

The women plucked and singed feathers over the fire. To this day, that burning feather odor nauseated Addie. By the time all the chickens lay in cold water for the night, the work was half done.

She'd never thought about it before, but where had Dad gone those evenings? So much hard work, but the women did it all.

She swerved around a bump, but thankfully, the bike settled down instead of sliding on loose gravel. Across the fields, the Benson Catholic Church spire rose like a slender finger. She'd never been inside, but the building's vaulted windows struck an artful chord when she biked past this morning en route to the elevator.

Ruthie once said Dad hadn't allowed Iva to help Mama butcher for several years because she'd married a Catholic. But eventually he relented, or more likely, didn't even notice.

Mama let the cousins sleep out in the haymow, and it was a wonder none of them fell out. They jumped on the hay until their ribs hurt, played hide and seek, and dribbled sticky watermelon juice. With the mow door open, the five girls and four boys stretched out for the night and counted stars. Time stopped in summer's fickle promise to last forever.

The next day, the work took on a party quality. Uncle Elwood never came along, but Aunt Iva and Mama worked as fast as they talked. Iva's eldest, Charlotte, cleaned the birds and Doreen, Ruthie's age, taught Addie how to slice through breastbones with ease.

Near the driveway, Jane's chrysanthemums welcomed her. She parked by the back porch in the shade of the tallest possible sunflower patch and in sight of gentle hollyhocks standing guard over melon vines. Was the soil here more fertile? Silly question—less than a mile separated the two places.

Knitting across from Jane vied with playing the piano with George on his accordion. You couldn't help but play faster. The rhythmic click of Jane's needles ate away at her yarn with singular intent.

Honored to go beyond the kitchen, Addie eyed the side door. Since the day that diminutive man approached, she'd hoped for another glimpse, and kept expecting Jane to offer some clue, like "By the way, the hand-sawing you hear in the distance? That's Simon out in his workshop." But it never happened.

Once, Simon's name appeared on a letter she carried to the house when George handed her the mail. Jane thanked her heartily. "George knows the walk hurts my knee in this humidity, and you've saved me the trip."

A perfect time to say, "By the way, Simon's my husband . . ." But Jane didn't.

Now Addie checked the mailbox every time she turned in, often finding letters addressed to Simon W. Pike, a dignified-enough name. Curiosity welled in her. Kate would have found a way to discover the truth by now.

"The truth will set you free." Harold preached on that verse last Sunday. These questions wouldn't circle like hungry hawks, had she found the courage to ask Jane. But something held Addie back, just as something freed her to wave Norman's post-war memories before Fern in the library.

Jane looked up from her work. "Need more tea?"

"Yes, thanks."

"Would you mind fetching it? This old knee likes to stay put once I'm sitting."

Addie leaped up to fire the gas burner. Out the north window, a light flickered. Maybe Simon in the cabin? She warded off her inquisitiveness and poured the hot brew.

"How's Berthea lately? I see her whiz by in a cloud of dust."

"Fine. Visiting the grandkids last weekend put a smile on her face."

"Haven't seen Bill in a coon's age, probably three or four years."

"They don't come often, with his business in the war effort now, and Sue's expecting their fourth child. Berthea says she's ashamed of having to beg rides to the city."

"Ashamed? I don't like that word. *Get over it* bothers me, too. That's what my Aunt Helen used to tell Mama about her fear of tight spaces." Jane's needles clicked even faster. "We come by our fears honestly, and with hard work we might grow out of them. But being ashamed leads nowhere except missing out on today."

They fell into silence. When Jane reached for her lamp switch, Addie clipped her yarn in place. "I get more done when we knit together."

"You're always welcome. What do you have planned for the week?"

"Chicken butchering. Harold needs me outside tomorrow, so I'll start on Tuesday."

"With Berthea?"

"No, she's got some meeting to attend. I think she's had enough of butchering." The clock ticked away a few more seconds while Addie headed out, but as she crossed the threshold into the kitchen, Jane stopped her.

"Would you like some help?"

Would she ever—with another worker, the wretched job would take only half the time. "Don't tell me you actually like to butcher chickens?"

Jane grabbed her cane. "Nothing I like better. Let me know what time."

September 18, London

Dear Addie,

About Daisy's birthing. Harold predicted difficulties, and as the expert on everything, his anger makes sense. His make-believe world failed to match reality.

It's the same with you, compared to the woman in his head. But what will he do when he realizes how strong you actually are? That's what worries me.

You must be your honest self, yet maintain your English dignity. It might not hurt to explore your tendency to turn the other cheek. I'm trying to understand why I take so many risks. We can share our discoveries.

Did I describe my latest outing with Evelyn? The right hand forgets what the left does. But Mr. Tenney says he likes that about me, and Alexandre does, too.

Harold couldn't begin to follow the talks you and I have. He'd call them impetuous and be shocked that the business world values flexibility. But we always return to our starting point, don't we? In this case, my concert with Evelyn.

We listened to a comedian, a classical pianist, and a local children's choir in a war fundraiser. They served currant buns—what a treat. Currants and blackberries are abundant right now, and pears. I fill up more easily lately, but still long for sweet corn and fresh eggs.

It was good to walk through a new area, in spite of the bombing debris. And then we had a warning, so Mrs. T put on rubber boots and a tin helmet and patrolled the road for incendiaries. I went along with her until the All Clear sounded around one a.m.

Mr. T: thirty-ish, with greying temples. His nose suffered some bad rugby breaks, and his dignity vanishes in a sea of freckles. His ear lobes have a cleft, which means something, I'm sure.

Gathering this data resulted in me missing a dictated word the other day. He caught me and asked, "Kathryn? Are you off your feed?

See how seriously I take your inquiries? Mr. T's military service precluded marriage, I think. As to Alexandre, no word yet. Prayer has become more a PRESENCE than an activity. Does that make sense?

The streets continue to tidy up, but people still await notification about their loved ones. During the heavy bombing, five-sixths of the children boarded buses for the countryside.

Many returned this spring to utter wreckage, and most families still eat at the meals service. Our 150 rest-centre stations tend the displaced and orphans. Fifty others accommodate ten thousand more. I can't imagine how Mr. T keeps track of it all.

Have any more of our friends deployed? Keep me up-to-date, please, and know that I always keep you close.

Your personal war correspondent,

Kate

For the second time in a week, Addie left the grain elevator with little to show for waiting in line. Berthea drove her home, barely disguising her impatience.

"Why don't you learn to drive, Addie? Kate knows how. So do Josie Branstad and Diane Colter."

"Harold says a woman's place is on the farm. Besides, he'd be after me for using too much gas. He says once we get a telephone. . ."

"*Harold says . . .*" Berthea stopped at the railroad tracks and tapped the steering wheel a little too loudly.

Clackety-clackety-clackety-clack. She tapped faster and Addie considered. Yes, her reasons for not learning revolved around Harold.

Kate would exclaim, "What are you waiting for?" And Jane would say, "No time like the present. We have to move ahead, even if we're afraid."

When the last car passed, Addie's request rose like a trapped bird taking flight. "Would you teach me?"

Chapter Twenty-four

*E*yes aglow, Berthea swiveled in the seat. "I thought you'd never ask. For years I was afraid to learn." She opened her door. "Come over here, Addie."

"I didn't mean now."

But Berthea already rounded the Chevy and opened the passenger door. "Slide under the wheel."

Goose bumps paraded Addie's arms, but she obeyed. The day's perspiration and Berthea's perfume wafted as she leaned closer to the gearshift.

"Neutral's in the middle, like the bar of an H. That's where the motor idles. You have to pass through neutral to first gear." Berthea pointed to the gearshift and continued. "Top left is first, second's straight down, third at the top of the other side, and fourth below that. Neutral is like . . . um . . . your garden. Seeds can't become flowers without soil. Neutral acts like soil for the gears." She angled her head. "Does that make sense?"

Addie nodded, but a tide of fear rode the pit of her stomach. "In my head, but I'm not sure my hands and feet will cooperate."

Berthea's grin never changed. "Oh, that'll come with practice." She adjusted herself in the seat. "First, you need to memorize the positions. How about repeating what I've told you so far?"

Addie did her best, and Berthea held up a palm. "I've always known you're smart, Addie. Now, see that pedal?"

"The clutch?"

"Yes. When it's pushed in, the car isn't in any gear. You hold it down to change gears. Gradually let up as you move into a gear until

178

the engine takes over. We don't stay in first long, unless we're crawling down a street or out in the field. Any questions?"

"It's a lot to remember, but I think watching Harold has helped me."

"Move into first, then second. We'll stay there 'til the road curves. At that little bridge past the curve, when the speedometer says about thirty, I want you to shift into third gear. Got it so far?"

"I think so."

After three false starts and a few gear-grinds, the car lurched ahead. Addie's heart pounded—so much power in her hands. But Berthea, as calm as if she stirred cookies in her kitchen, maintained her cheer.

"Good. Now second. There, see? You can do it!"

"We're coming to the crossroads, so shift into fourth now. Nothing's coming. Just keep your eyes on the road. Great, Addie— keep doing exactly what you're doing."

Keep doing what I'm doing. That's easy to say. But gradually, her tension gave way to a sense of accomplishment. At Jane's grove, Berthea said to let up on the accelerator and shift down to third. This time no lurching, and a smile niggled Addie's lips.

"We're halfway home from Jane's now, so shift down into second. Perfect. Now, into first."

Fully aware that the big test, their driveway, lay up ahead, Addie licked her lips. If she drove into the ditch, Harold would . . .

"That's right, now just turn the wheel—good, one smooth motion. There you go."

With the car parked in the Chevy's usual spot, Berthea let out a "Yahoo!" She rushed out, flew around the front fender and grabbed Addie by the shoulders.

"What a fast learner you are!"

"You must be kidding. It took us half an hour to drive six miles." Her fingers still clutched the wheel, and she let out a long breath.

Berthea ignored her comment. "Now nothing can stop you, dear. Let go of the steering wheel—take a deep breath and relax. That's how I feel when I'm driving. Don't know why I let it scare me for so long."

Her eyes glinted. "All right. I'll teach you to back down the driveway, for wintertime."

When they finished, Addie had navigated the driveway, backed onto the road and turned around at Jane's. Jane, out in her strawberry bed, straightened and waved. Back at the farm, Addie parked at Berthea's back step.

"I never dreamed I would learn so fast, and surely not today."

"Why not today? That's become my motto. For years I set things aside until another time. You don't know how often I repeated, *I'll have to ask Orville* when I had a chance to try something. But with his passing and this war . . . We never know if tomorrow will come. Next lesson, I'll teach you how to parallel park in town."

"You make a great teacher."

Berthea quieted. "I always wanted to be one." Silence sifted between them like a sermon.

"You did?"

"Yes. I used to practice teaching my brothers and sisters and friends. One of them even called me Bossy Bertie." She grinned at the nickname. "But I let that dream go once we married, because Orville wanted me here on the farm."

Addie wished she knew what to say, but Berthea threw up her hands. "What's past is past. No use wasting time on regrets. At least I can join committees now, and I just heard that the school secretary might retire. Been thinking I might apply for her job."

"That's so exciting—you'd be great, Berthea."

"We'll see. You did a fine job today, and on your very first try. When you want more practice, let me know. And let's schedule the parking lesson for Wednesday morning." She turned at her top step and surveyed the barn. "I imagine this would displease Harold. You won't mention our lesson to him, will you?"

Addie gave a slight nod. Berthea seemed to read Addie's silent agreement and went inside.

Now, nothing can stop you replayed as Addie smoothed a dark red dogwood branch between her thumb and forefinger. A list of female schoolteachers pranced through her head. Had any of them— especially Mrs. Morfordson—faced opposition from their husbands?

And then that Enquirer ad came to mind. What if she went in and talked with Spoon Caldwell, the editor?

She pictured the scene that might take place. Spoon would shake her hand and say, "Why, Mrs. Bledsoe, your English teacher told me what a good student you were. I'd be delighted to hire you."

Harold left the barn and puttered down the driveway on the Farm-All. Addie shook herself. "No, no, no—you mustn't think this way. It's one thing for Berthea to get a job since she's on her own now, but Harold would . . ."

If he patterned his picture of the perfect woman after Berthea, as Kate thought, that poor woman had spent the best years of her life unfulfilled. But Addie realized such a scenario would fit Harold's reality, leaving no room for the woman's satisfaction.

Early September sunlight dappled beautiful, full-grown bushes in a seamless botanical fence right where the farmyard needed one. "Whether Harold likes them or not, planting these lilacs was still a good idea, Addie Bledsoe. A very good idea."

Her own compliment floated around her like a prophecy, but Harold's perennial pout showed as he dipped a pail into the tank. Why couldn't he be happy on this pleasant fall day? Had he forgotten his opportunity to study this winter?

Suddenly, their big old frame house appeared in a new light. It needed a coat of paint, but otherwise, resembled several others around here. That's all it was, a typical farmhouse, desperate for a good painting and a new roof.

But this place didn't have to define her any more than it did Berthea. Orville's will stifled her mother-in-law for decades, yet Addie could learn from that. And then she saw something else. What Harold said about her in the chicken house was more than wrong.

You are this, you are that—you are disobedient, you are cursed, you are a temptress. In the depths of her being, she knew better, and acknowledged it out loud.

"I may have failed over and over, but I've always tried my best to please God. Even when I was little, I felt Him with me, and no matter what Harold says about me, God has never left me." She walked out into the pungent grove and turned a circle under the massive trees.

"Ruth whispered in my ear about divine love and care. Aunt Alvina allowed me to troop along to church and Sunday school, where

Ina Schmidt taught me to color and to pray out loud. All along the way, I learned so much."

A wind whipped up the pines, maybe enough to usher in a thunderstorm. Her back to one of the tall trees, Addie made a declaration.

"Before I became a Bledsoe, I was Addie Shields. I loved school and devoured books. I may never have learned to believe in myself, but I'm more than my feelings. We're all complicated, like Kate wrote, but that's not a fault. No, it's one of my strengths."

She stretched her arms. Even if she wasn't ready to make a move like talking with the newspaper editor, she could make progress in small ways. She could be sad about this situation with Harold, yet strive toward happiness. She could feel her anger to the full, yet still be capable of love.

The swish of low-hanging boughs seemed to hum, "You're all right just the way you are."

This summer's changes passed before her—a bright red Ford coupe, her own special tea stash, and even her own money, a fortune under Jane's watchful eye. Addie still had no idea what to do with it, but like Jane said, everything would become clear when the time was right.

"And this very day, I learned to drive an automobile." She hugged her arms tight, and the feel of her palms against her skin was good.

***

October 18, 1942

Dear Addie,

So much war news—Mrs. T's friend Blanche has a Canadian cousin who knows the Falcon of Malta's family. Have you heard of him, the ace with the most kills in the Force? He transferred to the RAF, and Alexandre met him —they trained together.

The Falcon received two Distinguished Flying Crosses and has already qualified for a third. Word has it they'll send him back to Canada for a victory load drive—their version of selling war bonds. The last time Alexandre wrote, he said if that's what they give you for being the best, he'd rather be down the line.

His letter had a strange air that still bothers me. He wrote about waking up some mornings to seven empty bunks in his hut—the men didn't return from last night's mission. He admitted it's nerve-wracking, and mentioned one fellow who'd flown his limit and should have gone home to his wife. But he stayed for one more mission with his bomber boy buddies. You can guess the outcome.

Americans take the daytime missions now, Brits the nighttime. Alexandre wrote that their teams find out ahead of time where they're assigned and have the whole day—or night—to worry about it. I can't imagine the pressure.

Anyway, Blanche's friend actually met the Falcon (his real name is Buerling). She stood in line for his autograph at a war production factory.

Other news here—the usual night raids and office work. I hope Harold is still intent on St. Louis, and know you're coping as best you can. Of course you are.

Cheerio,

Kate

"Come over and listen to tonight's fireside chat with me. You can bring your knitting, Addie." Berthea addressed Harold and Addie, but Harold turned away. A few minutes before seven, Addie hurried over, and after the preliminaries, her ears perked up.

. . . Perhaps the most difficult phase of the manpower problem is the scarcity of farm labor in many places. I have seen evidences of the fact, however, that the people are trying to meet it as well as possible.

In one community that I visited a perishable crop was harvested by turning out the whole of the high school for three or four days. And in another community of fruit growers the usual Japanese labor was not available; but when the fruit ripened, the banker, the butcher, the lawyer, the garage man, the druggist, the local editor, and in fact every able-bodied man and woman in the town, left their occupations, went out gathering the fruit, and sent it to market.

Every farmer in the land must realize fully that his production is part of war production, and that he is regarded by the nation as essential to victory. The American people expect him to keep his production up, and even to increase it. We will use every effort to help him to get labor; but, at the same time, he and the people of his community must use ingenuity and cooperative effort to produce crops and livestock and dairy products.

Berthea clasped her hands and sighed. "*Part of war production . . . essential to victory.* Oh, I do hope Harold is listening. This has to make him feel his work is worthwhile for the war effort."

"There's no question that he's listening." Addie leaned back against her chair, relishing being here without him. "But whether it makes any difference is another thing."

November 5, 1942

My dear correspondent,

Thank you for the description of Mr. T, but what about his eye color? And please describe his mother, too. I picture coifed hair, tasteful earrings, gold rings on slim fingers, and a nose less defining than her son's.

Her eyes are bluer than Mr. T's, and her husband is deceased? I love your depictions of life there.

Sometimes I open your letters behind the chicken house on these mild fall days. The pines lend a breeze, and best of all, the smell keeps Harold away.

Drum roll . . . exciting news! I should make you guess, but with your anxiety level, I won't. Berthea taught me to drive the other day. I already know you're proud of me.

The passenger cars of a train stirred me. So many on the move while I sat in a rut. Finally, I was ready to take the risk—we're such opposites about that. You're always ready.

Harold doesn't know, so I go nowhere. But I CAN, and now I can see why you like driving so much.

The tractor descends upon the yard, a sign from on high that I must close. Sending prayers for Alexandre, and for you. I don't know how those pilots stand the tension of facing 'the end' over and over and over.

Love,

Addie

"You found nothing of value to you?" Her forehead fretful, Fern blocked Addie on the church steps.

Jane was right. Fern must fear something. It would be difficult to harbor such a secret, only to have it spring up years later like a snake from tall grass.

"Oh, a few things. Norman had already given me Millie's tea canister, so I decided to use the rest of the set. The red and white enamel goes well in our kitchen."

"Is that all?"

"A nightstand fits just right beside our bed. Otherwise . . ."

"I assume Mr. Allen's sister already took his personal items?" Fern craned her neck in a most unladylike way.

"I think Mrs. Schultz took his clothes and his discharge papers."

Fern scraped her shoe against the sidewalk. "I mean, oh, you know, personal items—his Army uniform, mementos."

"I didn't think they would sell at the auction. Who would want a battered World War I uniform?"

"You never know about these things. Every penny counts these days."

"I never expected anything, so whatever the sale brings is fine with me, Fern."

Fern's fingernails, a gaudy red shade, bit into her arms through her sweater. "I must say, Addie Bledsoe, you can be most irritating."

"I'm sorry, Fern, I don't mean to be. Did you want something from the house?"

"Of course not. But a person's private items, you know, photographs, that sort of thing . . . I couldn't help but notice none of that showed up here."

"Mrs. Schultz must have sorted through them. I was glad, because I wouldn't know what to do with them anyway."

"Well, then." Fern's huge sigh seemed heartfelt. "I've hired a man to arrange thehay racks for the sale. When will you take your car?"

"I'll need to find a storage shed. Maybe whoever buys the house wouldn't mind if I left it there for a few weeks?"

"I'll certainly let you know. You'll surely come to the sale?"

"Saturday will be too busy. I'm sure you'll be relieved to have this over, but you must feel honored to have Norman trust you with his request."

Fern's eyes narrowed. "Don't forget to come by around four o'clock to pick up your earnings."

Watching Norman's possessions sold to the highest bidder didn't interest Addie, but Jane attended the auction. On Saturday afternoon, Addie poured a boiled frosting on her black walnut cake for tomorrow's church potluck and reminded herself to iron Harold's shirt after supper.

The auction never even crossed her mind until Jane wheeled her green Studebaker into the yard. She stopped as close to the back door as possible and beeped the horn.

Addie wiped her hands on her apron and hurried out. "Is everything all right?"

"Hurry and get in! They're closing down the auction and Fern's pacing like a cornered animal, upset with you."

"All right. Just a minute." Addie made sure she turned the oven off, tore at her apron strings and raced to the car.

Chapter Twenty-five

*D*ust roiled the curve and Addie stole a glance at Jane, gripping the steering wheel like Adolph Huhnlein. Harold used to have a picture of the famous German racecar driver in the '33 Autobahn groundbreaking ceremony. But when the Luftwaffe dropped its first bombs on London, he tore it to shreds and tossed them into the pigs' swill.

"Swine! German swine!"

The Studebaker swayed on the gravel, but Jane maintained control. "I heard Fern muttering on my way to the car and thought I'd better come for you right away."

She took her eyes off the road for a second. "The sale went well, but she could only fume about you not being there."

They roared into the alley and Addie ran around the car to open her door, but Jane waved her away. "The less I see of that woman, the better."

A dwindling crowd lingered near the emptyhay rack, so Addie straightened her work dress and headed toward Fern. Her brilliant hair and a bright yellow dress made her easy to find.

"A person would think you didn't care about this money at all, Addie Bledsoe. Maybe we should put it toward the orphanage fund."

Addie glanced around at the bystanders, beckoned Fern farther away, and lowered her voice. "We have no power to change Norman's will, right?"

"No, but you certainly do exasperate a person. Anybody with an ounce of sense would have been here a half hour ago, or all day long. I don't know how Harold stands it. A preacher needs an organized, timely wife."

Addie's heart thrummed faster, but she tamped her heating emotions. No use making a scene. Then Harold would hear about this for sure. She took a deep breath and looked Fern in the eye.

"If you have the money ready, I can take it now."

Stand up to a bully. For the first time, it occurred to her that Fern, more subtly than Harold, did her own share of bullying.

"All right." Fern's reply crisped, like the maple and oak leaves underfoot on this beautiful fall day. She handed over a wad of bills and Addie forced herself to stay calm under another tirade.

"I hold my tongue only because of my promise, but a good wife would find a way to get this money to her husband. I'm afraid Harold probably lost out on that score."

The same inspiration that overcame Addie that morning in the library when Fern attacked Kate swept her. Her reply issued forth with a life of its own.

"Why would you say that, Fern? I keep my promises, more than you know, especially to Norman about his war memories." Fern's blush darkened by two shades. "And he judged me capable of handling money, don't you think?"

With her stuck-out chin, Fern resembled a fox lunging at its prey. But strength flowed through Addie.

"I'll take some time to think about it, but I may donate to the thousands of orphans in London. Kathryn Isaacs knows firsthand about them, and would make sure not a penny was wasted."

Fern choked on whatever she intended to say. But Addie, aware of a strange tranquility, stood still. The sun on her back seeped into her spirit, and Fern stalked off, muttering under her breath. When she disappeared from sight, Addie hurtled back to Jane, who headed out of town.

Near the railroad tracks, she glanced over. "She was nasty?"

"Yes, but at least I don't have to deal with her anymore."

"Right, and it looks like you have more money for your dream basket."

"Dream basket?"

"Mama taught us girls to keep one. I'd saved almost a hundred dollars when I got married." Purpose outlined Jane's profile. "Let's stop at my place and see how much you've added to yours."

Within minutes, bills and coins spread across Jane's table like troops assembled for battle. "Make some tea for us, Addie. This will take a while."

They counted twice, and then Jane re-counted, "for safety's sake."

"Eight hundred and forty-seven dollars in this pile." Addie sipped her tea in wonder as Jane set the last dollar bill on a stack of ones, secured rubber bands around the other crinkled piles, and gave a low whistle.

"That makes more than two thousand dollars in all. Do you want me to keep this with the rest?"

The tally swirled in Addie's head. A few years back, she lacked five dollars to pay for the senior trip to Des Moines. At the last minute, Mrs. Morfordson came through with the money, and her comment resounded now: "An anonymous person supplied this without knowing who would receive the donation. You deserve to go on this trip, if anybody does. You'll have so much fun climbing the state capitol stairs with Kate."

Yet to suddenly have this much money for no specific purpose puzzled and overwhelmed her. Jane read her unspoken questions.

"Don't you fret. When the time is right, you'll know why this money appeared. You'll come asking for it, maybe in a dreadful hurry, and it'll wait here underneath my potato bin. If I'm gone, you can always find it."

Beneath the curved tin potato receptacle, a pocket-like niche created a cobwebbed shelf. No thief would think to run a hand under the bin.

"No one on earth knows about this place. Found it by accident myself."

"Anywhere is better than the best hiding place in our house. Harold has a way of going through my things."

"You don't say . . . just like he thinks he knows what's going on inside your head. But he doesn't, does he?"

For now, Addie set the question aside. Hiding Kate's letters in the storeroom made sense, but she shuddered at the responsibility of this much money. Far better to entrust it to Jane.

Her ears hummed like the grove in steady wind. Harold knew nothing about this treasure, and Jane would never let it slip. But inside Addie, a third Great War simmered. Keeping such a secret could lead to an unprecedented explosion.

Jane sensed her agitation. "Don't lose sleep over this. In wartime, people do things they would never do otherwise. We can't foresee the future, and who knows? Harold may still find a way to join the fight. We have no idea what other challenges might come up, Addie. You're only honoring Norman's wishes. Nothing wrong in that."

When they added the auction money, the pile overflowed a six-by-ten inch cigar box. Addie carefully positioned the bills and shut the lid with a queasy stomach. Even the mellow tea failed to quiet her fears.

"Every woman has a right to something of her own, but it takes us time to figure out what that is." Jane wound two wide rubber bands around the box and nudged it into the covert space.

"Thank you, Jane. I feel so much better leaving this here with you."

"Are you still planning to butcher chickens Tuesday?"

"Yes."

"Still want to come?"

"I surely do. We'll have the place to ourselves. Berthea's away and Harold will be in the field. I'd better get going now, but I don't know what I'd have done without you today."

"Want a ride home?"

"No, thanks. It's a perfect walking day."

Beside Jane's tool shed, a screen full of walnuts topped two sawhorses. What a good idea to gather them now and avoid the slippery mess when their husks blackened and fell in oily, slimy pieces. Every fall, the tractor smashed hundreds of them in the driveway.

A slight breeze rustled drying cornfields, and Jane's words resonated. *A right to something of her own . . . takes time to figure out what it is.*

One night years ago when they walked home from a neighbor's, Ruthie stopped in the middle of the road. "Listen to the corn."

They could, indeed, hear the corn stretching. Now, Addie felt like that cornfield, becoming a woman instead of a child. She could make decisions and claim her feelings and opinions, no matter how Harold reacted. Deciding what to do with that money hadn't been easy, but she'd joined the ranks of adults who made similar choices every day.

A screen stored in the corncrib caught her eye, so she hauled it down. Walnuts in various stages already littered the yard, some of them starting to blacken and ooze.

She propped the screen on two empty barrels and filled a pail with green walnuts, some smooth like rubber balls, some dried into the first rot, with the wavy exterior of mountains on a topographical map. Others already cracked at the ends.

Under the lilac bushes, busy squirrels worked at smelly black pulp that stained whatever it touched. Three pails full of the messy nuts spread across the screen.

Harold backed the tractor toward the shed, pulled out his two-row corn picker, and squatted to reach the machine's inmost joints with his grease gun. Then he spied Addie.

"You're wasting your time. They'll rot just as well on the ground."

He pushed back his cap and Addie considered. True, all walnuts shared the same destiny. Their husks disintegrated and dried, to be stowed in burlap sacks in the fruit cellar.

But who said it was better for them to rot on the ground? An urge to aim a walnut at Harold's stubborn head nearly overcame her. *A woman must take charge of her own life with the brain God gave her.*

Her life might consist of walnuts, squash and beans to pick, chickens to butcher, eggs to wash, floors to scrub, shirts and sheets to iron, and pies to bake. But it didn't belong to Harold. It belonged to her.

She needn't respond, nor tell him everything she thought. After all, what passed through her mind made her an individual, didn't it? And couldn't she decide how to handle her responsibilities? She never suggested improvements to him about his work, so why should he care how she managed the walnut harvest?

The old wheelbarrow's wooden handles felt grainy against her palms. She tossed her curls back and shot Harold a smile.

Actions speak louder than words. Who used to say that, Mama or Mrs. Morfordson? Maybe both.

"Don't you love the smell of fall in the air, Harold?"

"Hunnh." His frown jagged lower as she aimed the persnickety wheelbarrow toward the closest walnuts.

* * *

"I hate to tell you this, girls, but your time is almost up." Corralled into a makeshift wire enclosure, the chickens eyed Addie with caution.

The oldest stewing hen cackled furiously, sending the guilt of betrayal scuttling down Addie's backbone. She sharpened two butcher knives on Harold's tool shed file and waved to Berthea as she left the yard. "Have a good time."

"Here I am leaving you again," said Berthea "I'll make it up to you. Apple pie some night next week."

"That's all right, Jane's coming over."

"Really?"

"The other night, she said she liked to put up chickens. I can't believe that, but she'll be great help."

Berthea backed the Chevy around the windmill, whose metal flaps whistled in an east wind. Good—she and Jane could singe feathers off the slain birds without breathing in the fire's smoke.

Like a dirty chartreuse bug, the Studebaker entered the yard at precisely 7:10, and Jane emerged. Butcher knife in hand, she looked intent on slaughter. "Good morning. I'm here for my orders."

"Okay, look at my lay-out and tell me if anything's missing."

"Nope, you're all organized. We think alike, you know." Jane stood near the stump, axe at the ready and her hands open for a bird. "You catch and I'll chop. Just keep them coming."

In twenty minutes flat, they amassed fifteen chickens. Addie had half a notion to go for five more, but that would make her wearier when Harold walked in tonight, irritable and touchy.

The tinder she'd gathered from the grove leaped into flame when she struck a match, and by ten o'clock, the plucked, singed birds cooled in tubs on the shady side of the back porch. Jane cleaned up the mess with boiling water Addie carried from the house.

The pigs made a racket when she tossed chicken heads and feet into the swill. They barely looked up as she addressed them. "Your standards lower by the day, fellas."

After changing the water twice, Jane pronounced the carcasses cool enough to carry inside. They hauled them by the dishpan, and then Jane positioned a carcass on the breadboard, unsheathed her sharp knife and halved it in one wallop.

She grinned over at Addie. "My mother taught me to halve them first. Makes the gutting easier." They each gutted a half, and then another whack of Jane's knife produced quarters. Addie cut eating pieces and soon, five cut-up chickens boiled in two enormous pots.

At half past eleven, Jane laid down her knife. "I have to say, Harold's nail idea took some time off our work. I'll be back in an hour, have to check on something."

At noon, Harold came in and took three ham sandwiches with milk and a handful of cookies to the living room. When he passed through again, he glowered. "Stinks in here."

Maintain your English dignity. Without answering, Addie headed for the barn with another scrap pail. Before she returned, he chugged the tractor back to the field.

November 16, 1942

Dear Kate,

The chickens are laid to rest in the fruit cellar. Walt has relatives in St. Louis where Harold can stay free, but he's taking canned goods for lunches. Several chickens will end up there.

Jane cut the butchering time in half. In spite of her arthritis, she works like the wind, and as usual, she did my heart good.

Prayer is a presence—I like that. For me, thoughts, prayers, and wishes blend with war news these days, and with stirrings of something inside. I'm not sure how to describe it . . . maybe later. Anyway, back to Jane.

This morning, she said we think alike—wouldn't it be wonderful to marry someone like that? Do you and Alexandre think alike?

At four thirty, the last of the jars waited to be filled, and Jane gathered her belongings. "Think I'll go on home now." I tried to get her to take some chicken home, but she said it would be a while before she eats chicken again. Still, she insisted that she enjoyed the day's work.

Unpredictable as Old Brown's drool, impetuous words departed my mouth. The image of that man I saw coming to her side door flitted through my mind. Then I let something slip that I never meant to utter. I started to say maybe her husband would want some. She reddened and headed out fast.

"Oh no," I thought. "Now I've done it."

I followed along like a lost soul, hoping I hadn't ruined our friendship. I opened the car door for her, and after she got in, her normal cheeriness returned. "Come over real soon, Addie."

Dumbfounded, I waved her off. My tongue has rebelled before, especially in my adolescence. But why couldn't I rein it in now?

Ruthie wrote me this week. Herman works nearby and Dad keeps busy. Hard to imagine, but she could always handle him, unlike me.

You're saying, "Think of the good things about yourself." I'm trying.

Praying you'll hear about Alexandre very soon.

Your mouthy friend,

Addie

"Addie—are you down there?" Berthea's call echoed to the basement, where cobwebs fought Addie's reorganization campaign. She'd swept the ceiling and walls before she started, and with her feet straddling a shelf and an old wooden stool, she called up the stairs.

"Be right up."

Berthea's countenance crumbled when Addie entered the bright kitchen.

"What is it?"

"George dropped Willie off this morning, and I was working out in the shed. Willie pulled an old wagon the boys used to play with, but all of a sudden he disappeared. I've called and called."

Shivers coursed Addie's arms. "Where's the wagon?"

"Near the barn. I've looked all around the yard . . ."

"How about out by the driveway—I've seen him head for those cedars before. And the chicken house?"

"I'll check both places, but I don't think he could get the chicken house door open."

"I'll search the grove."

"Could he have gotten that far? If he gets in the cornfield, he could be . . ." Addie knew what Berthea meant—lost for good.

Addie patted her shoulder. "We'll find him."

Berthea scuttled out and Addie flew to the grove. A little fellow like Willie would be drawn here—so many pinecones, squirrels playing tag, and fallen logs to explore. The soft floor made tracking impossible, but the coolness and a quiet inner sense drew her farther.

"Willie! Answer me, Willie—where are you?" Berthea's frantic calls echoed from the driveway. Addie concentrated on the hum of the pines in the barest of breezes.

Near the west edge of the trees, a rhythmic *thrash, thrash, thrash* sounded from the corn rows, now russet-gold and ready for harvesting. Someone walked there, slow and steady, closer and closer. Addie took shelter behind a wide pine, since an adult obviously made all that noise.

Like curtains opening, scratchy dry leaves parted and someone sat Willie on the ground—a short man in patched overalls and a black wool beret. Addie held her breath as he bent low and shooed Willie toward the grove.

"Go on, now. Find Addie and Berthea."

Willie touched his fingers, but the man shook his head. "No—you can't play in the corn no more." His voice turned harsh. "Get back to the house right now—go on."

Willie's bottom lip protruded.

"Hurry up. Addie's waiting for you." The man's face twisted as Willie wavered between a pout and tears. "You hear me? Get going."

Finally, Willie took a few steps and the man crept back under cover. The corn took him in, and when Willie lost sight of him, he cried out, but Addie emerged.

"Willie—Aunt Addie's here. Come on, honey." She folded him in her arms, aware of wild running down the cornrows in the direction of Jane's house.

"Thank you," she called, certain that Simon didn't hear.

* * *

Dearest Addie,

Oct. 31, All Saints Eve, and this letter will be scattered, like my thoughts. I visited Westminster Abbey today. Crowds recalled those gone before us, and our status as children of the King. I suppose thousands more come in normal times.

I'm so unlike a King's daughter, yet remind myself God still claims me as His very own. Sounds selfish, but our feeble choices reflect on us, not on His faithfulness.

Amidst all the grandeur, I recalled Adolph Hitler sparing Westminster and Winchester Cathedral for his coronation as England's ruler. He sickens me.

Rumors float from occupied France of Jews deported by the thousands. Mr. T hints of this, and of Stalin's murders. Yet England's past reveals travesties, and so does ours.

Remember the Trail of Tears? I wonder if anyone rose up against that great wrongdoing.

I bought a Brownie camera and will send a photo of the Abbey when I fill up the full roll. Off the subject, did I tell you Mr. T's dark blue eyes turn indigo at bad news? You were right.

Mrs. T does take her tea with toast. Her garden begs for your touch, with poor soil and the worker shortage, but a salvageable wisteria and an old honeysuckle hold on.

You guessed right about her tastes, too—a suit with a silk blouse, sometimes a tuck here and there or a soft cravat. During one of my sleepless fits, I realized even her rose silk robe accentuates her coloring.

Her bearing reminds me of the Queen Mum, statuesque. Either she uses a powerful girdle or has strong muscles. And she always wears a gold ring.

From the mantel photos, I assume Mr. T senior served in the Great War. You'd be proud of me for curbing some questions, as you did with Fernella.

Rationing frustrates Mrs. T's penchant for entertaining, so she delights in the glorious packets you and Berthea send. She has friends all over the world—India, South Africa, Rhodesia, and they send us clarified butter by ship. What a treat.

I've laid off psychology for a while, to nurture my theological bent. Maybe God deals with us like Mr. T? We expect sharpness, but find Him gentle and kind with our foibles. "Come, let us reason together . . ."

Mr. T even admits his mistakes. Once, I posted a letter to the wrong office, and he acknowledged he'd given me the wrong address.

For days, I've searched for that Scripture about God reasoning with us. I bet you can open right to it—seems Isaiah or Jeremiah-ish.

Do you think the Almighty sets a standard we must attain or be damned, or takes us as we are, because as our creator, He's a realist?

About Alexandre—I pace my room nightly. By
bedtime, my mind wakes and I review our life together.
This thought train does no good, so adieu for now.

Kate

P.S. Did I say you struck out on Mrs. T's eyes?
They're as dark as yours.

Chapter Twenty-six

"*I*'m taking a bowl of stew over to your mother, Harold."

Harold barely looked up from the radio announcer comparing the Battle of Buna with Guadalcanal.

> Allied forces, lacking food and medicine, and attacked by Pacific island scourges like dengue fever, malaria, and tropical dysentery and bush typhus, engage the Japanese fortifications with inadequate weapons. This will prove to be a long, arduous fight. Pray for our boys.

Wet wind whipped the eight porch windows. The grove wailed as Addie pulled on her boots, but she still looked forward to going outside. Furious wind blew her prayer back at her, "Help them, please. Such an impossible mission, but help them somehow."

She tried to imagine those soldiers with so much against them, but succeeded only in mixing hot tears with the pulsing blast from the north. With her free hand, she captured the season's first lazy snowflakes, soft, sticky, and enormous, just right for snowmen.

She and Ruth had made so many snow forts, and taught Herman and Bonnie how. One Saturday afternoon, Aunt Alvina let Kate come over, and they dug seven feet into a drift to craft a winding tunnel that lasted until a March melt.

Remembering Kate standing on the wall six feet high and giving orders like a military commander brought a smile. Addie wiped her eyes with her sleeve and breathed in the cold.

"Come on in, Addie." Berthea's call led her into the cozy living room, and the heat warmed her cheeks. So did the scene she entered, with George Miller and Berthea nestled on the couch, listening to a radio show.

"Sorry, I didn't see your truck, George."

He smiled and waved her in. "I parked in the shed so I can shovel tonight and drive right out. Might save Harold some work in the morning."

"Good." Addie set the bowl down. "Beef stew from supper, Berthea. You won't have to cook tomorrow night."

"Thank you. I have a library board meeting in the afternoon, so that will be a big help. Will you sit down and listen with us?"

An advertisement on KXEL enticed Addie.

> Join the KXEL War bond club and tune in when Union Pacific presents "Your America," Saturdays at four p.m.

"I know Harold looks down on anything out of Waterloo, with its Negro population." Berthea squinched her nose. "But this new station is just as good as WHO. I think he misses out by shunning other stations."

"Surely he realizes Des Moines has its share of colored folks, too?" George reached across Berthea for the June *Life* issue. "Harold must've heard about the 761st Negro Battalion formed down in Louisiana—our boys surely need their manpower."

Berthea shook her head. "I've kept that one hidden. Don't want to set him off again."

George crossed his arms. "Besides, KXEL's the first station in the nation to be granted 50,000 megawatts of power—brings some shows in clearer."

> After the Cavalcade of America, we bring you the "Voice of America" and "The Firestone Hour."

Harold's warnings traipsed through Addie's mind. "It's best to stick with a channel you can trust. Charles Lindbergh defied American principles when he accepted that Nazi award, but WHO told us the truth."

His logic made no sense at the time, and even less now, but she acquiesced, and their radio dial seldom ventured away from WHO-1040.

"I'd better do some knitting tonight. Have to do some every evening if I want to keep up with Jane."

"All right. Thanks again for the stew."

Despite the cold, Addie took her time going home. Berthea and George had become good friends, but this looked more like . . . Through the window, in the soft light from the corner lamp, they created a contented picture.

"They both look so happy. And why shouldn't they be?"

At the back steps, the moonlit night, cool and mysterious, wooed her to linger. Why not circle the house?

Even out here, Edward R. Murrow's voice clarified the latest battle. His first broadcast, describing a full British moon, the gray buildings around him white, stayed with Addie all this time. Amazing that that "beautiful and lonely city where men and women are trying to snatch a few hours' sleep underground" was now Kate's home. As usual, she'd gone directly to the center of the action.

A fat flake plopped on Addie's nose and she pulled up her collar. Static filled the broadcast she could still hear, but it never kept Harold from listening.

Snow bunched on fence posts and barren maple branches, beginning winter's transformation. For Kate, change seemed inevitable. Maybe change employed different rhythms for each person, and hers moved at turtle-speed, like her hollyhock starts.

But things altered fast for Berthea, too. Not long ago, she nursed Orville. Tonight, she snuggled with George. She looked brighter by the day, as though hope burrowed in her heart now. But Harold still had no kind words for George.

"Ma can't be serious. Anybody with a name like Miller can't be trusted these days. George might even be related to that crazy Glen—

you know, the wild bandleader from Clarinda. His kind of music stirs everyone up—no good in it."

"Moonlight Serenade" and "Tuxedo Junction"? Addie kept quiet, aware that Kate would have plunged into a verbal tussle with Harold.

But he quieted down when Glen Miller petitioned the Army to allow him to join in September. Berthea told them about it one Sunday at dinner. "They rejected him because of his age. Mrs. Monson says he's in his late thirties and wouldn't have had to go at all. But he petitioned a Brigadier General. Can you believe his patriotism?"

Harold answered by screeching his chair back before he walked out. "Yeah, but I bet he won't fight."

"I don't know. Jimmy Stewart's been in since '41, and he's a pilot."

"Next thing we know, Charlie Chaplin'll join up."

The cold tweaked Addie's nose, as light from the living room window projected Harold's elongated profile over the dead grass. The sight of him holding his chin in his hands weighed her down.

A long-ago conversation with Ruthie came to mind. They discussed a neighbor girl who married young when she discovered she carried a man's child.

"Does Ella want to marry him?"

"No, she had dreams of becoming a nurse, but says she made her bed, so now she'll lie in it. I feel so sad for her. She can't finish high school, and the pastor in Benson won't even allow them to marry in his church."

"Why did she . . . ?"

"You ask so many questions, Addie. Mama wouldn't want us talking about this, but I don't think Ella had much choice. He forced her."

Addie heard nothing more about Ella after Ruthie left for Minnesota. What was her life like now? Did she ever think about her nursing dream?

"And what about *your* dreams?" The question floated like wayward flakes in the stillness. Kate set her sights on college, and then on an adventurous life with Alexandre, but after Harold invited Addie to the winter ball her senior year, she had no need to dream.

Everyone said she should thank her lucky stars—as Harold's wife, she'd be set. She agreed, since he offered her a good home.

A maple stump absorbed her kick. "And that night, we danced to Glen Miller's "String of Pearls" *and* "Chattanooga Choo Choo." Harold seemed to enjoy himself. Didn't he realize Glen's German heritage back then, or was he play-acting?"

Beyond the yard, the grove hovered like a dark lake. Clouds flitted across the moon, quickening the north wind with the promise of more snow. Addie rounded the house again.

Sometimes people like Berthea got a second chance. But second chances weren't guaranteed, just as babies didn't always come when you prayed. What if she never did become a mother? She paused to consider.

"What if, for the rest of our lives, it's just Harold and me?"

The frozen road stretched beyond their empty mailbox, but suddenly winter's artistry appeared stark and fickle. It all could melt tomorrow. Jane said the weatherman forecast an abnormally warm Christmas.

By the time Addie went inside, Harold already snored, but anxiety for Kate and the troops hindered her sleep.

Morning brought heavy clouds and low-hanging fog. Windblown snowdrifts and even the pines tinged dingy brown. Thanksgiving neared, always Addie's favorite holiday, but melancholy enveloped her.

On Wednesday, she helped Berthea chop onions, celery and boil turkey giblets for dressing. She made pies, deviled eggs, and walnut cake, but her heart wasn't in her work. That evening, she closed the chicken house door without even saying goodnight to the girls. Halfway to the house, she turned back.

"Sorry, ladies. I was lost in my own thoughts. Stay warm tonight."

By the time she washed the dishes and brought enough corn from the basement to scallop in the morning, Harold had already gone to bed. She waited until he snored and slipped in without a sound.

* * *

When Bill burst through Berthea's door midmorning with Sue and their youngsters close behind, Addie wiped her hands on her apron and ran to take the smallest child from him.

Bill sniffed the air. "Got anything to eat? Sue could hardly make it here, she's so hungry."

Berthea gestured toward a big basket on the table. "Have a roll, Sue. You're eating for two now."

Sue dropped at the table. "Addie, how are you? It's been so long since we've seen you." She draped a roll with raspberry jam and took a bite. "Oh, my. Who made this jam?"

Berthea piped up. "Addie. Isn't it wonderful?"

"Mine always ends up runny. Tell me your secret."

"I let a slow boil thicken the fruit instead of adding pectin."

"Really?"

"Mama taught us if you cook fruit long enough, the natural pectin rises." *That's the way you do it if you can't afford a luxury like pectin.*

"You're such a hard worker."

"She never stops. This place looks so much better since she joined the family."

After dinner, Addie and Sue sent Berthea to the living room with the grandchildren while they did the dishes. Harold and Bill pushed back from the table with their coffee. Then Harold threw a verbal dart, loud enough for everyone to hear.

"Next year at this time, you'll have another one crawling around the living room."

Bill crossed his arms over his bulging stomach. "Hopefully the powers that be will call four enough. Don't know if I can afford any more."

"If you have another, maybe Addie and I can take it. It's about as likely the war will end tomorrow as she'll ever have a baby."

Addie dropped one of Berthea's best glasses on the floor and sliced her finger when she bent to clean it up. Sue dried her hands and circled Addie's waist with her arm.

Harold whistled. "Whoo-hoo! She's as good at doing dishes as she is at producing babies, huh? But the problem is, she doesn't want to be a mother."

Addie willed the floor to open up and swallow her, but Sue pulled on her elbow. "Come with me."

"I'll clean this up in a jiffy." Berthea smoothed Addie's shoulder. Addie let Sue drag her down the hall, with Bill confronting Harold in the background.

"What's the matter with you? She can't help it if . . ."

Harold's voice rose to fever pitch. "She's driven me to this."

"Can't you see . . .?" Bill's voice took on an incredulous tone.

Sue slammed the bathroom door and clenched her teeth. "That selfish brute—I could wring his neck." She bandaged Addie's trembling finger, pushed her into the bedroom, and sank on the bed beside her.

"Sorry. I . . . "

"I'd be in worse shape if Bill spoke like that to me, hon."

"What if I never . . . what if . . . ?" The words stopped short in Addie's throat.

"I have a friend who's tried for years. She says it's not always the woman's fault. Her doctor believes things can go wrong in the man, too. What gets me is Harold acting like he can read your mind. Normally, men and women think differently. Why would he even pretend to know you don't want children?"

The unanswerable question revolved in Addie's head. She only knew she never wanted to face the family again. Thankfully, George's daughter invited him to her house today, so he missed this.

Harold stormed out, and was already doing chores when Sue and Bill left for Cedar Rapids. Their youngest clung to Addie when she carried her to the car.

"We'll see Aunt Addie soon, Lissa—maybe at Christmas. It all depends on the weather." Sue gave Addie a hug. "Thanks for helping me with them. Keep your spirits up, all right?"

But winter gloom descended in earnest, along with early December storms. Twice, Addie pulled on her heavy sweater and sat in the little room at the end of the hall to read Kate's old letters, but glumness stuck to her like winter sludge.

Harold's wall of silence tore at her worse than if he hit her. She might as well be dead, for all the notice he paid her. She gave thanks for every minute he spent in the barn, but one thing kept her expectant during his stonewalling. December twelfth, he would leave for St. Louis.

Day by day, Berthea created excuses for Addie to come over. "All kinds of things to do around here, but I have so many commitments. Would you mind helping me carry some boxes to the basement?"

One day, Addie stopped in with the mail and Berthea was scrubbing her kitchen sink in a fury. An invigorating scent filled the kitchen.

"Lemon juice and Borax—it's a miracle worker. Come see, Addie—I'm trying this on my saucepans next. I doubt the stains in that old sink of yours would respond, but would you like a little of the mixture?"

"Sure. You ought to write a book about all the uses for Borax, Berthea. You could title it, *Household Transformation, Cheap and Simple* or *Fifty Inexpensive Ways to Cleanliness.*"

Arms akimbo, Berthea grinned. "You have no idea—it's good for fleas, rust, and washing combs and brushes. Orville even took a little in water for—you know—when he had trouble in the bathroom. Besides that, did you see the Mercantile ran a special on lemons the other day?"

Addie shook her head.

"Can't imagine why, but I took advantage of it. Here, I'll send some home with you."

Although she felt a little guilty because of the shortages in London, Addie gave her own sink a thorough going-over. It looked a little better, but Berthea was right—those stains were here to stay.

She packed canned goods for Harold's trip, ironed everything in sight, and baked cookies for him to take. But when evening came, none of her accomplishments cheered her.

Even her hens produced pale, placid yolks these days. Old Brown lazed in the most protected corner of the back porch, and George brought no news from Kate. On the eleventh, Berthea invited them for supper, giving Addie extra time during late afternoon while Harold worked on a barn stall.

Through the dining room window, she eyed the closed barn door. Should she risk writing Kate with him so near? Hopefully, Kate's silence didn't mean bad news about Alexandre, but if it did, she needed support more than ever.

In the broad window seat where she could see Harold coming and stash her paper and pen under a cushion, Addie wrote a couple of pages.

As Harold emerged from the barn, she addressed the envelope and buried the letter in her coat pocket to give to George.

While Harold was still washing up, she met George on Berthea's steps.

He smiled at the address. "Aha—good girl. Mighty rough times over there. Gotta keep Kate encouraged."

He ushered her into the homey scent of scalloped potatoes and ham, buttered corn, and rich cherry pie. George set the table and Berthea drew Addie into the pantry.

"I have something to tell you first. I got the job!" Her eyes sparkled as she accepted Addie's hug. "Shhh . . . I want to break the news to Harold with other people around,"

"Good idea."

Harold meandered in, and George tried to make conversation with him. Once they started eating, Berthea cleared her throat.

"I found out something today, and want you all to know." She waited for Harold to look up.

"The school principal has hired me as his secretary, starting January third."

Addie clapped her hands. "Oh, that's wonderful. I'm so proud of you."

Harold balanced a biscuit midair. "At your age, working in an office? What can you be thinking, Ma?"

George opened his mouth, but Berthea touched his arm and stood, hands on her hips. "Harold Duane Bledsoe, I'm sure you have no idea what I'm thinking, and if you knew, you wouldn't like it at all. I've wanted to work in a school my whole life."

"Oh, come on, Ma."

"No, you come on—stop acting like your father. I rejoiced at your opportunity to go to the seminary. Why can't you do the same for me?"

The vein in Harold's forehead burgeoned to Mississippi River size. Addie thought he might leave the table, but he lanced Berthea a stormy look.

"You'll be facing roads that need plowed. Remember, I won't be here to pull you out of the ditch any more, or plow the driveway."

"I've thought ahead about that. I do have a brain, you know! I'm going to practice with the tractor and loader. I've driven it before, and besides that, I have a back-up plan."

Harold fidgeted under Berthea's smug smile. When she gestured toward George, Harold's lips twisted like a gargoyle's.

He made no attempt to hide his scowl, and Addie leaned back to study his jaw's firm set. George had been their mail carrier for over twenty years. Didn't that count for anything?

A few days earlier, Harold tramped into the house livid, threw down his coat and tore off his boots as though attempting to break his ankles. He muttered under his breath, then exploded. "That Miller's parked at Ma's again. Some men have to work, but he has nothing better to do than visit her. *German vermin*, they say. For all we know, George might be a spy."

For once, Addie couldn't hold her tongue. "He works hard, Harold. He starts his route at five in the morning and goes until three. And I've never known George to speak German. He was born here, and even fought in the Great War."

Harold huffed and switched on the radio. After supper when she went in to knit, he looked up from his book. "I have a notion to talk with the postmaster. It's dangerous to have a German for our mail carrier."

Addie gulped down her retort. Mama would say, "Why borrow trouble?"

After Berthea faced off with him tonight, Harold hung his head, but he still ignored George. Over the dishpan, Berthea fumed.

"I don't know how you put up with him, Addie. Guess I spoiled him, because we'd wanted another child for so long, and . . . " She took out her frustration on the plates and soapsuds spilled on the floor. Addie raced to keep up with her.

"After his accident, I let him have his way too much. But I have a life of my own now, and he has to accept it." Wrinkles wrapped her forehead. "Do you understand?"

"That you need to start a new life?"

Berthea nodded and swiped bubbles across her forehead.

"Yes, and I'm so happy about your new job. I've wanted to work, too, maybe at the newspaper office, but Harold is so. . ."

Berthea interrupted. "Stubborn and selfish and bigoted when it comes to women. And Germans. And Negros. And a few others, I suppose. The next thing I know, he'll be saying George spies for the Nazis."

Better to let that one go. Berthea fumed on about Harold, and the tiny kitchen's warmth stole over Addie. Hearing Harold's mother fuss warmed her heart. When they hung up their aprons, Berthea took her hand.

"Thanks for your help, and for listening."

When the evening news ended, Harold yawned. "Time to get home. I have to clean out the barn in the morning."

Berthea touched his sleeve. "What time does the train leave?"

"Midafternoon. Mr. Lundene's taking me, since you're always gone."

Berthea blinked at the ice in his voice. "You know I'd have been happy to drive you."

He left without a word, and let the door slam behind him. Berthea's face fell and Addie felt she should apologize for Harold.

"Thank you for dinner, Berthea. Don't let him make you miserable."

Berthea squared her shoulders. "I won't. My whole life, I've asked people to *let* me do something, but now things have changed. Instead, I ask, 'Who's going to *stop* me?' And Harold's attitude certainly won't." She gave Addie a hug.

"Thanks for mailing my letter, George." The warmth in his eyes increased Addie's desire to stay longer, and the way he squeezed Berthea's hand revealed his tenderness.

She wouldn't be surprised if they married, although that would make Harold even more livid. But for Berthea to finally have someone interested in what she wanted . . . how wonderful would that be?

Aunt Alvina had said George's wife died when their children were young, so he raised them alone. She and Kate benefitted from his neighborliness, and now, finding a companion like Berthea seemed ideal for him.

In a flurry, Harold left the barn, covered the yard in a few long strides, and shut the porch door as Addie started home. Knowing icy silence awaited her, even this cold night seemed warmer than their living room.

Chapter Twenty-seven

*H*arold craned his head out the back porch door as Addie started around the house. "What're you doing now?" His impatience strengthened her resolve to stay outside as long as possible.

"Going for a walk."

"Why would anybody want to do that?" His eyebrows hit the bill of his cap. The icy air stung Addie's cheeks, but her realization smarted even more.

She might have said, "See how the moisture cleaves to the pine tips? I want to walk over the garden, to remember that seeds wait their chance. I want to let the cold penetrate me, and then get warm again. I want to feel something—anything."

She could have added, "We're as different as Hitler and Churchill, Harold, as different as north and south. But what hurts most is that you don't even try to understand me."

The loud monotony of a news report already spewed from the living room. She'd nurtured a faint hope that tonight would be better, with him leaving in the morning.

Mrs. Morfordson's words came on a slight breeze as she rounded the west side of the house. "Donne, Dickinson, and Kipling create parcels of life so real they take our breath away. Novelists reveal who their characters are little by little. When they do, it behooves us to believe them."

Harold made that kind of statement tonight, like Rhett Butler walking out on Scarlett in *Gone With The Wind*. Scarlett pursued him, but when Addie and Kate first saw the movie, they both uttered the wistful phrase "It's too late," in unison.

In the following weeks, they re-enacted the scene a dozen ways, rendering Scarlett less willful and Rhett just a bit more patient. He took her along to Europe, and their daughter had no riding accident. But when the movie came back a second time, Scarlett still paved her way to misery and missed the true love right before her.

"Harold is as willful and stubborn as Scarlett. Does he even have the capacity to enjoy this crystal night?" But the most important question swirled inside Addie as she forged a trail to the garden. What did his behavior tell her?

He viewed even Berthea as though she must obey his desires. The truth glared like their broken-down garden fence. Berthea and George did nothing to contribute to Harold's attitude except to *be who they were*.

Could that hold true for her, too, as Kate believed? Addie always thought her personality triggered the worst in Harold, so she bore responsibility for his attitudes. But maybe deception had her in its clutches.

With a stick, she traced a heart in the snow. Could she have been so far from reality this whole time, just as she failed to see the truth about Dad until Ruthie pointed it out?

What do you think he had in his coffee cup all those years, Addie? Sleep walking through life . . .

Before her stood the garden fence she'd plotted so long to hide. A shaft of snow from a bough jiggled the weather-worn wood, and something else came clear. A few axe blows could topple it. One of the boards swayed easily when Addie shoved it with her boot.

Her thoughts pummeled faster than the snow. "You're just a broken-down fence—that's all. I don't know why I didn't see it before. And Harold's been showing me who he is this whole time, too."

Snow-cover brought the grove closer and made the house into a huge, eerie ship anchored in an ocean of white. A light appeared in their bedroom, where perfect rows of shirts, pants, undershirts and socks lined the old suitcase she'd packed for Harold.

Jars of chicken, jam, and vegetables, loaves of bread and two beautiful pies filled several boxes on the kitchen counter. There was nothing left to do for him, but did he notice all her work? And if she stayed out here a few more hours, would he even care?

A white mound made the front steps unrecognizable. Like a fine meringue topping, graceful folds hid brick and cement. Then George started his car and he rounded the yard. The lights shone on Addie and he rolled down his window.

"You're going to freeze, young lady." His good-natured comment rolled like laughter.

"Then you'll find me in the morning, like Lot's wife—a pillar of salt."

His chuckle resonated. That's what she needed, smiles and laughter and joy. And starting tomorrow, she would find them and hold them close. Her curls, wet through, clung to her cheeks, but her heart felt lighter than it had in weeks.

Normally she had little energy at this time of night, but she shoveled a path to the chicken house, another to the barn, and scooped off the dusting that accumulated on Berthea's steps since George left. When she finally went inside, exhilaration replaced the pall that had settled over her since Thanksgiving.

A subdued but joyous rumble began low in her chest. Harold was leaving tomorrow.

"Gas man's due in the morning. Be sure to get me from the barn when he drives in." That was Harold's goodnight, and he turned away after she slid beneath the covers.

In the regularity of his snore, another revelation emanated. His concern wasn't so much about having a baby, or he would have seized this last chance. The thing he cared about most was power.

Actions speak louder than words. All about power, all about power.

The phrase circled until Addie finally slept. A pleasant dream of flower buds opening to the sun lingered with her in the morning.

Before breakfast, Harold piled boxes on the back porch. Soon, Paul Johansen backed his coal truck between the big soft maple tree and the undulating drift dressing the side of the house.

Harold crossed his arms and groaned. "Paulie works even slower than he thinks."

"But he sure has a good aim toward the coal chute. That must take a lot of practice."

Harold squinched at her. "How would you know, Miss Smarty?"

But she did know, and practiced great self-control not to tell him about her driving lessons. She went back to fluting her pie crust and slid her work of art into the oven as he went out to open the chute below the kitchen window.

Cascading black nuggets echoed from the chute. Even their clatter struck Addie as hopeful. Loads lasted about three months, so with an early spring, she shouldn't have to order again. Filling the bin reminded her of all Harold's work around here. No matter what, he was a hard worker, unlike her dad.

Sometimes Dad ordered coal to keep their family warm, sometimes he didn't. When Reuben still lived at home, he exchanged his labor with the coal company for their winter supply. But one cold night after a run-in with Dad, Reuben took off during the wee hours. The next morning, Mama's voice rose to a near-wail.

"Avery, we don't even know where he's gone."

"At least he left the coal bin full."

From then on until Herman grew strong enough to work, the hodgepodge three-room house welcomed winter drafts like old friends. Of course, Addie still saw her breath in the upstairs now, like most people around here. But the cold in her childhood went deeper.

She and Ruthie put Herman between them in bed when the fuel ran out, and Bonnie slept with Mama and Dad. When a truck finally brought coal, light returned to Mama's eyes.

Slam. The kitchen floor vibrated when Harold dropped the chute lid. A few seconds later, he clumped down the basement stairs.

The aroma of baking apples and cinnamon engulfed the kitchen, and Addie checked his suitcase one last time. Then she dropped dumplings into the beef broth, and chatted during the meal.

"Are you excited, Harold? What do you think it will be like at the seminary?" His calculating glance asked what it mattered to her, but she persevered.

"Don't you wonder about your classes and the new people you'll meet?"

"You think I'm going on a vacation or something?"

An hour later when Maynard's pick-up chugged into the yard, Harold issued instructions. "Don't let the pipes freeze, now. I showed you how to use the blow torch in the crawl space over the basement ceiling, remember?"

"Yes." Not a pleasant memory of scooting into a cobwebby hole in the foundation to hold the torch to the pipes under the un-insulated back porch pipes. Addie waited for something more, but he hefted canned goods and his suitcase into the pick-up box.

He was about to get in when Berthea stepped out and waved, but Harold turned his back. Maynard goosed the engine up the driveway's slight incline, and that was that. Berthea put her hand to her chest.

Later, Addie walked to get the mail with a mix of emotions battling inside. A dull throb of disappointment reminded her nothing had changed last night, but stronger than that came a sense of relief.

"Guess we women are on our own." Berthea's cheerful greeting belied the softness in her eyes when Addie delivered her mail. Her voice perked when she glanced through the letters.

"Oh good, here's one from Bill and Sue. Maybe Lissa scribbled me a picture this time." A lemon and Borax scent laced the sparkling kitchen.

"You've been busy cleaning again—looks great, Berthea."

"Won't be long and I'll be a working woman, so I figured I'd best get things in order. Let me know if you need anything, and come over for supper tonight. It's fun to listen to radio programs with George."

"Thanks, I will." Addie crossed the yard, entered her back porch and ambled through the rooms. With the whole house to herself now, why not spread Kate's letters out on the table, along with the map she'd drawn, and study the lay of London?

London
November 22, 1942

Dear Addie,

   Your chicken factory reads like a movie. So does the Simon mystery. Jane's reaction to you mentioning him fits a thought in one of Mrs. T's books. (I'm back to my psychology.)

"Individuals often submerge deep sorrow, but their silence implies no lack of integrity. Honesty with oneself reveals the maturity to keep one's own counsel."

And for goodness sake, you're not mouthy. When pressed, you finally garnered the courage to level with your dad. What do you call rebellion, attending the Methodist Youth Fellowship meeting? I'd say your dad's incoherence contributed more to his railings than your honesty did.

Here's a thought—maybe Jane needed to hear you mention Simon. Truth speakers can't let people's reactions beach their craft.

A few questions: shouldn't each of us be FOR ourselves, since God is? If we judge our every move, who would ever do anything? Aren't our ideas and passions given us for a reason?

Things continue here as normal. Mrs. T invited me for my first plum pudding. She says no news is good news, and maybe Alexandre will come. Why not assume the best? And wonderful news: we've bombed Berlin.

Everyone here has been waiting for that . . .

Revenge is sweet . . .

What will you do the 25th, besides all the chores? I wish I could transport you here for a few hours. As for thinking alike, I can't imagine living with someone without freely sharing your thoughts. Yes, Alex thinks like me, though not as much as you.

Did your news carry Mr. Churchill's speech at the Lord Mayor's Luncheon, about Montgomery turning back Rommel at El Alamein, nearly finishing the Nazi army? After our defeats, we had to win—had to. And the Prime Minister reminded us.

Mrs. T adores W.C. If we didn't already believe in word power, his speeches would convince us.

"The bright gleam has caught the helmets of our soldiers, and warmed and cheered all our hearts. This is not the end. It is not even the beginning of the end. But it is, perhaps, the end of the beginning."

Ahh . . . eloquence. Mr. T brought a radio to work and the performance brought to mind your struggle with Harold. Maybe his absence will mark the end of the beginning.

Mr. Churchill continued, "We mean to hold our own. I have not become the King's first minister to preside over the liquidation of the British Empire."

Everyone in the office applauded, many shed tears, and we all took fresh hope. Check the library for a copy of the November Tenth New York Times. Maybe Churchill's words will stir Harold.

On a Hollywood note, did you hear Henry Fonda enlisted? Remember watching Wake Island? Amazing to think those actors might soon be in the thick of battle.

Your letters cheer me, as well as the Thanksgiving packet. Your jam is definitely number one with Mrs. T, and Charles, too. (It's strange to call him Mr. T when he visits his mum.)

Onward, then . . .

Kate

Chapter Twenty-eight

"You introduced me to oyster stew on Christmas Eve, Berthea. It's a German tradition, isn't it?" Addie took a second helping of the mellow soup and another biscuit.

"Now we can say that word out loud. Harold forgets he spoke German with his grandmother until she died, and he loved her sauerbraten."

"And I'd vote for sauerkraut any day." George's eyes twinkled, but his voice sobered. "Did you hear that some general stores around here cancelled their normal oyster order this year, for fear of provoking more local anger?"

Berthea shook her head. "I understand, but that's too bad—wish we could detest Hitler without hating all that great German food. Mama always made mulled cider, red cabbage and spatzle when I was growing up, but my Norwegian aunt married into the family and introduced us to oyster stew."

George gave a Christmas Eve-sized grin. "And tonight, we've got it all, thanks to you."

Berthea squeezed his hand, but couldn't hide her wistfulness, so Addie chimed in. "This'll be a different Christmas, with Bill and Sue not coming, won't it, Berthea?"

"Yes, I have to admit, I miss those little ones, but wouldn't want Bill driving with them in this weather, either. They're forecasting blizzard conditions around Cedar Rapids. But with you and George around, we still make a family."

She brought more stew from the stove and George took another helping. "Can't forget all those sons or husbands thousands of miles away tonight."

"I can't figure out why the seminary called Harold down there before the holidays, but maybe it's a good thing." Berthea reached for something on the floor. "I have a little gift for you, Addie, since Jane's due to pick you up soon." She handed over a paper sack and Addie peeked inside.

"Oh, this is the best surprise ever, so thoughtful of you."

"Well, I know Harold frowns on you buying tea."

George cleared his throat. "I didn't bring you a gift, but promise to clean out the driveway every morning when I do the chores."

"You already brought my Christmas yesterday—Kate's letter. It took twice as long as usual to get here this time."

"Lots of Atlantic war traffic these days. Has she heard from her husband yet?"

"No, not lately." Addie finished her second roll, but George's next question made her gulp.

"Have either of you heard from Harold?"

In the awkward silence, Addie forced a smile. "I'm sure he's busy."

Berthea set down her fork. "That's no excuse." Tires crunched in the driveway. "That's Jane—tell her hello for me, and that I still remember that wonderful supper she brought over last winter."

"I will. Have a blessed Christmas Eve, you two—sorry I'm leaving you with the dishes."

George brought Addie's coat and saw her to the door. "Enjoy the service tonight, and we'll see you tomorrow."

When Addie looked up from putting on her boots, he studied Berthea with devotion. Harold hadn't even sent her a postcard, although she'd mailed him a scarf.

A clear, starry sky hid the Studebaker's dents, and Jane seemed particularly talkative. "Isn't it beautiful out? I'm so glad you're coming, like the old days when you visited with Alvina. Oh, before I forget, we'll pick up your coupe before January first—some day next week"

"That's right. I'd forgotten."

A friendly parishioner ushered them into the sanctuary, where soft blue light enveloped the oak altar. Someone handed out small candles, and Jane led the way to a pew on the right, where Aunt Alvina said the women always used to sit.

Right for women, left for men, that's how it used to be, with a door on each side—never the twain shall meet.

After they sang "I Am So Glad Each Christmas Eve," the pastor read the nativity story. His strong, resonant voice drifted over rows of worshippers clad in wool coats, though the massive iron floor grate belched heat with a musty tinge.

"We have prayed through the darkness and possibility of Advent, 'Come to us, make straight paths through the wilderness of our lives. Reduce the mountains our pride has raised and shore up the valleys formed by guilt.' Now, we beseech Thee, build in our hearts a wide way for Your Son to enter anew. We embrace the joy of our Savior's birth with gratitude. Amen."

In the front pew, his youngest son shifted in his seat next to a gaggle of sisters and brothers. Down the row, their mother sent the lad a sharp look.

"Our Lord came into this world in the shadow of a cruel oppressor. His was not an easy life, and under Roman rule, he was no stranger to tyranny. Tonight, we remember our brothers and sisters around this hurting world in similar circumstances.

"We all plead daily for deliverance from great evil unleashed on many nations. As we gather in this warm place, tens of thousands are cast from their homelands and wander the earth tonight, and our soldiers suffer for our sake far from home."

Pastor Bachmann endured his own share of suffering, some of it stemming from First Methodist, fueled by Harold himself. *The mountains of our pride* and *the valleys formed by our guilt* sat in Addie's consciousness like a familiar melody.

Which troubled her most, pride or guilt? As Pastor Bachmann spoke of the longing for peace, guilt won easily. At home, surrounded by reminders of all the times she disappointed or displeased Harold, not a day went by when she felt free of guilt.

At least now, with him gone, no fresh evidence mounted of her failures. But he obviously had no desire to share Christmas with her in even the smallest way.

Shoring up the valleys . . . guilt had gouged plenty of them in her soul. How could they be shored up? Then, like a Christmas Eve angel sent just for her, Kate's analyzing came to mind. Harold's behavior made a statement about him, not her, so why should she allow guilt to harass her?

Jane chose that moment to glance over with such kindness that Addie's eyes stung. Maybe *shoring up* was what Jane and Kate did, refusing to let her blame herself for everything.

"We look forward to our Easter hope, for the gift of the baby Jesus means the Father highly values us. His coming to earth tells us we are worthy, for he bears our grief and carries our sorrows. Whatever loads we shoulder, He longs to share."

Pastor Bachmann faced the altar and bowed his head. "As we enter a new year, Father in Heaven, reveal Thy benevolence and help us believe that He who sent His only Son for us will also with Him freely give us all things."

He carried the flame to two parishioners who walked down the aisle, lighting candles all the way. Row by row, individual flames multiplied until their joined warmth became tangible. In the glow, people's faces took on an ethereal radiance.

"Come to us anew this night, Lord God. Invade our darkness and shine eternal light into our hungry hearts. Grant us to carry the light with us wherever we go, whatever we face."

The altar lights dimmed, and a bulky man hurried out the side door. As everyone sang "Silent Night," the pale blue light once again cast friendly shadows on the high walls. Such tender harmony touched Addie, and she hated having the lovely song end.

Pastor Bachmann's firm handshake strengthened her as the people filed into the cold. Along frozen roads out of Currier and Ives, Jane kept silent. But near the Bledsoe farm, she turned to Addie.

"Would you mind stopping over for a while? I have a little surprise, and I'll drive you home later."

"Oh, I'd love to. I wasn't looking forward to that big, empty house."

December 25, 1942

Dear Kate,

Your letter arrived—I hope you see Alexandre today.

It's quiet here, but I'm thankful for a warm downstairs and for our kitchen pump, since it's twenty below zero. Most of all, I'm so glad Alexandre's all right.

Last night, Jane gave me an unexpected gift. She invited me over after church, and in her living room sat her mystery man. He seemed boyish, sinking back in his over-stuffed chair when I entered.

"We have company, Simon." Jane flung her coat over a chair. "Remember, I told you it's Christmas Eve?"

He smiled shyly and brushed his fingers over his flannel shirt. "Yeah. Baby Sarah came to us on Christmas Eve."

Jane introduced me to him and asked if I'd mind heating some tea water. My mind raced. Who was Sarah? In this bitter cold, did Simon still stay in the cabin? He looked too delicate to clear that long path.

Even Berthea has nothing good to say about him, yet he seemed so innocent. Had he undergone a personality change? The burbling teapot and a simple Bible verse stilled my questions.

Love one another.

All my wonderings vanished as Jane read from a big black family Bible, and Simon drank in the story. When she finished, Jane handed me a package, and gave a larger one to Simon.

I rummaged in my coat pocket for her gift. The day we canned corn, she'd exclaimed over my sharp knives.

"My sharpener's missing, and I can't imagine how I lost it. I've looked everywhere."

Norman had a sharpener like mine, so I set it aside. This morning, I wrapped it in one of the embroidered dishtowels the church ladies gave us for our wedding. Knowing Jane's love of country, I chose the American flag design.

Simon giggled with anticipation when he told Jane to open her gift first.

She arched her brows and tugged at the ribbon. Then her face lighted with pleasure, and she remarked on my good memory.

I asked if she'd ever found her sharpener, and she said she hadn't, though she'd searched and searched.

Simon gasped. Then he wriggled forward until his feet touched the linoleum. He crossed the room in a haphazard lope, slid his hand along a shelf, and pulled out a gray metal piece—a knife sharpener much like the one in Jane's hands.

"Simon Pike!" Jane's voice rang sharp. Simon ducked his head and her tone softened. "Were you playing a trick on me?"

He tightened his lips in a charming O. "Merry Christmas, Janey."

She fingered the sharpener and patted his hand. "All right, then. Sit down and open your gift."

He clapped his hands over a Five and Dime puzzle of a sleigh and horses. "'Member how we used to ride, Janey?"

Jane's moist eyes matched his. "It's Addie's turn now."

I hoped she hadn't spent much. The package held a gold locket, and under its tiny latch, what do you think I found?

"How did you . . . ?"

"Letha Cady cleaned out Alvina's things and saved a few items back for Kate. But when I told Letha about our neighboring, she gave me this picture of Kate to give you. The locket belonged to my mother."

I hugged her hard—to think she would give up this treasure for me. And the gift goes on—now you can delight in this story.

My "Who is Sarah?" will be answered in due time, I'm sure of it. Ambiguities improve my patience, thanks to sharing your experiences this past year.

Write and tell me all about your plum pudding, please.

Near at heart,

Addie

Addie cleaned the chicken roosts and baked cookies for George, but apprehension about Alexandre hovered over her like a cloud tracking the grove.

When she checked the animals, the filly raised her great dark eyes. One day last week, she sauntered over for her usual carrot, and a name occurred to Addie.

"Missy. That's what I'll call you. We won't tell old Harold."

She inched her fingers toward Missy's nose and waited for her to adjust. Little by little, she worked her way to her muzzle, but Missy still startled, even after all these weeks. Hopefully, the reflex would fade, along with Addie's fear of horses.

Reuben had sometimes saddled the workhorse for her and Ruth, but one time, he disappeared after helping them on. The next thing Addie knew, they struggled on the ground in a tangled mass of legs and arms.

Luckily, the horse stood still until they crawled away. Ruth grabbed the reins and tightened the cinch. "Get back on, Addie. Otherwise you'll always be scared."

But Addie stepped back, and to this day, that fear troubled her. The summer after their wedding, Harold invited her along when he leaped onto Daisy to check the fencerows one evening. She put her foot in the stirrup, but her hand trembled.

"Come on, don't be a scaredy-cat."

Addie cowered, and Harold never offered again. Now, in the quiet barn, Missy offered hope. Touching her softer-than-snow muzzle fired Addie's desire.

"Maybe once you're grown, you'll give me a little ride."

The temperature dropped that evening, so she checked the chickens a second time. "You girls stay warm, though it won't be easy."

In the morning, the tank evidenced more ice than water, even though George broke it earlier. Addie bore down on the ice pick and picked out the largest chunks with a set of tongs.

Her hands hurt with the cold, so she buried them in a ewe's woolly fleece. As her fingers thawed, a vehicle rolled down the driveway and a man hurried toward the house, the black rubber flies of his unbuckled overshoes flapping in the wind. Emmet Lardner from the post office? Addie opened the top door and yelled her loudest.

"Emmet!"

He retraced his steps, his thin nose red and eyes watering. He carried an envelope in his gloved hand.

"Mrs. Bledsoe?"

"Yes?"

"Addie Bledsoe?"

Her heart did a flip-flop.

"Telegram for you."

Emmet fished in his back pocket for a paper folded in thirds, splayed it on the doorsill, and handed her a pen. "Sign here."

The cold ink finally flowed while Emmet shifted his feet in the snow.

"Thank you kindly, ma'am."

Back in the barn, Addie broke the seal and pulled out a note-card-sized message.

January 6, 1943 Stop A's plane found Stop Pray Stop
Love you Stop Kate

Telegrams cost by the word, that much Addie knew. Even with this dire news, Kate spent extra money to include "Love you."

Harold's face flashed before her, distant and strained. Berthea's pithy Christmas Eve statement ran through her mind. *That's no excuse.*

No, busyness was no excuse. How long had it been since he said, "I love you?"

But she put the question aside and headed for her desk—the kitchen table, now that she could write to Kate anytime she wished.

January 6, 1943 Stop Dear Kate Stop Holding out hope Stop Love YOU Stop Addie

Her egg money can produced five dollars, and she raced to catch Berthea before she left for school. They met near the Chevy.

"Sure, I'll send it for you." Berthea's brow crinkled. "Something's wrong?"

"Alexandre's plane went down at Dieppe."

Berthea shuddered in spite of her fur collar and perky knitted hat. "I'll be praying."

The hens, stricken with the cold, laid only half their normal amount. When the truck came last Thursday, only ten dozen eggs waited in cardboard containers. Addie addressed her best laying hens, like brown mounds hunkered down on their perches.

"You girls are hoarding your resources. Guess that's what we all have to do right now."

The cowgirl on the open egg money can sipped her perennial cup of steaming coffee, and Addie noticed the pockets on her leather skirt. "With your fancy fringe and your hot coffee, you don't have a care in the world."

She put the lid on and slid the can back on its shelf, cooked some oatmeal with raisins, and turned on the weather report. The bay window's bleak sunshine invited her in to eat breakfast, so she turned on the radio.

"There's no getting away from the cold today, eighteen below zero, and it's too icy to drive, folks. Stoke your furnace. Expect winds up to thirty miles an hour, but we can be glad there's no snow in the forecast."

The stubborn sewing machine awaited her attention. She could knit on the sweater she'd started two days ago, and had a new sock pattern to try. But the desire to talk with someone pressed at her.

The wind howled through the abandoned chimney between the living room and dining room and rattled the windows without mercy. The day stretched ahead like a long, weary road.

"I'll go to Jane's, that's what." Addie bundled Harold's overalls over her clothes, wriggled on his chore coat, and wrapped an extra scarf over her head. Then she wound another one around her neck.

Maybe Jane would enjoy a jar of apple butter. She shuffled down the basement steps and put a pint in an oversized pocket. When she emerged, the egg man drove up, so she watched him retrieve her eggs from the milk house and met him halfway for her payment.

His nose shone red with the cold as he handed her a few dollar bills and some coins. "Cold 'nuff to blister a fella's skin today."

He hurried back to his truck and shifted out onto the road. Addie's determination increased. "If he can still make his rounds in this bitter weather, and Kate can somehow manage this intolerable news, I'm not about to let the weather stop me from making it over to Jane's."

In the house, she dropped the money into her coffee can and warmed herself thoroughly by the stove, then marched outside with resolve.

Chapter Twenty-nine

A strong southerly wind made the going difficult. Matchstick fence posts blurred and every breath hurt. Halfway to Jane's house, Addie considered going back, but why waste all this effort? She pushed harder, and by the time she knocked on Jane's door, she was spent.

"My goodness, child, out on a day like this? I was sure I saw someone coming down the road, but thought to myself, no, it just can't be. Is everything all right?"

Addie's teeth chattered, but Jane threw her arms around her and warmth reached through her heavy layers. Jane unwound her frozen scarf, pulled off her coat and boots, and wrapped her in a thick woolen blanket from the other room.

The warm air made Addie's nose and lips tingle. At the same time, Kate's news poured out in gasps. Jane wiped away tears with the back of her hand as she boiled tea water.

"That kind of searching can take a long, long time, especially this time of year."

"I don't know how Kate handles all this waiting."

"You heard about the Owens boy? Killed last week on some island."

"Yes, George told us. Roy's sister Lila was in Harold's class." Once again, Addie wondered if Roy ever got those soldier cookies she and Berthea sent him.

While Jane poured her tea, a bloody scene from *Wake Island* made Addie tremble. Back when she saw the movie, the battle seemed surreal, but Roy likely died that way, far from home, in great pain, and all alone.

"What do you hear from Harold?"

"He hasn't written."

Jane's eyes darkened to the color of the lowest pine boughs.

"I'm happy for him, though. He hates being stuck here."

Jane worked her mouth as if she tamped down some feisty response, and friendly quiet descended. Here, there always seemed to be plenty of time. No scrabbling to think of an answer that would please, no holding back. But Addie's mind went blank, except for thinking about Kate's telegram.

The clock's steady rhythm melded with some chicken bubbling in broth on the back of the stove. Jane rimmed her cup with her forefinger and refilled Addie's tea.

"How about a molasses cookie—it'll cure what ails you." Jane grinned and brought out a plate full, as crinkly as a washboard.

"We haven't talked since Christmas Eve, and I would expect you'd have questions about Simon." She set out the topic like Addie's gloves drying near the stove.

"It's all right. I've been too secretive for far too long . . ." Jane's gaze shifted to the cabin's distant slanted roof, stark against barren trees.

"That's one of my besetting sins. But I suppose we all make choices we later doubt." She tapped her fingers on her teacup.

"I used to think we were here on earth to make sense of things, but I've come to believe we're meant to take care of each other as best we can. The Almighty trusts that to us, since He still gives us breath. If any sense comes of anything in the process, we can be extra thankful."

They sat together for a while in stillness with a flavor different from silence with Harold. *I can be quiet here, or ask any question I want.*

"About ten years ago, Simon began forgetting where things were . . . his truck, the barn, our bedroom at night. Once, he even forgot how to feed the pigs. He'd always been a jokester, so at first I thought . . ."

Jane gestured toward the grove, where Simon, a scarf bound over his stocking cap, plunged through hip-high drifts. With a long stick, he touched random trees in some sort of ritual.

"Doc found him wandering on the railroad tracks south of town one day, and sat down with me after he brought Simon home. Simon fought other folks when they tried to guide him home, and they called him cantankerous. I heard later that some even swore he hit me."

Jane scowled and sighed over her teacup. "People—it's hard to know who you can trust. But Doc had a way with Simon, and said his mother changed the same way as she aged. They had to watch her night and day, and he knew how hard it was to see a loved one slip in and out of this world.

"We had an old castoff table outside the door, and Simon stayed out there. Doc and I watched him jiggle his finger along the boards behind a big black ant, like he did something important.

"Doc knew of places he could live, he said. One was down in Independence, where nurses watch the patients day and night."

Jane snorted. "I asked if that's what he did with his mother and his mouth contorted. That settled it for me. He said his mother roamed so much, he and his wife constantly waited for her next disappearance, so they could protect her and pick up the pieces. It was no way to live.

"He told me to keep things as simple as possible, allow Simon in only one part of the house, away from the stove—things like that. Otherwise, I'd spend my whole life in fear instead of living each day.

"That's when I thought of the cabin. Years ago, when a neighbor planned to burn it down, Simon said he'd take it, and one afternoon, eight men, two to a side, hauled the building across the field. It's not often you see a cabin on centipede legs. I met them and asked Simon what he was doing.

"'Don't worry,' he said. 'I'll make something nice for you.' Simon's good with wood, so he built cupboards, a chest of drawers, and a bedframe. He patched and shingled the roof and reinforced the hearth, too. The work kept him busy during the winters.

"Ten years later with Doc, I realized Simon had created his own safe place. Back there behind the grove, he feels better, without seeing traffic pass by.

"That day, the three of us took a walk, and when Simon opened the cabin door, he sat down in an old armchair and leaned his head back real peaceful. Doc and I exchanged a look and sealed the decision."

"Simon's been fine, for the most part, ever since. Before my knee went bum, I cleaned houses and saved up a nest egg. His pension from the meat packing plant pays for gas and fuel oil, and that's about all we need."

"And flowers."

Jane's eyes brightened.

"Thank you for telling me. I liked meeting Simon."

"We haven't done much on Christmas all these years, but I decided to take the risk. You're the first person I've trusted enough, and I thank my lucky stars you live so close. You mean a lot to Simon, too—he mentions you every day."

"That's the best compliment I've had for a long, long time. I never told you, but last fall, Simon saved little Willie Miller. He wandered into the cornfield when Berthea was watching him for George, and Simon brought him to the edge of our grove."

"So you knew about him ..." Jane shook her head. "Goes to show how much good all my hiding did, eh?"

Back at home, Addie found the house freezing. Still in her coat and boots, she descended to the dank basement and checked the furnace.

"Urgh . . . can't believe I let the fire get so low. Harold would have a fit."

After shaking the ashes from the grate, she scraped up hot coals, scooped on some corncobs, and added enough coal to ignite a good fire. When the peculiar dry odor of burning cobs filled her senses, she left the draft open a little and started back upstairs.

Light on the moist limestone wall caught her attention. Such a small rectangular window, and so little light today, but rays found their way to this wall to create a show. Something Jane said this morning wafted through Addie's mind.

No way to live . . . I'd spend my whole life in fear instead of living each day.

"That's exactly what I've done for three and a half years. I don't ever want to miss out on today again." She shivered in spite of her coat and went up to open the stovepipe damper.

January 22, 1943

Dear Addie,

God spared me a long wait. I knew in my heart, but the RAF confirms Alexandre's death. He'll never surprise me again as he did on Christmas Eve when he knocked on Mrs. T's door in time for plum pudding.

He had few answers—a paperwork mix-up, he said, but he finally made it to London and read all my letters. The day after Christmas, he left again on his final mission, and I've heard no details of the crash.

I used to wonder if anything could render me speechless—now I know. I wish I could talk with you. Mr. T offered me a week off, but my nervous fingers crave work.

We've had some bombing this month—I can't sleep, so I patrol with Mrs. T. She found me a tin cap like hers. It's another world out there, with shrapnel in the air, searchlights everywhere, whines and wails and multicolored lights flashing.

I suppose it sounds crazy, but in the flames of rocket guns and the bang and BOOM of their recoil, I feel Alexandre near. Maybe that's how it was when his plane went down. The wild colors remind me I'm alive, and somehow, I feel his presence.

Mrs. T says it's getting more like the Blitz by the day. We never know where it's safe—some people died in a restaurant recently, and a bomb hit a school. So we patrol for incendiaries—they fall by the dozens at times, and we helped a neighbor smother one near his front door the other evening.

Please don't be afraid to write me. I'm still the same Kate. Thank you so much for the telegram. You can't imagine how much it meant to me.

Love,

Kate

The road grader passed early in the morning, mashing January thaw like potatoes and pressing the oozy mess to the frost line. Addie checked the road's condition after the big gold machine passed.

The gravel had firmed up enough to give the red coupe a run. For days she'd thought about it, ever since she followed Jane home from Norman's garage. Tucked in the corncrib, the coupe stayed hidden. But today, the timing seemed right.

Berthea normally left for work by now, yet the Chevy sat unmoved. After only one knock, Berthea opened the door. "Morning, Glory! Come on in. I have a surprise for you, Addie." She pointed to a rectangular wooden box hung on the wall.

"Wow—I've only seen telephones in town. How did you manage?"

"The principal said I'd need one, since he might have to call me after hours. The company strung the wires last fall, so he convinced them to install this in spite of the cold. You didn't see the workmen yesterday?"

"No, maybe I was over visiting Jane."

"Want to try it out?" Berthea lifted the shiny receiver and turned a smooth black crank on the right side.

"Say hello to Selma." She thrust the receiver into Addie's hand.

"Is that you, Addie?"

"Yes."

"Oh, sorry. Got another call. Take good care of Berthea, now. 'Bye."

"It's wonderful."

"They say all the farms on our road will have one by summer."

"Don't you have to go to work today?"

"Not until noon. The furnace acted up and Mr. Woods called to let me know. The ring almost sent me through the ceiling."

"I have something to show you, too." After the words left her mouth, Addie had second thoughts. But it was too late. Berthea bundled up and gaped when Addie slid the heavy wooden door down its track. Then she rushed in and opened the passenger door.

"Why, this car's in much better condition than the Chevy. Wherever did you get it?"

"I can't say. It's been in storage."

"Ah . . ." Berthea ran her hand over the leather dashboard. "Maybe I can guess. Aunt Alvina?"

Addie sealed her lips.

"Does Harold know?"

"No, he would never approve. I brought it here that day George drove you down to Bill and Sue's."

"This car is yours, title and all?"

"Yes. When you taught me to drive, I had no idea, and I can't . . . I wish I could explain."

Berthea's thoughtful look lasted a long time. "God has a way of providing what we need before we need it sometimes." Addie wanted an explanation, but decided against asking.

"Take me for a ride, why don't you?"

Relief washed through Addie. Berthea thought Aunt Alvina bequeathed her the car. It wasn't true, but she'd kept the secret.

You don't have to say everything you think. Wasn't that Kate's advice? Addie looked guilt in the eye and watched it shrink. Another snitch of Kate's wisdom came to mind, something about outer and inner words. Right now, she could let outer words carry more weight than the constant negative stream that flowed through her mind.

Just this morning she memorized something about that from the book of Romans. *There is therefore now no condemnation to them which are in Christ Jesus, who walk not after the flesh, but after the Spirit.* Harold used this passage in his Thanksgiving sermon.

"To walk after the flesh paves the easy route to perdition. Giving our bodies to fleshly desires like seeking money, physical pleasures and self-gratification instead of the will of God . . ."

That morning, she wondered if this might be one reason their attempts to have a child became so emotionless over the past months. Did Harold believe being together as husband and wife was sinful?

The passage revolved around freedom from condemnation rather than what it meant to walk after the flesh, although Harold focused his sermon on condemning human needs and desires. But hadn't Jane said her besetting sin was being so secretive?

What if "the flesh" included that, our own harsh self-judgment, and a narrow view of God and life? Kate would understand the difference, but Harold would say she misinterpreted Scripture, and when he came home from the seminary, he would have some theological education to support his view.

Addie shuddered. His time away was one-third over. She took a deep breath and inserted the key in the coupe. After one false start, the engine cooperated, and she steered north down the center of the road. The seat gave a more comfortable ride than Jane's Studebaker, and Berthea's smile widened.

"Good springs, Addie. It's odd I never saw Alvina drive this."

"Um . . . I'm going to turn around up there, in that driveway."

"All right, take your time."

The abandoned farmstead's steep grade tightened her shoulders, but she shifted without the car stalling, and turned to Berthea. "From the tracks, it looks like somebody's been here lately."

"Alfred keeps his cattle here during the winter."

A circle around the windmill sent them back toward the road, with Berthea navigating. "Nothing's coming from this way."

The wheels spun on the last few feet, but they made it onto the road. Addie shifted past white fields with golden brown stubble etching zigzag lines to the horizon.

When she parked, Berthea accepted her invitation to tea. "How will you tell Harold?"

"The will said I can't give him any details, and he won't like that."

Berthea shook her head. "You're right on that account. But you have a full three months before he comes home. We'll put our heads together. Who knows how things could change by then? By the way, has Harold written you yet?"

Addie shook her head, and Berthea glanced around the kitchen. "I really like what you've done in here. The yellow and white appeal to the eye. That dark wainscoting was so gloomy. Harold didn't bother you any more about it after that first morning, did he?"

"No." It seemed so natural to discuss him with Berthea now. Just a year ago at this time, Addie would never have guessed their relationship would change so much.

"And you're happy with the results?"

"Oh, yes. Although at the time . . ."

"I know—but you plowed through it, Addie. You've been an inspiration for me, you know?" Berthea took her time with her tea, and after she put her coat on, she hesitated with a thoughtful expression.

"Change is hard work. People like Harold aren't ever going to like it, but that doesn't mean we should back away from our ideas. Wish I'd known that thirty years ago. Things might've been different."

Addie held the door open for her, and Berthea gave her a confident smile. "Don't you worry about Harold. I have a feeling everything will work out."

Chapter Thirty

A lazy, late Sunday afternoon after a lovely nap made the perfect time for letter writing. Even with Kate's bad news, Addie figured it would be easier to write her than to answer Harold's recent note. For the fourth or fifth time, she reread the single, typed page.

January 24, 1943

To my wife,

My first class, The History of Methodism, makes me proud to be Methodist. All things have a method, as I always have believed. Our professor centers on three tenets: Shun evil and avoid partaking in wicked deeds at all cost; perform kind acts as much as possible, and abide by the edicts of God the Almighty Father.

It will take a lifetime to fulfill these. If I cannot be on the front lines, then this is second best.

Another professor here, Dr. Wesley, speaks boldly about marriage, and believes great tension between man and wife can reduce one's chances of procreation. He attributes most marital trouble to disobedience to clear-cut biblical instructions.

He says his own wife had many lessons to learn, which gives me hope. But are you willing? I had given up, but now have begun to pray for a miracle.

Our early morning prayer group keeps in mind the troops. Many of us were denied, so we volunteer at the railway station USO.

The soldiers have eyes only for the girls, but we do the heavy lifting and cleaning, and sometimes hold chapel. You might be surprised how many attend.

You don't keep up with the war news, but in the Pacific, our forces have finally attacked. I still hold out hope to join the seven million now serving.

Keep an eye out for Mother, for I fear she attempts to replay her youth with George Miller. A widower of long standing, he ought to squelch fleshly desires, just as our troops must.

I hope this winter is not too hard on the ewes and sows. We need their litters for hard cash.

Harold

If he knew how much George helped her with the sheep and pigs, or how happy Berthea was, Harold would be even more irritated. Addie closed her eyes and pictured George's smile. Such a wonderful man, but Harold only saw his "fleshly desires."

She gritted her teeth. "How can he believe I don't keep up with the war? What could she write about the ever-present foreboding that filled her since Alexandre and Roy's deaths?

And what could she write about Harold's prayers for a miracle? At least she agreed with his premise—a breakthrough would require divine intervention. But since he blamed their marriage troubles on her, he meant she must change.

"Change ... oh, Harold, I *am* changing, but you're not going to like the new me, either."

His meaning baffled her, and she couldn't share what he'd written with anyone but Kate. Did he think she failed to conceive because she painted the kitchen? If obedience were required, most babies would never come into this world.

But what he said about the war bothered her most. Just three days ago, she'd received personal war news about Alexandre, yet Harold insisted she didn't care. Kate said it exactly—he was convinced he knew her mind.

She tried to make sense of the part about Wesley, but maybe Jane was right that making sense of things didn't always work. Instead of reacting, Addie listed the temperatures for the past five days, the news about the animals, and the bills she'd paid.

She twiddled her pen between her fingers. She couldn't mention Berthea and George . . . could it be this hard to write her own husband a letter? Finally she ended with, "You're wrong about me and the war news. Have you heard Roy Owens died in the Pacific? And Alexandre has been killed, too."

Tempted to add, "I hope you're happy now," she signed her name and sealed the envelope.

George entered the yard, so she stoked the furnace, bundled up and went outdoors. As usual, he whistled through the stalls, and when she carried water for the chickens, he took the pail from her with a headshake.

"No kind of weather for you to be out. Sometimes I think you take better care of these animals than you do of yourself." The look he gave her mixed sternness and concern, the way Aunt Alvina sometimes looked at Kate.

"Go in and get warmed up. Have a cup of tea and enjoy the sunset."

Before going inside, Addie petted Missy and Daisy. Now, for Kate's letter. What could encourage her at such a time? Maybe everyday things would be best. Her whole life had changed, but not their friendship.

January 28, 1943

Dear Kate,

Your sad news arrived yesterday. I had so hoped Alexandre survived the crash. I'm glad you two could share Christmas—you kept believing he'd come, and he did.

Berthea and Jane cried for him. Mrs. M visited First Methodist on Sunday, and her chin quivered at the news.

I wish you were here, so I could halve your sorrow. As usual, I imagine you active, working through everything walking to work, typing like crazy, and stamping out those blaaaaasted incendiaries.

Tell me about London's birds. Is Mrs. T's courtyard home to some over the cold months? Or don't they fly south like they do here? Our cardinals never tire of proclaiming ownership of our grove.

George visits Berthea every night—the porch light still shines when I go to bed. This would trouble Harold beyond telling. His one letter bothers me, but I'll save it for later, when you're up for a puzzle.

Berthea's relief to have him in St. Louis rivals mine. I'd never have believed she'd become an ally.

Does Evelyn know about Alexandre? Can you talk with Mrs. T? Does anyone there speak his name? I'd think that might bring you solace.

Here's my favorite memory of him. We all searched for something, maybe a flashlight to take to that little room above your aunt's carriage house. Anyway, remember when Alexandre pulled quite a large corset from behind the washing machine? We laughed 'til we were sick.

He loved life, and made a good partner for you. Maybe eloping wasn't so impertinent—that decision gave you more time together. As you often remind me, don't be too hard on yourself.

I'll return to local news. Due to her new job, Berthea's had a phone installed. She invites me over every evening, and usually I go—why sit alone with the war news?

For Christmas, she gave me a sack of tea, and said she should have braved Harold's wrath before. Still, I dare not show her his letter. I said I'd mention it later, but have changed my mind. I'm enclosing it, and once you figure out what he means about childbearing, please tell me. Then destroy it, please.

Since I cannot visit London, I'm scrubbing the dour living room and dining room walls. The next time I get to town, I'll buy some paint. Berthea offered to trade her hardware coupons for my gasoline ones.

George loves the lambs and baby pigs. He whistles the whole time he does the chores before his route and again in late afternoon.

He says sitting in the mail truck is making him fat and old, and he hopes I don't mind him taking over. Mind? Would I mind if rising temperatures spared us a grim February and March, or a mighty wind transported me to Westbourne Grove?

I've run out of news. When I think of you (all day long), I pray you cling to your best memories.

Love to you always,

Addie

Thinking of the chocolate rationing in London, Addie baked a double batch of soldier cookies for Kate and took the box to Berthea's for George. At the last minute, she grabbed a bag of walnuts to crack while they talked.

"I'm glad you came over. George had to sort mail tonight, so I'll get this package to him tomorrow." Berthea set her embroidery hoop aside and turned off the radio.

She scooped nuts from Addie's sack and reached for her picks. Addie cracked a walnut, scraped around its edge and dropped the nutmeat into a bowl. They worked in silence for a while before Berthea cleared her throat.

"What would you think if George and I were to marry?"

"I'd think you got exactly what you deserve."

"People will say I didn't wait long enough after Orville died, and Harold will balk for sure. But that's one reason for us to marry soon.

May as well let the town talk about us now as later. By the time Harold comes home, we'll be old news and George's servant heart will have won over the church members. Harold won't be able to find anyone to take his side."

"Take his side?"

"I've realized since Orville died that Harold's intent on arguing. Guess I didn't see it before, since we didn't have to work on farm business together. Surely you've noticed when someone disagrees with him, he attempts to win them over?" Berthea grabbed another walnut.

"As I look back, he's always been that way, while Bill accepted others' views. I meant to treat them the same, but after Harold's accident, I wish . . ."

Addie picked at a nutmeat. Most of the time, instead of trying to win her over, Harold ignored her. His self-confidence made him effective on the debate team where, of course, he aimed to win. But as far as she knew, he had only Joe for a friend.

"Have you set a date?"

"February 2, Groundhog Day. I've never put much stock in that old legend. Who cares if a hairy rodent sees his shadow that day or not? No amount of wishing or hocus-pocus will change winter's schedule."

"Why, that's only a few days away. Can I help you get ready?"

"We want you to stand up with us, dear. I almost drowned in my own self-pity the last few years, but I've always admired your spunk, Addie. Would you witness our vows?"

"I'd be glad to. What else could I do?"

"How about baking one of your walnut cakes? I'll bring a couple of pies for afterward." Berthea rubbed her hands together and leaned closer.

"The ceremony will be really small, and keep this a secret, all right? Harold wrote that he's discovered the Rural Letter Carriers' Association is fascist, and George was voted in as the county president. I think that means I become the Women's Auxiliary president when I marry him. Harold will have a fit."

Berthea made a clucking sound. "That boy. If he found out, he might try to stop the ceremony."

"Your secret is safe with me. Besides, Harold has only written once since he left."

Berthea's lips formed a thin line, but she said no more. The nutmeats formed a growing mound in her bowl, and the clock's comfortable *tick-tock* enveloped their labor. Brown stain covered their forefingers and thumbs, and the almost bitter black walnut odor permeated the small kitchen.

"Can't say as I like how these taste all by themselves, but I can't imagine your glory cake without them. And they're good for what ails you, my aunt always used to say.""

About twenty minutes later, George roared into the yard and they heard his door slam shut. A while later, Berthea smiled.

"He must be checking the sheep. Warms my heart the way he's taken this place right into his heart."

In a few minutes, she answered a bang on the door. There stood George with a wet gray mass in his arms.

"So glad I stopped out there. Can you quick warm up a bottle? Gotta see to the mother."

"Ooh, my." Berthea received the quivering lamb. "Addie, there's a black nipple in the pantry, top shelf on the right. Would you heat up some milk, please?"

A few minutes later, Addie whet the baby's appetite with warm milk on her fingertip. Then she offered the bottle. Berthea fixed a blanket bed near the stove and heated a towel in the oven.

"It'll be a long evening, I expect."

"Do you want me to stay around?"

"No, thanks. George will handle this like he handles everything."

Addie bundled up and closed the door behind her. Frozen mud replaced the afternoon thaw, a bitter wind whipped the farmyard, and the frosty back porch offered slim welcome.

She left her coat on a kitchen chair, stoked the furnace, and wandered through the downstairs. This big old house with its high ceilings and crown molding, deep window seat and beautiful oak floors, seemed far too large tonight. The upstairs was so drafty, why not read and fall asleep on the davenport?

Bunching Mama's quilt around her, she opened a poetry volume. Suddenly, Mama's voice flitted through her mind, from those days just before she died.

Your grandmother made this quilt, Addie, stitch by stitch. I still remember her telling me how it needed an odd number of squares for the design to be centered. That didn't make sense at the time, but now I understand. Sunshine and shadows—even and odd—everything needs balance.

Addie leaned into the cushion and let her mind wander before she flipped to one of Emily Dickinson's poems.

"Hope is the thing with feathers, that perches in the soul, and sings the words without the tune, and never minds at all."

In the living room's shadows, an image rose from last March, the night Addie found Harold out in the barn, sleeping with a newborn orphan lamb in his arms. Right then, she'd known that she still loved his well-concealed compassion.

No matter how he raged about the draft board, blamed her or shunned her, she'd still believed in that side of him. Even as his shows of tenderness became more miserly and finally disappeared altogether, she'd believed.

Tears dropped onto her book, so she switched off the light and buried her face in a pillow. She'd had tears that night, too, yet still hoped everything would work out.

But in Harold's indifferent letter, everything depended on her changing, while she felt exactly the opposite. A year ago, seeing him change seemed possible, but not anymore. That *thing with feathers* seemed to have found another roosting place.

She hugged Mama's—Grandma's—quilt close. . . . *an odd number of squares . . . to be centered.* Maybe that's how Norman grew so wise—all the oddities of his life, the war and his choices afterward, melded together into a clear focus as he matured.

But with Harold, something went missing along the way. Somehow, his challenges in life refused to meld together, rendering him capable of sending her that indifferent letter. *Indifferent*—a fitting word for her psychologist friend in London to analyze.

Chapter Thirty-one

*O*n February second, a beautiful walnut glory cake accompanied Addie down the Halberton road in her red coupe. She couldn't stop smiling, because Berthea and George made such a photograph of happiness. And she felt a little smug—Harold would give anything to know about this wedding.

Berthea's comment about him trying to change people stuck in her mind. Did he think he must persuade her to want a child? He had no idea how even suckling that orphan lamb the other night ignited her desire to mother a little one.

Turning down Jane's driveway, Addie punched the steering wheel. "And he thinks I don't care about the war. Doesn't knitting sweaters and growing a victory garden count for anything?"

Jane made her careful way down a recently shoveled path, and Addie scurried out to open the passenger door. No sign of Simon today.

"Good to get out of the house. George shoveled us out and promised to stop by again tomorrow to clear out some more." Jane heaved into the seat with a mighty groan.

"Best man I know. Used to bring the mail with a team and buggy or on horseback, even came on skis a couple of times. First car I ever saw was his Model T."

She caught her breath. "Once a blizzard snowed him in up north, but he made it through. That day, he stopped for a cup of coffee. Said things could be worse, and I knew he was talking about his time overseas.

"He served in France, only he was years younger than Norman. Joined up at sixteen, nobody even questioned him, and they put him in the Prisoner of War Escort company.

"People have no idea how much he does around here, in his quiet way. Mighty proud to have him for a neighbor, and I'm so glad for Berthea, too. Have you heard we'll have telephones by next winter?"

The right side of the front window frosted over—clearly, Jane hadn't talked with anyone for a long time. She regaled Addie right up to the door of First Methodist.

"Such a bright, sunny day for their wedding. I'm so glad that storm gave out last night. Simon gets awfully antsy being cooped up, but the walk between the cabin and the house helps. I set him to cracking hickory nuts this afternoon, and he's arranging them in long lines on his table."

The high windows shed radiance over the sanctuary. Everyone in the small gathering wore a smile. Sue was about to deliver, so they didn't make the trip, and most of George's children lived too far away. But his son brought his wife, their two daughters, and little Willie. When Willie saw Berthea, he leaped from his daddy's arms and raced to her.

The school principal, Mr. Woods, handed his wife a corsage to pin on Berthea's dress and a fill-in pastor from Cedar Rapids performed the ceremony. He cleared his throat to still the chatter. "We gather here today in the sight of God to join this man and this woman in holy matrimony."

He paused to look George and Berthea full in the face. "I suspect no one in this room would take exception to your intent."

Berthea glanced at George, then at Addie with a secret message. *If only the pastor knew how much a certain young man would take exception.*

"I, George, take you, Berthea, to be my wedded wife, to have and to hold from this day forward, for better or for worse, in sickness and in health, to love and to cherish . . . until death do us part . . ."

Berthea dabbed her eyes with her hankie. So did Addie and Jane. There was no doubt George meant every word. After Berthea's vows, Addie signed the marriage license and Berthea embraced her.

"Oh, thank you, Addie. No matter what, we'll always be family." George took Berthea's elbow and half-turned to a well wisher.

"I'll go down and pour the coffee—take your time, Berthea." The basement was warmer than usual, since someone left the heat on after church this morning. Addie sliced cake and pie onto plates, the fresh vows swirling in her mind. *For better or worse, in sickness and in health . . .*

Surely Jane lived that meaning with the peculiar illness Simon suffered. Simon's image came to mind, intent over his growing rows of hickory nuts.

To love and to cherish . . . George's expression touched her more than anything. Mrs. Morfordson would take time to discuss what the word *cherish* really meant.

The Woods came down first, and Mr. Woods shook Addie's hand. "We hear there's some scrumptious desserts down here. You must be Addie? You must've graduated just before we moved here."

Mrs. Woods extended her hand. "Oh, what a lovely cake. Who made that?"

Before Addie could answer, her husband went on. "I appreciate having your mother-in-law handling the office, but I suspect that makes your workload heavier?"

"No, not really, and she loves her new job, sir."

"Good. She definitely lightens *my* workload. Oh, my—pie and cake, too. Suppose I'll have to taste both."

After cleaning up the kitchen, Addie drove Jane home. The festivities only increased Jane's talkativeness. "Never met the Woods before, or George's son. Such cute little ones, but his wife seems standoffish."

"Maybe she's a little shy?"

"Yes, probably as friendly as pie in other circumstances. Some folks close down in public places, don't they? So that little fellow, Willie—he's the one Simon brought out of the cornfield?"

"Yes. I don't know what we'd have done if he hadn't found him."

"Wonders never cease." Jane shook her head as she opened her door. "If only I had an idea what goes through Simon's head. How could he have known know Willie was in trouble that day?"

"It's a mystery, isn't it? I'm just grateful he did."

"Would you like to come in for a while?"

"Thanks, but I'd like to be home when George brings his things. Maybe I can help him move in."

When he and Berthea drove in with his boxes and a suitcase, Addie carried a few things. When she left, Berthea joined her out on the steps.

"I can't believe it's all over already. Harold would be beside himself if he knew a German Lutheran not only joined the Methodist Church today, but moved in right across the drive."

"That's for sure."

"Thank you for being such an important part of our wedding, Addie."

"Thanks for asking me. Enjoy the rest of your day." Addie went home to the quiet house and tried to nap, but those vows circled like vultures in summer. *Cherish . . . cherish.* Finally, she looked it up in the dictionary.

> *From French cher (dear)*
> *To hold dear, feel or show affection for;*
> *Cultivate with care and affection: nurture*
> *SYN: appreciate*

There was only one thing to do—write Kate to discuss this, the way they used to tackle vocabulary words in literature class. She settled in the window seat and wrote until afternoon shadows fell and she heard the barn door open. She counted the pages she'd amassed, amazed to find six.

Reading her musings produced a lump in her throat and stopped her short. "I can't send this. All this talk of cherishing someone will make Kate even lonelier for Alexandre, and Harold must never see it, either."

She tucked the pages into her notebook of quotes and sayings. "I'll throw this out before he comes home."

George crossed toward the chickens, so she joined him. "Have to visit my girls today, even if you're doing all my work."

He chuckled. "They'll be happier to see you than me." The hens clucked up a storm at the entrance of two people, and George made cackling noises to them.

"You don't mind the chickens, do you?"

"Mind? Nope. Can't say as I mind anything about farming. Why?"

"Harold hates them. He says they're women's work."

George's chuckle incited the hens again. "The way I see it, manure is manure. Chicken manure smells worse than most, I have to admit."

"You grew up on a farm?"

"Sort of. After my folks died in a fire, Grandpa and Grandma took us in. I'd always liked visiting them, but being there all the time was even better. There's something comforting about farm animals."

Addie followed him back to the barn to pet Missy and Daisy, and for the first time, Missy accepted her touch without startling. "Why you good, good girl. We're going to be great friends, I can feel it."

"Ready?" George shut the barn door behind them. "This day's a new beginning for me. Besides marrying a fine woman and moving to the country, I'll see more of you now. Coming over for supper? You're always welcome."

"I think Berthea might like you all to herself on your wedding day." He colored under his deep tan and turned toward home. Halfway across the yard, Addie realized her throat no longer harbored a boulder.

* * *

As if she had an inkling Addie would come, Jane poured tea. At the grove's edge, Simon aimed a long stick like a gun. After chatting about the wedding and the weather, she introduced a new subject.

"Last night I listened to *You Can't Do Business With Hitler* from the war information office. Douglas Miller spent fifteen years in Berlin, and says either we wipe out Hitlerism or they destroy us. That can only mean more suffering by the time all this is over."

"Does Simon listen to the shows?"

"Usually not. They upset him something terrible, but last night, I let him, and you see the results." She gestured out the window.

"Does he know how to use a gun?" Too late, Addie recalled Jane's brother's death and wished she hadn't asked.

"He used to hunt pheasants and rabbits, but it's been a while since he showed any interest." Jane nudged a plate of shortbread her way, and the mellow, buttery concoction satisfied Addie's hunger for something homemade and sweet.

She took another piece and they observed Simon as daylight faded. Close to the house now, he yelled "Pow, Pow!"

Jane groaned. "That's the last show he'll hear for a good long time."

February 29, 1943

Dear Addie,

More bombing here, willy-nilly. As Mrs. T says, no rhyme or reason to it, and the stories of death and destruction continue. The weather's unseasonably mild, violets peek out, W.C. and Roosevelt met in Casablanca, and we've gained control of Libya.

Sorry I haven't written. I've been sick for a week. A cold? No. Sick to my stomach, mostly in the mornings. A few days ago, Mrs. T asked with great care if I'd had my monthly since Christmas.

Being dignified has its shortcomings. I'd never heard her stammer, but silently applauded her courage as the inchworm of truth squirmed down my spine.

At first, I couldn't stop crying, but not all sad tears. This baby will be Alexandre's legacy, although I still fall into a dreadful panic at times.

After taking me to a doctor at an almost-free clinic, Mrs. T begged me to stay home, but it's not as if I'm contagious. I must get out.

Mrs. T grieves the anniversary of Singapore. Her circle knew some of the officers killed, and now so many wives are imprisoned. These Brits had such faith in their Navy—it's hard to accept.

Coal is scarce, the coke supply late, and even fish have become scanty. The office overruns with deadlines, which helps me cope with everything.

Sorry for all the negatives here, and my scattered frame of mind. Your goofy memory of Alexandre with Aunt Alvina's massive corset made me laugh out loud. I'd forgotten that day.

Berthea and Mrs. M sent gracious sympathy letters. You were right about Mrs. M and John Donne.

Friends always,

Kate

On March sixteenth, Addie woke with Kate's news pulsing through her. Two hours earlier, she heard George shut the chicken coop door, but turned over and slept until the sun rose. Harold would have slapped her backside and sent her out of bed.

The very thought motivated her to linger a while longer. When she finally went downstairs, the wrinkled sheets in the back bedroom stared up at her, waiting to be ironed. But Addie tossed her head.

"I never slept on ironed sheets before I married Harold. We were lucky to have sheets at all." She punched the soft cotton pile. "The world won't end if you never see the hot side of my iron again."

In the living room, the new rosy paint she applied last week made the day so much brighter. Outside, Old Brown barked at a teasing squirrel, a spring breeze warmed the air with the scent of change, and in unspoken cooperation with the season, the hens already increased their egg count.

Last week, Berthea's newspaper announced the onset of shoe rationing. Surely, England rationed them, too, although Kate hadn't mentioned it.

Kate Isaacs sick and scared—hard to imagine. She always found her way. If only they could drink tea together this morning. Sunlight bathed the kitchen in warmth and Addie's prayer ascended with the steam. "Help her. Please help her."

But her petition echoed back as she sank into a chair. Bright rays splayed the tablecloth and warmed her hands. She rubbed her thumbnail as the water kettle rattled above the flame, and then a suggestion swept her.

"*You* help her."

A shiver traced her shoulders. The injunction seemed so real, it might have been spoken aloud. An idea had taken root in her mind the moment she first read Kate's letter. Day by day it grew, but Addie kept it at bay.

Now, she studied the objects of her daily life—her enamel dishpan, the terrycloth towel on its hook, the bright-eyed cowgirl on her egg money can, surrounded by these spanking white walls. She let out a long breath.

Energy stoked her imagination, and she ran upstairs to change into a shirtwaist and sweater. Before she left her bedroom, she grabbed the photo Aunt Alvina took so long ago. In today's sunshine, her resemblance to Myrna Loy finally came through. Why not keep this on the kitchen table where she could enjoy looking at it?

A younger Kate eyed Addie from the photo while she poured herself more tea, and a breathless sense of destiny danced inside her. What did this inner stirring mean?

With each swallow, she breathed, "Show me."

The outdoors called to her. Even from here, green peeped up in her flowerbeds. Mama would say she bargained with fate to go out without her winter jacket, but Addie passed the coat hooks without guilt.

"It's all right, Mama. Half of spring's joy is shedding our heavy winter coats."

As if led by an unseen force, she made her way to the shed where she parked the coupe and screeched the door open. The dimness of the enclosed space gave way to beckoning sunlight, and Addie tapped her fingers on the cool fender. With an odd mix of tension and exhilaration, she slid under the wheel.

When she pushed on the accelerator, tingles like thousands of lights radiated her arms. The coupe's bright red exterior agreed with the sunshine. She drove south past Jane and Simons', past the turn to Norman's house, and beyond Main Street. Within minutes, the Red Cross Office came into view.

A new window poster featuring a black and white photograph of high browed, clear-eyed Myrna Loy sent a tremor through Addie. But more than the Queen of Hollywood's turned-up nose and perfect lips obsessed Valentino, Barrymore, and Spencer Tracy. One morning during their senior year, Kate had supplied the details.

"Did you hear? Myrna sent Gable away for 'getting fresh.' What a woman, eh? The reporter said even President Roosevelt admires her."

After Kate moved in with Aunt Alvina, the two girls attended every one of Myrna Loy's box-office hit. For some reason, Kate's impassioned pleas worked with Mama.

"Aunt Alvina won't let me go alone, ma'am. But her arthritis won't allow her to sit through a feature, either. I *need* Addie to go, pleeease, Mrs. Shields?"

Presenting her ticket to the theater clerk, Addie felt like a princess. Plunging her hand into the warm, salty bag of buttered popcorn included in the outing made her forget all about her dad disappearing for days, someone bringing a box of groceries to their door, and the mice scrabbling in the attic. She even forgot Mr. Andrews stopping in again, and Mama sobbing on Ruthie's shoulder.

Kate informed her of each new moving picture coming to town. During their senior year, Harold's attitude put a damper on the outings, but the girls still attended Saturday afternoon matinees when he was busy working in the field.

One day, Kate produced a newspaper clipping about Miss Loy's courageous remarks against Hitler's treatment of Jews. "She's suspending her acting career for wartime commitments. How gutsy is that? She and Charlie Chaplain head the Nazi black list."

Today, more than a provocative actress gazed back at Addie from the shiny poster catching morning rays from the east. Myrna Loy's determined expression exuded willpower, strength and self-sacrifice.

How many times had she and Kate mimicked that look? But this morning, it was Myrna Loy's courage Addie craved.

Join Miss Loy. Work the canteens as she does in Hollywood. Do your part for the war effort. Get on Hitler's black list!

The powerful invitation became more than a dream when Elma Crandall unlocked the office promptly at eight. The middle-aged matron carefully sprinkled sand from a bucket to protect patrons from thick sidewalk frost. When she spied Addie, she waved her in.

Only a few people were out, mainly in front of the café and the Mercantile. One or two cars chugged by, and a pick-up Addie recognized as Maynard Lundene's. When she waved, he raised his hand, but his face showed no recognition. Did Kate share that same vacant look now, since they'd both lost a loved one to the war?

Addie hurried across the glaze. Long ago, she learned that crossing ice goes better if you head straight for your destination without hesitating.

In the well-organized office, Elma looked up from straightening the literature table.

"Hello, there. Addie, isn't it? Need some more yarn?"

"Yes, and some for Jane Pike. But I have other business, too."

Mrs. Crandall's eyes widened. "How may I help you?"

"A friend of mine needs me. I'd like to find a way to London."

"Do you wish to volunteer your way there?"

The easy way she asked made Addie gulp. "Could I do that?"

"Quite possibly. Volunteers attach to ships, and you could become one. In London, the Rainbow Corner Club welcomes volunteers. They serve upwards of fifty thousand meals a day. Is your friend incapacitated, so you would need to stay by her side at all times?"

"Oh, no. But she . . . uh . . .lost her husband a month ago and . . ."

"It's okay. I don't need to know all the details. I'll make a phone call to our headquarters and see where you might fit in. How soon could you go?"

"What would be the earliest possibility?"

"I'm not sure, but I'll find out. How can I get in touch with you?"

"I'll drive back into town this afternoon."

"I hope to have some word for you by then. We're open until six."

Addie stepped back in a daze. She might hear today. This was far more than she hoped for when she entered.

"And here's your yarn. We just received a new shipment."

"Thank you. I . . . I'm shocked things could go so quickly."

"It's a hurting world, with no end to the needs." Elma raised her shoulders and eyebrows at the same time. "We do our best to put able-bodied volunteers to work as soon as we can. When they sent me here, I thought there wouldn't be much activity, but that's not true at all."

The thin ice already melted, and springtime seemed tangible. For passersby, this must seem like any other day, but Addie's fingers shook as she turned the key. A jittery now-or-never awareness enveloped her, and sent her toward the school, though she hadn't been inside since she graduated.

But this couldn't wait. For the first time, she considered the practicalities of such an undertaking. What if she could leave in a month, or in two weeks? Whenever it was, she needed Berthea's support.

Outside Norman's house sat a child's red wagon. A wave of homesickness for him ran through Addie. It seemed impossible that last year at this time, she hadn't even met him. After the first visit, she hadn't wanted to go back, but now she treasured that unique friendship.

Norman taught her so much, and knowing him led her to this very morning, when all things seem possible. He gave her far more than money and the coupe. He broadened her outlook and motivated her to believe in herself.

For a minute after she parked in front of the school, she stared at the red brick building. Having Mrs. Morfordson for English classes proved the difference one person could make. Their senior year, she and Kate reveled in the nuances of literature and history, but also in Mrs. M's attention.

The wide central hallway welcomed her, and on tiptoe, Addie peeked through the office window, where Berthea sat with the attendance list, looking even younger than on her wedding day. So much had happened since last March, with Orville's death, Harold's job at First Methodist and getting to know Norman.

Then George and Berthea started seeing each other, and now they were married. The sweep of all these changes rolled over Addie, even as transformation knocked on her own door.

"Things are changing for me, too. I own my own car and have more savings than my eggs would have produced in a lifetime." Breathing the words strengthened her. But a tall high school student who looked a lot like Harold approached, and she suddenly lost her breath.

It was as if he'd looked into her heart again. Sudden negative thoughts assailed her. *What do you think you're doing, anyway? How can you consider leaving, when I'll be home soon to plant the crops? The farm is the only place for you. It's Kate who was born for adventure.*

Perspiration broke out on Addie's forehead. Could she sneak out before anyone saw her? She closed her eyes and forced herself back against the cool brick wall. Then a door cracked nearby, and Berthea's cheerful voice reached her.

"Why Addie!" She clutched her throat. "Is something wrong?"

"I . . . would you have a few minutes to talk?"

"Go on in and sit down. I'll be right back."

Chapter Thirty-two

*B*erthea's cramped office once housed a cloakroom. An instantaneous memory overwhelmed Addie—the clinging odor of wet wool, muddy rubber boots and sweaty boys. In this space, those boys jabbed each other and the girls whispered secrets. But for her first few years of school, her classmates treated her like a stranger.

Then Kate came to town, and someone finally shared secrets with her. She didn't even recall how their friendship began. It took some time for her to feel comfortable, but she gradually let a few of her own secrets slip out.

Settled into an oak chair near Berthea's desk, her pulse drummed in her ears. If Berthea didn't understand, what would she do? She glanced around the walls, pausing on a framed World War I discharge just like Norman's, and his advice calmed her.

Don't have t' know everything 'bout the future to do somethin' today. When ya feel somethin' strong, it's time to act.

"There now." Berthea's eyes, brighter against her royal blue cardigan, encouraged Addie to begin.

"You know Kate lost Alexandre, but . . ." Addie lowered her voice. "Can anyone else hear me?"

Fingers laced under her chin, Berthea leaned forward. Addie wrapped her leg around the chair rung and whispered. "She saw Alexandre on Christmas Day, and she's expecting a baby now."

Berthea's eyebrows arched, but she didn't frown. "Humm. . . "

"This will be so hard for her in a strange place and . . ."

Berthea's chin rose a fraction of an inch.

"With Harold gone to St. Louis, I . . . " *How can you expect my mother to bless this strange state of affairs?* Addie rubbed an old burn mark on her wrist. The wall clock ticked louder and louder.

"I might want to go to London to help Kate." The words streamed out like a fast train. Intrigued by Berthea's impassive expression, Addie plunged ahead. "I've been thinking about this since I read Kate's letter, but the idea of volunteering with the Red Cross came to me this morning. The lady down at the office . . . she said such a thing is possible, Berthea."

"Well." Berthea glanced over her shoulder at Mr. Wood's office door. "I wish I had half your spirit. Being a school secretary is one thing, but to work on a Red Cross ship, take on a newborn baby, and London . . ."

Her encouraging hand squeeze kept Addie in reality. She could hardly believe her ears as Berthea continued.

"If you think God wants you to do this, maybe you ought to go. You've got a level head on your shoulders, so I know you're not being flighty."

"You . . . even with Harold coming home soon?"

Berthea dabbed her eyes. "This wretched war . . . Your news from Kate, how they go without butter and applaud at a packet of cheese or tins of sausage over there, and now she's expecting a baby . . . Things are so dire, and you're as resourceful as can be. I do believe your instinct is right. Kate needs you."

"But I thought . . ." Addie faltered. "My garden. I would hate to leave it . . ."

"George and I can tend that." She caught her upper lip with her teeth. "We can always ask Jane's advice."

"I'd hate to leave her, too."

"I haven't been much of a friend to her, but I'm adjusted to work now, and to George. Those are good changes, but our whole nation, I mean the whole world . . . " But she said nothing about Harold.

"I'll find out more this afternoon. I don't know how Harold will . . ."

"Has he written you lately?"

"No."

"I should have told you right away. A letter came a couple of weeks ago, and . . ." Berthea's pause lasted forever. "This will be a shock, but a St. Louis infantry unit has registered Harold."

Addie felt her jaw drop like the power takeoff lever. What she saw in Berthea's eyes stunned her—relief and pain.

"I've been hoping he'd let you know, but George and I had decided to tell you tonight. Harold's unit deploys in April." Her cheeks fired. "I apologize. Harold has never . . . I should have known something was wrong, starting with the county fair when you were first married."

"The fair?"

"Don't you remember, your first summer with us? Harold said Bledsoe women always bring canned goods to the fair. That should have alerted me, but I was so . . ."

Addie vaguely recalled seeing her name on jars of vegetables and preserves she'd never touched. At the time, she thought Harold had used foresight to keep her from being embarrassed. But now, Berthea's other news consumed her.

"A unit has accepted Harold?"

"Must be that he was away from Iowa and his agricultural restriction. It's awful he didn't tell you. Here, take a tissue, dear."

"I'm sure he wrote you because of the farm . . . "

"Don't make excuses for him. Hasn't he written you at all?"

"Once, and I sent him reports on the stock." In the hallway, boisterous students hurried outdoors for recess. "Actually, it's not much different when he's here."

Berthea sniffed. "I'm so sorry about his behavior—you deserve better. I wish there was something I could do."

A mix of emotions swarmed Addie. Harold's dreams were coming true at last, but he hadn't bothered to tell her. Her limbs went weak, and the walls seemed to shrink in on her. She was a hen's feather floating on air. Berthea might have to see her to the door.

* * *

"Mrs. Harold Bledsoe?"
"Yes."

"We have an order to run a telephone line and install the apparatus. Not supposed to do this 'til warmer weather, but as long as we're out here working on your mother-in-law's system . . . "

"Do you need to come inside?"

"Not for a few hours. If you show us where you'd like the telephone, we can come in later, if you don't mind."

Considering all the earth-shattering things going on today, this decision seemed about as important as the pigs' swill. Addie let the men in and turned a circle in the kitchen.
"Maybe between the window and the cupboard?"

"Should work." One of the workers made a mark with a thick pencil. "You sure it's okay if we install it when you're not here?"

"Yes, but I won't be gone long."

The men left and Addie flopped on the davenport, exhausted. Less than two weeks ago, she painted this room. The rosy hue soothed her, though Harold would hate it.

Now, she would have a telephone right in the kitchen. And the Army had accepted Harold—for the eightieth time today, she rehearsed the news.

The davenport's dry velvet scratched against her skin, and she closed her eyes to a whirlwind of images. Even as she'd listened to that old internal tirade outside Berthea's office, Harold had been happily anticipating his deployment.

A twinge of hurt crept in, but compared to facing him in the chicken house, this seemed minor. One thing he'd shown her without a doubt: he had no intention of treating her as his wife.

Across the driveway, the workmen kept at their job. Would they hide something so important from their wives?

Oddly, Berthea's news grounded Addie, like the wires the men attached to a pole across the yard. Harold regularly accused her of hiding things, but he hid even more. Coming now, his secrecy confirmed her desire to help Kate. And the way might be opening up before her like the Red Sea for Moses and the Israelites.

She dozed, woke ravenous, and devoured leftovers from Berthea's Sunday dinner—roast chicken, mashed potatoes, and some Jell-O fruit salad. That brought Kate's last letter to mind.

No tinned fruit to be had until month's end, so Mrs. T is saving her points to buy some. The soap ration is cut again, and no sugar for weeks. Never thought I'd be starving for eggs, butter and toast.

In another air raid warning last night, we hurried down to the tube station. A single plane had broken through the clouds, but the fighters got the blighter before he did much damage.

Makeshift shanties spring up all over the city. Football field-sized areas welcome recent bomb victims.

Things look bleak here, but Mrs. T met an old friend in the station. Seeing them so excited reminded me how much our friendship means.

Energy flooded Addie, and when the faint one-o'clock whistle sounded from Halberton, she could wait no longer. She started the coupe. At Jane's, Simon skulked around the northwest corner of the house with a long stick.

Greening trees added a springy touch to Halberton's streets, and hatless folks raked their yards or cleared garden patches. Even the sidewalks looked brighter somehow. Elma's smile greeted Addie as she walked in.

"Hello. I just hung up from a return call." She reached for a notepad. "A Red Cross ship arrives in New York Harbor on May thirtieth to reload for her third journey to an undisclosed port relatively near London.

"More specifics will be available from New York, or later, aboard ship." Elma pushed her glasses up the bridge of her nose. "Six civilian slots remain open—kitchen jobs, organizing supplies, that sort of thing. Are you interested?"

"How long does a voyage usually take?"

"The average . . . let me see." Elma consulted her notes. "Oh yes, from sixteen days to ah . . . three weeks . . . requires security clearance, an up-to-date passport, proof of citizenship, statement of purpose, and you would have to sign a safety waiver. We can help you with all that."

"Did they say when the ship would leave?"

"Usually within a week of arrival, so you would need to be in New York by May thirtieth."

Excitement and trembling fought in Addie's stomach. She could be with Kate even before her baby came. Be in London, on the Thames, where Shakespeare walked—what would Mrs. Morfordson say?

"When do you need to know?"

"The sooner, the better, lots of paperwork to attend to. If you decide to move ahead, we'll need a birth certificate to start with."

"Thank you. I . . . I'll get back to you."

Standing before the Myrna Loy poster again, Addie focused on the glint in her eye. *Join Miss Loy. Do your part . . .* Could it be that traveling to join Kate could be her part in the war effort?

Addie opened the door of the coupe, and received her next guidance.

A wobbly bicycle careened around the Fourth Street corner bearing Fern McCluskey, who clung to a handlebar with one hand and grabbed her hat brim with the other. Addie almost yelled, "Be careful."

At the same time, Paulie backed his coal truck diagonally toward a chute under the Mercantile.

The scene unfolded like a slow-motion movie, and seeing what would happen next, Addie thrust out her hand. But Fern's concentration on her new spring hat and her high heels' tight fit on the bike pedals assured what happened next.

Paulie's perfect aim escaped Fern's notice, and she pedaled blithely on. When the truck halted in the intersection, one of the gate latches gave way, sending coal onto the street. The other latch broke and an inevitable pile formed, while a conglomeration of rubber tires rolled every which way.

Their diameters garnered Addie's attention—from small to bulky tractor size, but still, Fern remained unaware. Powered by the impact, one tire passed in front of Fern and a second smashed into her front wheel. She yelped and swerved toward the growing coal pile. And then came the sound effects.

Paulie's door screeched open and he sprinted toward Fern, who sprawled helpless on the lumpy black bed. Her screams drew spectators like flies.

"Ma'am, I'm sure sorry. Didn't mean to cause you no trouble."

Fern planted her elbow in the slippery pile. "Any *trouble*?" She launched into a shriek. "You've just wrecked my new outfit. And you could have killed me! Trouble? Why, you're nothing but trouble. I don't know why they let you out on the roads."

Paulie extended his gloved hand, but Fern waved him away. A renegade breeze whipped her skirt as she attempted to stand. Then she spied Addie and sputtered, "What're you doing here?"

Minor Randolph ran out the side door. "What . . .? Who made this . . ." He loped into the street. "Who's going to clean up this mess?"

Paulie doffed his cap. "That'd be me, Mr. Randolph. Looks like a latch busted, but if you could help Mrs. . . ."

Minor boosted Fern under the armpits as she pawed the air and grasped for her smashed hat. "Somebody ought to prosecute that . . . How dare he . . .?"

"Now, Fern, Paulie's just doing his job."

"So am I! Our new pastor told us to save on gas, and I was just . . ."

Walt joined the growing crowd and Fern limped into his arms. Minor kicked at a couple of tires as Paulie rescued his shovel and set to work, beset by Minor.

"Why were you hauling old rubber tires in with that coal, anyway?"

"Doing my part for the troops, Mr. Randolph. Left half a load of coal at the gas station, so they asked me if I'd tote the tires over to Benson for the rubber drive."

"Well, hurry up with this."

"You bet. If you want to help, I got another shovel in the front."

Minor muttered a curse. "I have customers to tend to. Poor Fern broke a heel on top of everything else. Try to be more careful, will you?" He huffed back inside. Folks went on about their business, but Addie still stood there.

"You okay, miss? Looks like that lady don't like you much, neither."

"I think you're right, Paulie, but I saw the whole thing. You didn't do anything wrong. Fern just wasn't paying attention to where she was going."

The urge to laugh almost overtook her, but at the same time, she felt sorry for Fern. Nothing she said about Paulie was true. In fact, she was the one deserving to be barred from the streets.

Paulie merely scratched his head. "It's all right. We all make plenty of mistakes, but I don't let 'em get me down. My pap used to say, 'Don't pick up your mistakes and carry 'em with you. Let 'em lay there and use 'em for stepping stones.'"

Back in the coupe, Addie gathered her thoughts. *Don't carry your mistakes with you—use them . . .*

A cavalcade of her errors filed before her. She hadn't realized Harold's true nature, and assumed his behavior was her fault no matter how badly he treated her. Also, she was slow to learn from Kate and Jane.

The list went on and on—letting someone else control her like Mama did, allowing fear of Harold's anger to smother her intuition, and neglecting her own desires. Over and over, she'd refused the quiet voice that declared her worthy and loveable.

"But I can *learn*. I can stop carrying my mistakes and start over." She set the coupe in motion and bypassed the bedraggled Fern, leaning on Walt en route to the bank.

The yarn still sat on the seat, and she rolled down her window for some fresh air. Soon she might breathe the salty Atlantic. The possibility swelled like a rainbow, but at the same time, doubt reared its head. What could she be thinking to consider such a move?

"Jane will hear me out, and won't mince words if this idea is too far-fetched." Addie turned the coupe down the Pike's driveway.

Whack . . . thunk. In the distance, Simon rounded his cabin, striking a tree now and then.

Jane fished tulips from the muck and nodded in his direction. "He's made up some new game. It keeps him occupied."

While Addie reached for a distressed tulip, Jane shifted on her weather-worn stool and wiped the back of her hand across her forehead, leaving a black trail.

"What's going on with you?"

"I brought you some yarn and need your listening ear."

"Something's happened. Those brown eyes carry signs, you know."

"Kate is in a family way."

Jane's face paled.

"I just talked with Elma Crandall and at the end of May, a ship needing six more volunteers leaves New York for England. I could go and help Kate." The admission emerged so quickly, puzzlement crossed Jane's face.

Her ragged overalls, faded plaid shirt, and mud-streaked forehead made quite the picture. She added a final touch when she scratched the end of her nose.

Addie burst out laughing. "You look so funny. You ought to see yourself."

"You're not the Queen of Sheba, yourself."

Addie took stock. Already, mud dripped from her skirt and splotches peppered her legs.

"Pull up that old chair. No better place to talk than right here in the full sun. I've had plenty of experience with war turning everything around, but it sounds like this one may unite old friends clear across an ocean."

"Kate's not one to ask for help, but she needs me, more than I'm needed here . . ."

Jane leaned on her cane. "And what do *you* need?"

When Addie shut her eyes for a moment, heat built behind them.

"Sometimes, my friend, we need to stop thinking so hard and listen to what our heart says."

"I thought if I could just figure out how to make Harold happy . . . " Addie uncovered a fledgling tulip willing to rise from its muddy captivity.

"The truth is, I've been so much happier with Harold gone. And now, Berthea tells me he's deploying with a Missouri unit."

Jane scraped at grit under her fingernails. "Berthea told you?"

"Yes. I don't know if he would ever have let me know."

"So what does she make of all this?"

"She's upset with Harold, and said if I found a way, if I thought this was God's will, I should go."

Simon's playful patter wafted in the still afternoon, and Jane mulled over the information. For a moment, Simon's simple life out there in the grove seemed enviable.

"Do you think it would be wrong for me to leave?"

Sunshine formed an aura around Jane's hair, and a budding oak dispersed shade in spiked designs on the shed behind her.

"People talk about God's will, but I don't believe it's always black and white. I doubt it was for Kate when she decided to search for Alexandre." Jane leaned back. "Maybe it's better to leave the judgment to God, especially when it comes to ourselves."

"It's warmed up twenty degrees this afternoon, a sure mark of spring. You've watched for your own signs all winter, but they don't mean a thing unless you're ready to take action. Are you strong enough? Only you can tell, Addie."

Driving home through mud that sucked at the wheels, Addie feared hitting a frost pothole and sliding in the ditch. But halfway there, she smiled. If she did slip off the track, George would rescue her, they'd have a good laugh, and Harold would never know.

In the kitchen, her new oak telephone's black handle and receiver offered a steady buzz connecting her with the outside world. She entered the stuffy living room and opened the windows in a daze.

"I might really get to go." She eased against the davenport's thick arm. In a breeze lush with scents of thawing earth and budding trees, her thoughts wavered between wild dreams of a lurching ship and visions of Harold dashing into battle.

When she rose, late afternoon shadows decorated the yard with faint prickles of chartreuse grass poking through the soil. She stretched her arms and everything came clear. She needed something to eat, and then she'd better contact Kate right away.

Chapter Thirty-three

Dear Kate,

Your news flashes in my mind like a blinking light. You're having a baby. Do mornings still find you sick?

I hope not, and am glad you're with Mrs. T rather than in some hotel room.

I have a surprise for you, too. Harold deploys in late April with a St. Louis unit. After all this time, I can barely believe it.

Berthea told me, and apologized for his secrecy, but it hardly hurts anymore. I'm taking that as a good sign and am thrilled he's not coming home.

I finally realize my determination to please him was grounded in fear. Jane mentioned her besetting sin once, and I think mine might be letting others control me. After all, if I hadn't let him, Harold wouldn't have ruled my life.

I don't know what all this means, but I'm trying to take responsibility for myself.

Today, some workers installed a telephone above our kitchen table. I successfully tried it out tonight, and thought, why not call you?

So I sent you a telegram with our number— Halberton 421, or two shorts and a long. Is your office tele still intact? I await your number, and tell me a good time to call.

I ran another errand today. I'll be naughty and give you only clues. What flies a flag, propels without wheels, and carries a friend?

Oh, we sent you two packages. Wish I could pack up eggs and butter, but cookies will have to do.

Until we talk,

Addie

The clock struck twelve, but Addie felt more awake than she had in a long time. A slice of moon drew her into the yard. Elma said her chances were better the sooner she decided, so why put it off? She spoke her feelings to the midnight moon.

"The Great War brought Fern and Norman choices, and this one has forced Kate into action. Harold finally has his chance to prove himself, and now, I have to choose, too."

Her throat parched with the decision's enormity. She wandered back to the house, recalling Gideon's need for signs. In the ship's availability, Berthea's advice and Jane's wisdom, three arrows pointed toward London. But everything happened so fast, maybe she ought to seek one more sign.

By now, Kate should have received her telegram, and the reply might already be waiting in Emmet's office downtown. A long night stretched ahead, but it was never too late for tea. Without even a twinge of guilt, Addie brewed a pot.

***

The black soil behind Jane's house produced ample earthworms. Careful not to disturb them, Addie cultivated the spinach row. Across the driveway, Jane sat on her stool hoeing the first batch of weeds around her peony bushes, her lively elbows in company with a pair of red-winged blackbirds chirping from an oak tree. A purple finch raised a lovely melody right above her head.

Simon fitted his hands to some trees and tapped a big stick on others. When Addie stopped hoeing to watch, she could see no logic to his movements, but as Jane said, he hurt no one.

She came over nearly every day this spring, since Jane's lame knee frustrated her gardening. Splitting the days between her garden at home and Jane's brought such pleasure. Several times, Simon skittered closer to wave to her, his pale forehead gleaming in the mid-April sun.

Trucks loaded with seed sacks whizzed back and forth from Halberton, and tractors put-putted along, transferring heavy raised plows from one field to another. George, elated at the opportunity, plowed the west forty acres every day from mid-afternoon until full dark.

A mild breeze brought the peaceful sensation Addie sought last year at this time. Back then, the "Bucket Brigade" began protecting vessels on the eastern seaboard, so German U-boats attacked ships in the Gulf, off the Passes of the Mississippi.

This news nearly drove Harold to distraction, and his howl, "The Mississippi. Do you realize how close that is?" echoed through the house. But he yelled even louder after American and Filipino troops fell into Japanese hands. "Twenty-four thousand sick and starving soldiers stranded on the Bataan Peninsula—what's wrong with our leaders? What idiot thing will the generals and colonels do next?"

Nearly every evening, she discussed the day's war news with George and Berthea, but without Harold's eruptions, the tension dissipated. With her London trip just around the corner, she relished these days with Jane. Rich, black Iowa soil filled spring breezes with its heady scent, and the trees became a riot of nest-building and territorial squabbles.

Simon stared up into the branches near his cabin, observing one such dispute. Jane pulled weeds west of the driveway, and Addie manhandled tenacious weeds in the flowerbed east of the house. Blighters, Kate would call them.

A sudden screech broke the serenity. Tires scrunched on gravel, and partially hidden by the corner of the house, a blue swatch lurched into the driveway. Could that be the bubbletop? If Berthea came home early from school, why would she drive it over here?

The door banged. A familiar gait sent a sharp slash along Addie's collarbone. No one except Harold walked like that. Her heart stopped when his voice rose over a manure spreader's hum in a nearby field.

"Hello, Mrs. Pike. Have you seen Addie today?"

"Why Harold, haven't seen you in a coon's age. Nice of you to stop in. I hear you're deploying soon. Do you know your destination?" Jane maintained perfect control, but raised her voice louder than normal.

A suffocating weight crushed Addie. She backed into the shadow of the porch and clutched the wood siding.

Pride buoyed Harold's reply. "An undisclosed European destination, but I'd say we're going to invade France."

An internal racetrack claimed Addie's heart as it had a thousand times before. She palmed her collarbone and tried to think. Jane was giving her time to hide. She eased closer to the side door, her pulse hammering like a woodpecker. The door gave way with a squeak Harold surely could hear.

She locked the door and slunk into the kitchen, where Jane's calico curtains prevented detection. Ever so slowly, Addie secured the lock and plastered her back to the wall. The clock, the stove, Jane's yellow teapot . . . all these familiar items gave her a sense of safety, yet she had no idea what to expect from her own husband.

"I hitched a ride home, but go back on tomorrow's early train. You see, Mrs. Pike, I simply couldn't leave the country without seeing Addie again."

"Ah . . . I understand. If she stops in, I'll let her know you're home. God go with you, Harold. This war's a mighty terrible thing."

He cleared his throat and Addie sent a plea heavenward. *Give me the sign I need.* At the same time, she chastised herself for behaving like a child. Why did she quaver to face Harold? She couldn't hole up here until he left for the train, could she?

"Yes, but God is on our side. Did you hear that Admiral Yamamoto's been shot down? And word has it the final attack on Tunisia will soon be underway. I'm absolutely sure we will prevail, just as I believe certain other things are God's inevitable will."

"Umm. Like what?"

Addie took her first real breath. Jane knew Harold would never pass up a preaching opportunity.

"Providence decrees specific earthly ordinances, such as gravity's pull. People are to marry and men must manage their households. Wives obey their husbands and produce children to glorify God in the rightful order of things, the set method of the universe, like spring and summer, fall and winter."

"And if things don't happen according to that method, then what happens?"

Addie circled her thumbnail with her finger. She recalled Simon's tearful look when he mentioned baby Sarah on Christmas Eve. Surely Harold knew the Pikes had no children and would switch his tack.

"You mean like producing children? Then there's sin in the camp, that's all there is to it. The Almighty punishes disobedience."

Addie risked a peek through a crack in the curtains. Harold's spread feet, jutting jaw, and thumbs laced into his belt took her back to that day in the chicken house. But he faced someone much stronger this time.

"This is Addie's last chance to obey the divine will. Then, even if I die in battle, an heir can carry my name."

Addie clamped her lips between her teeth and swallowed down her revulsion.

Jane toed clumps of soil. "I see. What do you believe, Harold, about a baby that lives a few months but suddenly passes from this world, perhaps on account of disease? Would that be God's will, or do you think the child's parents sinned?"

"There's a method to everything, Mrs. Pike, and sometimes people inherit the wind. You're probably talking about generational sin, visited on the children's children to the third and fourth generation."

"So you'd conclude their parents' or grandparents' actions may have caused the death?"

"I'd say so, but sometimes such tendencies can be difficult to track."

Jane struggled to her feet and leaned on her hoe. "My, my. Seems only yesterday you were toddling around here, mimicking your father's every move. Now, you've learned so much at the seminary. Glad such a wonderful opportunity came your way."

"Let me remind you, Mrs. Pike, this wasn't chance. Everything's ordained, just as it's ordained that Addie bear my child, according to the law of inheritance."

Though her throat throbbed, Addie couldn't look away. In utter earnestness, Harold bobbed his head up and down, but a hint of a smile piqued Jane's lips.

"Speaking of an inheritance, that reminds me. Addie mentioned wanting to ride her bike over to her home place sometime. Maybe she pedaled down there this morning. That girl has so much energy . . ."

"I'll check around there. I've got to drive to the Benson elevator and make sure Ma's been making our payments. And then, I need to visit Joe's dad—I'm sure you're aware, the Bible commands us to visit the sick and grieving."

"A praiseworthy thing. *Praiseable*, my grandmother Fitzmeier used to say. You take care now, Harold. What time does that early train leave tomorrow?"

"Seven a.m."

"Rest well tonight, son."

The bubbletop's engine fired. Once the tires spun on the gravel, Addie exhaled in parcels. The same urge that spurred her to make a train reservation for New York now instructed her to seek a better hiding place.

When a thin spiral of dust trailed the spot of blue toward Halberton, she collapsed, as weak as corn silk. Jane's homey kitchen, still bearing the aroma of chicken and homemade noodles, spun around her.

"Oh, God, I don't want to disobey, but if I become with child now, how can I help Kate? Please show me what to do."

The doorknob wiggled, and she unlatched the lock. Jane's forehead showed first, then her eyes, like fresh-rubbed emeralds against ruddy, weathered skin.

"Oh, child. Did you hear what he said? I'd like to smack that boy's smart, prideful mouth."

Jane shut the door and spread her arms wide. When Addie's trembling ceased, she led her to a chair and filled the kettle.

"You're as pale as hominy grits." She ran a cool rag over Addie's forehead and the back of her neck. "Sit here and collect yourself while I check on Simon."

Dropping her head on her arms, Addie questioned everything. What happened to all the confidence she enjoyed the past few days? How could she manage a transatlantic journey with such a puny constitution?

Jane talked with Simon outside, and snitches came through the screen. " . . . if he should come back, stay inside the cabin. Do you understand?"

In a few minutes, Jane set a hot cup of tea with a sprig of crushed rosemary before Addie. "Rosemary stands for remembrance and for healing. Did you know that?"

With her first sip, terror released its iron hold, and Addie focused on those warm green eyes. They shone with a plan, and Jane rubbed her hands together.

"Well, now. What do you want to do?" The quiet inquiry caressed Addie like balm. Could her answer be one and the same as God's will?

Her thoughts flitted to Norman. *Fernella couldn't stand up to him, and no one else could do it for her.* But if she returned home, could she speak her mind to Harold?

"I want to hide. It sounds spineless, but . . ."

"Sometimes what looks fainthearted is actually courage, and what would normally count as daring equals foolhardiness."

"You really think so?"

"If you go home, you'll have no choice in the matter. Harold made that clear. For him, God's will is black and white, and that's that. If he has to force you to comply, so be it. "

She paused for some tea, and outside, the red-winged blackbirds twittered in unison. "The way I see it, your urge to hide is self-preservation, and since Harold brought up the topic, I'd say it's God's will, too." She poured second cups.

"I'd be happy to have you stay here, but he'll be watching. There's the cabin, but that might upset Simon." A faraway look came into Jane's eyes.

"What if we hide your bike, and I'll drive you to . . . I know! We'll take the back road out to Emmanuel. You can sleep in the organ loft tonight. Pastor Bachmann locks the door at five, and by the time he comes into the sacristy in the morning, Harold will have left for the train."

"Stay there all night? Should I tell Berthea?"

"I'll visit with her if you want me to. Harold had several stops to make, so he won't be home for a while."

"You would do that?"

"She's stopped in a few times lately, and I think we have an understanding." Jane pushed back from the table. "You're sure this is what you want?"

A parade of scenes tumbled before Addie, but Harold delivering judgment on Jane and Simon's tragic loss topped them all. As usual, everything had to be somebody's fault. Close behind came his vehemence in the chicken house. She'd stood her ground, but with his single-minded, theological focus, could she do it again?

"Yes."

"All right. I'll round up some food and have Simon hide your bike behind the cabin. We'll make a quick stop at your place to get whatever you need."

Chapter Thirty-four

*L*ike an old friend, the cool sanctuary brought back the peacefulness of Christmas Eve, but Harold's perennial judgment still circled Addie.

"Those Lutherans worship a statue just like Catholics. I can't believe your mother let you go to church with Kate's aunt, even if her grandfather's a judge."

The close, dry scent of tattered hymnbooks and old dust drew her to the loft stairs, whose waxed wooden floorboards cracked under her step. Like a Sherman tank on a mission, Jane followed with a box of food and a lantern swinging from one arm. On the way to Emmanuel, she'd explained her plan.

"You know the parsonage sits beyond that thick pine grove? Pastor Bachmann takes his family into town on Saturday nights, but they come home early and go to bed with the chickens. You'll be safe walking in the field straight behind the church this afternoon, and no one'll see your light tonight."

"What if someone drives by?"

"No windows face the road, and since the river runs on the diagonal, no one lives beyond the grove. Now that I think of it, I wonder if your old farm lies straight south, as the crow flies."

She handed over a flashlight. "In case the lantern fails you—I just put in a new bulb. I'll be here with some crocus and tulips for the altar when Pastor unlocks the door. He goes back home then, so we'll get you out with plenty of time to spare."

She grasped Addie's shoulders. "You'll be all right? I'd stay with you, if it weren't for . . ."

"I'll be fine, thanks to you. And Jane, Harold says Lutherans worship a statue. I know that's not true, but . . ."

Jane chortled. "Oh, for heaven's sake. He's in for some big surprises in the army. He'll bed down with men from every corner. A Lutheran may well save his life. As for the statue . . ." She stepped back and eyed the altar. "That's only an artful reminder of God reaching out to us."

Before she disappeared out the back door, she fortified Addie with a bear hug. "It's only two o'clock, plenty of time for a walk before Pastor Bachman locks up. I'll speak with Berthea, and we'll both be praying. See you in the morning."

Dragging Jane's thick quilt up the stairs made Addie pant. The food box revealed that Jane thought of everything. A quart of water filled one corner, a jug of milk the opposite. Two dried beef sandwiches, a boiled egg, some cheese chunks and a paper bag of dried apples and oatmeal cookies completed the feast.

In the pew beside the organ, Addie leaned against the polished wood and closed her eyes. Right now in Europe and the Pacific Islands, people hid from real tyrants. All those troops taken by the Japanese huddled in horrible prison camps. Her danger didn't even compare, yet her wild heartbeat acknowledged no difference.

Finally, in the stillness, she relaxed. One thing was sure, Harold would never set foot in here. How could he see such a refuge as evil?

A glass chandelier balanced about five feet out from the balustrade, with twelve orbs extending from a central burnished globe. Five more like it interspersed throughout the sanctuary. Jane said the first settlers brought each hand-worked piece from the Old Country in the 1860's.

"Someone trimmed the wicks and climbed a ladder to light and extinguish them before and after each service. You can be sure I voted for electrification."

In spite of Jesus' outstretched arms, the barrier between Catholics and Protestants ran through this section of the country like electric wires. Even now, when Baptists fought side by side with Catholics overseas, one gravel road south of Halberton still divided families by their denomination.

One day in high school, Mary Faye Huntington said her parents threatened to disown her if she went to the Christmas ball with Patrick O'Neal.

"I told Mother I'd fallen in love with Patrick, but she yelled at me."

"'You just fall out of love, then. No daughter of mine marries a Catholic. You'd sign your children over to the Roman church, and Lutherans are about as bad. Why can't you pick a good Presbyterian boy?'"

Sounded like Harold's vehemence toward Pastor Bachman, whom he'd never met. The pastor's humility and kindness shone on Christmas Eve, and he worked with Mr. Wood to make sure poor rural children went to school. He even struck the final *n* from his name to prove his patriotism.

But Harold and others assumed the pastor's German relatives fought for the Nazis right now. Could he help it if they did? Addie imagined Kate broaching the subject with Harold.

"Our views are like these two sets of pews. In olden days, women sat on one side, men on the other. But that changed, why can't you?"

Another of Kate's questions prodded Addie. Had she ever argued with Harold? Every conversation seemed like arguing, but hearing Jane talk with him today brought a revelation. Jane played word games, like Kate. Her mind stayed a little ahead of his arguments, and she asked strategic questions.

"Why can't I do that? He must have some sort of spell over me."

Afternoon sun touched the altar, and Addie's words bounced back to her. Jane and Aunt Alvina loved this church, but others could still appreciate its beauty, couldn't they? Did faith have to be narrow to be real?

So many mysteries, but as sure as this building stood, the same Providence that saw Kate safely to London dwelt here. And He dwelt in Kate's whoop over the telephone last night. Her reaction made the journey seem final, as though this audacious plan could really work.

But now Addie caught her breath. What if Kate had called tonight instead, with Harold in the house? Surely, her angels were taking their duty seriously. Mama and Ruthie believed in guardian angels . . . had hers kept Harold from hitting her that day in the chicken house?

Downstairs, the same hymnbook Addie practiced from at Aunt Alvina's fell open to a favorite, "Open Now Thy Gates of Beauty."

Gracious God, I come before Thee; come thou also unto me. Where we find Thee and adore Thee, there a heaven on earth must be. To my heart O enter Thou; let it be Thy temple now . . .

Harold would say she gave in to temptation in coming here, but Kate would declare that this so-called disobedience proved her faith. All Addie knew for sure was the security she felt here.

The stanzas ended with a fitting request. *How so e'er temptations thicken, May Thy Word still o'er me shine as my guiding star through life, as my comfort in all strife.*

The sunlight climbed to soak her back. Sunshine—she needed more of it. And Jane said she could walk this afternoon.

The north field dried enough for a walk, but years of hoeing soybean fields taught Addie to skirt thick, fibrous stems that could grab you by the toe and throw you to the ground. The straggly rows led a full mile south.

She never dreamed Emmanuel lay so close to their old place, but Jane was seldom wrong. When the river sparkled to her left, Addie turned to get her bearings.

"Why, Ruthie and I always took Herman and Bonnie to play at that little pond."

Benson's Grain Elevator and the Catholic Church spire needled the eastern sky. On this curve, old Finn Edwards' team ran aground in a storm one night. On their walk to school the next morning, Reuben ran for help while Ruthie dragged Addie down the road. But she remembered Finn's groans, and his hand extending from the wrecked wagon.

A staggered line of hard maple, oak and cottonwood marked the creek's course. Like Moley in *The Wind and the Willows*, Addie soon stood in the rubble of her childhood home. Scattered limestone and a pile of once-red boards marked the barn's foundation.

Early in their marriage, Orville spouted his opinion of that barn.

"If I lived down there, the first thing I'd do is paint my barn white." Addie missed the derogation in his tone, but Harold explained.

"Germans paint their barns red and English farmers paint them white. Didn't you know that?"

Today, springtime held court with budding trees, weeds waking in fencerows, soil fertile with worms, moss, and seeds. But the wintry gloom that settled over Addie last November threatened again in the decaying odor from the sunken outhouse.

Traces of the kitchen door dangled listless on wall remnants, and scattered chunks of grimy floorboards splayed over the yard. The windmill lurched, startling a long-tailed rat from the old root cellar.

Something tripped her—the remains of the rain barrel. Thick rust crusted the metal circle where Ruthie taught her to wash her hair. A few feet farther, the old garden plot boasted a gangly milkweed mass.

Nothing for her here, exactly how she felt when she stopped by the house to gather her things. Even her white kitchen and the freshly painted living room failed to cheer her. She gathered her photograph, notebook and Kate's letters, just in case.

By the time she hurried through the back door of the church, the sun slipped lower. Already four o'clock. In all these years, she'd never spent a night away from home, but Jane's comfortable quilt folded perfectly between the banister and the first pew.

At seven, she would miss hearing the radio announcer say, "Here's your own Johnny Girl, Bonnie Baker!" Since Harold left, Miss Baker's candied-apple voice immersed the old farmhouse in lighthearted wartime romance stories on Saturday nights. Addie even transcribed one song for Kate.

> On Monday he told me he was One A,
> Tuesday he said he would go any day,
> Wednesday night he told me how he'd miss me,
> And then he took me in his arms and he kissed me . . .

Her relationship with Harold had few similarities to Bonnie Baker's lyrics. He didn't really court her. And he didn't even propose.

"I gave him no reason to." Addie sank into the comfort of Jane's quilt. "Everyone said we made a good pair, and it was meant to be. What a fool I was, so glad to have him take over my life."

An image pressed at Addie—Mama crying in the kitchen. Why had she spent so much time like that, forcing Ruthie to be the adult?

Not once did she recall Mama standing up to her dad. Her illness brought him regret, but his tardy changes made little difference. Mama curled toward the barren wall and responded only to the hymns Addie crooned or little Bonnie's voice.

With Bonnie and Herman in school, witnessed Mama passed from this world one quiet afternoon. A woman from the Presbyterian Ladies' Aid sat with her and Addie. Ruthie hurried down from Minnesota when the church ladies let her know.

A cardinal's clear call split the cooling evening air, and from the squat window, his brilliant coat gave him away, a splash of red amidst forest green.

"Hi, little fellow. Calling your mate?" His warble resembled one two-syllable word. *Agree ... agree ... agree.*

Maybe her parents once treasured dreams, but just as likely, Mama had blindly followed Dad—just as she followed Harold. At that time, having a warm house and a new family meant so much.

But now, it came down to this. Like a helpless child, she hid from her husband. Addie's cheeks flamed as the cardinal repeated its distinctive summons. Fern would say a wife must answer her mate's call.

The truth, as vivid as the cardinal, faced Addie down. The war called Harold away from here—for that, she felt only gratitude.

The sinking sun reflected deep gold through the balcony. *Agree, agree, agree.*

Against the pine background, Mama's face appeared, chin down, jaws clamped, eyes averted. It took such hard work to pretend you agreed with someone all the time.

The suffocating weight of all that effort filled Addie's throat. And even though she'd come so far, she still couldn't face Harold. When she looked up again, brilliant orange flared against a purple cloudbank, and a footfall sounded below.

Chapter Thirty-five

*F*ootsteps echoed, up the aisle to the front door, then slowly back—Pastor Bachman, here to lock the door. But instead, a raspy resonance rose to the tin-paneled ceiling.

"Fader Gott . . ."

Hiding was one thing, but eavesdropping on a prayer? After the first phrases, his voice fell into a heavy German rhythm. A few words made sense to Addie, but then his throaty "r's" dissolved in sobs.

Something slammed into protesting wood, and he cried out in English, "The children mock my little Peter at school, and people cross the street when Brita goes to market. We came here for freedom, but my family suffers for my sake."

There was no shutting out his anguish, though Addie shrank back and clapped her hands over her ears.

"To America I came, according to Thy leading. Shall I leave my family helpless now? Who will provide for them? And this flock entrusted to me—who will shepherd them? To come here at Thy call, yes! But for honor's sake, must I serve in this dread war?"

Pastor Bachman, go to war? Would the congregation allow his family to stay in the parsonage? Harold's accusations swam through Addie's mind.

"I'd bet our grain check he's a spy. Came just before the Luftwaffe's first strike—how convenient." Others joined in, though Jane pronounced her pastor a patriot. But now he considered leaving his family to fight for the Allies?

Knees popped as he trod the aisle. The floorboards directly below Addie squeaked, and somehow, her bag containing Kate's letters stirred from its perch in the front pew.

Though she grappled for it, the bag tipped, and like an autumn leaf, one envelope sailed out and came to rest on a pew.

Oh, please, don't let him see it.

But Pastor Bachman retrieved the letter. Guilty as sin, Addie caught his eye as he looked up. In seconds, he climbed the balcony stairs.

As his head appeared above the first pew, her face flamed. Her finger might have worn through her thumbnail. And then he stood a few feet away. The worn toes of his shoes made a statement all their own.

"You are Jane's friend? I have seen you in town with her."

Heat enveloped Addie. "Yes."

"She brought you here?"

Addie nodded. It was all she could do, for he held far more in his hands than Kate's letter. What if he insisted on taking her home?

But he sank into a pew. He handed her the letter, and his gaze demanded nothing. She let out her breath.

"You are afraid. What can I do to help?"

"I . . . I cannot go home."

"You seek refuge?"

"If I could stay here, just for tonight?"

"You have food?"

She pointed to Jane's box.

"Of course. Stay, or come with me to our house." His lips twisted. "Whatever troubles you, I am sorry."

"Thank you. Jane will come for me early tomorrow morning."

He pointed out the window. "We live beyond the grove. If you need anything, come to us. I cannot leave a light burning because of the black-out, but the back door will be open."

He rose with a faint heathery scent and touched her forehead with the sign of the Cross. "Remember that God wraps you in His love, and is always near in times of distress."

For a moment, she wanted to tell him everything, but his red eyes testified to his own tears. Long after the key turned in the back door, his pleas still roosted along the walls and nestled in her heart.

"Such a tender soul. Help him know what to do, and please help his family."

More than once, Norman shed tears over Fernella and the life they might have shared. Dad never cried, but he might have if someone discovered him wasting his third paycheck in a row. George? Yes, Addie could picture him weeping, and Simon, too.

But Harold? Never. Instead, he might ransack the house. She sat bolt upright in sudden panic—Kate's letters! Then she calmed down—no, she'd brought them along. In fact, one of them gave her away.

She stroked her clogged throat and whispered, "See—your fears are groundless, Addie Bledsoe. They have no place in a grown woman's life." Yet how could she free herself from them?

Light faded, and Jane's sandwiches, downed with cheese and milk, tasted like a special recipe. A dark blue book lay in the last pew—how did the Small English Prayer Book land in a German Lutheran Church loft?

War turns things upside down.

She flipped through the pages, and one line stood out:

> May Thy beloved take failure not as a measure of self-worth, but as an opportunity to begin anew, leaving all mistakes to Thy great Mercy. Give grace to relinquish the vain attempt to understand all things.

The words struck a deep chord. Addie closed her eyes. "Kate saw it all, but I kept plotting to fix things, to change Harold. I let stubbornness be my guide, and fear. Maybe I've been so afraid to fail as a wife that I . . ."

She leaned into the hard oak pew, limp as baby sister Bonnie's hand-me-down rag doll. Right now, she'd give anything to hold Bonnie once again or feel Ruthie's embrace. The clock made the only sound except for the old structure's moans.

Love your neighbor as yourself. The message wafted from the wooden altar. Kate wrote that verse in one of her letters, didn't she?

Addie rummaged for the lantern and sought until her fingers touched her notebook of hopeful thoughts.

The quote came not from Kate, but from one of Harold's books. "Help us to accept our faults and love ourselves, that we might also love our neighbor." Below it, she'd copied the London bookseller's advice.

> . . . We must refrain from apologizing and celebrate our tenacity. Otherwise, we shall look down on ourselves forever—not a pleasant prospect, eh?

When the lantern sputtered, she switched it off. In thick twilight, smoke spiraled like a balloon rising.

"I worked so hard to make Harold happy." Even though only God heard, saying the words strengthened her, and in the shadowy stillness, Addie arranged Jane's quilt around her. It smelled like her house— home cooking, hot tea, the earth, and flowers.

Gradually, sleep overtook her, then wakefulness, back and forth like a pendulum. Once when she woke, a chandelier reflected faint blue. Had Pastor Bachman adjusted the altar light for her before he left, in spite of the black-out?

The Shepherd's arms extended for her, Addie Shields Bledsoe, a woman running from her husband. Jesus reached her way, just as He invited children, his imperfect disciples, and the woman taken in adultery.

Warmth enveloped her head to toe. Unlike Harold with his condemnations, the Almighty welcomed her.

All the *shoulds* and *oughts* of her marriage crowded into a heap at the Savior's feet. She ought to be at home in bed right now, since she vowed to obey Harold before God and witnesses. She ought to put his wishes first and submit like a good, obedient wife, ought to . . .

But his pronouncement haunted her . . . *one last chance to become a mother—God's will.* Of course a man going off to war would want an heir, but why hadn't he done his part before he left in December?

"I might have conceived that night. I've never said no to him before."

But he has said no to you.

Her thoughts gained clarity. "He can choose, but I can't—it's about him being right, not about having a baby. That should be all about love."

No choice in the matter . . . Jane's kind eyes united with the Savior's—no harshness or accusation.

Addie retraced the cross Pastor Bachman made on her forehead. "Is this what it means to accept my faults and love myself?"

Kate might have been here beside her, with just the right questions.

> *Shouldn't each of us be FOR ourselves, since God is?*
> *If we judge our every move, who would ever do anything?*
> *Aren't our ideas and passions given us for a reason?*

"All this time, I've made excuses for Harold, but held myself to his standard of perfection. I've been just as judgmental as him. I thought he was my worst enemy, but maybe I am. How could I not see this before. . .?"

Weariness washed her, and she slumped against the banister. "Help me leave my mistakes to your mercy, dear God. Oh please, help me."

Later she found Jane's quilt and slept until the back door opened. Papers rustled behind the altar. Steady footsteps retreated, so she ate an egg and an apple, folded her blankets and took a load down the stairs. A short time later, Jane's whistle ascended.

"Did you sleep?"

"Even the mice and bats made me feel at home."

"No sign of anyone at your place. Probably left for Cedar Rapids hours ago. Still, it might be good to stop by my house for a while. I left tea steeping."

Jane had done enough for her already, and yet . . . "Whatever you think, if I won't bother Simon."

"Ach! He's making war on the weeds—won't even realize you're there."

They unloaded the car and Jane smiled. "I'll be back from church in about an hour and a half. Lock the door and make yourself some tea. By then, we'll both feel better about you going home."

She put one foot on the top step, but a blue whirlwind roared in beside the Studebaker, and Harold rushed toward the house. Addie shrank back, but Jane stood as solid as concrete.

"Harold?"

"Give me my wife, or I'll get the sheriff." His voice became a shrill whine.

"If you'll just . . ." Jane navigated the steps one by one. Gravel crunched under the Chevy and Berthea emerged.

Harold half-turned with a snarl. "Get home, Ma. I'll handle this."

But Berthea kept coming. "Jane, I'm sorry, you shouldn't have to . . ."

"What? Keep my own wife from me? I come home for less than twenty-four hours, and I can't even see her?" Harold launched a wail. "She refuses to obey God, and keeps me from pleasing Him, too."

"Listen to me, Harold. You can't force love." Berthea touched his hand, but he shook her off and approached Jane. When he grabbed her arm, Addie lost control and ran out yelling.

"Take your hands off her. She's my friend."

"Right. That's why she turns you against me."

"No one turns me against you, Harold. No one but you."

Berthea tugged at him, but he wrestled away and shoved Jane. Without her cane, she swayed against the house. Addie flew down the steps. Did the urge to kill count as God's will outside of war?

But a streak tore around the house. Before anyone realized what happened, Simon held a long-necked shotgun to Harold's back.

"Get outta my yard, Mister. Nobody touches my wife. Addie Bledsoe, neither. No, sirree."

The steel barrel glinted in the sunlight. Whether Simon loaded it was anybody's guess. Jane gawked at him in wonderment.

Harold's flexed his biceps and sidestepped toward Berthea. But Simon kept up with him.

"She . . . Ma, Addie painted our living room pink. And there's a strange car parked in the shed. She's my wife—I have my rights."

"Son, Addie's taken care of everything since you left, and the living room has needed painting for twenty years. I let it go for way too long. I like the color, and the car . . . George and I are buying it for his mail route."

"You and George? What's that supposed to mean?"

Berthea looked him full in the face. "George and I have been married since February."

The vein in Harold's forehead nearly ruptured. "Ma!"

"Yes. Sooner or later, you'll have to accept it. And about Addie— if she doesn't want to see you, that's her right."

His upraised arm stark against blue sky, Harold sputtered. "You would stand against your own son?"

"And you would hit your own mother?" Not a tremble in Berthea's voice, but her unmistakable sad undertone drifted to Addie.

"You don't want to miss your train, do you? You can still make the afternoon one out of Waterloo. I'll drive you."

Simon gave another push with the gun. Berthea pulled Harold to the Chevy and shut the door, but as she opened the driver's side, he burst out again.

Addie's mind said, "Run," but her feet froze.

Like a villain in a movie scene, Harold pushed Simon aside and the gun fired. Harold's fingers bit into Addie's wrist, and his gravelly tone imploded in her ear.

"You will do as I say." He nearly wrenched her arm from its socket, and ire wakened in her. She kicked him in the shins and clawed his face with her free hand. Berthea sped toward them, and another loud crack sounded.

Harold sagged against Addie as Simon raised the gun butt. But Jane held out her hand over Harold's crumpled figure, gentle and steady.

"Simon. Simon. Now, that's enough."

Harold muttered something as Berthea checked his head and held her fingers up, clear of blood.

"Harold, now think. This is your last chance."

He shook his torso like a stunned bull.

Berthea supported him and turned to Jane. "Forgive us, please. Addie, would you bring the pick-up home later?" Harold staggered beside her to the Chevy. Doors slammed, the engine kicked into gear, and Jane collapsed against the house.

Simon lowered the gun and approached her, solemn as a statue. "You okay, Janey?"

"Thanks to you, Simon. You certainly saved the day. Everything's all right."

His chin quivered. "I ain't gonna let nobody . . ."

Jane held her arms out to him and waved Addie into their embrace. "I think we'll all be fine now."

Chapter Thirty-six

"*I*'m so pleased you came, Addie. Let's sit on the back porch, where we can enjoy my flowers."

Mrs. Morfordson led the way to white wicker chairs poised over sprouting sumac. Sheltered by blue-green spruce trees meeting a white wooden fence, her back yard could have appeared in a Burpee's catalog.

"How about a glass of lemonade?"

"That would be fine, ma'am."

Mrs. M stepped into the kitchen, an expansive room with white cupboards. The pale yellow porch walls reflected sunlight, and even the ceiling's white beaded board sparkled.

A Robert Frost volume nearly filled a wicker table between a settee and Addie's rocker, but before she could reach for it, Mrs. Morfordson returned with a delicate tray of quartered egg salad sandwiches and lemonade. She took several sandwiches on a small plate.

"Help yourself. My, it's good to see you again. Having you and Kate in my class was such a joy. But I hear you're leaving us tomorrow?"

"Yes." Memories from their wonderful literature classroom came to life. So much good came to her through this teacher, right here in tiny Halberton. Was it foolhardy to go so far away?

"I would imagine you entertain both excitement and foreboding. I know I would at such an undertaking."

"You said that just right, ma'am. I want to see Kate and help her out, but to think of the ocean voyage . . ."

"You're only being realistic, which is wise. That's how we prepare ourselves. Leaving one place for another is no small thing, and this war makes everything seem even more capricious."

"Kate taught me the word ambivalent this winter. It fits my circumstances, don't you think?"

"Still increasing your vocabulary, I see, even without the benefit of English class."

"With Kate as a correspondent, I can't help it. She's so full of words and ideas, I have to keep my dictionary handy and visit the library to keep up with her."

Hearty laughter filled the sunny room. If Addie had any misgivings when she accepted Mrs. M's invitation, they vanished.

"That's why we're still here on earth, to learn and grow. But Kate has always shown a realistic side, too. Instead of complaining about things, she stirs them up to create change."

Like not showing up for graduation? Addie bit her tongue. No use bringing up a difficult moment, but Mrs. M. surprised her.

"I'll never forget her absence at your graduation. You must have missed her terribly."

"Oh, I did. I had an inkling where she slipped off to, but it was hard to see Aunt Alvina's dismay. She was always so good to me."

"Yes—an incredible woman. Did you know about her Great War exploits?" When Addie shook her head, she went on. "She kept them quiet, but some of us never forgot. Kate's mother worked for Bell Telephone at the front lines in France, and Alvina volunteered with the YMCA in Paris.

"Just think what their ships must have been like. I would think them far more primitive than what you'll experience."

"She never mentioned . . ."

"No, that was just like her. But you see, you're in good company. Imagine how much you'll learn living on another continent. If I were younger, I might join you."

A male cardinal's familiar "Agree, agree, agree" echoed from the back yard. Agreeing with Mrs. M wasn't difficult at all.

"May I ask what puts the tang in your egg salad?"

"A dash of dry mustard, a squirt of vinegar, and finely diced onions and celery. It's my mother's recipe. Small things can make such a difference, can't they? Back to Kate—because of her, the valedictorian committee made some important changes—you might let her know."

The cardinal fluttered to the stair railing and called again.

"That little fellow thinks he owns the back yard." Mrs. M's chuckle deepened her eyelid folds. "I've always thought our Creator's whimsy to fashion such a striking creature. The blue jay, too, and those little yellow goldfinches—birds might all be dull brown, like sparrows."

"You like birds?"

"Almost as much as poetry, which lands on the railing of our consciousness and sings its heart out when we need it most."

"That sounds like Emily Dickinson's *Hope*. Oh, I have missed all your wonderful metaphors, ma'am!"

"There's nothing like a good comparison. Take Robert Frost." Mrs. M leafed through the book. "Just last night I read this."

Our very life depends on everything's
Recurring till we answer from within.

"This describes my life from childhood on. Sometimes I wonder why I have to learn lessons so many times, but without the irritating recurrences, I'd never have been forced to finally answer from within. And that's the point of the journey."

"Could I . . . would you mind if I copied that down? I'm awfully slow to learn things, although I can't imagine that being true for you."

"You were never slow in my class. You see me as your instructor, but I'm a traveler just like you, with all sorts of sticky conundrums. Everyone is, except those who concentrate only on what's before their eyes. I saw you as a thinker even as you walked down the hall."

"I don't know if that's good or bad."

"Neither—it's simply who you are. That's why I always felt such an affinity with you and Kate. At your age, I'd have wanted to be in your circle—girls who contemplate, yet still take risks."

"The risk-taking would be Kate, ma'am, not me."

"Humpf." Mrs. M. refilled Addie's glass. "You must rethink that, my dear. You took quite the risk when you married Harold. Years ago,

I did the same thing. Having been Harold's teacher, I suspect that living with him could pose quite the challenge."

Addie nearly dropped her lemonade—another woman besides Berthea and Jane saw beyond Harold's exterior? As far as she knew, no Mr. Morfordson lived here, and today's visit showed no signs. She'd always assumed Mrs. M's husband died long ago, maybe in the Great War. Yet her teacher's mysterious expression hinted otherwise.

"It takes women time to find their voices. All we have to do is study the history of female writers. You may have had to work up to it, but anyone at the precipice of an adventure like yours knows how to look risk in the eye and keep moving ahead, Addie."

Warmth flooded Addie. She was who she was, before marrying Harold, afterward, and—suddenly, *now* became a category all its own.

* * *

The first hint of dawn frosted the horizon as George revved the coupe's engine. From the back seat's depths, Addie whispered, "Goodbye garden. I'm leaving you in good hands, but I'll miss you." She glanced at the chicken house and barn. "And good-bye, girls, Missy, and Old Brown."

The staggered grass where the fence once stood gradually filled in. The other day, every step of tearing it down—kicking, hammering, pulling out nails, toting some wood to the woodpile and some to the burn pile, increased her lightness.

Harold would find a reason to lament the loss, and blame her impulsive nature. But Berthea exclaimed how the fence's absence improved the yard. Best of all, Addie already thought so, and enjoyed the process.

At Jane's, Simon skulked around the edge of the house, even this early in the morning. She'd said good-bye last night, but he lurked in the shadows and let Jane do the talking.

"Don't know what I'll do now, Addie, without your visits to look forward to. I'll feel guilty drinking my tea alone. But I've had an inspiration about those hollyhocks. Maybe we need to plant seed, rather than starts. If you don't mind, I'll go over and scatter some this fall."

Addie accepted the offer, but heaviness bore down on her. Who knew how long she'd be gone or what might happen before she came back? As usual, though she tried to hide her anxiety, Jane read her misgivings.

"Mind you, no second thoughts. You have a mission, and I'm so proud of you. But we're going to miss you every single day."

"Me, too." Simon bopped into the kitchen, his voice muffled. "Janey said you're coming back, Miss Addie. I'll watch for you."

"Yes, and I'll bring Kate. You'll like her, Simon. Take good care of Jane for me, won't you?"

Simon clasped his hands and shifted his feet. "Yeah, but no more guns. Janey said so."

"Well, she's almost always right."

"Yep." He backed out the door, and Jane handed Addie a small piece of paper.

"Mr. Lincoln's my favorite President. He suffered so much, yet encouraged so many. Once, he wrote to a friend, 'Always bear in mind that your own resolution to succeed is more important than any other one thing.' Keep this handy and think on it if you run into any trouble."

When she saw Addie out, they paused to watch Simon near the shed. Jane sighed and cleared her throat.

"You have no idea what a difference you've made for Simon and me. For a long while after I got him situated out in the cabin, I stayed away from folks. They wouldn't understand, so why take a chance? It was far easier to hole up here and plant flowers.

"But when you rode over on your bike that first afternoon and told me about opening up the living room in the old house, beating the dust out of the drapes and pulling them back, I knew I could trust you.

"You've been such a good friend, and you've helped Berthea come out of her shell, too. You've brought us two together. In my book, there's no one quite like you, Addie Bledsoe." Her eyes glinted. "Take care of yourself."

As George turned into Halberton, Addie pulled the paper from her pocket. *My own resolution to succeed ...* She rummaged again and handed George the extra gas coupon Jane gave her.

"Jane sent this. She said even though you have a C gasoline sticker for your work, you might need extra for this trip."

"Her week's four-gallon gasoline coupon—well, I'll be. That woman's always thinking of others. With the new speed limit at thirty-five miles per hour, we shouldn't need it, but it's better to be on the safe side."

Berthea twisted in her seat and patted Addie's knee. "We heard from Harold yesterday. His unit sails for the English coast in a month."

"Mrs. Morfordson would call this ironic—I'll be closer to him now."

"He didn't write anything else." Berthea shook her head and clicked her tongue on the roof of her mouth. "But I'll let you know if he does, all right?"

"Sure."

George caught Addie's eye in the rear view mirror, a gentle look that bespoke camaraderie. They navigated the rest of sleepy Halberton in silence. The mercantile, the theater, Olson's café and the Red Cross office might have been a movie set, false storefronts that stood only four feet deep.

She and Kate used to walk Main Street on Saturday nights, hailing friends and stopping to talk. Sometimes Kate treated her to a nickel cherry drugstore Coke, but Harold refused to come to town when everyone else was out and farm wives did their weekly grocery shopping.

"Too many people too close for my taste."

"Wonder how Harold's handling the swarms of soldiers? He's never liked crowds. Ah, well . . . what will be, will be. At least he got his wish."

Berthea and George kept talking, but Addie stopped with Harold. Resolution of their problems seemed as impossible as perfection, but there was no use revisiting that old thought channel. Things would work out, one way or the other. Why not adopt Berthea's view? *what will be, will be*

Past the McCluskey's turn, the sunshine highlighted the first pale green alfalfa sprouts, row on row. As Halberton faded, corn seedlings already formed rows in a few fields. Farmstead after farmstead passed, some with long lanes, some hedged entirely by thick groves, some with red barns, others painted white.

German and English. And I'm on my way to England because of the Germans. The concept boggled Addie's mind, and this day seemed unreal, like something she'd read in a book.

For one thing, George determined to drive to Davenport, two hours farther, although regular trains left from Cedar Rapids. All the way to the Mississippi—farther than Addie had ever gone.

"Connections are better down there, and I haven't seen the Mississippi River in years. We'll get a hotel for the night, Bea. This'll be our wedding trip."

Every time he called Berthea by the new nickname he'd coined, she smiled. The name fit her—short and efficient, and as Mr. Wood said, a perfect school secretary. Bea Miller, so much easier to say than Berthea, just right for her new figure and her fresh outlook on life.

Flat farmland gave way to undulating hills in a gradual decline to the great river. Morning sun inundated lurking shadows and stirred the scent of lilacs, ever-present manure, and earth hungry for seeds.

Once George stopped at a gas station to fill the tank. Berthea visited the ladies' room first and handed the key to Addie.

"Not so pleasant, but here's an extra hand towel I brought along. You'll need it in there."

Just like her to think ahead. She'd lost a few more pounds since the wedding, gained color in her cheeks from Saturdays spent in the garden, and rarely scowled. Her entire bearing declared her happy.

For the rest of the trip, Addie let the world fly by. In a few hours, she opened her eyes to the highway sign outside Davenport. *Population 66,039.* The smooth ride must have put her to sleep.

"There now. That didn't take long at all. Did you know this is the only place where the Mississippi bends and flows east to west for a while?"

George parked at the train station and went in to buy Addie's ticket. When he handed it to her, her fingers trembled. Berthea noticed and squeezed Addie's hand.

"In three days, you'll meet your ship in New York Harbor—it seems impossible." Whatever she saw in Addie's eyes caused her to continue. "You've become so strong. You'll do just fine, I know you will. Kate paved the way for you."

Like it had in the chicken house that long-ago morning with Harold, Addie's stomach flip-flopped. "I'll have to borrow your faith, because right now I'm thinking, 'How can I possibly embark on such a Kate-like adventure?'"

"In your own way, and with the courage that's grown in you, that's how." Berthea opened her purse for her hankie. "Now, no more such talk—set your mind. The deed is already practically done."

"I'll leave you ladies at Petersen's and make the hotel arrangements." George pulled to the curb in front of a red brick building, taller than any in Halberton.

"Come on, Addie. We have some shopping to do." Berthea led the way through heavy double doors underneath a *Peterson Harned Von Maur* sign.

"We'll start with new shoes." She whisked down a wide aisle and halted at a map of the store.

"The lay-out hasn't changed much. My aunt Elise used to live here, did you know that? I stayed with her my first year out of high school. Although she was nearly bed-ridden, she still had a taste for style, and sent me down here on errands. I always liked this store."

"You lived here? Why, I didn't know . . ."

"Of course you didn't. When I came to the farm, I buried the past. Some day, I'll show you my old pictures. Once, a neighbor included me in an outing aboard their boat. Can you picture me, young and out on the wide Mississippi?"

She shook her head. "Those days are long gone, but having George bring me back here means so much. Now, let's find you a pair of sturdy shoes for those London sidewalks."

An hour later, new black Mary Jane wingtip shoes with a two-inch heel carried Addie around the store. Every few minutes, she glanced down in wonder.

A plush gray wool coat draped her arm, and a warm rose hat enhanced her hair. When they passed a long mirror, she stared at this stranger, someone who might work in an office, maybe even a writer.

Berthea also insisted on leather gloves, a new nightgown, a silk slip, and two pairs of stockings. Her energy propelled them from department to department.

But as they maneuvered the curving granite stairs, Addie clutched Berthea's arm. "Really, this is too much. You don't need to buy me any more. I'm fine just the way . . . ."

"You are fine. But a beautiful young woman like you deserves a decent set of traveling clothes. I should have been a better mother-in-law to you all along, and today's a good day for starting to set things right."

At a grand piano on the first floor, a male pianist attired in a black tuxedo played with such grace, Addie could have listened for hours. But Berthea urged her on.

"You need a new purse. Choose a high-quality one, and don't look at the price tag—I want this to last you for years. My purse becomes part of me, and I hate to change it."

So many grains to choose from—alligator, suede and tanned leather buffed to a shine, as soft as Missy's nose. Addie ran her fingers over a supple black creation with long braided handles.

"Try it out. Here, put on your coat, and ... Oh my, it goes so well with your shoes . . ." Berthea smoothed Addie's sleeve and gave a low whistle. "And it has plenty of pockets. Like it?"

Addie adjusted the straps over her shoulder. "It makes me feel like a woman about town."

"Well then, it's the one for you."

While Berthea paid the bill, Addie tapped her toe to the piano music. Maybe Mrs. Tenney had a piano, or she could play at a nearby church.

"All right, let's sit down. Go ahead, clean out that old purse so I can throw it out."

"Oh, I know—you can fill it with treasures for Willie to discover the next time he comes over. I'll picture him going through it, looking for whatever you've added since his last visit."

"What a great idea—I'll do just that."

The new purse boasted two inner zipper compartments, one for Addie's ticket, along with half of her cash. The other half, she slipped in the inside pocket of her coat.

George ushered them to an early dinner in the basement cafeteria, but she could barely finish her meal. On the way to the station, her throat tightened.

Berthea turned and placed a shiny gold compact in her hand. "When you look in the mirror, remember who you are and how far you've come." She reached for a small paper sack. "And take this, too. You may find some use for it on your crossing."

One sniff of the white powder brought a chuckle. "Oh, you would give me Borax—now I'm prepared for anything!"

George carried Addie's suitcase. In the spacious women's waiting room, a USO poster invited women to participate. When Addie and Berthea came out, a line formed near the train. Addie's breathing went wild and she reached blindly for George.

"I'm going to miss you so much. Thank you for driving me here, for doing the chores and cleaning out the . . ."

"Ach. You take care, now." He hugged her hard and turned her over to Berthea, whose accordion embrace brought more tears.

"If you need anything, write me." She drew back. "I should have sent something along for Kate. Let me know what she needs, will you? Jane and I can send a package for the baby."

"Oh, yes, Jane can knit something." Addie struggled for breath. "You've been so good to me . . ."

"Not half as good as I should have been. The Lord gave me the daughter I never had, but it took me way too long to see it." Berthea wiped her eyes.

"But regret never changes anything. Remember, no matter what happens between you and Harold, nothing will ever change our friendship. I'll write you every week and watch your garden. And I'll report on any hollyhocks that come up."

George took over as she broke down. "Let us know when you get to New York, and when you arrive in London, too. Call us and reverse the charges, all right? You have plenty of money, don't you?"

Plenty of money? More than Addie had ever carried, plus three times that amount sequestered in Jane's unique hiding spot in a locked metal safe to replace the cigar box. "In case the house burns down."

Berthea and George insisted on banking the payment for the coupe in Addie's name. "I'm doing the same thing with my paycheck. When the war's over we'll start collecting interest. From now on, a woman can grow her savings as well as any man."

George handed the conductor her ticket and patted Addie's shoulder. "Be careful."

Three steps up, a deluge of interesting hats and expressions faced her, as colorful as her garden in July. One small group drew her toward the back. A slight woman with a flushed face and her hat askew balanced an infant in one arm and grasped a squirming toddler's ankle with the other.

Addie wormed her way down the narrow aisle and slid her bag into the seat ahead of the little family. Her purse strap caught on the buckle of her Mary Janes, so she reached down to set things aright. Before she even settled her things, warm clammy fingers touched her neck, so she twisted with her best smile.

"Michael, you mustn't . . . " The woman grimaced, but the two-year old reached for Addie like Willie Miller, his big brown eyes intent.

"I'm so sorry, ma'am. Michael, come here right now." His mother's voice trembled, and she looked too exhausted to fight.

The cuddly little fellow wiggled into the crook of Addie's arm, releasing his weight against her. Almost immediately, his eyelids shuttered.

"He's fine. I don't mind at all. My name is Addie, and I grew up taking care of my baby sister. Have you come a long way?"

"From Grand Island to Cleveland. My husband left for the Pacific front, and we're going back to stay with my parents until he comes home."

"You must have been traveling so long already."

The woman nodded as if speaking required too much effort.

"Really, I don't mind holding this sweet guy at all."

"Oh, thank you so much. Michael's at that age where he's so squirmy I can hardly handle him anymore. And my name's Lorraine Connors."

She blinked back tears and Addie gave her attention to the cuddly child fiddling with her coat button, already so at ease in her arms. She took a deep breath. The suffocating sensation in her throat gave way. Michael's smile won her heart as she smoothed her finger over his soft cheek and murmured in his ear.

"Little one, you're on your way to a safe place where your Grandma and Grandpa will help your mommy care for you. And I'm on my way somewhere, too."

Outside, Mississippi River views faded as Illinois cropland came into sight. Just like that, Iowa was gone—the farm, her garden, and her people. Against the rhythmic clackety-clack of the train and the chatter of folks throughout the car, Addie whispered to the slumbering boy in her arms.

"I'm on my way to see a friend—to help with her baby. And maybe someday, I'll still be blessed with a beautiful child like you. It's spring, little Michael—spring of 1943. No one knows how long this war will last, but I do know one thing for sure. My life belongs to me. I'll never return to the way things have been—I'll never again be Harold's slave."

Addie let her glance range around the car until it fell on two young men in uniform napping in a front seat. She lowered her head again and breathed in Michael's baby scent. "I'm glad Harold's finally a soldier, and I'll pray for his safety. I don't know what the future holds, or how long I'll stay in England. I only know I'm on my way."

The End

Gail Kittleson taught college expository writing and ESL. Now she focuses on writing women's fiction and facilitating writing workshops and women's retreats. She and her husband enjoy family in northern Iowa, and the Arizona Ponderosa forest in winter.

WhiteFire Publishing released Gail's memoir, *Catching Up With Daylight,* in 2013, and her debut women's historical fiction, *In This Together* (Wild Rose Press/Vintage Imprint) released in 2015. She also contributed to the Little Cab Press 2015 Christmas Anthology,

The first novel in her World War II series releases on June 6, 2016—D-Day, and the second is contracted with Lighthouse Publishing of the Carolinas for release in February, 2017. You can count on Gail's heroines to make do with what life hands them, and to overcome great odds.

Meeting new reading and writing friends is the meringue on Gail's pie, as her heroines would say.

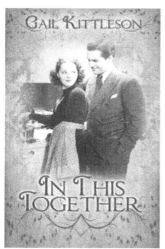

After World War II steals her only son and sickness takes her husband, Dottie Kyle begins cooking and cleaning at the local boarding house. The job and small town life allow her to slip into a predictable routine, but her daughters and grandchildren live far away, and loneliness is Dottie's constant companion when she's not working. Then, complications arise at work that challenge quiet Dottie to speak up for justice.

Al Jensen, Dottie's long-time neighbor, has merely existed since his wife died. Al passes his time working for his son at the town's hardware store, while still coping with tragic memories of his WWI service. Being with Dottie makes him happy, and their friendship grows until, for him, love has replaced friendship.

Health threats to her daughter in California increase Dottie's desire to travel west, but Dottie's fear of crowds thwarts her taking a train trip halfway across the nation. She finds that second chances also present challenges. Embracing them requires newfound courage and a life-changing fight against fear.

Available in print and Kindle ebook through Amazon.com at http://amzn.to/1VBjwBJ

Just as old houses need renovation, our spirits require replenishment. Women's friendships nourish us, as do their stories. This redemptive memoir blends contemporary women's stories with those from bygone generations, plus truths exhibited by the mystics and female Bible characters. The author invites us to share her experiences after her husband's military deployment as they move to a new community and refurbish a very old house. She also shares how the ancient meditation method of Lectio Divina can revolutionize one's devotional life.

Available in print and Kindle: http://amzn.to/21imWZK

Made in the USA
Monee, IL
13 November 2019